STAR OF PEACE

Books by Jan de Hartog

Star of Peace
The Trail of the Serpent
The Lamb's War
The Peaceable Kingdom
The Children
The Captain
The Call of the Sea
(including The Lost Sea, The Distant Shore, A Sailor's Life)
The Hospital
The Artist
Waters of the New World
The Inspector
The Spiral Road
A Sailor's Life
The Little Ark
The Distant Shore
The Lost Sea

PLAYS:

William and Mary
The Fourposter
Skipper Next to God
This Time Tomorrow

STAR OF PEACE

A NOVEL OF THE SEA

Jan de Hartog

A Cornelia & Michael Bessie Book

HARPER & ROW, PUBLISHERS, New York
Cambridge, Philadelphia, San Francisco, London
Mexico City, São Paulo, Sydney

This book is based in part on a play by Jan de Hartog entitled *Skipper Next to God.*

FIRST EDITION

Designer: Sidney Feinberg

This book was set in 11-point Video Comp. Janson Alternate. It was composed by ComCom and printed and bound by Haddon Craftsmen, Inc., Scranton, Pennsylvania.

Library of Congress Cataloging in Publication Data

De Hartog, Jan, 1914–
    Star of Peace.

    "A Cornelia and Michael Bessie book."
    1. World War, 1939–1945—Fiction. I. Title.
PR6015.A674S8 1983   823'.914   83-47552
ISBN 0-06-039029-8

84 85 86 87 88 10 9 8 7 6 5 4 3 2 1

CONTENTS

Part One
DEPARTURES

CHAPTER ONE

I

Dr. Hendrik Richters could best be described as a radiantly bad physician. Young, blue-eyed, blond, irresistible to older women, he had the worst record of his class of interns at the Amsterdam University Hospital. G.P.'s looking for a *locum tenens* during their summer vacations turned him down after seeing his record, whereas their wives urged them to take him on: "The best of the lot! So amusing! And such good manners!"

The summer of 1939, the wives did not prevail. Hendrik Richters, M.D., at the end of his tether and low on faith, climbed the stoop and rang the doorbell of an old house on one of the canals in Amsterdam, his last chance. It was July; even he, glandular optimist, had little hope that this late he'd be lucky. Circumstances seemed about to force him to follow his father's advice to go and see a business friend who ran the new Mercedes-Benz agency in town and had openings for "high-class salesmen."

The front door of the gloomy, somewhat disreputable-looking house took a long time to open; when finally it did, an old housekeeper peered out morosely. Her expression of dyspepsia softened, however, at the sight of Hendrik's cherubic countenance. "Yes?" she inquired.

"My name is Richters," he said engagingly. "I've come in answer to the ad."

"Ad?"

"The advertisement in this month's *Lancet,* where a Dr. Halbertsma of this address asks for a young physician to replace him as ship's physician on—" he looked at the slip of paper in his hand —"*a challenging voyage to South America.*" He knew that the housekeeper was unlikely to have any influence on his fate, but the boyish grin full of hollow promise was second nature by now.

It never failed. "Come in, come in," the old woman suddenly said, opening the door wide. "This way, please."

She led him down a long, echoing hall and ushered him into an old-fashioned doctor's office. "You wait here, sir; I'll tell the doctor. He won't be long. Would you care for a cup of tea?"

"You know, I'd simply adore it!" He'd have preferred Scotch on the rocks, but added radiantly, "How *did* you guess?"

"Ah," the housekeeper said, "I know men. I've been working for gentlemen for—well—a long time, heh heh heh . . . " She shuffled back into the gloom.

Dr. Halbertsma's office was as decrepit as his housekeeper. A case full of ancient books, their backs discolored and scarred by roaches, topped by a row of glass bottles with human organs in formaldehyde. A sepia photograph of a Victorian elder with a paunch and a beard. A lithograph of *The Monarch of the Glen.* The only cheer in the room was spread by the grin of a skeleton in one corner.

"Yes?"

Hendrik rose smiling, ready to seduce the newcomer with his charm; seeing the man, he faltered—a small, swarthy pugilist with a low brow and a flattened nose, who peered at him through rimless glasses with an expression of distaste.

"I've come in answer to your advertisement."

"Qualifications?" the man growled.

Hendrik reeled off the short, dismal list while Dr. Halbertsma, with obvious lack of interest, sat down in a chair behind his desk, from where he observed his visitor with the blank stare of glasses mirroring the window. "I see," he said, finally. "Not very impressive, eh?" He fell silent for a moment—then sighed and said, "Well, what the hell. I'll put my cards on the table. The job I have for you is badly paid, probably illegal, certainly unrewarding, and I have reason to believe that the ship concerned will sink after an explosion. What did you say your name was?"

"Richters."

"Richters," Dr. Halbertsma repeated, as if the name somehow confirmed the poor opinion he had formed of his visitor. "Well, Richters, do you want me to go on, or have you had enough?"

"I—er—yes, go on, please," Hendrik replied, smiling uneasily.

"All right." Dr. Halbertsma leaned back in his chair, which tilted backward. "The job is that of resident physician on board a dilapidated freighter called *Star of Peace* which has been converted into, quote, a passenger ship, unquote. Destination, Montevideo. She sails tomorrow from Hamburg with two hundred and fifty passengers. She's due in Le Havre to take on coal three days from now; that's where you'll join her for a crossing of four weeks. She's a slow boat."

"Sounds interesting," Hendrik murmured.

"It's even more interesting." The eyeless Dr. Halbertsma flashed him a smile reminiscent of the skeleton in the corner. "The passengers are German Jews: old men, women and children. They've been expelled by the Nazis, with immigrant visas for Uruguay. Any political convictions?"

"Who—me?" Hendrik realized his startled reaction might not be helpful, but he had been taken unawares.

"Are you a Nazi?"

"Good heavens, no. Why?"

"Well, what the hell." Dr. Halbertsma's chair tilted forward; he took off his glasses and retrieved his eyes. "The way the skinflint converted that ship is a disgrace. He'll run you off your feet, the bastard. What's more, you'll have to share a cabin with him."

"Who's that, sir?"

"Her captain. Young fellow by the name of Kuiper. He owns the ship; mortgaged to the hilt, I'd guess. How does it sound to you?"

It sounded awful. Hendrik was inclined to say he'd have to think it over, but it was his last chance to add some practical experience to the meager little list: *ship's doctor on a 250-passenger liner, Le Havre to Montevideo, summer/fall '39.* "You mentioned —er—an explosion?"

Dr. Halbertsma once again gave him a skeletal grin. "I did," he said with an odd hint of satisfaction, "and I'm telling you because I know your type. You'd sue a man for offering a job under false pretenses—in case you were to survive, that is."

"I don't understand." It was an understatement. He began to suspect that Dr. Halbertsma was crazy.

"It's been my custom over the years to take my summer vacation by serving as a ship's doctor for one voyage," the doctor explained. "I applied for this one because it suited my schedule and because, once we'd delivered the immigrants, I could spend a week or two there and return by passenger liner. I talked to the captain, saw the vessel and was unfavorably impressed. But there was nothing else available, so I thought: What the hell? Last week, Thursday, I went to sign the articles. As you may remember, it rained all day. I went by car to the harbormaster's office. The full crew was there, and the water sheriff before whom the articles have to be sworn. As I sat down to join them, something happened. I looked around the table and all I saw, believe it or not, was corpses. All except the water sheriff. Are you psychic?"

"Well—er—can't say I am." Dr. Halbertsma was definitely crazy.

"I should have had more sense, but I told myself not to be a fool and signed the articles. When I got back to my car, it was still raining. I turned on the windshield wipers. The moment I did so, I saw a death's-head on my windshield, shaking 'no,' slowly, like this: 'No—no—no—no,' in time with the wipers." His impersonation of the death's-head was evocative. "When I got home— Yes, what is it, goddammit?" The sudden change of tone startled Hendrik. He looked around and saw the housekeeper standing in the doorway with a tray.

"I've brought the young man his tea, Doctor."

"Tea? Are you insane? What are you giving him tea for? He's here to apply for a job!"

The housekeeper glared at him and put the tray on the desk in front of Hendrik.

"Well, I'll be . . . " Dr. Halbertsma started furiously.

"Sugar?"

"Yes—please," Hendrik stammered. "Two, please . . . "

"Go away, woman!" Dr. Halbertsma shouted. "Let him take his own goddam sugar! Get out!" She fled. When she was gone, Dr. Halbertsma sneered, "You've chosen the wrong career, my boy. You should try selling from door to door, you'd make a fortune. Now, do you want that job, or don't you?"

"Do you seriously think the ship'll go down?"

"I think nothing," Dr. Halbertsma said. "I received a flash of precognition and decided to heed it. It's not your precognition, it's mine. Maybe she'd have sunk only if I had joined her, who knows? I'm telling you just in case. If that goddam ship does go down, I'll write about it for the *Journal of Parapsychology,* and I don't want you to sue me for offering you a job under false pretenses. Understand?"

"You—you have my promise I wouldn't sue you," Hendrik said with conviction.

"Your promise is worthless." Dr. Halbertsma put his glasses back on; his eyes went blank again with the reflection of the window. "Anyhow: now, if you take the job, you'll know exactly what you're letting yourself in for. The pay, by the way, is poor." The doctor mentioned an amount. It was poor indeed.

Hendrik felt conflicting emotions. He said, "I'll take it," even though he knew he really should think this through first. But then, he could always change his mind later. He hadn't signed anything yet.

"All right," Dr. Halbertsma said, "I've written a note to the water sheriff. All I've got to do is fill in your name." He lifted his blotter and brought out a sheet of paper. "First name?"

"Hendrik. I wonder—"

"Nothing to wonder about." The pen scratched. "The contract specifies a paid return voyage by liner. Don't let that bullying Calvinist swindle you out of it."

"Who?"

"Her master. He's Skipper next to God, as it says in the Dutch Articles. Not 'Master under God' as the British call it, or 'After God,' like the French, no—" he licked the envelope and banged it shut with his fist—"to him, God is standing right by his side on the bridge, as an equal." He handed Hendrik the letter. "Here you go, have a nice trip. Know your way out?"

"Yes, er—goodbye, sir."

The tea remained undrunk. The housekeeper, waiting for him in the passage, whispered, "I heard him! Don't touch it! He's psychic! He knows things before they happen! Don't you *touch* it!"

"Thank you," Hendrik said, beaming mechanically. "I appreciate that."

"Don't touch it!" the housekeeper urged, opening the front door. "He *knows*, believe me. Stay home!" She closed the door behind him.

Hendrik stood on the stoop, looking at the letter in his hand. Maybe he should have a look at the Mercedes-Benz showroom before making up his mind; but no, he couldn't pass this up, bizarre though the whole thing might sound. It was the only offer that had come his way all summer and it would be ludicrous to let it slip through his fingers just because an obviously deranged old quack had been hallucinating about death's-heads on his windshield.

Pity there was no one he could talk it over with. Despite all his years at the University, he had made few friends there, mainly because most of his classmates had passed him by academically, so each year he had found himself among a new crowd. But then, he had never had any male friends; they had all been girls. Come to think of it, one of them lived right nearby.

He decided to go and see her.

2

Her name was Molly; she ran a little shop of yarns and needlework which could not possibly produce enough income for her to keep body and soul together. Hendrik suspected she had been set up in the business by an admirer twice her age, some capitalist from the city, but he had never probed into her private life. They had met one evening at a rather desultory party to which he had escorted somebody's Lesbian sister who made dolls. Molly, plump and huge-eyed, had sat enthroned on an ottoman in a tentlike dress she had designed and sewn herself which made her look like a giant tea cozy. The Lesbian girl had found a soulmate and so he and the tea cozy had talked about Hitler and health foods and the latest Jean Gabin film, which neither had seen; it was reputed to be very good, so he had suggested they leave the party and see it together. She had seemed delighted, in a startled, round-eyed way, and had risen to go; only then did he discover that whether she sat or stood made little difference in her height: the tea cozy just moved toward the door, footless like a ghost. She had worn an interesting perfume, rather reminiscent of the lavender-scented dressing-up trunk in his grandparents' attic.

They had not gone to see the Jean Gabin film; instead they had gone to her little shop, where she floated footless past the counter, up a narrow winding stair, to the smallest apartment he had ever seen, almost entirely taken up by a double bed. There he discovered that inside the tea cozy was hidden a plump child-like body which, unleashed, made for a memorable experience. She was utterly delicious, with surprising abandon; the only trouble was that she screamed so piercingly that his rapture was dimmed by the nervous expectation that the police would come banging on the door downstairs, drawn by the sounds of murder. But nothing happened; obviously, the neighbors, if not the neighborhood, were accustomed to her shrieks.

He had since visited her occasionally; she would be delighted to see him—if she were alone, that is. He decided to try his luck; she was certain to be fascinated by the story and might even give him some level-headed advice, once his ears had stopped ringing and they lay peaceably entwined in the contentment of the afterglow. Despite her round-eyed look of startled innocence, she must have a pretty sharp eye for the realities of life, or she wouldn't be set up the way she was.

The reversible sign on the inside of the glass door to the little shop said CLOSED, but when he tried the knob, the door opened.

He entered the still air and the faint scent of wool and lavender that evoked her sleek, ample nakedness.

"Yes?" her voice called from the top of the spiral stairs.

"It's me, Hendrik. Have you got a moment?"

"Oh! Hendrik!" The joy in the cry of recognition was gratifying. Footsteps came drumming down the stairs and there she was: tiny, round-eyed, her hair pulled into a bird's nest on top of her head, her muu-muu another tent job hiding what she called her unfashionable figure. "What a surprise!" she cried. "I was just thinking . . . " Then her face changed as if a shadow passed over it. "What is today? Not Friday, is it?"

"No, it's Thursday."

She sighed, a happy sigh of relief. "Thank God. Come! Come on up!"

He followed her up the winding stairs. So her lover visited her on Fridays. It did not bother him; what he hated above all was scenes, and single women without secret lovers made scenes.

He expected her to tumble onto the double bed at once, but she must have sensed his preoccupation. She looked at him with a frown of concern. "Anything the matter?"

He told her, pacing up and down in the tiny bedroom, head bent because of the low beams, about Dr. Halbertsma and his hallucinations. She listened, round-eyed, sitting on the bed, her knees drawn up, not a tea cozy this time but a Punch-and-Judy doll at rest, her muu-muu spread around her. He told her everything, down to the tea he had not been allowed to drink.

"Well, what do you think about all this? Think there's anything to that business of the ship sinking? He struck me as a nut."

"You wouldn't be here if you were sure of that."

"Well—what do you think?"

"I think you should take it seriously. But you need that job, don't you?" She hesitated, then she gathered her muu-muu about her, slid off the bed and made for the door. "I'm going to take you to Mrs. Karelsen."

"Who the hell is that?" He followed her downstairs.

"She's a medium, the most gifted sensitive in Amsterdam. I've consulted her many a time. She's terribly busy, but I'm sure that if I give her a tinkle she'll see you right away. This is an emergency."

He wasn't at all sure that was what he wanted; by asking one innocent question he seemed to have handed over the reins of his life to a bossy young woman. She made for the telephone in a corner of her shop, dialed a number and said, in a voice he suspected she used to her lover, sweet and cloying, "Mrs. Karelsen? Oh, how *lovely* you're there. This is Molly Boda. I have a dear, *dear* friend who has had a most *extraordinary* experience and is now faced with an *extremely* important decision which he has to make *this minute*. Do you think you would have a moment for us?"

The telephone mumbled.

"Oh, how absolutely *super* of you! I *knew* I could count on you in an emergency. Yes, we'll be *right* with you, Mrs. Karelsen! Right *now*. We're *there!*" She put down the receiver and turned around, triumphant. "Well, you see? There's no such thing as chance. She just happened to be there."

"How splendid," he said lamely.

"Come, let's go. It's right around the corner. Oh, you'll see! She'll tell you; she'll tell you exactly what to do."

Full of misgivings, he gave in.

3

Mrs. Karelsen's apartment turned out to be at the top of an intimidating flight of very steep stairs. Molly preceded him; there seemed to be no end to the rustle of her climbing. They passed the doors of two lower apartments on their way up: one produced the smell of Brussels sprouts, the other the *Kleine Nachtmusik* played by a child on an untuned piano.

"Ha! There you are!" a sergeant-major's voice rang out as they approached the top. "Come in, dearie! Come in! Is this the sitter?"

"Yes. Dr. Richters—Mrs. Karelsen. Hendrik Richters. He has a *very* ticklish problem for you."

The woman who looked him up and down was a tall, middle-aged blonde wearing a full-length purple robe and a number of huge bracelets. She dwarfed Molly, who gazed up at her with a look of awe and adulation. The scrutiny to which he was subjected seemed uncomfortably reminiscent of Dr. Halbertsma's.

"All right," the woman said in that unnerving barracks bellow. "Come in and we'll see what we can do. Charlie may not be available, you know, but then that's the luck of the draw. In here."

Hendrik passed through a door she held open for them. He was not sure he was going to like this; but maybe Charlie, whoever he might be, would turn out to be unavailable.

"Sit down!"

He obeyed and sank into the overstuffed chair Mrs. Karelsen indicated. It stood facing another one into which she lowered herself with a massive twanging of springs. Although dusk was just starting and apt to linger for hours, the room was lit like a stage set: orange and yellow. On the walls were mystical paintings, at least Hendrik assumed that's what they were: vague pastels of what looked like shrouds picking submarine flowers in the blue gloom of the bottom of the sea. There was a third overstuffed chair in the room, occupied by a large orange cat, fast asleep, which looked as intimidating as its mistress. Molly sat down reverently on a stool in the corner.

"Charlie? Hello, Charlie," Mrs. Karelsen said in a conversational tone.

Hendrik looked around, startled, but there was no one. She sat, hands folded, eyes closed, speaking into space.

"Charlie, we need you, sweetheart."

Hendrik watched her, spellbound. Would Charlie materialize behind her? Would a voice sound from a corner of the room? Maybe she had a loudspeaker hidden somewhere, successor to the fraudulent trumpet of nineteenth-century séances. But nothing happened. The stage of the room remained empty. Its center was slowly taken over by the orange cat, which stretched, yawned and rolled onto its back, displaying a surprisingly large expanse of white belly.

Mrs. Karelsen opened her eyes and gazed at Hendrik, blinking. "Well, Charlie doesn't seem to want to cooperate. You'll have to come back."

"But it is *terribly* important," Molly's voice urged from the corner of the room. "Hendrik is facing a *very* important decision which is a matter of *life* or *death!* He has to make it *today!*"

"Ah?" Mrs. Karelsen's eyebrows rose and she focused on him with a vengeance. "Don't say a word!" she commanded, raising a hand of surprising size. Then she held it out toward him and said, "Your watch."

"Excuse me?"

"Your watch! Take it off and give it to me."

Obediently, he took off his wristwatch and handed it to her. It disappeared completely as she folded her hands. She closed her eyes and began to hyperventilate. The cat yawned and turned its back on the scene. Next to Mrs. Karelsen's chair was a bookcase. Surreptitiously, Hendrik glanced at the titles. *The Secret of the Pyramids. How to Develop Your Third Eye.*

"Balloons . . . " Mrs. Karelsen's voice sounded distant and somnolent, like a dreamer mumbling. "I see balloons, huge . . . white . . . sweeping in low, over water . . . I hear people cheering . . . a sound of gushing water . . . " She halted; it seemed to Hendrik, despite the orange lighting, that she went pale. "Flood!" she gasped. "It's a flood! The water is rising! I'm in a barn . . . the barn is filling with water . . . the floor is tilting . . . Oh my God, oh my God, I'm climbing to—to a—a hayloft? I can't see; total darkness; I . . . Oh, no! *No!* Oh my God! Oh Christ! Oh God! Oh dear God, no, no! *Help!*" She pressed herself back into the twanging chair as if trying to escape from some horrible vision. Despite himself, Hendrik had to admit that it was very impressive; the only one who remained unaffected was the orange cat in the other chair. "Holy Mother of God! Oh Christ, oh God, oh Mary, mercy! Please, please, don't let me drown!" It was really becoming a bit much; Molly rose from her stool in the corner, ready to rush to the aid of the woman who now lay sprawled in her chair, legs spread, chest heaving, trying to fend off imaginary horrors, but still firmly clutching his watch. "I'm drowning!" she gasped. "Jesus, I'm drowning! Mercy, God, mercy!" Now even Hendrik began to feel that maybe he had better do something: slap her face, or at least get his wretched watch back.

But, as suddenly as it had started, the woman's terror collapsed. Even though tears were running down her face now, she smiled beatifically, eyes closed, and breathed, "Oh, what a darling child! Oh, what a sweetheart! Oh, I'm so delighted the little girl turned up! Saved by a little girl—who would have believed it? And a lovely . . . " She inhaled deeply as if sniffing something. "A lovely smell . . . Flowers . . . I know that smell, I know it . . . What *are* those flowers . . . ? White . . . " She opened her eyes.

At first, they were glazed and unfocused, then her sergeant-major's regard zeroed in on Hendrik in the chair opposite her and she said, in what he supposed was her normal voice, "I have it on the tip of my tongue."

Molly asked, audibly shaken, "What, Mrs. Karelsen? What is on the tip of your tongue?" Her voice was full of ridiculous awe.

"The name of the flowers," Mrs. Karelsen replied. "I know it, I know it! I can *smell* those flowers, but it's leaving. It's going now. What *are* they?" She closed her eyes and gave herself such a resounding smack on her forehead that this time the cat twitched in its slumber.

"Is—is it *he* who was drowning?" Molly asked quaveringly.

"He?" Mrs. Karelsen retorted as if it had been a ludicrous suggestion. "*He's* not about to drown. No, it was a girl. Beautiful young woman: dark-eyed, brunette—gorgeous. Saved by a child! Extraordinary; but I was there. I saw it. Oh my God, the terror! Do you know this poor girl was trying to climb some kind of a scaffolding, in total darkness, while the water was rising? My God! Never been so afraid in my life. But there came this little girl in a white dress, and all became light. A sunlit garden. What are those white flowers? I know them, I know them!"

"But—but is he in danger?" Molly persisted.

Mrs. Karelsen eyed him untenderly, then she said, "Yes, but not from extraneous forces. You're endangered by your own Parsifal, my friend."

"My what?"

"You're a very foolish young man. If you allow your life to be dominated by your carnal urges, you starve in the midst of plenty. My God! Surely you aspire to a higher awareness?"

"I'm sorry," Hendrik said with an uncharacteristic edge of asperity, "I don't have the faintest idea what you're talking about."

Mrs. Karelsen did not appear to be listening. "No wonder Charlie had nothing to say to you."

"But—but would he be *wise* to expose himself to the possibility of a shipwreck?" Molly urged in a hushed tone of reverence.

"Shipwreck? I see balloons. A flood. A girl drowning inside a barn. I see no shipwreck. The danger he runs is self-determined; all his chakras are closed except the one at the base of the spine. What you should do, young man, is master the biological imperative and start to live on a higher plane of consciousness."

The cat yawned and rolled onto its back again, its hind paws spread, its tail lashing in slow, sensuous movements.

"So he *can* go?" Molly urged.

"Why not? Let him go and sail the seas. Better than allowing his Parsifal to force him down to a lower plane of life in his next incarnation."

Hendrik decided he'd had enough. "Thank you very much. May I have my watch, please?"

"Certainly." Mrs. Karelsen handed it back in a manner that suggested she was surrendering to violence.

"But, *Hendrik*," Molly pleaded, "maybe Mrs. Karelsen has more to say . . . "

He decided to ignore it. He rose. "How much do I owe you for this consultation?"

Mrs. Karelsen somehow managed to strut sitting down. "You keep your money, young man. This was a favor to my friend Molly. She needs friends."

"Shall we?" He went to the door.

Molly said, looking unhappy, "Thank you *so* much, Mrs. Karelsen. I can't tell you how *impressed* we are."

"Thank you, my dear."

For some reason, Hendrik felt the temptation to poke the

huge tomcat's exposed belly. "Let's go," he said, taking Molly by the arm and urging her out the door onto the landing.

He descended the stairs ahead of her. Mozart was still being butchered behind door two; when they entered the smell of Brussels sprouts in front of door one, the sergeant-major's voice bellowed above them, "Honeysuckle!"

They stopped and looked up the virtually perpendicular stairs to the top landing. There she stood, massive and overbearing, and bellowed once more, "Honeysuckle! The flowers are honeysuckle!"

"Oh, *thank* you, Mrs. Karelsen, thank you."

Hendrik mumbled, "For God's sake!" and dragged her down the rest of the stairs.

Outside, as he opened the front door, a Jewish rag-peddler pushing a handcart solicited discarded clothing with an Arabian chant that caromed off the façades of the narrow street.

"Why were you so irritated with Mrs. Karelsen?" Molly asked, as he pulled rather than guided her in the direction of the Yarn Shoppe. "I thought what she said was *remarkable!*"

"Absolute nonsense," he answered angrily. "Balloons! Drowning brunettes climbing haylofts! Honeysuckle! The whole thing is a patent hoax. And what the hell is my Parsifal?"

He squawked like a hen when she grabbed it. "For Pete's sake! Not in the *street!*"

Behind them, the rag merchant wailed his melancholy chant. There were seagulls in the sky, orange birds lit from below by the setting sun. The bell of a streetcar clanged. The town suddenly seemed precious to him, a place of youth and love. As they entered the little shop, with its faint aroma of the dressing-up trunk, he was overcome by a feeling of farewell.

"I'll make you some orange-blossom tea," she said, "but first . . . "

She lifted her face and closed those huge, round eyes to receive his kiss.

CHAPTER TWO

As the freighter *Star of Peace* approached the Elbe River on her way to Hamburg, Captain Joris Kuiper made a final tour of inspection through the holds of his vessel before his passengers arrived.

What he saw made him feel pleased with himself. Admittedly, the accommodations were primitive. The three-tiered bunks, built close together in long rows in both the fore and aft holds, looked makeshift and uninviting in the unpainted starkness of their scaffolding; but he tried one and found it to be surprisingly comfortable. The straw mattress, which he had expected to be lumpy and unyielding, proved to be soft and fresh-smelling. The chemical toilets, though only semi-private and with the odor of a morgue, were adequate; the wash bays businesslike and without frills, but better than those in most Army barracks. After all, these people were not passengers in the usual sense of the word, but emigrants, traveling in bulk at bulk rate. At ninety-six dollars a head, the passage was a bargain; immigrants traveling steerage to the United States had no better accommodations and paid the same, yet Montevideo was almost twice the distance. Even the catering problem had been solved satisfactorily in the end: the temporary extension of the ship's galley in the port catwalk amidships, made up of two Army-surplus coal ranges, could amply provide simple fare for two hundred and fifty. The tables and benches in the starboard catwalk could seat one hundred and fifty, which meant two sittings for each meal with space to spare.

No, he had more than lived up to the terms of the contract with World Tours Inc. His crew had been cooperative and viewed the undertaking with obvious sympathy—no wonder, considering the fifty-dollar bonus each man would receive after the passengers had disembarked in South America and the mess they were sure to leave behind had been cleaned up.

Kuiper strode in high spirits past the tiers of bunks, climbed the ladder to the deck without pausing, emerged smiling in the sunlight and strode to the midships—a stocky figure in a worn blue uniform, the four gold rings on its sleeves oxidized by salt water to a coppery green. He looked young for his years: blue eyes, a shock of unruly brown hair, a ready smile—his father would have welcomed him as the prodigal son.

In the officers' messroom, converted into a temporary hospital, the unfamiliar presence of the medic he had hired awaited him, a morose man in his forties with hollow cheeks and dark rings under his eyes. He looked the victim of a hangover, but—so his testimonial said—he had been released reluctantly by Rotterdam University Hospital for temporary duty on this errand of mercy. The testimonial smelled of forgery, but at a wage of fifty dollars a month, you could not expect top labor. The man's license had been checked by the water sheriff and accepted as genuine, so the requirements of the law were met.

"Well? How are you getting on, Vinkemans?"

"Okay, I guess, Captain," the cavernous medic replied, in a tone implying a melancholy disposition and a tendency to complain. "I wish the doctor was here, though. I don't know where he wants all this stored." He indicated the five beds littered with urinals, bedpans, emesis basins and boxes of bandages.

"Well, use your own judgment. We have plenty of closet space." That was true: three temporary storage cabinets had been put up in the passage. It had seemed an excessive expense at the time; now, judging by the amount of litter on the beds, they would need every inch.

"And then I'd like to see the passenger list."

"Why?"

"Because I want to address my patients by name, for God's sake."

"Ask the doctor," Kuiper said curtly. "And I advise you that here no one takes the Lord's name in vain. This is a Christian ship. Remember that."

He left the man in an even more lugubrious mood. He would have to watch this joker—looked like a born sea lawyer. Well, you got what you paid for.

The distant ring of the engine-room telegraph and a change in the vibration of the ship alerted him that the pilot was about to board, so he left the inspection of the consulting room until later and went to meet the man at the rail.

Looking over the edge, he saw, three stories below, the pilot launch bouncing alongside in the eddies of the still-traveling ship. The rope ladder had been lowered; a figure in oilskins and a sou'wester began to claw his way up. The pilot boat veered away, gathering speed with a roar of engines. The pilot heaved himself over the rail. It turned out to be the fat, florid one he'd had on board twice before. *"Guten Morgen, Herr Kapitän!"* the man exclaimed, pumping him vigorously by the hand with a heartiness that had an edge to it—a change that had come with the Nazis taking power. Germany was no longer a pleasant country; his future passengers were lucky to be getting out. Especially as they were Jews.

"Which quay is it to be this time?"

"We go to the Hamburg America Line," the pilot said. "First-class service there, Captain. You'll be in and out in a matter of hours."

Kuiper was not happy with the idea. He knew the dock: high and heavily padded with floats and shock-absorbing dolphins meant for big passenger liners. "I'll look like a mouse in a barn there, and too far away from the dockside for my gangway."

"Don't you worry about a thing, *Herr Kapitän*," the pilot said. "The H.A.L. has graciously allowed you the use of two of their own passenger gangways. You'll see: you'll be out of there in a jiffy."

Kuiper grunted.

The pilot climbed the stairs to the bridge and the wheelhouse with the agility of his profession. He greeted Mate Meyer and Johansen, the helmsman, and gave the course. "You'd better go down and prepare for loading," Kuiper said to Meyer. "There's apt to be a lot of baggage." He turned to the pilot. "Or is there?"

"Pardon?"

"Are these people likely to have much with them?"

"No—no, no," the pilot said airily. "Just the usual. A suitcase, maybe; more likely a duffel bag . . . "

"That many suitcases or duffel bags call for expert handling."

"You have the use of the H.A.L. nets," the pilot said. "You'll see, you'll be in and out in a jiffy."

"Where are they now?"

"*Verzeihung?*"

"The passengers. Are they waiting on the quayside?"

"I suppose so." The pilot seemed ill at ease. "They're in the terminal, I think. You'll see: we'll turn you straight around. You are bunkered up, are you?"

"Yes." No point in telling the man that they would bunker in Le Havre, where the coal was cheaper. The Germans were touchy on the subject, always had been; it was one of the things that hadn't changed.

The pilot lit a pipe. Henky, the messroomboy, came with mugs of coffee.

"And how are things in your neck of the woods?" Kuiper asked, as the ship was nosing up the central channel.

"Oh, so-so," the pilot replied. "There are good things and bad things. That's life."

"Are you going to take us out too?"

"I suppose so. If you leave during my watch, which is the expectation."

"I didn't know they were going to turn me straight around."

"Well, you don't mind, do you? Time is money."

"No, I don't mind." Kuiper didn't. But it was odd all the same. He had counted on laying over in Hamburg and sailing with the outgoing tide early in the morning. "I have some provisions on order. They have to be loaded."

"Everything is ready and waiting. You'll see: with the H.A.L.'s nets and their stevedores, you'll be in and out in no time."

Kuiper did not press the subject. The pilot's discomfort was embarrassing to both of them. "Nice weather for this time of year," he ventured.

"Ah, yes!" the pilot exclaimed, relieved. "I remember this same day, sixteen years ago; we had driving rain, freezing temperatures—*Mensch!* It was like winter. I remember because, to tell you the truth, it was sixteen years ago that my good wife and I were married. It seems like yesterday, let me tell you. She was dressed in gray taffeta—know what taffeta is? Well, she looked a picture, let me tell you. She was a lot thinner then. Well, so was I . . ."

The man rattled on. It was a lovely day indeed. The river glinted in the sunlight, patches of floating oil shimmered like mother-of-pearl. There was a lot of traffic of small boats and barges; there were even some sailboats out, tacking to and fro between the river's banks despite the heavy traffic. A big liner detached itself from the silhouette of the city on the horizon. "That's the *Bremen* on her way to New York," the pilot said with obvious pride. "It's her place you're going to take. Fortunately, our ships always leave on time."

Kuiper said nothing.

They both watched silently, side by side, as the huge vessel passed them, with a sudden drop in the wind. Its decks towered high above them, their rails thick with people waving, shouting; a few threw paper streamers.

"Look at them," the pilot said beside him with a sudden change of tone. "Lucky devils."

Kuiper did not respond. The man was probably sorry he had let the words slip out. But, to his surprise, the pilot continued in the same tone, "America! That's where I'd like to go. That's where people are still free. Odd thing, freedom. You only realize you had it when you've lost it."

Kuiper still said nothing. He did not want to be involved in

the problems of the Germans. Let them work it out for themselves.

"Well, we're almost there," the pilot said. "Your men ready
fore and aft?"

"I'll check." Kuiper took the megaphone and hailed Meyer on
the forecastle. "Throw line ready?"

Meyer lifted his hand.

Kuiper walked to the starboard wing of the bridge and hailed
the poop. "Throw line ready?"

Second Mate Wybrands lifted a hand.

He put the megaphone back and rejoined the pilot in the
wheelhouse.

"Well, here we go," the pilot said, putting his pipe away. He
put the engine-room telegraph on DEAD SLOW, and said, "Don't
worry about a thing, Captain." It was an odd thing to say; odder
still was that he touched Kuiper's arm in an awkward gesture of
reassurance. "You'll be in and out in a jiffy, you'll see. Steady as
you go, helmsman." With that, he stepped over the high threshold onto the bridge and went to the port wing.

Kuiper followed him. The dock and the passenger terminal
of the Hamburg America Line were in full view now. There was
quite a crowd on the quayside, and a lot of police. Kuiper didn't
have any experience of crowds, but it seemed to him that there
must be more than two hundred and fifty waiting there: one solid
mass of people, four rows deep, from the terminal building right
to the end of the dock. They were being kept in line by the police.

"I had no idea there would be that many."

"*Verzeihung?*"

"That's more than two hundred and fifty people, isn't it?"

"Oh, no, no no." The pilot sounded shifty again. "Those are
not your passengers, Captain. That's just people who—who've
come to see them off."

"You mean relatives?"

"No," the pilot said. "I don't mean relatives." With that he
turned away and went back to the wheelhouse to give an order
to the helmsman.

Kuiper became preoccupied with the maneuver as his ship
was being moored to the quayside. The German stevedores were

very professional and fast with the ropes; but his own men worried him. His crew wasn't used to these pyrotechnics, they were
fumbling with the aft spring line and he was calling a command
to young Wybrands when sounds on the quayside caught his
attention. Shouts, screams, curses—it sounded like a riot. He
hurried to the port side of the bridge; on his way there he met
the pilot, walking in the opposite direction. "What's going on?"

The pilot did not answer, but walked straight past him as if
he had not heard.

At the rail he had a view of the quay and saw a confusing
scene: angry people trying to advance toward the ship, held back
by police; other people, fleeing, stumbling, dropping things: parcels, purses, paper bags. He realized that these latter were his
passengers, running from the doors of the terminal toward the
two gangways the stevedores had put up. The people trying to
get to them were the crowd he had seen waiting on the quayside.

He stood there, bewildered, and watched the police trying to
separate the shrieking crowd and the terrified passengers; then he
registered what the mob was screaming: "Jews! Foul Jews! Jew
bitches! Jew whores! Whores! Get the whores out of this country! Whores! Kikes!" What stunned him was that the most vocif-
erous were children: little boys no older than his own two sons
shrieked with high-pitched childish voices, *Juda! Juda verrecke!"*
They threw things, made obscene gestures, stuck out their
tongues at terrified old men, at mothers dragging small children,
at women carrying babies and trying to protect the infants from
the projectiles the crowd was now hurling: stones, bottles,
wooden hatch-cover wedges from the stacks on the quay. The
Jews running the gauntlet of the mob panicked as their tormen-
tors pressed closer, cursing, spitting at them, shouting obscenities. Terrified, they tried to flee up the gangways, where stumbling old men who had lost their glasses caused bottlenecks in
exhausted confusion. Babies yowled, women screamed in panic.
It was a situation the like of which Kuiper had never seen before.

For a few moments he stood in indecision, then he could stand
it no longer. He pulled out his whistle, blew it shrilly and
shouted, "Stop! Stop that at once!"

He might as well have shouted at a gale. He ran to fetch the megaphone; on his way back to the rail, he ran into the wheel-house and pulled the cord of the ship's foghorn.

First there came a hoarse gurgle; a jet of water splashed down on the wheelhouse roof. Then the steam took hold and a deep-throated roar set the windows rattling. He ran back to the rail and saw that the startling bellow of the foghorn had served its pur-pose: the crowd had fallen silent and was now looking up at the bridge. "You stop that, you hear!" he shouted through the mega-phone in his pidgin German. "Leave those people alone and go home!"

Obviously, his words had an effect; then someone shouted, *"Sau-Juden! Venerische Schweine!"* To his astonishment, he saw it was a police officer.

The crowd, as if in obedient response to the rabble-rousing yell, began to harass the remaining passengers with redoubled fury. A few shook their fists at the bridge and screamed, *"Kommu-nist!"* Another bully in uniform bellowed, *"Holländischer Käse-kopf!"* But Kuiper's attention was caught by the last of the passen-gers: an elderly man trying to climb the steep gangway with a footlocker on his shoulder. The man staggered under the load, threatened to lose his balance, then looked up at the bridge with despairing eyes; Kuiper saw that he had been hurt, his forehead was covered with blood. During one hallucinatory moment, as the old man gazed up at the bridge, Kuiper saw Jesus carrying His cross, halting, exhausted, on His way to Golgotha, gazing up at him through the blood of the crown of thorns. It lasted only a second; then it was just a confused old man again, stumbling as he fled from the howling fury of his persecutors.

But the vision so deeply moved Kuiper that he ran down the stairs to the deck, made his way through the crowd and went to the old man's aid. By the time he reached the gangway, the man had reached the deck; Kuiper took the footlocker from his shoul-der, hoisted it onto his own and said, "This way." He guided the old man through the milling mass of hysterical women and screaming children to the sick bay.

There was quite a crowd in the passage outside what had once been the messroom. He had to shout commands to make way for

himself and the old man; when he got to the sick bay, he saw why
there were so many people. The old man was not the only one
who was wounded. The place was full of people with bloodied
faces, bruises, nosebleeds—it looked like chaos, but, to his surprise, the medic Vinkemans radiated calm and confidence. In the
midst of hysterics, sobs and wails, he was a center of soothing
authority. He was bandaging a child's arm.

"Here's one more," Kuiper said. "This gentleman has a nasty
wound."

Vinkemans patted the child before he got up. He looked at the
wound on the old man's forehead. "Looks worse than it is, sir.
I'll have you fixed up in a moment. Why don't you sit down with
the others there? I'll be right with you."

"I'm putting your footlocker here in the corner," Kuiper said.

The old man began to cry; Vinkemans put an arm around
him. "Nothing to worry about, sir. You're safe now. Nothing
will happen to you on board this ship. We'll look after you and
take you safely to Uruguay. Why don't you sit down here and
have a rest? Here, on your own footlocker. There now. I promise
you I'll be right with you."

Kuiper asked, "Need any help, Vinkemans?"

"I could do with a couple of nurses," the medic said dourly.
"But, for the time being, maybe the messroom boy? Somebody
to hand me stuff from the cupboards. They're kind of difficult to
get to, with all those people in the passage."

"I'll send him down, and see if I can spare a sailor."

"I'd appreciate that," Vinkemans said. Then he turned back
to the child. "And, Lieschen? Shall we finish wrapping you up?
Give me your arm again."

Someone outside in the passage shouted, "Captain! Is the
captain there? Captain!"

"Yes!" Kuiper made his way to the door and stepped over the
threshold into the passage. At the far end, Meyer waved to him
over the heads of the crowd. "Someone to see you, Cap! Immigration officer! In your cabin!"

"Okay! Thanks!" He made his way through the crowd to the
steps leading to the lower bridge, but before going into his cabin

he went to the port rail and looked down at the quayside. The shouting and the screaming continued unabated, but there was a change. He looked at the gangways and saw why: now that all the passengers were on board, the crowd had been released by the police and allowed to rush the ship. They stood right below him, screaming, shrieking, their faces distorted with hatred, shaking their fists, spitting, some woman holding up a crying toddler and shouting, "*Juden! Sau-Juden!*" A little boy, perilously close to the edge, expressed his emotion by urinating at the ship. A woman thought this went too far, pulled him back and smacked his face; his angry shriek could be heard briefly over the howl of the crowd.

"*Kapitän!*"

It was a command, shouted behind his back, without the customary prefix, '*Herr.*' Kuiper turned around and saw, standing in the door to his quarters, a youth in uniform, with jackboots, his eyes blazing with rage. "Come here at once!" The youth pointed at a spot in front of his boots as if calling a dog.

It was the straw that broke the camel's back. So far, Kuiper had been shocked, outraged, but essentially confused. The experience was so new, so far outside his frame of reference, that he had not yet been able to get it into focus. Now it focused on the sallow youth in that ludicrous uniform with those ridiculous boots. He strode toward him; when the youth, in the shrill voice of intimidation he had heard occasionally over the radio when some Nazi made a speech, started to yell at him, Kuiper cut him short. He pushed him into his cabin, slammed the door shut and said, "Now you listen, friend! You may carry on like that in your own country, but here you are on Dutch territory. This ship flies the Netherlands flag. I am her master. You will behave like a civilized human being, or I'll fling you down the gangway and let your cronies pick you up!" When the youth took a breath to respond, Kuiper pushed his face close to his and yelled, "*Is that understood?!*"

It was astounding how quickly the bluster and the bullying collapsed when confronted with a fearless adversary. The youth swallowed, said, with a remnant of martial bluster, "*Du Lümmel!*

I represent the forces of law and order here, and I command
you—"

Kuiper had had enough. "You command *nothing!*" he
shouted, his face close to the boy's. "If there's any commanding
to be done on board this ship, *I* will do it. Now get the hell out!"

"I command you . . . " the youth quavered, but Kuiper wasn't
interested. He ripped open the door and said, "Out!"

The youth hesitated, then set his jaw, snarled, "You'll be sorry
for this!" and strode out, tripping on the high threshold.

Only as Kuiper was about to close the door did he realize that
someone had stepped aside to allow the jackbooted clown to pass.
A man in a dark suit, with a sallow face, his hair plastered to his
skull. He had a briefcase and a gray metal strongbox with him.
"Captain Kuiper?"

"Yes."

"May I come in?"

"Who are you?"

"I represent World Tours Inc. I've come to give you your
check."

"Check? But we agreed—"

"Let's discuss that inside, shall we?" The man brushed past
him without waiting for permission. After Kuiper had closed the
door behind him, he said, "That was most unwise, *Herr Kapitän.*"

"What was?"

"That officer was a *Sturmbannführer,* the wrong person to
insult."

Kuiper was not impressed. The very rank of the youth
sounded like a music-hall joke. "Let's get down to business, shall
we? You say you have a check."

"Indeed I have." The man opened his briefcase.

"But it was specifically agreed by your representative in Amsterdam that I would be paid cash before departure. What good
is a check to me? Where can I cash it?"

"Now, Captain, calm down," the man said, with a great deal
more authority than the jackbooted clown. "Let's handle this in
a rational manner. Here's your check. It's a cashier's check; when
you get to Le Havre, where I gather you are going to take on coal,

go to the Crédit Lyonnais and they will pay it out for you."

"But it's in German marks," Kuiper cried, shaken by the fact that the German knew he was planning to bunker in Le Havre.

"The German mark is legitimate, negotiable tender," the man said. "The bank will pay out this check in German marks, you will take your German marks to another ticket window and there have them changed into dollars. The whole operation will take no more than a few minutes."

"But the agreement—"

"*Herr Kapitän,*" the man said, with an edge to his voice, "don't let's flog a dead horse. Currency regulations will not allow me to pay you in U.S. dollars. Now, here's the box with your passengers' passports . . . Here's the key . . . "

"I want to see those passports, right now."

"Oh? I see . . . Of course." The man opened the box and handed him one.

"Thank you." Kuiper leafed through the passport; its identification page was disfigured with a large stamped letter J. "What's the J for?"

"*Jude, Herr Kapitän.* It stands for 'Jew.' "

"That stamp renders the passport invalid." It was a wild shot which he hoped would fluster the man.

It did not. The man shrugged his shoulders and said, "Allow me." He took the passport back and pointed at another page. "If you please: a visa for Uruguay, duly stamped and legalized by the Uruguayan Consulate."

"And where's my letter?"

"Excuse me?"

"The letter we agreed upon, the one from the Consulate."

"Ah, yes—of course. *Verzeihung.* I forgot." He brought out a wallet from his inner pocket and extracted a folded letter. "There you are."

Kuiper took it from him and read it. It stated that the accompanying passports of two hundred and fifty passengers had been duly checked and that legal entrance visas had been granted to all concerned. The Uruguayan Consul, authorized by the Uruguayan Foreign Minister, represented by the Uruguayan

Ambassador in Berlin, declared herewith that said immigrants were permitted to enter Uruguayan territory for the purpose of settlement prior to naturalization. The document was sealed with a large stamp, validated by a legalized signature. No one could reasonably ask for more.

"All right. But as to the check—"

"Take it and get out as fast as you can. That is my advice." The man snapped his briefcase shut.

"But I insist—"

"Captain, you've thrown your weight about enough for today. Let's hope, for your sake, that the authorities are so eager to get the Jews out of their hair that they'll overlook the incident. But don't you expect to ever pick up another cargo in this port, or any other German port, for that matter. Insulting an S.A. officer is not a trifling matter here. You have effectively black-listed yourself. Goodbye." He held out a thin hand, which felt fragile and bony as Kuiper shook it. Then the man clicked his heels, raised his right arm and gave a startling shout. *"Heil Hitler!"* He made an about-turn, marched to the door, let himself out and flung the door shut behind him with a show of force. Even as his anger flared, Kuiper realized that it was a piece of showmanship intended not for him but for those who might be watching outside. Obviously, the man had felt obliged to create the impression of outrage.

Now that he was alone, Kuiper felt the overwhelming need to pray. He wanted to go down on his knees, invoke the presence of Christ, put the whole confusing conflict before Him, but he was not given the chance, for there was a knock at the door. It was the pilot; his ruddy face looked pale and fearful, his voice sounded hoarse and secretive. "We must leave at once, *Herr Kapitän!* There's no time to lose: at once! Go to the bridge, get your men to the hawsers!"

"But what about my stores? I ordered—"

"Never mind stores," the pilot whispered with the urgency of fear. "Leave! *Now!* To the bridge!" He turned around and strode to the stairs. Bemused, Kuiper followed him.

Seen from the bridge, the ship was in a state of chaos. Hundreds of people, mainly women and children, crowded the deck. The hatches to the forward holds were open; he saw the second mate guarding the ladder leading down into number-one hold, the chief engineer the one into number-two. He had ordered that no one be allowed to go down into the holds until all the passengers were on board—that order seemed to have been given a long time ago, in a different world.

He took out his whistle and blew it to attract the officers' attention over the hubbub of the crowd. They heard it and looked up at the bridge. "Wybrands! Davelaar! You can let them go down! But get crew to help the women and the elderly! They aren't used to those ladders and we don't want any accidents!" The men each lifted a hand to acknowledge the command. "You yourselves get to your posts!" he concluded. "We're leaving now! Where's Meyer?"

Mate Meyer turned out to be waiting in the wheelhouse. The pilot must have got to him, for he looked intimidated; but then he was easy to intimidate. "Get yourself to the forecastle," Kuiper said. "We're about to cast off."

"But—but what about the baggage?"

"What about it?"

"It's still on the quay, tons of it!"

"All right, get it winched on board, on the double!"

As Meyer went to leave, the pilot stopped him. "No! No baggage! There's no time. We must leave it behind!"

Meyer, intimidated, looked from one to the other.

"We can't leave their baggage, Mr. Pilot," Kuiper said. "All their clothes are in there. Their medicines, their personal belongings."

"Now, you listen to me, young man," the pilot said in a low voice, "you're lucky if we get to the outer buoy without their coming after you!"

"To do what?"

"To arrest you!"

"For what?"

"For insulting an S.A. officer! Do you know what the penalty is for that? Concentration camp! *Konzentrationslager.*" The pilot whispered it as if the mere voicing of the word were an offense. His eyes were full of such genuine terror that Kuiper bit back the contemptuous remark he had been about to make.

"Mr. Pilot," he said, "I'm not in your shoes, so I can speak only for myself. I say I cannot leave without my passengers' personal belongings. It says so in my contract: their baggage shall be delivered on board. So, Meyer, go ahead and have it winched on board."

"*Herr* Meyer! Please listen to me!"

But Meyer ignored him now. "Do I sort it out on the quayside, Captain?"

"*Herr Kapitän* . . . "

"No, don't let's hang around any longer than necessary. Dump it on deck."

Meyer left.

"You'll be sorry," the pilot said. "They'll come for you, you'll see!"

"Mr. Pilot, don't you worry about that. This is Dutch territory, according to international law."

"Captain!" The pilot grabbed his arm. "Understand, *please:* they have *Scheisse* at international law! They make their own laws!"

"Maybe so, but still they cannot arrest the master of a foreign vessel on board his own ship."

The pilot gave him a searching look, then let go of his arm. "You'll be sorry, Captain," he said resignedly. "You're an honorable man, but innocent. Too innocent. On your head be it."

"That's right."

Kuiper did not show that the pilot's alarm had got to him. Maybe the man was right; maybe he had gone too far with his undiplomatic reaction to the obscenity he had witnessed. Maybe he should call Meyer back and arrange . . . He turned to the pilot. "Could you arrange for their baggage to be forwarded to Le Havre by train? Or by truck? We'll be there through Sunday. It's Thursday."

The pilot looked at him in an odd way before he answered, "Captain, I know it's difficult for you to understand, but the chance that they'll allow that baggage to be forwarded is nil. Zero. You see, they use every opportunity to torment the Jews. It's their pleasure. It gives them satisfaction. What you'd be doing is offering them another opportunity to play their game of cat and mouse. If they can procrastinate and keep you marking time in Le Havre, losing money, they'll keep you there for as long as the traffic will bear."

Kuiper had had enough of the pilot and his messages of doom. He went out onto the bridge to make sure that his order was being carried out and the passengers' baggage winched on board. He looked for Meyer on the quayside, but could not locate him in the crowd. Then a voice said behind him, "No go, Cap." He turned around; it was Meyer. "They won't allow me off the ship. And as to the baggage—forget it. They ordered us to cast off at once."

Kuiper stood in doubt for a moment. Then the pilot joined them. "Think of your passengers, *Herr Kapitän.* What do you think they would prefer? To leave without their baggage or be held up here at the quayside indefinitely? Be sensible, Captain. You are playing with lives. Believe me."

After a moment of thought, Kuiper said, "Let's ask *them.* " He leaned over the rail above the foredeck and called through his megaphone in his private German, "You people down there on the deck! Listen to me! Listen!" Silence fell. The deck changed into a white expanse of upturned faces. "Do you have any leaders?" Kuiper continued. "If so, I want to see them here on the bridge, *now.* It is urgent. *Oorgent.* " He did not know the German word, he just pronounced it with a German accent, hoping they would understand.

The white expanse below him darkened as people started to talk among themselves with a hubbub of voices. Then someone called out, "Yes, *Herr Kapitän!* They are coming! They are on their way to you, now!"

'They' turned out to be a frail, elderly man with a beard and ringlets and a wide-brimmed hat, and a big, blowsy woman with hennaed hair made up like a Russian doll. They introduced themselves as Rabbi Hirsch and *Frau* Goldstein.

"Do you represent the passengers?" Kuiper asked.

They nodded.

"Can you speak for them?"

"Well . . . " the Rabbi began thoughtfully.

The blowsy woman cut him short. "Of course we can, Captain. What is it you want?" She sounded completely matter-of-fact and unimpressed by what had happened.

"The baggage is still ashore," Kuiper said. "The pilot urges me to leave, because he thinks for us to hang around waiting for your personal belongings may lead to complications."

"In what way?"

"I had a run-in with an officer, to whom I gave a piece of my mind." Kuiper felt somewhat sheepish now; in retrospect, it had been an intemperate outburst, not only unintelligent and impulsive but somehow selfish. "The pilot thinks they may want to hold me for questioning; so he advises we sail at once, leaving your baggage behind."

The Rabbi said, "*Ach, Weh! Ach, Weh!*" and put his hands on his face; the woman asked calmly, "What would you like us to decide?"

"I cannot really judge what I'm dealing with, but I'm prepared to risk it. The pilot thinks that by hanging around here I may be putting your freedom in jeopardy. It's up to you. What do you want me to do: wait for your baggage or leave without it?"

"Leave!" the Rabbi cried, obviously under great stress. "*Um Gottes Willen,* leave!"

"Madam?"

"I agree with him," the woman said.

"Thank you. We'll leave at once." As they turned to go, he added, "As soon as we're under way and I can be spared here on the bridge, I'd like you to come up to my cabin for a conference. There are many things to decide."

"I'll be happy to," the woman said. "*Komm, Rebbe.*" She put her arm around the shoulders of the frail old man and led him to the stairs.

"Right," Kuiper said, "let's get going. Meyer! To the forecastle." Meyer scurried off. Kuiper crossed to the back of the bridge and saw that the second mate had already taken up position on the poop. He blew his whistle. "Wybrands! We're leaving! Cast off the main hawser, but keep the spring line going! I'll back into it, to swing out the bow!"

Wybrands lifted a hand.

Meyer cast off both the forward spring and the hawser. The engine was turning dead slow astern and the bow swinging away from the quay when suddenly there came a cry from below, "The baggage, Captain! There comes the baggage!"

Indeed, there it came: a huge net full of suitcases and duffel bags, parcels and boxes, suspended from a large mobile crane. By now, there was a gap of forty feet between the forward part of the ship and the dock. "Hard port!" Kuiper called to the wheelhouse, dashed for the telegraph and put the engine on DEAD SLOW AHEAD. The pilot was standing idly by; Kuiper couldn't help saying, "You see, *Herr* Pilot? You were wrong. They're sending over the baggage now."

The pilot looked as if this were an alarming development; the man obviously suffered from persecution mania. Suddenly, there was a tearing noise and a massive cry of anguish and disbelief on the deck below. Kuiper looked and saw an avalanche of baggage cascading down into the water between ship and shore. For a second he thought it had been an accident. Then he saw that the net was undamaged; one side of it had been deliberately released.

It was an act of such wanton viciousness that he stood for a moment transfixed, staring at the mass of suitcases, bags and parcels bobbing in the oily water. Then he put the telegraph back on DEAD SLOW ASTERN. "Hard starboard!"

Slowly, the bow swung away from the quay.

"All right, *Herr Kapitän*. I'll take over," the pilot said. His face was expressionless.

"Very well. She's all yours."

The ship was about to head downstream when Kuiper, glancing at the quayside, saw a spectacle that filled him with a sense of unreality. This could not be true!

But it was: there came, swinging out in the net, a second load of bags and suitcases. The crane swung it out to where the ship had been, then one side of the net was released and the load dumped in the river to loud cheers and boos from the crowd on the dock. "I don't believe it," he said to no one in particular.

"It's all very logical, *Herr Kapitän.*" The pilot was standing behind him, hands clasped behind his back, stoically watching the scene. "Your contract says that the passengers' baggage shall be delivered on board; they're living up to their end of the bargain and putting it on the deck of your ship. Only, the ship is no longer there; but that's not their problem. Do you see now? That's how the Nazi mind works."

"But it's the mind of a madman!"

"Maybe. Maybe they're mad. Maybe we're all mad and some terrible wrath for past sins is being visited upon us. Who knows? God knows."

"He docs indeed," Kuiper said with conviction.

But it was difficult to recognize God's plan in what he had seen this day.

CHAPTER THREE

Hendrik Richters' departure from Amsterdam was chaotic—last-minute signing of the articles at the harbormaster's, last-minute shopping—because he had overslept in Molly's bed and made copious languid morning love, oblivious of the hour. This time, she had not screamed but passed out; as he stood, stretching and yawning, in front of the window, wondering if she had indeed fainted or pretended to, the clock of the Southern Church struck the hour. It seemed to go on forever—when he counted twelve, he decided that either the clock had gone haywire or he was insanely late, considering that the train he was supposed to take left at four. And he *must* make that one, or he would miss the connection in Paris.

He made it by the skin of his teeth, loaded with suitcases, parcels, a shopping bag, a tropical helmet on his head and a tennis racket under his arm which he dropped when groping for his ticket at the gate to the platform. The train was about to leave; as he stooped to pick up the racket, his tropical helmet fell and rolled, limping, toward the track. Only with the help of an indeterminate number of porters, costing him an indeterminate number of quarters, did he manage to lug all his belongings into the compartment through the window with the train, shuddering, clanking and hissing, already in motion.

The change of stations in Paris in the small hours was equally chaotic and expensive, as there was scandalously little time to make the connection. Only in the second train, as it clanked at a snail's pace through the flat and unattractive countryside in the pale dawn, did the realization strike him. Absent-mindedly scanning the front page of *Le Figaro* behind which a priest was hiding, he suddenly stared at the date. *Jeudi.* That was Thursday, wasn't it? Or was it Friday? No, Friday was *Vendredi.* Maybe it was yesterday's paper . . . *"Monsieur—excusez!"*

The priest lowered the paper slowly and glared at him with a marked lack of Christian charity.

"Is that today's paper? I mean, is today *Jeudi?*"

The priest slowly turned the paper around to contemplate the front page. Then he said, *"Oui,"* and retired once more behind the paper.

It couldn't be! There must be a mistake! *"Pardon, Monsieur . . ."*

This time the priest took so long to lower the paper that Hendrik was about to reach for it. The look he received was frosty to the point of hostility, but he had to know.

"Jeudi is Thursday, isn't it? I mean, *Lundi, Mardi, Mercredi, Jeudi . . . ?"*

Now the priest, judging by his expression, was sure he was dealing with a lunatic. *"Oui,"* he said, then he hid behind his paper once more.

Dammit! He was a day early! Of all the insane, moronic . . . Now he would have to kill a day in Le Havre, stay overnight in a hotel and pay for it himself! Damn Molly! Damn women!

As he stood, morose and furious, in front of the station in Le Havre in the midst of the luggage, the tropical helmet on his head because there was nowhere else to put it, a taxi cab crawled up. He was about to ask for the nearest cheap hotel when, in a flash of inspiration, he said, *"Le bateau Hollandais* Star of Peace. *Est-ce en port?"*

The driver grinned and replied enthusiastically, *"Bateau Hollandais! Oui, oui!"* He leaped out to help pile the luggage into the trunk.

It was an incredible stroke of luck! The ship must have docked a full two days ahead of time. But when the taxi drew up alongside a huge white liner moored to the dock of what appeared to be a passenger terminal, Hendrik's heart sank. *"Non, non! Ce n'est pas bateau Hollandais!"*

"Oui, oui, monsieur! C'est le bateau Hollandais! Regardez!" The man pointed at the mast of the liner; there indeed fluttered the Dutch flag. On the gangways it said ROYAL NETHERLANDS LLOYD; on the life buoys TUBANTIA—AMSTERDAM.

As Hendrik stood in a quandary as to what to do next, a sailor with a beribboned cap came up to him and asked with well-schooled courtesy, "Can I help you, sir?"

"As a matter of fact, yes," Hendrik replied. "My name is Dr. Richters. I'm the ship's surgeon of a freighter with passenger accommodation called *Star of Peace,* home port Amsterdam. I'm supposed to board her here in Le Havre. Have you seen her by any chance?"

The sailor frowned. "No, Doctor. I couldn't say . . . " He looked around in a vague effort to be helpful; then, suddenly, his face lit up and he exclaimed, "Wait! There's Dr. Willemse! He'll be able to help you. He's our own ship's doctor. Doctor! Doctor!"

A uniformed character on one of the decks of the floating wedding cake shouted back, "Yes?"

The sailor pointed at Hendrik and shouted, "He's a doctor too! Ship's doctor of . . . What did you say the ship's name was, sir?"

"Star of Peace."

"Star of Peace!"

The natty figure on the distant deck shrugged his shoulders and pointed at his ears. The sailor hollered, between his hands, "A doctor! A ship's doctor! He's looking for the *Star of Peace!"* Hendrik felt foolish, standing there like an inanimate object under the scrutiny of his distant colleague. On impulse, he saluted at his tropical helmet, which made him feel even sillier. But it seemed to have a beneficial effect on the character up there, who shouted, "Wait! I'll come down!"

"You see, Doctor?" the sailor said. "I knew he could help. Anything else I can do for you, sir?"

"No, thank you; you've been most helpful. Have a nice jour-
ney."

"Yessir." The sailor saluted.

Hendrik returned the salute, which made the helmet wobble
on his head; he would have to practice this. Maybe he should have
got himself a peaked cap instead.

"*Monsieur . . . ?*" The taxi driver, whom he had forgotten,
sounded plaintive.

"Just hang in there, will you? I'm waiting for someone to tell
me where to go. *Comprenez?*"

The driver raised his shoulders and lifted his arms sideways
in the French gesture of incomprehension.

"*Attendez.* We must *attendez.* We need *information. Com-
pris?*"

That produced a torrent of words. "*Mais, monsieur, ceci est
bien le bateau Hollandais! Vous m'avez dit à la gare . . .* " The man
sounded like an accusing mistress.

"Well now, that's a surprise!" a cheerful voice said. It was the
character off the wedding cake; he had arrived so speedily that it
seemed as if he had made the descent by parachute. "I'm Dr.
Willemse. I gather you're a colleague off some other bucket." He
looked young, successful, debonair, all the things Hendrik himself aspired to.

"Yes. My name is Richters, Hendrik Richters. I'm waiting for
a converted freighter full of Jews."

"I beg your pardon?"

"Emigrants. Two hundred and fifty. Picked up in Hamburg.
I'm supposed to board her here."

"Well, sounds like you're going to have your hands full!"

"Yes, that seems a safe bet. You haven't seen the thing, have
you? I don't mean here in port, for she isn't due in until tomorrow, but at sea?"

"*Monsieur . . . !*" The taxi driver wailed.

Hendrik had forgotten about him. "Okay, okay," he said
impatiently, then turned to Dr. Willemse again. "Look, do you
know of a reasonable hotel nearby?"

"Hotel? You're nuts. Come and stay on board. We're held up
here for another twenty-four hours; there's been a delay in the

train connection from Germany. We'll find someone to take care of your luggage . . . Hey, you there!"

The same sailor came running, obligingly. "Yes, Doctor?"

"The doctor here is going to stay on board. He has some luggage. Will you take care of it?"

"Right away, Doctor. What cabin?"

"I don't know yet, I'll have to ask the purser. Put it in the First Class infirmary."

"Yes, Doctor."

"*Monsieur . . .* "

"*Oui, oui!*" Hendrik pulled the envelope of French banknotes from his inside pocket. "*Combien?* How much?"

The man, in the plaintive voice of the jilted mistress, named an astronomical figure.

"You're crazy. *Vous êtes fou!*"

The driver started the sorrow scene from *La Bohême*. Willemse asked, "Where did you come from? The station?"

"Yes."

"They're all robbers here. Leave him to me." There ensued a vivid exchange between the two, which the driver seemed to lose. He took his loss badly; it looked for a moment as if he were going to hang on to the luggage as ransom. But a second sailor turned up, so he was outnumbered. When the last parcel had been removed, he slammed the lid of the trunk and, cursing unintelligibly, drove off, bouncing across the railroad tracks.

"Well, welcome aboard! Let's go upstairs, and I'll introduce you to our staff."

Chatting, they climbed the gangway and walked through the movie-set opulence of a series of public rooms to an infirmary, where Willemse called in "the troops" and introduced him to two pretty young nurses, Myrtle Sedgwick-Jones, thin, blonde and very British, and Susan Foster, a compact brunette. They had drinks together in his quarters, then lunch in the First Class dining room, coffee in the First Class library, drinks in the Coconut Bar, and decided in high spirits to go ashore for dinner. Susan Foster put her arm through Hendrik's as they went down the gangway.

Dinner was a festive affair with lots of wine and gales of laughter. Hendrik was a great success. He discovered in himself a fountain of wit that, thus far, had remained untapped. Later, when it came to the dessert, he ordered *"Le mousse au chocolat"* instead of *"La mousse,"* which changed it into "the chocolate-covered cabin boy." It had everybody in stitches, including the headwaiter; Hendrik nimbly pretended the joke had been intentional, convincing everyone except Nurse Foster, who, eyeing him like an expert, said, "I think it's time we packed up," and thereby started an argument between the two men over the bill. Hendrik insisted he take care of it; finally he handed the envelope with the money to Nurse Foster, saying, "You sort it out, honey, I'm bored with the Frogs and their stage money."

She scrutinized the bill, had a tart exchange with the head-waiter, who recovered at once from his fit of laughter at *le mousse;* then she said, "I'll need another ten, Frans."

"What do you mean?" Hendrik asked, angered when he saw Willemse reach for his wallet. "There's enough in that envelope to buy the damn restaurant."

"Ten," Nurse Foster said calmly, hand extended.

"Here," Willemse said.

"But this is ridiculous!"

Nurse Foster rolled the empty envelope into a ball, tossed it into the ashtray and said, "Come. I'm going to take you home."

Hendrik did not like her tone; he hated bossy women. "Let me tell you something," he started, but he was not given the chance until they sat squeezed in the back seat of a taxi. There he resumed. "As I was saying a moment ag—" The rest was a gurgle, for Nurse Foster gave him a kiss that would have turned a prince into a frog.

Pity he was drunk, for when he found himself kissing her again in some cabin—either his or hers, he wasn't sure—he seemed completely in control of the situation until she said briskly, "Well, are we going to remain fully dressed?"

They weren't. They had a high old time, once they had managed to sort out their limbs in the narrow lower bunk where they soon found themselves. She was an eager lover, very competent and in control, as she had been from the moment they met. If he had been sober, he could have taught her a thing or two; now he was somewhat disoriented by the confines of the narrow bunk. She proved more expert at making love in a coffin than he was; even a chaise-longue was a king-size bed compared to this. Also, the fact that he went on hitting his tailbone against the lid of the coffin—the bottom of the upper bunk—was dispiriting. But once he had accepted the fact that she was in control, he had a whale of a time. Even her climax sounded controlled, like the competent extraction of a tooth. "Okay, Hank," she said, slapping his behind, "that's it. Time for bye-byes." When he protested feebly, distressed by the clinical expertise of the whole thing, she said, "Don't be difficult, sweetie. Just stay where you are, I'll bring you a cup of coffee in a couple of hours, okay?" She cantilevered him off her sweat-slick body, slipped from under, leaving him lying on his stomach, mewling; then she covered him up and turned off the lights. "Bully," he muttered, and sank into sleep like a stone.

Within minutes, so it seemed, the lights were turned on again and there she was, in crisp, starched white, shaking him by the shoulder and saying, "Wakey-wakey! Time for little boys to do wee-wee!" All things considered, he decided, he would have preferred *le mousse*.

He was having breakfast with her and Willemse and the British nurse in a corner of the First Class coffee shop when the sailor who had accosted him on the quayside the day before came in with an air of urgency and said, "Doctor! Your ship's coming up the channel!"

"It is? Where?"

"Right there, sir—over on starboard."

Hendrik threw down his napkin and hurried to the nearest porthole on the opposite side.

Indeed, there came a scruffy old freighter, looking tiny and toylike, with an upright thin funnel and a perpendicular bow, slowly working her way upriver. His heart sank at the sight; suddenly, mad Dr. Halbertsma's prediction came back to mind: she did indeed look as if a minor explosion would sink her. He hoped for a moment, foolishly, that it might be another vessel; but there was the Dutch flag fluttering at the stern, and when she was broadside, he could decipher the name on her bow: *Star of Peace.*

"Is that her?" Susan Foster asked, beside him.

"Yes," he answered, "I'm afraid so. It's going to be a—well —different experience, by the looks of it."

She briefly touched his arm, an unexpected expression of tenderness. "So what?" she said. "*Vive la différence.* Come, finish your breakfast."

As he turned away from the porthole with a feeling of malaise, he saw that Willemse and the other nurse had been watching the ship through another porthole.

"Looks like a nasty old bucket," Willemse said expertly, as they walked back to their table. "I know the kind. Made a voyage on one just like that: Tandjong Priok to Djedda, with *hadjis.*"

"What's that?"

"Moslem pilgrims for Mecca." Willemse pulled out his chair and sat down. "They were stacked three deep, both holds stuffed to the gills, and you could hardly move about on deck. And hot! They died in swarms, poor devils. I can still smell the stench occasionally, at odd moments."

"Well, he isn't going to treat *hadjis,*" Susan Foster said protectively. "His passengers are normal people."

"German Jews? Women and children? The old and the infirm? I wouldn't call that 'normal people.' "

"Here," Susan said, "have some coffee." She filled Hendrik's cup; then, seeing his face, she patted his hand and said, "Don't you worry, we'll all come and see you off. Won't we, Frans?"

"Of course," Willemse said without enthusiasm. "By the way, do you think you'll need help fitting out the lazaret?"

"I haven't seen it yet, I've no idea."

"Well," Willemse said, buttering his toast, "we've got more stuff here on board than we know what to do with. After breakfast, let's go and take a look and— Oh, good morning, sir!" He rose.

Hendrik looked up and saw an intimidating figure loom at their table, a grizzled, large man in uniform, with gold stripes up to his elbows.

"Commodore, may I present a colleague of mine: Dr. Richters, ship's surgeon of the Dutch freighter that just came in. Immigrants, German Jews, Hamburg to Montevideo. Er—Hendrik—this is Commodore Bruinsma."

The commodore extended a golden arm. "Doctor."

Hendrik shook a hand that felt as if it were carved out of hardwood. "Commodore . . . "

That was all. The commodore moved on, massively, to the next table, where he sat in solitary splendor until the purser joined him, bringing a list.

Their table was within earshot; the intimidating presence inhibited their own conversation. They finished their breakfast almost in silence; it was not until they were standing in the lobby to the public rooms that Willemse said, "If you like, we'll have a look at our stores now. And maybe I can give you a few tips. I don't suggest that you need them . . . "

Hendrik needed them desperately. He had not given much thought to his future patients, largely because he was scared stiff. He had a fairly accurate idea of his own worth as a physician; the prospect of having to care for two hundred and fifty potential patients intimidated him; he certainly needed all the help he could get. "I'll be delighted," he said.

"Okay, let's go."

They all trooped to the infirmary, where Willemse took him on a guided tour of their stores of supplies and equipment, then the pharmacy and the accommodations. "I have a fair amount of experience with elderly patients," he said, holding open the door to his office. "We've done a couple of cruises of late, and they're virtually geared to the geriatric set. Shall we go in?"

"Thank you."

It was a splendid office in the heart of a small but model infirmary. "I can't hope to have anything resembling your facilities . . . "

"Oh, you won't need all this," Willemse said, sitting down behind his desk. "Let me just give you a list of things that I think are essential. I'm sure you have drawn up one yourself, but you may find one or two items on here that you might want to add."

He handed Hendrik a few sheets of typed paper. "This is the pharmacy . . . " He proffered another set of pages. "And this the instrumentarium. You won't need anything as fancy as this, but, with that passenger list, I think you should be prepared for three types of emergency: pediatric, obstetric and geriatric. Do you have any pregnant women on board?"

"I haven't the faintest idea."

"Well, I expect you do. So, better get equipped for the possibility. Then, of course, the usual children's diseases, which always look like emergencies and rarely are. And then your main problem, given the age of your male passengers: cardiovascular incidents. So, make sure you get all the stuff on the first list I gave you. You may also find that you'll need lots of bromide. I'd take a barrel of it, if I were you. By the way, I suppose you'll be allowed to add to the ship's pharmacy as you judge necessary?"

"If I can't, I won't sail."

"Fair enough." Willemse rose. "I expect you want to get a move on. Anything else I can do for you?"

"No, thank you. You've been more than helpful."

"You'll need some help with your luggage. Let me get you somebody."

While Willemse was getting somebody, Hendrik had a look at the lists. They were pretty extensive, and some of the medication he knew to be very costly. He remembered Dr. Halbertsma's definition of the captain as 'a skinflint' and doubted he'd find much of this stuff on board.

As they stood at the head of the gangway with the two girls, who had come to see him off, Susan asked, "By the way, when are you due to arrive in Montevideo?"

"Four-weeks from now."

"Well, what do you know! We may meet again!"

"You're headed for Montevideo too? But aren't you much faster than we?"

"This is the last run of our summer schedule: Curaçao, Paramaribo, Rio, Monte, B.A., and back to Amsterdam after another stop in Monte. We might catch up with you there. Would be nice, wouldn't it?"

"Very," he said.

He turned around at the bottom of the gangway to wave to Susan and her English friend, who stood at the rail. Only in the taxi, as it made its way, bumping and rattling, across the cobbles and rails, did he realize he had no money. He recalled, like a dream remembered, Susan crumpling the envelope the night before in the restaurant and tossing it into an ashtray. This was an awkward situation; the first thing he would have to do on board the new ship was ask for money. Well, his travel expenses were supposed to be paid.

It became a long ride to what looked like the shady part of the harbor. The sheds and shacks on the dock they finally rattled onto were dilapidated and in disrepair; the freighters tied up to them looked in no better shape. Passing one after another of a dismal row of vessels, peering at them from the window of his taxi, he saw a diversity of flags: Greek, Liberian, Panamanian and some that were unrecognizable. In any case, not one of them was French.

It looked as if the *Star of Peace* was going to be the last of the row; to his unpleasant surprise, the taxi driver stopped at the far end of the dock, where there seemed to be an inordinate number of policemen loitering, and said, *"Le voilà, Monsieur."*

"Où ça?"

"Là! En rade!" The man pointed across the water, and there she lay: at anchor, at least two hundred yards off the pier. One of the policemen came sauntering over and asked what his business was. He explained, and *"Médecin de bord du bateau Hollandais"* seemed to bring about a sudden concentration of policemen, who, each in turn, checked his passport and his musterbook. Despite his grandmother's advice never to become angry with a policeman, he became angry. "Gentlemen, would any of you have the kindness to indicate to me what this is about?" he inquired in his best French.

The head of the posse looked him up and down and said, as if bestowing a favor, "You may go on board."

"How, may I ask?"

"Ici, Monsieur le Colonel!" It took him a moment to locate the

origin of the cry: a roguish head sticking up over the edge of the pier.

It turned out to be *un rameur libre,* 'a free oarsman,' which proved to be a euphemism for floating highwayman. It took an embarrassing amount of haggling with both taxi driver and *rameur libre* under the disapproving gaze of the police before the three of them set out in a rowboat for the distant ship, his luggage in a desultory heap between the coils of rope and baskets of coal. The taxi driver came along to press his claim, price for the two-way trip for one: nine francs. In Arabia he would have had his hand chopped off.

As the boat, rocking and plunging, made its way across the river restless with the incoming tide and turbulent with the wash of passing traffic, Hendrik had the opportunity to have a good look at the *Star of Peace.* She turned out to be even less prepossessing than when he had watched her trundle by from the porthole on the *Tubantia.* Seen from close quarters, she looked ancient; her buckled plates sunken between the ribs, patched in many places; she seemed to carry many layers of paint in a vain effort to subdue the rust. Her rails were lined with people on different levels, silently watching the boat's approach; it looked as if every available inch of space on main deck, boat deck and lower bridge was taken up by staring spectators.

They moored, messily, to the bottom of a gangway slanting down the side of the ship; no one came down to help them. All Hendrik could do was get out of the perilously bobbing boat in an undignified scramble and set off up the gangway. As he clawed his way up, hanging on to the swaying rope banister for dear life, all those silent spectators peered down at him.

The one closest to the gap in the rail where he finally ended up turned out to be a hobo-like old man with a peaked cap and a three-day-old beard. Despite the fact that he wore a greasy blue coverall, he appeared to be someone in authority, so Hendrik said, holding out his hand, "Good morning! I'm Dr. Richters. Your ship's surgeon."

The man seemed startled by the outstretched hand. He looked at it in apparent indecision, then pulled a wad of cotton waste from his back pocket, cleaned his right palm with it and gingerly shook hands.

"With whom do I have the pleasure?"

The man looked around, then realized it was he who had been addressed and replied, "I'm the chief engineer. Davelaar's the name."

"Good morning, Chief, I have a taxi driver as well as a boat-man waiting below. Both have to be paid, but I don't have any French money left. Would you kindly take care of it for me?"

That seemed to put the man on familiar territory. He growled, "I don't handle money. Go ask the captain," and shuffled off.

"Where do I find the captain, Chief?" Hendrik called after him.

"In his cabin. Up on the lower bridge." The man pointed without looking around and disappeared into the crowd of silent watchers, which closed behind him like water. They were unlike anything he had ever seen. He had no picture in mind of the "Jews" who were to be his patients; he had thought of them, if at all, as just people like anyone else. Now, for the first time, it was brought home to him that they weren't. They looked ordi-nary enough; it was their attitude that made him experience them as totally alien. All of them, old men, women of all ages, children, seemed to gaze at him with incipient terror, as if one sharp word, one impatient gesture on his part would set off a reaction of panic and flight. It was most unnerving, but he had to make his way through their silent ranks to find the captain. He gave a jocular wave to the taxi driver and the *rameur libre,* who peered up at him from their bobbing boat with expressive distrust, then set out to look for a flight of stairs. "Excuse me . . . " The spectators silently stood aside to let him through; he found a set of stairs, climbed them and was welcomed on the lower bridge by yet another wall of gazing, motionless figures on the brink of panic.

He was beginning to get a feeling of claustrophobia when a woman's voice said, "Doctor, sir? Are you the doctor, sir?"

"Yes!" He turned around, relieved, and discovered it was not a woman but an urchin. The boy could be no more than thirteen years old; he was dressed in rags and his face was so grimy that it looked like makeup.

"I'm Henky, the messroom boy," the urchin said breathlessly; he must have climbed those stairs like a weasel to catch up with him. "You want the captain, sir?"

"That's right."

"This way, sir, this way . . . " The urchin dived ahead and tackled the crowd. "Come on! Gangway for the doctor! Come on! Gangway!" His voice was strident and imperious, as if he were on a cattle drive. "This way, sir! This way!"

Hendrik followed, touched by unease. So far, his encounter with the crew of the *Star of Peace* had been less than promising.

"One second, sir . . . " The boy had stopped in front of a closed door. He listened at the crack; after a brief hesitation, he knocked tentatively. When there was no reply, he knocked again, louder this time. Somehow, the pantomime gave a thumbnail sketch of the captain, at least as far as the messroom boy was concerned.

"Come in!"

The boy opened the door and stuck his head in. "The doctor's here, Captain. Shall I let him in, Captain?" Obviously reassured, he turned to Hendrik and opened the door wide. "Here you go, sir. The captain will see you now."

"Thank you." Hendrik stepped over the high threshold into a dark, low-ceilinged cabin. A surprisingly young man rose to greet him behind a table covered with papers. "Good morning. My name is Kuiper. You are Doctor— er—?"

"Richters."

"Ah, yes. I've got it somewhere . . . " The young man gestured vaguely at the mess on the table. "Kind of you to come at such short notice. I take it you saw the water sheriff in Amsterdam?"

"Yes—he told me to give you this . . . " Hendrik produced the muster book he had received after signing the articles. He handed it to the captain.

"Thank you. I'll write you out a shore pass." The captain looked around for a place to put the booklet, then added it to the pile in front of him. "You want to see the sick bay, I expect? Let me take you there. Or do you prefer to unpack first? This half of the wardrobe has been cleared for you." He opened the door of a small cupboard. "The rest of your *barang* will have to go under the seat of the settee over there. It's yours." He pointed at a narrow built-in couch against the outside wall, underneath a porthole.

"You mean, that's where I sleep?"

"Yes."

After Susan's cabin on board the *Tubantia,* this looked so dismal that Hendrik was tempted to turn on his heels, and never mind the articles. "Before I do anything else," he said, "I have a taxi driver and a boatman waiting below, and I have no French currency." The captain's face changed, so he added hastily, "The whole thing was a bit of a scramble, you know. Sorry about this."

"How much is it?"

"Ten francs fifty for the taxi, eighteen for the boat."

The captain reluctantly opened a drawer of a desk next to the couch and took out a billfold held together with a rubber band. As he selected a banknote from the wad, Hendrik noticed the four stripes on the man's sleeves. They looked worn and unimpressive after the commodore's golden arms.

"Here you go." The captain took a purse out of his back pocket and produced a coin. "Let 'em keep the change."

"A fifty-centime tip is hardly enough for the two of them."

The captain reluctantly took out another coin. "Here. That'll have to do."

"All right. Thank you."

A skinflint, Dr. Halbertsma had said. How right he was. Hendrik made his way back to the gangway through the silent, staring crowd, and was joined by the urchin darting from behind a ventilator. "Need help, Doc?"

"Yes indeed. You can carry some stuff on board for me. It's in the boat."

"Sure, Doc!" Eagerly, the boy ran ahead of him, shouting his cattle drover's yell: "Gertcha! Gangway!" The silent crowd obeyed.

At the top of the gangway, Hendrik found an emaciated man in an orderly's uniform waiting for him. "My name is Vinkemans, Doctor," the man said plaintively. "I'm the medic. Shall I take you to the infirmary?"

"Ah, delighted. The name is Richters. I'll be with you in a minute. First, I have to pay the two men down there."

"Want me to do that for you, Doc?" the urchin asked, bright-eyed.

The prospect of having to do battle with those cutthroats in a bobbing boat over a fifty-centime tip was so dismal that Hendrik hesitated.

"You can leave it to him, Doctor," the medic said lugubriously.

"Sure can, Doc!" The boy seemed so keen and so street-wise that Hendrik said, "Well, thank you. Here." He gave him the banknote and the coins. "Tell them to keep the change."

"Yes, Doc!" The boy raced down the gangway with the zest of a terrier; Hendrik didn't stay to watch. The worst that could happen was that the Frenchmen would make off with his luggage; right now, he didn't care if he never saw it again.

"This way, Doctor, if you please . . ." The medic sounded like an undertaker taking a relative of the deceased to the last viewing. He made way for them by saying, *"Verzeihung, Herr Schwarz—Verzeihung—Verzeihung, Frau Adler . . . "* As Hendrik followed the man through the crowd, it somehow seemed as if by the wave of a magic wand the anonymous ranks were dissolved into individuals. Hendrik became aware of intense distress, a harrowing melancholy in the faces that, so far, had seemed expressionless. Even the children, of whom there were a good many, seemed to watch him with grave eyes, adult with grief.

"Jawohl, Frau Pauli, the doctor is here. He'll see your husband as soon as he can, I promise. Just allow us a few moments to get things organized, will you? Thank you. Thank you, *Frau* Sturmer. Yes, yes, the doctor's here; he'll see you in a little while." The individuals looked at Hendrik unsmilingly, without a word.

"Well, here it is, Doctor. After you."

Hendrik stepped over the high threshold into a narrow passage where in the darkness scores of people seemed to be packed together, barring his way.

"*Komm, meine Damen und Herren,*" the plaintive voice of the medic pleaded, "*machen sie doch ein bisschen Raum für den Herrn Doktor!*"

Slowly, the mass of people receded. More striking than their meek obedience was their silence. From the moment Hendrik had set foot on board, he had not heard any of them utter a word; those who had addressed the medic had done so in an inaudible whisper.

"Here we are, Doctor," Vinkemans said, opening a door.

It was a fair-sized room with three portholes, crammed full of beds. In each bed was a patient, one of them in traction. "Good morning—*guten Morgen!*" Hendrik said, to no one in particular.

"This is Dr. Richters," the medic explained. "He will be coming to see each one of you in turn. Right now, he and I have to sort out a few things first. The doctor has just arrived, so would you kindly give us time to find our bearings? Thank you."

Hendrik realized that his first reaction needed revision. At the gangway, when he discovered that instead of a pretty young nurse he was being given a cadaverous, middle-aged orderly, the man had made an impression of morose incompetence. Now it occurred to him that he might have been lucky and hit an experienced old-timer. The best thing to make a doctor look good, so the saying went, was a first-class Head Nurse.

In a small office next door, Vinkemans produced two lists. "This one, Doctor, contains our pharmacy and the instrumentarium Dr. Halbertsma ordered when I met him in Amsterdam. This second one is a list of items I feel we should take on before we sail."

Hendrik glanced at the two lists. The first contained more or less what Willemse had suggested, the second the medication he had recommended in view of the age of the passengers. Indeed, the unprepossessing Vinkemans was a professional.

"Isn't this rather meager?"

Vinkemans looked. "Ah, the bromide. Yes, I know it doesn't look like a lot. I personally would have ordered twice the amount, both tablets and suspension, but that was considered too expensive."

"By whom? The captain?"

"Actually, it was Dr. Halbertsma. His budget was tight, he had to make choices."

"All right, I'll order some more. Now, about the patients in there. I see you have one in traction."

"Yes," Vinkemans said somberly. "When we took the passengers on board in Hamburg, there was a scuffle. That one fell and was roughed up—a fracture of the tibia. I also have two cases of cranial trauma. But before you go to see them, maybe you should present these two lists to the captain and get his okay for me to go and buy this stuff while there's still time. We're about to start taking on coal, and sail at first light tomorrow. I'd like to get my pharmacy—excuse me, *your* pharmacy . . . "

"Our pharmacy."

"All right, our pharmacy in order before the ship chandler's office closes."

"But why didn't you arrange this before you came into port?"

The medic smiled wanly. "I'm afraid you're the one to make the request, Doctor. You're the ship's surgeon; I'm just the male nurse. The captain, I'm afraid . . . "

"Is a skinflint."

"Well—yes. He owns this ship. It seems he inherited it from his father fairly recently; most of the staff served under the old man. If you ask me, he has a chip on his shoulder."

"All right, let's go and see him together. The two of us can put on more pressure."

"If you wish . . . "

"You don't look convinced."

"Well . . . "

"Come on, Vinkemans, spell it out, man!"

"In my estimation, the question of authority is less likely to arise if you keep it between the two of you. Don't forget, to him I'm an N.C.O. You're his equal."

"All right, let's play it your way. But you're prepared to take care of all this once he agrees?"

"Oh, yes."

"Any idea how much it's going to cost?"

"I have it right here . . . "

Hendrik looked at the figure and whistled. "That much?"

Vinkemans smiled. "No, Doctor; it's about half that. But the captain likes to bargain."

"I see."

"One argument you might use is that a number of passengers lost their medication in Hamburg. That should be replaced."

"How did that happen?"

"The Germans dropped their baggage into the harbor."

"The Germans did *what?*"

"They swung two nets full of baggage out over the water, and just dumped it."

Hendrik looked at him in disbelief. "You're kidding! Why would they do such a thing? Weird people . . . Well, all right. I'll go and see what I can do." With that, he set out for the lion's den.

2

When Henky, the messroom boy, finished stacking the doctor's belongings in the center of the cabin—*his* cabin—Captain Kuiper was outraged. There was hardly room left for one person to move about, let alone two. What in the world had the man thought this ship was? The *Majestic?* A tennis racket! A topee! Ballroom pumps! Where did the city slicker expect to store it all? Half of the junk would have to be dumped into the sick bay; better still, over the edge. Kuiper's heart sank at the prospect of having to share his cabin, his intimate private world, his meeting place with the Lord, with this nincompoop.

Grimly, he sat down at the table and continued sorting out the bills. There was still hope that he might have made a miscalculation, but as he added up the amounts once again, checking each figure with the original bill, the hope was fading. He was going to be thirteen hundred Dutch guilders and thirty-one cents over the original estimate. How was it possible? He had checked it all twice, on the way to Hamburg. Had he picked up two bills at once without realizing it? The only way he could trace the origin of his error would be by—There was a knock on the door.

"Come in!"

It was the doctor, smiling, self-confident. "You needn't knock each time you come in," Kuiper said, "it's your cabin too now." Worse luck, he added to himself.

"Oh, sorry. Ah, I see! The boy brought it in. Good for him. Sorry about the mess. Tell me, when is the best time for me to unpack?"

"It's too much."

"Pardon?"

"You've got too much stuff with you, Doctor. You have half the wardrobe and three drawers in yonder desk and that's all."

"Oh . . . " The doctor looked around. "And the space under the settee, I gather?"

"That's where your bedding goes during the day. All it will hold is your night gear, a robe and a pair of slippers."

"Oh, well . . . " With a shrug of the shoulders, the man dismissed the problem. So he was one of those: 'I'll think about it tomorrow.' Lot of good that would do him on board *Star of Peace!* Here, people were expected to cope with problems *today.*

"Er—Captain, I have checked the pharmacy and the consulting room and there are a few essentials lacking. I won't take up your time with technical details, but here's a list of medications and medical equipment I'll need for that number of passengers over a period of four weeks."

"Twenty-three days."

"Okay, twenty-three days." Again the man dismissed reality with a shrug. "Here's the list. I'll send Vinkemans to collect the stuff, but he'll have to be nippy about it, it's almost closing time. What time are we leaving?"

Kuiper looked at the list; when he saw the final figure, he said, "No."

"I beg your pardon?"

"Dr. Blankema, or whatever his name is, gave me a list of his requirements. Those I got before we left. What was good enough for him is good enough for you. This is not the *Majestic.*"

The doctor smiled at him engagingly. Kuiper felt an acute dislike for the man. "In that case, let's settle for two-thirds of the amount, Captain. But that will have to be the absolute minimum."

"No."

"Can you tell me why?"

"Unnecessary expense. This whole trip has been budgeted to the penny. I based my budget for medical care on what Dr. Blankenspiel told me he needed to fit out a sick bay for up to three hundred according to the law. I already have an overrun. The spending has to stop."

"What you'll find on that list are essential needs for particular passengers! Dr. Halbertsma could not foresee—"

"He knew exactly what type of passengers to expect. He knew the men would be elderly, the children prone to children's diseases—"

"He did not know there would be nine gravidae."

"Nine what?"

"Pregnant women."

"Are all of them going to give birth in the next twenty-three days?"

"Well—er—one of them may."

"Then that's one less than he expected. I have his written estimate here . . . somewhere here."

"Did he also expect broken bones, concussions, emotional trauma caused by a riot on the quay in Hamburg? The loss of their medication when their luggage was dumped in the river?"

"All right, you show me what on this list applies to whatever resulted from the business in Hamburg. That I'll pay for."

"Very well." The man's response was so nonchalant, it proved the whole exercise to be a waste of time.

"Now, if you'll excuse me?" Kuiper said. "I have these papers to finish."

"Of course." The doctor rose. "Goodbye, Captain. I'll send the boy to collect my luggage." He went to the door.

"No need to do that now. Later tonight will be soon enough."

"Sorry, Captain. Now."

Frowning, Kuiper looked up.

"You see, Captain," the man continued with a smile, "I'm leaving."

"Leaving?"

"That's right. You find yourself another patsy. I'm pulling out. Goodbye." He opened the door.

"You seem to have forgotten something," Kuiper said calmly.

The doctor came back and leaned on the table. His face was vacant and pretty. He smelled of a woman's perfume. "Look, old man," he said with a show of bravado. "I'm not about to sail if I'm not given the tools to do a proper job."

"You have to, Doctor. You signed the articles."

"Okay, sue me. But I'm leaving."

"I'm not talking about suing you, Doctor. I'm talking about reporting you to the police as a deserter. They'll bring you back on board, handcuffed."

"You must be kidding!" He seemed genuinely surprised.

"You were appointed by Dr. Blankenstein to act as his replacement. You'll have to accept his arrangements. So, don't give me any lists; give me a sheet of paper with on it the following information: name of patient, nature and extent of injury or illness, and specific medicine or equipment not provided for by the physician whose place you have taken. That, I'll consider. The rest is hogwash."

"But I insist—"

"Dr. Fritters, you're wasting my time and your own. Good day."

There he went, slamming the door behind him. Tennis racket! Ballroom pumps! Maybe he went to bed wearing his topee. Not his own bed either. Judging by his belongings, he had come equipped for a busy social life, rather than for work among the sick. He looked more gifted for making babies than delivering them. Kuiper wondered dourly what God could have in mind, sending this lounge lizard to share his cabin rather than a straightforward ship's doctor who knew his job and his place.

There was a knock on the door. They were coming thick and fast this morning. "Come in!"

This time, it was Davelaar. He looked grimier and more foul-tempered than usual. "I've got to talk to you, Joris!"

"Must it be now?"

"Yes! Those goddamned women go on stuffing God knows what down my toilets in the holds! I've told them at least twice that if they do that, they block the works and I have to take it all apart. Now, I'm prepared to do extra duty for these people, but I'm not prepared to lie there up to my elbows in shit every other day just because they are too lazy to—"

"Enough already! To start with, I don't want to hear any blasphemy in this cabin."

"The hell with that! What I want to know—"

"All right: write out a notice saying in large letters: 'Do not dispose of refuse in this toilet. Use bag provided.' With an arrow."

"Pointing where?"

"Pointing to the bag you are going to put beside each toilet."

"But I ain't got no bags!"

"Then go to Meyer and ask for some."

"Meyer ain't got no bags either! What do you think this is, a grocery store?"

"Chief," Kuiper said calmly, "get out of here."

"Huh?"

"Out. I've got work to do."

The old man stood breathing heavily through the nose for a few moments, growling like an old, feeble bull; then, shaking his head, he said, "One of these days."

"That's okay. One of these days. Now leave me alone, will you? Do what I told you."

"Never!" the old man shouted, and went to the door. As he opened it, he found Meyer standing there, awaiting his turn. "There he is!" he shouted. "Ask him! Ask *him* about the bags!"

"About what?" Meyer asked, frowning.

"Bags! The boy says I've got to use bags down below for those damn women to stuff their garbage in! Have you got any bags?"

"Yes," Meyer said.

The old man stomped off.

"Captain?" Meyer asked tentatively.

"Yes, come in."

"It's about Cook. He says the two helpers we hired for him are no good. They're lazy, they don't know their job—you know the kind of thing. He wants three sailors detailed to do table duty and to help with the washing up."

"He's not going to get them."

"He'll make trouble if he doesn't."

"Tell him— No, better if I do it. Go and look for that thick-set lady, red-haired, middle-aged—you know, the one representing the women. Tell her I want to see her."

"Mrs. Goldstein?"

"Yes. And tell Cook I'll take care of it."

"You want me to detail the sailors?"

"No. Send Mrs. Goldstein."

"Okay. There's one more thing—"

"Not now. I've got to finish what I'm doing. Unless it's urgent."

"It's about the medic, but I suppose it can wait." He moved toward the door.

"What about the medic?"

"Well, he's raiding my stores all the time, and I wonder what's the proper procedure."

"What do you mean, raiding your stores? What's he taking?"

"Oh, just stuff. Pieces of two-by-four, nails, tools he doesn't give back . . . "

"What's he up to?"

"Well, by the looks of it, he's building a house. Sheets of plywood. A drill. Boxes of screws."

"All right, I'll talk to him."

"And then . . . "

Kuiper sighed. This was a typical Meyer performance. He obviously had something important on his mind, but, like a street Arab, it took him half an hour to get to the point. "All right, let's have it."

"Frederiks is gone."

"What do you mean, gone?"

"Jumped ship."

"When?"

"The moment we arrived."

"Well, he may be drunk somewhere. He may be shacked up with a woman. He'll turn up."

"No, he won't."

"How do you know?"

"He left a note."

"Well? What did it say? For Pete's sake, Meyer, get on with it!"

"Here it is, Cap." Meyer pulled the note out of his breast pocket and handed it over. It was written in pencil in a childish hand. *I am sick of women and emptying slop and buckets of piss. I am a sailor, not a ——.* The word was unreadable; some of it had been crossed out and written over; it looked like *boney* something. *Do not try to find me. I know this town better than anybody you can send after me. Greetings, G. H. J. Frederiks Jr.*

"Well?" Kuiper asked. "Do you want me to alert the police?"

"Suit yourself," Meyer answered evasively.

"Do you want him back?"

"Well, if you want to send the police after him, I'll be the last to stop you."

"Meyer," Kuiper said patiently, "I'm asking you a straight question, give me a straight answer. Do you want him back, or don't you? Is he going to be any good to you after he's been dragged back on board by his ears? As far as I can see, he was more trouble than he was worth."

"Well, if that's your opinion . . . "

"Blast it, Meyer, I'm asking *you!* Do *you* want him back or don't you?"

"No, I guess I don't . . . " Meyer opened the door.

"All right, that's all I wanted to know. Now clear out."

Meyer left, closing the door softly.

Kuiper sighed and rubbed his eyes. Both Meyer and Davelaar were part of his inheritance. They had sailed with his father for over thirty years; the relationship was fraught with emotional hang-ups, or he would have got rid of them both when he took over the ship. Suddenly, he felt suffocated by all these picayune concerns; he needed a breather. A sense of space, peace, tranquillity.

He rose, went to his bunk and took the Bible off the shelf under the porthole. He meant to open it at random, but his eye was caught by the inscription from his father. It was in Anna's handwriting; the Old Man had dictated it to her, as he himself could no longer write after his stroke.

For my son Joris, as he takes over command of Star of Peace. Son, in this book you will find your true north. If you get the devil on board, hoist the flag of the cross that you will find in the drawer with the ship's papers, and I will be standing behind you on the bridge. Never despair, even when you are facing the forces of hell, for one thing I know from experience after a long life in the service of the Lord: once God makes His will known to you, He will provide you with the means to obey it. Father.

Despite Anna's prim, schoolmistressy handwriting, the power of the Old Man came through. Kuiper had never felt it so strongly as at this moment. It was typical of the Old Man: the bombast of the flag of the cross and the clarity and majesty of that last line. Well, if God had indeed made His will known to him when He sent him that vision of Christ carrying His cross up the gangway in Hamburg . . .

He became aware of a knocking on the door, put the Bible back on the shelf and called wearily, "Come in!"

The door opened, the red-haired woman stuck her head in. "You wanted to see me, *Herr Kapitän?*"

"Yes, Mrs. Goldstein. Come in, please. Sit down. Please."

She obeyed and sat down on the couch. Again he was struck by her composure. She exuded a quiet but formidable authority. "Mrs. Goldstein, there are one or two things I would like to discuss with you. To start with, it seems that the women are putting—er—paper napkins and other materials in the chemical toilets, which causes a lot of problems. I've asked the chief engineer to write a notice warning them not to do so; maybe you could translate it into German and announce it. It's unimportant, but it would help."

"With pleasure."

"Then it seems that my cook wants more help than I thought he would need. Would it be possible to get some volunteers from among the women to help at table and with the dishes?"

"Of course."

"Well, that's fine. Is there anything I can do for *you?*"

"Well, I don't know, Captain, if this is something you want to handle yourself or leave to me. But your little boy, whatever his name is, the little cabin boy, is stealing."

"You mean money? Valuables?"

"No. Toys, mainly. Trinkets. Like a magpie. What's his age? Eleven, twelve?"

"No, he has to be fourteen. The law won't allow me to hire anybody below the age of fourteen."

"Well, I may be mistaken, Captain, but I have a pretty sharp eye for children's ages. That boy managed to sell you and the authorities a bill of goods. He's not a day older than twelve."

"Be that as it may, Mrs. Goldstein, we can't have him stealing children's toys, whatever his age is. I'll tell Cook to put a stop to this once and for all."

"That's what I'm afraid of. I thought you should know about it, but I think maybe it would be better if you left him to me. He's a child, not a criminal. I can just see how your cook would handle it."

"Are you a teacher, by any chance?"

"No, Captain." She smiled. "I ran a small, select hotel. For gentlemen." She said it charmingly, but with a hint of steel in her eyes.

"That should qualify you for most anything," he said non-committally. "I'll be happy to leave him to you."

"Thank you. Then Mr. Vinkemans has asked me to appoint some volunteer nurse's aides to help him out in the sick bay and in the holds."

He smiled at the 'appointing' of volunteers; she was one formidable lady. "Well, if you have some ex-nurses among your women, that seems an excellent idea."

"That's where the rub is, Captain. I don't have any nurses. I have three or four women who might be suitable, but I want to make sure first that we won't run into any legal problems. Will the law allow untrained help in nursing the sick?"

"Mrs. Goldstein," he said, smiling, "on board this ship, I am the law. *I* give you permission." Then he added, as an afterthought, "But keep an eye on them. I want you to be responsible for them."

She gave him a shrewd look. "In what way, Captain?"

He was tempted to share with her his low opinion of the doctor, but decided against it. "As it will be an arrangement among the passengers, the passengers should carry the responsibility. And that, I presume, means you."

She gave him a knowing look, then she said, "All right, Captain," and rose. "Now I'll leave you to your work."

"Any time, Mrs. Goldstein," he said, following her to the door. "Whenever you need to see me, I'm at your disposal. We are running this operation together. Let's meet again and discuss whatever needs discussing."

"Let's," she said, and they shook hands. He opened the door for her. She turned and added, "The same goes for me: should you need me, call on me. Any time."

"I will. Thank you, Mrs. Goldstein."

"Thank you, Captain."

After he had closed the door behind her, he went back to his Bible.

3

"And these, then, are the ladies who have volunteered to help us," Vinkemans said mournfully. "*Frau* Adler—Dr. Richters."

The big-boned woman must be in her forties, Hendrik estimated. She looked competent and turned out to have the hand-shake of a farmer.

"*Frau* Hoflein . . . "

Another snowplow, bosomy and forbidding. "Delighted to have you with us, Mrs. Hoflein."

"*Fräulein* Nachtgeist—Dr. Richters."

Now, this was something else: a tall, willowy redhead with striking green eyes, about eighteen years old. Hendrik had noticed her before, but had seen only her red hair, moving among the crowd like a fishing lure on murky water. "Welcome, Miss Nachtgeist. How kind of you all to come and help us out. Mr. Vinkemans will take care of your training—or are any of you trained nurses, by any chance?" They shook their heads. "Have you had any nursing experience at all?" He asked it to be pleasant, not because it mattered. Vinkemans, he suspected, would bring them up to snuff in short order.

Frau Adler had nursed an aging father; *Frau* Hoflein had been a cleaning woman in a hospital and occasionally helped out with the patients; *Fräulein* Nachtgeist had only had experience with children.

"Ah? What kind of experience?" He gave her his number-one smile.

She blushed while telling him in a shy whisper about a kindergarten in which she had been an assistant.

"*Fräulein* Nachtgeist also has the care of her little brother who is with her," Vinkemans said, like an undertaker intoning a condolence. "Haven't you, Tovah?"

'Tovah'—what a lilting name. "Is that so? And your parents? Are they with you?"

The girl shook her head; eighteen was too young an estimate, Hendrik decided. Nineteen, more likely.

"Her parents are deceased," Vinkemans dirged, in his element at last. "Tovah and David are on their way to Uruguay alone."

"Very courageous," Hendrik said. "Delighted to have you on board, Tovah."

The girl whispered, "Yes," and blushed again.

"Well, I'm glad you can help us." Hendrik smiled at them.

"We'll be in touch with you. Thank you." He shook hands with each of them; Tovah's hand turned out to be soft and narrow and very young.

They turned and trooped out; the girl Tovah was the last to step over the high threshold into the passage. Very nice legs indeed, compact little tail.

The moment they were gone, Vinkemans said, "Doctor, we're having some problems."

"Ah? What's up?"

"One of the old gentlemen is having an emotional crisis. Then there's a laceration of the knee waiting to be sutured: a small boy fell down a ladder."

In the small ward Hendrik found an elderly male sitting on the edge of one of the beds, picture of dejection. Tears were running down the gray stubble of his beard; he looked at the doctor and the medic with such utter hopelessness that Hendrik, almost instantly, felt inadequate. He took Vinkemans aside and muttered, "I want a word with you."

"Yes, Doctor."

But in the consulting room a little boy was waiting, also in tears, so they had to talk in the passage. "What can you tell me about the old man?" Hendrik asked. "I need some background information before I tackle him."

"Well, nothing in particular, Doctor. I've not had him as a patient before. But he seems typical of a lot of them: single elderly male, probably professional background, either a widower or separated from his wife. It's the fact that the French keep us in quarantine and refuse to dock us that set them off. They are all in a state of high tension."

"How do you mean, separated? Divorced?"

Vinkemans smiled dourly. "No, Doctor. Just physically separated, by the Nazis. They did that, it appears, in quite a number of cases: tell one of the couples, usually the wife, at the very last minute before boarding that she could not go, but her husband could. Things being the way they are in Germany right now, these people had little choice but to comply. It seems that the wives urged the men to go, assuring them that they would come later, by the next boat—that's what they were told."

"But why? Was the ship overbooked or something?"

Vinkemans shrugged. "More likely pointless torture. They are sadists, Doctor. It gives them satisfaction to torment the Jews. They think of a thousand ways, I'm sure. Let me help you into your coat."

Hendrik put on the white coat and, picking up his stethoscope and sphygmomanometer, went back to the ward. "I'm Dr. Richters," he said pleasantly. "Would you take off your jacket, please, so I can take your blood pressure. We'll start by doing that, shall we?" The old man turned out to have arthritic shoulders, so he needed help. Hendrik also helped him roll up the sleeve of his shirt; the old arm was thin and fragile and, somehow, expressed loneliness and disorientation. Now, that was clearly a worthless romantic observation, Hendrik thought, as he put on the cuff of the blood-pressure gauge. It was the kind of diagnosis that would have provoked angry scorn in his professors. He inflated the cuff and listened to the artery. Both diastolic and systolic were elevated; the pulse was rapid and slightly irregular. But, again, the real message he received was in the way the old man sat there, staring straight ahead of him, tears running down his face. A lost, confused soul, overcome by utter weariness.

It was difficult to get through to him. He barely registered the questions and answered with grunts and shakings of the head. It was a curious situation, almost like the opening stage of a court-ship with a reluctant partner—another of those romantic interpretations that were anathema to the scientific mind. But the similarity to the process of seduction was so tempting that even though Hendrik rejected it intellectually, he found himself employing the same technique he had applied so many times to unresponsive young females. He felt the intellectual and moral obligation to approach his first patient as a physician, yet found himself entrapping Mr. Himmelbaum with the wiles of a lover. What seduction amounted to was identification; in this case, it turned out to be very effective. As Mr. Himmelbaum relaxed, he spoke haltingly of his wife, who indeed had stayed behind on the quayside in Hamburg, and of the medication lost with his luggage, the anti-hypertensive drug the name of which he could not remember, but which had given him a stuffy nose.

In all, Hendrik spent some twenty minutes with him; if Mr. Himmelbaum had been a young woman, they would now have reached the stage of the first shy smile and the agreement to meet again. When *Herr Doktor* was through, a poker-faced Vinkemans provided Mr. Himmelbaum with twelve tablets of bromide, three a day with meals, the dosage under no circumstances to be increased; Mr. Himmelbaum agreed to come back after three days for a re-evaluation. When Mr. Himmelbaum left, he replied to an inaudible question put by someone waiting outside in the passage, saying, *"Grossartig,"* the German equivalent of 'terrific.' So Hendrik's first consultation as G.P. of this village of two hundred and fifty souls had been an unqualified success.

His suturing of the laceration of the little boy's knee was less so. The child screamed like a stuck pig, struggled and kicked; the stitches were wide and irregular; only Vinkemans' deft assistance saved Hendrik from a total fiasco. As a finishing touch, the little boy managed to kick over the suture tray, splashing Hendrik's white coat with green Mecressin, shrieking, *"Metzger!"*—butcher —thereby canceling out any rapture induced by Mr. Himmelbaum. After being abducted by his doubtful mother, he left behind him a battlefield and a sense of defeat.

But Vinkemans seemed to be mysteriously reassured. "I thought that went very well, Doctor," he said, clearing up the mess with expert efficiency. "Let me give you another coat. Maybe this would be a good moment, if you could spare the time, to make a tour through the holds? Show the flag, so to speak?"

The prospect dismayed Hendrik. "I should really be stowing away my personal belongings in the captain's cabin. Right now, they're in a heap on the floor."

"Oh, that can wait," Vinkemans said airily, helping him out of his coat.

"But I don't want any conflict with His Nibs on minor details."

"I wouldn't give it a second thought, Doctor," Vinkemans

said behind him. "Your patients are more important. Thank you. I'll get a fresh one."

"But they aren't my patients! At least, not yet."

"Ah, make no mistake, Doctor," Vinkemans said, opening the door of the linen closet. "They are all your patients. The sooner they see you, the better it is. Today of all days, your presence is important, what with the French behaving the way they are. We might as well have yellow fever on board."

Given the choice between the captain and the medic, Hendrik decided that Vinkemans had priority; without the help of this experienced old fox, his chances of making a success as ship's doctor would be slender. "All right," he said, "let's go."

They started with the women's holds. The ladder would take some getting used to, Hendrik decided when he stood at the top and looked down into the hold—a sheer drop of at least forty feet. The ladder, no more than a narrow perpendicular fire escape, was rusty and rough, and its rungs far apart. Despite its gritty appearance, it was slippery to the feet, he noticed as he followed Vinkemans down into the void with his heart in his mouth. How did the women manage? If it frightened the daylights out of him to go down that gerbil staircase, where did they find the courage? He was an athletic man in his twenties—how about the old biddies he had seen, the pregnant women, the children? No wonder the little boy had lacerated his knee—there would be a lot more suturing before this trip was over.

At the bottom of the ladder, he entered a gloomy cave with tiers of bunks jammed close together, running off into the darkness. It seemed a twilight world unfit for civilized habitation, yet the women gave it an atmosphere of cheerful neighborliness. Lots of children were running about; at the sight of him, they scurried and hid behind their mothers or clambered into the bunks with the agility of monkeys. A buxom woman with the orange hair he associated with Turkish harems emerged from the gloom; Vinkemans introduced her as Mrs. Goldstein, the passengers' representative.

"Are the women satisfactory?" she asked Hendrik.

"I beg your pardon?"

"The nursing volunteers I sent you."

"Ah, yes. Excellent. Mr. Vinkemans and I are most grateful."

"Do you need any more?"

Hendrik did not know why, but she evoked an atmosphere of corruption—protection money, political chicanery, cops on the take. "I'm not the one to ask, Madam. Mr. Vinkemans here is going to do the training, it's up to him to decide how many he can manage at one time."

Vinkemans seemed quite at ease with her. "Three's enough for the time being, thank you, Mrs. Goldstein," he said. "When I need a few more ladies, I'll let you know. How is Mrs. Kohnstamm?"

"Doing fine." She turned the beam of her uncomfortably perspicacious eyes back onto Hendrik. "Mrs. Kohnstamm is blind and fell from her bunk," she explained. "Mr. Vinkemans very kindly looked after her." She seemed to be scrutinizing Hendrik's soul—at least, that was how it felt. "Do you want to visit the sick first, or get an idea of the layout before you do your rounds?"

"Let's go and see the patients. I'll get my bearings as we go along."

"This way, please."

She guided them down one of the narrow passages between the bunks, poorly lit by naked lightbulbs. She and Vinkemans were accosted on their way by women with questions, making Hendrik feel like the invisible man as none of them seemed to notice him. He realized that in his white doctor's coat he represented a figure of authority whom no one dared approach directly when Vinkemans said to one of them, "Ask *Herr Doktor*; tell him."

The woman in question seemed flustered by the suggestion. She curtsied, then whispered, standing virtually to attention, "I ask permission to be examined, if you please, *Herr Doctor.*"

It was such an odd way of asking for an appointment that Hendrik countered, jovially, "It should be I who asks permission to examine you. Isn't that the proper way?"

He had intended to put her at her ease, but the consternation he caused in the poor woman was alarming. Vinkemans said, "It's all right, Mrs. Spiegel, it's all right," and Hendrik realized she was afraid. "Mrs. Spiegel is in her last month," Vinkemans explained. "She wonders what the facilities are for delivery."

For someone in her last month, Mrs. Spiegel's pregnancy was discreet indeed; in the half-light between the bunks, Hendrik had not spotted her condition.

"We're ready for all comers," he said. "We are fully equipped for even the most difficult complications. So, Mrs. Spiegel, don't you worry. We'll take good care of you and your baby."

"*Zu Befehl, Herr Doktor . . .* " the woman whispered, and curtsied again.

As they walked on, Hendrik asked Mrs. Goldstein, "Would you explain to me what was the matter with that woman?"

The red-haired woman said, "Don't you worry, Doctor, They'll soon get the message."

"What message?"

"That you are harmless."

"I don't understand."

"They're not used to kindness in a doctor, not if he's a goy. They think there's a catch to it."

"I see."

The rounds of the women's hold took the better part of an hour. Hendrik was shown various patients whom Vinkemans had taken care of most capably. He visited wash bays, latrines, the nursery—and it was there that he set eyes on the girl Tovah again. She was reading a story to a circle of toddlers, and looked up when they came in. When she saw him, she blushed again; at least, so it seemed. Maybe she was a congenital blusher. By this time, Hendrik had had enough of the women's hold. It all seemed organized and orderly, and obviously it was running smoothly; even so, to transport people across the ocean under these conditions was a disgrace. Dr. Halbertsma had been right: Captain Kuiper, with his Christian pretensions, should be ashamed of himself.

"Let's go and take a look at the men's department," he said. "I gather they're in the forward hold?"

"Very well," Mrs. Goldstein answered; to Hendrik's amazement, she came with them. She must really be the boss lady around here.

If the women's section had been barely acceptable, the men's was an outrage. The layout and the facilities were the same as in the women's section, only here there was no gloss of order or organization. Clothes hung out of almost every bunk, shoes and packages cluttered the walkways; there was an all-pervading stench of unwashed bodies. There were a number of patients, most of them confined to their bunks; those on the top layer were difficult to evaluate, as Hendrik had to cling to the edge of the bunk, perched on the edge of the one below. Vinkemans, in his reports, included in virtually all cases the formula, "Mr. So-and-So is on bromide, T.I.D. with meals, for five days." Only a few old men had a real problem; in ninety percent of the cases, the complaints were psychosomatic.

As they looked in on what had been the nursery in the women's department, they found a religious service in progress: a dozen men with hats on and shawls around their shoulders, rocking in prayer, a frail, bearded old man chanting. "I wondered where the Rabbi was," Mrs. Goldstein whispered. "Let's leave them to it, you'll meet him later." They retired.

The wash bays and the latrines were foul. Obviously, the men could not be bothered to clean up; maybe they didn't know how to. When Hendrik commented, Mrs. Goldstein shrugged her shoulders. "What do you want? Men are pigs. I have arranged for three women to come in every morning and clean up the place, but look at it. Pigs? Give me pigs any time. At least they're productive."

"I think it would help a great deal if the Rabbi could talk to the men about this," Hendrik said. "Most of the cases I've just seen are psychological. And no wonder—in an atmosphere like this, I'd fall sick myself if I had nothing else to do."

"All right," Mrs. Goldstein said, unimpressed. "I'll mention it to him."

It was a relief to re-emerge on deck; as he did so, Hendrik realized to his surprise that the ship was under way; he had not noticed their leaving. He went to the rail to look for *Tubantia*, but the big liner lay far behind them. The current of the river, combined with the tide, carried them swiftly out to sea.

"Well, there we go," he said. "Now, unless you have any other suggestions, I think I should unpack while His Nibs is gone. I suppose he's on the bridge?"

"Yes, Doctor." Vinkemans looked as if he had something on his mind.

"What is it, Vinkemans?"

"Well, you see, Doctor, I've only been around these people for a few days, but one thing is obvious: they're all terribly on edge. You saw the way they reacted to you. God knows what they went through in bloody Germany prior to boarding in Hamburg, where I saw Nazi bullies chase them onto the ship." He described the scene to Hendrik with surprising passion. "They still haven't recovered," he went on, "and the French haven't helped. So I wonder if you and I could sit down together and maybe come up with a game plan."

"Game plan?"

"Well . . . " Vinkemans looked around as if to make sure that they were not overheard. "I'm not a psychiatric nurse, but my guess is that once these people realize they're free and that the possibility of their being pulled back into the net is gone, we may have some surprises."

"Such as?"

"Irrational behavior. Letting it rip. Explosions of joy and relief that could get out of hand. This is a ship, after all, and these people aren't used to that."

"Well, what do you suggest?"

"Why not pre-empt the psychological reaction and channel it into something we can control? A sort of ritual of liberation? I was thinking in terms of a carnival."

Hendrik observed him. There was something intriguing about the man. "Have you known situations like this before?"

Vinkemans looked away at the shore. "Not exactly."

"You must have had a similar experience, to come up with this?"

"I was in Spain."

"You mean the Civil War? As a soldier?"

"No. A medic."

"What side were you on, Vinkemans?"

"No side. Neither were the wounded and the dying, once they got to me."

There was a silence in which Hendrik watched the shore too. "Are you a Quaker or something?"

"No, no specific religion. Let's say I'm not in this for the money."

"Well, God knows, neither am I," Hendrik said fervently.

"I heard about this voyage in the canteen of my hospital, and I felt it was something I'd want to do. So I applied for leave and here I am."

"Which hospital was that?"

"Rotterdam University."

Thank God it wasn't Amsterdam, where Hendrik himself had served as an intern with a marked lack of distinction. "What did you do there?"

"Oh," Vinkemans said casually, "nothing particularly impressive."

"Like head nurse or something?"

"Well—yes."

"I thought so. Which department?"

"I.C."

"Well, happy to have you on board." Head nurse of Intensive Care was about as prestigious a post as an R.N. could attain. Hendrik felt a mixture of relief and wariness. It was like doing your stuff under the eagle eye of a professor.

"Occasionally, we need this," Vinkemans said, somewhat obscurely. "After all, ours is supposed to be a vocation, isn't it?"

"Oh, that. Yes indeed."

"Well—I suppose I'd better get back to the shop. It's time for the vital signs. I'm trying to keep regular hours for the observations."

"I'll come with you."

"No need. I've got nothing else to do anyhow. You go ahead and unpack. See you at supper."

With that he walked off, white and slender and somewhat effeminate among the people from the abyss.

4

The officers' meals, so Hendrik discovered, were served in the starboard catwalk, at a table separate from the long ones at which the passengers were given their food. Henky served; apart from Hendrik and Vinkemans, the captain, Mate Meyer and the chief engineer were present. The ship was well out to sea, the sun had set; despite the warm day, there was a nip in the air. They dined under an immense cobalt sky tinged with red; a pale moon floated between the masts swaying to and fro with the swell, as if she were slowly being bounced from one mast top to the other.

The meal started with a long and rather embarrassing prayer by the captain, in which Jesus was invited to occupy Himself with their digestion; during it, Henky waited respectfully in the background with the soup tureen and the chief engineer picked his nose. It was quiet on deck during the blessing; Hendrik realized that the passengers at the tables adjoining theirs had respectfully fallen silent. After the "Amen," Henky came forward with the tureen and put it in front of the captain.

"Take your thumb out of the soup, boy," the first mate said; and the captain, "Gentlemen, your bowls, please."

The gentlemen passed their bowls down the line, the captain ladled them full of soup and they were handed back down the line. The ritual had a patriarchal aspect.

There was no small talk; everyone listened to the chief engineer drinking his soup with the sound of a bath emptying. Then the captain said, "Have you unpacked yet, Doctor?"

"I'm in the middle of it. I made my rounds first."

"After supper might be a good time. I'll be on the bridge through midnight."

"Yes, Captain."

Silence.

"Vinkemans?"

"Yes, Captain?"

"That list of medications lost by the passengers in Hamburg —do you still have that?"

"Yes, Captain."

"I'd like to file it with my insurance claim. Let me have it back, please. At your convenience."

"Very well, Captain."

Silence.

"Yes, boy. Next course."

"I haven't finished my soup," the chief engineer growled as Henky reached for his bowl.

"Then finish," the captain said.

Slurp, slurp, in silence. "Okay, boy, take it away."

"Yes, Chief. Thanks, Chief."

Growl. Silence.

"Meyer?"

"Yes, Cap?"

"Have you arranged for those tarpaulins to be put up here when it rains?"

"Aye."

"Let's hope it won't blow at the same time," the chief growled.

"Did you have the struts made up, Meyer?"

"Yes, Cap."

So it went, all through the meal: the captain in the father's seat, querying his brood one by one as to their activities during the day. Hendrik felt a growing resentment against the captain; no man had any business lording it over other men like that, certainly not over men old enough to be his father, like the chief and the mate. The food was poor, the service slow, Henky's thumbprint marked the inside of the rims of all dishes. Finally, after a gray semolina pudding swimming in red sauce like a brain in blood, a mug of dishwater coffee was served up and another prayer thanked Jesus for His cooperation, after which the captain said, *"Mahlzeit"* and rose to leave. Everybody mumbled *"Mahlzeit"* in response.

The moment he was out of earshot, the conversation started —not only at the officers' table but at those of the passengers as well. Whatever might be said about Kuiper, he was an intimidating presence. Hendrik smoked a cigarette with the rest of the staff and had another mug of the awful coffee, then he excused himself and went to the cabin to finish unpacking.

In the twilight, the room seemed even more cramped than before. Switching on the ceiling light made little difference, it merely deepened the gloom. This was the cabin where he would have to spend the three weeks between now and their arrival in Montevideo, sharing it with that tyrant. It was an unattractive prospect; but then, three weeks went fast if they were busy ones, and there certainly seemed to be plenty to do. He explored the cabin, not only to reconnoiter but in a search for a clue to the captain's persona.

There weren't any clues, other than the books on the small shelf in his bunk: the Bible, a Concordance, the *Celestial Ephemeris* for 1939, a *Ship Captain's Medical Guide* dated 1908, and four dog-eared books on religious subjects, three of them to do with angels. Hendrik had never been one for religion; the books made the lack of privacy more acute. He wished there were a place on board this ship to which he could retreat for a few hours each day, a sanctuary where he would be out of reach. But that was likely to be a pipe dream, what with all those people milling about.

He unpacked the rest of his belongings and stuffed his half of the wardrobe with them; opening a drawer in the desk, he found a pair of handcuffs, an antique-looking pistol and a box of ammunition marked SOFT CENTERS. The gun looked fierce and yet oddly antiquated, a pistol for pirates. After filling the wardrobe and the three drawers allotted to him, he still had a pile of stuff left. Where in the world could he store it? Well, Vinkemans would help out. Splendid fellow, Vinkemans. He hated to think how this first day would have shaped up without the gloomy medic. He tried the couch and found it extremely uncomfortable as well as narrow. For a moment, he thought it would be preferable to claim a bed in the infirmary; then he got up, opened the lid to look at the cavity underneath and saw that it was indeed filled with blankets, sheets and a pillow. Even so, with a bit of assiduous packing, he might be able to stow away some more.

He tried; when he was through, the lid would barely close. He still had a stack of shirts left, a tennis racket, a pair of tropical shoes and the miserable helmet. He finally took all the stuff out from under the damn settee, put it back in a suitcase and replaced it with the shoes, the helmet and the tennis racket. That made one full suitcase to be stored. Well, Vinkemans would have the answer.

Only on his way out did he see the photograph. It was fixed to the wall between the door and the coat rack: the picture of a youngish woman hand in hand with two children. It had obviously been taken by a professional photographer who had managed to make the woman pose with her hands in a position she had probably never achieved before. The two little boys stared into space with fixed grins, each in a slightly different direction; the woman looked ill at ease and somewhat cowed. She was pretty in a working-class way, with, somewhat incongruously, an aura of sexual experience—what old Schulbe in his lectures used to call 'a fornicatrix.' The brooch she was wearing turned out to be, on closer scrutiny, a silver whistle. There wasn't a clue anywhere to the captain's private persona, except maybe the whistle. It seemed to deepen the enigma rather than solve it.

Vinkemans was busy with a bedpan in the smelly little ward. The problem of having to store a suitcase somewhere did not seem to faze him. He asked, politely, what the accommodation was like; when Hendrik mentioned the acute lack of privacy and voiced his daydream of a sanctuary to which he might be able to retire for an odd hour or so every day, Vinkemans said, "Oh, I can probably fix that for you, Doctor." Then he proceeded to put the patient in traction onto the bedpan.

"Need any help?"

"No, thank you, Doctor. I'm used to this. Now take it really easy, *Frau* Kahana . . . "

It was almost dark when Hendrik, gazing at the sea, smoking a cigarette, leaning on the rail of the lower bridge outside the captain's cabin, heard a voice say, "I think I found it, Doctor."

It was Vinkemans, ghostlike in his whites in the dusk.

"Found what, friend?"

"Your retreat. I took it up with the bo'sun; he suggested the number-three lifeboat. It's out of the way, and can't be seen from the bridge. Why don't you give it a try?"

"Well! That's remarkably civil of you, I must say! Which one is it?"

"The last one from here, over on the starboard side."

"Starboard is over there, is it?"

"Yes, Doctor."

"Thanks! I'll go and take a look. Thanks again!"

"You're most welcome."

A few minutes later Hendrik found himself lying on his back between the seats of a large rowboat, gazing at the moon, musing about that odd idea of a carnival and liking it.

Good old Vinkemans! Some people could truly be called the salt of the earth.

CHAPTER FOUR

The idea of a carnival, once it had passed the hurdle of the captain's dour suspicion, turned out to be a brilliant bit of mass therapy. The passengers—men, women and children—set to work on the preparations with zest, manufacturing funny hats, streamers, lanterns, masks and even noses, all made out of old newspapers, the wrappers of medical equipment and empty cardboard drug boxes. The ingenuity of the elderly men was amazing, and, more important, the activity turned them from hypochondriacs with intermittent melancholia into children at play, lost to the world, concentrating wholly on the dream taking shape in their hands.

Vinkemans was much in evidence, planning, organizing, and going into solemn huddles with Mrs. Goldstein, the Rabbi and Mr. Himmelbaum, who had become Hendrik's prize patient. The old gentleman's transformation from a neurotic in a permanent catatonic state into a brisk and authoritarian organizer of the festivities might, in part, be due to Vinkemans' occupational therapy, but undoubtedly owed much to Hendrik's own private session with the old man that first day.

Vinkemans' social activities did not leave him enough time to train the nurses, so Hendrik took on the task. The red-headed Tovah was willing enough but so inexperienced that she had to stay after class; the other two were battleaxes who could fend for themselves after having been shown a few basic procedures. He found that for him and his student to concentrate they needed a non-intrusive environment, so he suggested she join him in his secret hideout, on condition she would not divulge its existence to anyone. Tovah—an innocent, trusting soul—was prepared to follow him into the lifeboat without second thoughts, but her ten-year-old brother David presented a problem. He clung to them like a leech: a stocky, carrot-topped brat with the same green eyes as his sister's, only his were a good deal more perspicacious. The dislike between little David and Hendrik was instant and mutual; to get her into the lifeboat without the ever present brat climbing in with them, or perching somewhere in the rigging for an unobstructed view, seemed a practical impossibility. But here, too, Vinkemans provided the answer, be it unwittingly.

There came a moment, toward the end of a first-aid class, when a box of medication had to be taken down into the men's hold. Henky had promised he would help, but Vinkemans waited for him in vain; luckily, there was David, hanging around outside in the passage, waiting for his sister. "Why, there's David!" said Hendrik, smiling. "He's a strong boy, he'll help you. Won't you, David?" It took the little private eye unawares; before he knew it, he was on his way down, carrying the box. Three minutes later, Hendrik and Tovah were sitting side by side in the lifeboat, going through the procedure of taking blood pressure.

"You see, sweetie? This is where the artery is, on this side in the crook of the left arm. Here . . . " Her skin was silky and white, the vein showed blue through the translucent epidermis. "In the right arm, it's on the other side. Here, you try it. On me. Put the cuff here. That's right. Now put your stethoscope in your ears. Right. Don't bang the head against the seat, it'll hurt your eardrums. Now—pump up the cuff. Enough! Enough! Two-twenty is enough, or you'll hurt the patient. Now put it here where my finger is. That's right. Now release the air—slowly! Slowly. Now listen. Do you hear the pulse coming on? Whoosh—whoosh—whoosh?"

Whether she did or didn't became immaterial as she bent her head and gave him a whiff of the scent of her sun-warmed hair. "Yes!" she whispered, happy and proud. "I hear it!"

Well, no wonder: his heart was thumping, blood must be coursing through the artery in gushes. But he knew enough not to press his advantage. Softlee, softlee catchee monkey. Next time, it would be a great deal easier to shake little David with the knowing eyes, for next time she would cooperate.

The night of the carnival was starry and bright. The weather had held ever since Le Havre; it was a beautiful, balmy summer evening, with Venus shimmering above the horizon as bright as the toplight of an approaching vessel, and the Milky Way an almost solid sweep of luminous dust overhead. The moon rose, a huge orange disk, from the haze on the horizon; Chinese lanterns, candlelight flickering inside, were strung on flaglines between masts and funnel. Cook and some women had made *Mandelkuchen* and *Leckerbissen*. Vinkemans had contributed two bottles of Dutch gin to go into the non-alcoholic punch. Only he and Hendrik—and possibly little David, who watched everything the doctor did—knew why, once the punch had made the rounds, the party really got into its stride. Even the sailors collaborated, a mouth-organ-and-haircomb band provided dance music; before long, a fantastic crowd of pigs, cavaliers, clowns and mermaids was foxtrotting and waltzing in the catwalks to the tune of *Roll Me Over in the Clover* and *When Irish Eyes Are Smiling*. After the second round, a circle of masked revelers went in for a Jewish tribal dance to which they themselves sang the tune and the onlookers beat time by clapping their hands. It involved pulling the children into the center of the circle, and little David, although he struggled, was sucked in with the rest.

Suddenly Hendrik, who was watching with Tovah by his side, sensed the mood change from exuberance to something deeper. As the crowd danced arm in arm around the children in their midst, the carnival turned from just any old party into a celebration, solemn and moving, of something unspoken, mystical. The dance changed from a conga into a ritual that seemed of ancient standing, a dedication of this moment to the children, the future. Even though Hendrik's attention was with Tovah, he felt moved by what was taking place. A threshold was crossed, away from the past, its horrors and despair. It was the transformation canny old Vinkemans had predicted. Hendrik looked at Tovah, her earnest face, her shining eyes. Her lips were parted, she looked innocent and young and irresistibly desirable. "Come," he said, "let's get out of this stampede. How about having a look at the moon?"

Tovah, after a moment's hesitation, followed him. She could do little else, as he had grabbed her hand and was pulling her along, up the stairs, into the darkness of the boat deck.

"We could have a look at the stars from the boat. How does that sound to you?"

He did not wait for her answer; he grabbed her by the waist and lifted her into the boat. To see her outlined against the starry sky with her paper crown, the silhouette of a princess in a fairy tale, was very provocative.

Suddenly, a woman's voice said, "Doctor! Could I have a word with you?"

He put the girl down and turned around angrily. Facing him in the darkness was Mrs. Goldstein. "I think this is hardly the moment—" he began.

She cut him short. "I need to see you. It's extremely urgent."

"What happened?"

"We can't talk here. Let's go to your cabin."

He stood for a moment in doubt, then turned to tell Tovah to wait, but she was gone. "What on earth is all this about?"

"I'll tell you," the woman said. "Let's go."

He followed her to the cabin and opened the door for her. The ceiling light was on; the room was empty.

"Close the door," she said.

He obeyed. "Now, what on earth—"

She faced him with grim authority, her hennaed hair an orange halo in the lamplight. "Tovah Nachtgeist," she said, "is a seventeen-year-old orphan who at age fourteen lost both parents in a pogrom. Her father was beaten to death in the street. Her mother died soon thereafter. They were civilized, cultured people like your own parents must be. How would *you* have reacted at fourteen if, suddenly, the world you grew up in was invaded by a horde of bullies with axes and nightsticks, smashing furniture, windows, pulling your father out into the street, beating and kicking him as he lay bleeding on the ground, then dragging his body away, never to be seen again? And then to watch your mother die slowly from shock, and find yourself alone with your seven-year-old brother in a nightmare world? Think about it." She went toward the door. There she turned. "Tovah Nachtgeist is emotionally damaged. She is, as we all are, temporarily entrusted to your care. You abuse that role by seducing her, unless you are planning to marry her."

"Look, Mrs. Goldstein, I—"

"Are you, *Herr Doktor?*"

"Well, no, of course not! And let me explain: nothing has hap—"

"One more thing: she's betrothed to a cousin of hers, a young man called Yakov Koblenz. He's not one of your cowed, cringing Jews, he's a fighter. He was captured, escaped, and made his way to Palestine. As God is my witness: should anything happen to that girl because of you, Yakov Koblenz will pursue you to the ends of the earth. He's an Old Testament Jew: an eye for an eye, a tooth for a tooth. Good night, *Herr Doktor.*" She opened the door and stepped across the high threshold into the darkness.

After a few moments, he went out and wandered down the boat deck toward the shindig below. The Jews were singing and dancing; the rhythmic stamping was so exuberant that he could feel the vibration under his feet.

Yakov Koblenz. Captured, escaped, now in Palestine. An Old Testament Jew; an eye for an eye, a tooth for a tooth. As he stood gazing at the carnival below, he remembered Mrs. Karelsen. 'In danger? He? Not from extraneous forces. He's endangered by his own Parsifal.'

Right then and there, he decided to leave Tovah Nachtgeist severely alone. He had no gift, nor taste, for heroics. Imagine! 'Molly darling, could you put me up for the night? There's a Jewish freedom fighter out gunning for me . . .'

No, old Parsifal would have to take a holiday.

CHAPTER FIVE

I

After *Star of Peace* passed the limit of her radio transmitter's range, she entered a timeless, peaceable world of total self-containment which, to Kuiper, was the best part of a sailor's life.

The crew settled down in their familiar routine; the passengers adapted to it too; peace and tranquillity descended on the ship that had been so restless, so haunted by unspeakable memories of the shore, the flashing lights of which were now forever out of sight beyond the horizon. Bells counted the half-hours of each watch, doing away with the rhythm of day and night; at the end of each watch, the log was brought up to date, the weather and the height of the waves reported. *No cloud; slow moderate SE swell; Wve ht 5/10 ft; no other vessels sighted; all well on board.*

The weather held and day after day the reports in the log remained much the same, until *Star of Peace* seemed to be coursing in an orbit of her own around the sun. The Big Dipper sank lower each night; the trades took hold, making the wave troughs deeper and the swell longer—but still: *No cloud; no other vessels sighted; all well on board.*

Life with the doctor in his cabin proved less of a strain than Kuiper had expected. The man was there only to sleep, or pretend to be asleep each time the door was opened after the captain's night watch. There was little conversation, no gossip and no complaints. The only quirk was that the man took to calling him "Skipper" instead of "Captain," for reasons of his own, but that was all right.

One night, shortly after the carnival, Kuiper stood leaning against the rail of the port wing of his bridge, gazing aft at the luminous wake of the ship, a whirling green furrow in the dark sea, with a feeling of timeless isolation. The ship was alone on the ocean.

In moments like these, it seemed to him that his life before his conversion was a legend, a fairy tale someone had told about a big, bad boy who battled his father and ended up being transformed into his father when the Old Man was felled by a stroke and died. It had not happened quite like that, but to all intents and purposes *Star of Peace* had continued with the same master after his father was carried off the ship paralyzed, unable to speak. There she had been: rudderless vessel with a fatherless crew, and all eyes had looked to him. But he had wanted no part of it, and he had fled to the red-light district, damned if he'd take over that old bucket, those cantankerous old men. But God had waylaid him by tricking him into a mission post, and contrived to change him from a boozing, brawling rebel into a God-fearing ship's captain. What was amazing was that it had happened so quickly. There seemed to have been no transition, no period of adjustment, no awkwardness or moments of doubt. The new life had been there, waiting for him to step into, ready-made.

As he stood gazing at the ship's wake, lost in thought, he caught a surreptitious movement in number-three lifeboat. The night was bright with stars, and the sea so phosphorescent that the curling waves hissing past lit up the boats from below. He waited for the next foamer to come swishing past; yes, there was someone there. He went down the steps to investigate; as he approached the boat, a man was getting out of it. "Who's there?"

"Me, Skipper."

"Doctor? What were you doing in there?"

"Having a quiet moment, if that's all right with you."

Kuiper's first impulse was to tell the man that the lifeboats were out of bounds, but life was easy, the mood of the ship peaceful; he decided against it. It was not his affair what the doctor did in his spare time. Live and let live. "All right, Doc. Good night."

"Good watch, Skipper."

No clouds; slow, moderate SE swell, no other vessels sighted; all well on board.

2

_____

When *Star of Peace* entered the tropics, an unexpected transformation took place, seemingly triggered by the captain turning up on the bridge in a white uniform. Later that same day, as if a giant flowering bush had suddenly burst into bloom, decks and catwalks broke out in a rash of awnings. They were makeshift affairs put up by the passengers and made out of bedsheets, blankets and bits of tarpaulin the bo'sun had lent them. The effect was bizarre: the staid old Calvinist freighter was suddenly transformed into a village marketplace jammed full of covered stalls. The flimsy structures, billowing precariously in the breeze, had an incongruous air of conquest about them. Once, when *Star* was anchored in the estuary of the Rhône in the Mediterranean, Kuiper had seen the ship covered in a matter of hours with a blanket of a zillion fluttering moths, called *éphémères*. They came in so thickly that they had to be removed by the shovelful. They could not be caught separately because they were too fragile, yet they had brought about a sense of insecurity; so, now, did the rash of covered stalls as he looked down on them from the bridge. It was as if they changed the personality of the ship. Suddenly, old *Star* revealed a side that would have outraged his father and the stern whitewashed church of his childhood. She was like a staid old dowager suddenly putting on a hat full of bows and ribbons that fluttered in the wind, ridiculous, faintly scandalous and somehow irrevocable.

With the awnings, the multi-colored blankets, the sheets and the flopping pieces of tarpaulin came a new sound. Underneath those giant moths, the passengers began to sing and laugh and squeal and giggle and babble. Then they began to sunbathe, in skimpy homemade garments composed of kerchiefs and panties, on unshaded parts of the ship—the forecastle, the winch covers, open spaces in the catwalks.

Kuiper considered ordering the damn tent village struck because it was dangerous. One good blow and the thing would turn into a shambles; there might be accidents. But the air of finality of the transformation was so compelling that, as in the face of the onslaught of the *éphémères*, he felt powerless. *Star of Peace* changed into an oasis of gaiety, music and laughter in the featureless solitude of the ocean. The slow motion of the ship, slowly raising her bow, slowly plunging back into the trough, seemed mysteriously to add to the illusion. This was no longer the sea; Jews had no truck with the sea. They had struck out for the promised land, and somehow managed to turn the sea into a desert, at least after dark when the illusion seemed to become eerily confirmed in the star-blazed night, haunted by a multitude of fires. Porpoises, giant squids, whales that occasionally surfaced in the distance created whorls and fountains of flame. The slightest movement of wave or fish struck showers of green fire, touching the darkness with the magic of the Arabian Nights. People stayed up late, chatting, laughing. Staring down at them during the midwatch, Kuiper felt like a stranger on board his own ship.

The new spirit among the passengers expressed itself in other ways. The doctor reported that underneath those billowing awnings classes in Spanish were being organized, the history of Uruguay, bookkeeping, child care, shorthand. It was hard to believe that these were the same poor wretches who had been chased on board in Hamburg, terrorized out of their very humanity. As Kuiper walked the alleys of their tent village in his white uniform, hands clasped behind his back like a cop on the beat, he came to the conclusion that these people would make a living, even strike gold, anywhere as long as there was fire, water and a musical instrument. It didn't matter what: homemade drum, improvised ukulele, comb and paper; failing those, their voices, singing as they had done for five thousand years to please the Lord. There was no getting around it: for the duration of the crossing, the God of Calvin had temporarily retired to make room for the God of Israel.

As they approached the equator, it became unbearably hot in the captain's cabin and in the crew's quarters, even in the shade of the awnings on the decks. Life of the village withdrew into the holds during the hottest hours until the sun began to sink, fiery ball of menace and glory in the west. Everybody slept during most of the day to emerge, like the Bedouin, under the sickle of the moon and the shimmering scythe of the Milky Way. Music, laughter, lectures, chanted prayer services—Kuiper and the doctor lay open-eyed on their bunks, sweating, hearts pounding with the heat, and listened to those incredible Jews who, instead of sailing into the unknown, seemed to be on their way home. Gradually, it brought about a communication between skipper and physician that went somewhat further than the terse monosyllables to which it had been restricted so far. The doctor began to talk about himself, which turned out to be an unexpected boon as it put Kuiper to sleep within minutes. Kuiper began to talk about the sea and strange lands he had known, which, he discovered, had the same effect upon the doctor: within minutes, the hubbub of voices on deck, ever present in the background because of the open portholes, became laced with discreet snores from the direction of the settee. Strange, that boring each other to sleep should create a bond, but there it was. The doctor, Kuiper decided, might be a rake and a butterfly, but he was good value for the money; and it appeared the doctor no longer regarded him as a penny-pinching ogre. Their more relaxed relationship led to their sharing a sundowner before dinner, after sloshing their sweat-slick bodies with buckets of water on the lower deck with the boy Henky standing guard against Mrs. Goldstein.

Mrs. Goldstein, as might have been expected, turned into the queen bee of the ship. She appeared frequently on the lower bridge with some request or announcement, and both captain and doctor began to look forward to her appearance because somehow she managed to turn up in a different outfit every day. Despite the fact that all their baggage had been dumped in the harbor in Hamburg, she concocted flimsy robes, flowing gowns, startling shorts and bulging blouses out of whatever she rifled from her subjects' meager possessions or bullied out of bo'sun and cook. She must have brought with her a variety of powerful perfumes in her voluminous reticule when she came on board, for neither cook nor bo'sun could have furnished them. She brought a daily report on the state of her nation, pointed out who needed special attention from either doctor or captain, reported on the general mood and how it could be improved by some edict from the bridge which, as she hastened to say every time, was none of her business of course, merely a suggestion. For some reason, Kuiper's tomato juice and the doctor's gin tasted better after her visit; their maleness seemed more hale, the ship less of a ramshackle cattle-runner and more of a dignified vessel on which these good people could cross the ocean in security, comfort and dignity.

The relaxing of the relationship between captain and doctor induced the latter to innocently broach ticklish subjects which earlier in the voyage would have roused Kuiper's hackles. Like, for instance, the life rafts.

The doctor mentioned the rafts casually one evening after they'd had their communal shower on the lower bridge and Henky had brought glasses and a bowlful of the cook's pretzels, which would have defanged a tiger but provided the illusion of a savory nibble. "By the way, Skipper," he said, as they stretched out in their deck chairs in the shade of the cabin, "you aren't seriously planning to use those rafts in the event of an emergency, are you?"

Kuiper bristled. He had been unexpectedly lucky with the inspection, but preferred not to think about it. All he did was grunt and crunch a pretzel.

The doctor persisted innocently, "Aren't there regulations banning those things? I thought they were strictly for submarines or something. At least, that's what Vinkemans says."

"Doctor," Kuiper said calmly and he hoped with finality, "Vinkemans is a bathtub sailor, and so are you. Stick to your patients, and let me sail the ship."

"Oh, sorry," the doctor said. "I didn't mean to tread on any toes. It's just that I couldn't help wondering about them. The damn things aren't actually rafts at all, are they? Merely rings of something—"

"Balsa wood," Kuiper grunted.

"Right, just a ring of balsa wood with a net in the center. Are people expected to sit in those nets with their legs sticking through? What about sharks? And they'd be squatting up to their midriffs in water. Are they just for show?"

Clearly, this conversation had to be brought to an end. "Doctor," Kuiper said, as to an eager but tiresome teenager, "I have room in my lifeboats for a hundred and eighty souls. That leaves seventy, not counting the crew. I think we have seventy sturdy people among our passengers who in the case of an emergency wouldn't mind roughing it. Those rafts are perfectly acceptable. I bought them, Navy surplus, in Amsterdam. They cost me a pretty penny, I'd have you know."

"Well, they must have passed safety inspection, I suppose." The man said it casually, just to make conversation. The gin was what did it; he was into his third, so the warmth of good fellowship must have begun to spread in his chest and the miracle of fleeting brotherhood which once had made the Old Man say that the devil could bring about with half a bottle of gin what had taken Christianity two thousand years to achieve. "To tell you the truth," Kuiper said, "if the scramble nets and rafts had been inspected by the German authorities, I might have had a problem. As a matter of fact, I worried about them when I sailed upriver that morning on my way to Hamburg. But because of the business on the quayside, we left so fast that I never saw an inspector."

"H'm." The doctor tested his teeth on a pretzel, gave up and took a sip of gin instead. "Well, from what I gather, I don't think the Germans were about to inspect you anyhow. The Nazi authorities probably didn't give a damn whether you put their Jews into boats or colanders. Be that as it may, I'd rather dog-paddle to safety in one of your nets than in anybody else's lifeboat. I suppose that's the sign of a good captain, eh? Mind if I indulge in another snort?"

It was the first time that anybody had told Kuiper he was a

good captain. Maybe it was the gin. "Tell me, where do you get that stuff?" he asked brusquely. "Did you bring it with you?"

"No, no," the doctor said. "It's acquired locally. I know this is supposed to be a dry ship, but there are sources, you know."

"If you got it from the cook," Kuiper said, "it probably came straight from the lamp."

The doctor changed the subject. "How long would you say this heat's going to last, Skipper?"

"Oh, another week or so. Then we get the trades again. After that, we'll be heading into winter."

The prospect filled Kuiper with a sudden sense of regret. Merely to talk about it broke the spell of timelessness

Unexpectedly, he had become attached to the tent village and its emotional inhabitants. The return voyage would be very different, whatever cargo the market brought.

"Well, time for the evening round," the doctor said, rising. "I don't suppose I'll see you before you go to the bridge. Good watch, Skipper."

"Good night, Doc."

After the man had left, Kuiper concluded that he'd miss him, too. Well, what do you know?

3

The euphoria of the Chosen traversing the desert headed for the Promised Land did not last. The mood changed shortly after *Star of Peace* had crossed the Tropic of Capricorn.

The first high wind came blustering out of the gray void of the South Atlantic; it ripped the awnings, which had to be hastily taken in. The sea turned angry; small, vicious, foam-spewing waves ruffled the rising and falling slopes of the hill-sized swell. It happened very fast; the moment the wind began to whistle in the rigging, the laboring old ship, her blunt bow rising and plunging, turned from a village back into a scruffy freighter crowded with refugees headed for an uncertain future.

Maybe it was the seasickness that did it. So far, the passengers on the whole had been free of it; now the long refectory tables which had witnessed such jollity became deserted, and those who did appear for meals had to clutch their mugs to prevent them from sliding off with the rolling of the ship. The smell in the holds acquired a new ingredient: the acrid stench of vomit.

Kuiper, watching the transformation of his ship from the bridge, had a sudden sense of foreboding, which he shook off irritably. It was just a patch of bad weather; tomorrow or the next day, the high wind would die down, the sun would be out again and all would return to normal. The trouble was that the carefree village with its happy people laughing and singing underneath the awnings had not been normal. It had been an illusion, a dream. Now, under the gray sky, on the gray, foam-scarred sea, lashed by swirling spray as the blunt bow plunged and shipped tons of water, reality returned.

As he stood there watching the heaving foredeck, hanging on to the rail of the bridge as the ship heeled, his eye was caught by a slight figure standing in the wind, gazing out over the angry sea. It took a moment before he realized there were two of them, a tall girl sheltering a small boy whom she pressed against her protectively. There was something so sad, so apprehensive about them, and such loneliness, that it seemed as if they personified the sadness of exile, the curse of the Diaspora. When the wind whisked aside the kerchief the girl was wearing on her head, Kuiper saw it was the red-headed one and her little brother.

"Captain?"

Henky stood behind him with the midwatch coffee.

"Thank you, boy."

Henky's oilskins fluttered with a paper sound as the wind whisked them.

"Hang on to your tray, lad. Mr. Wybrands is in the radio room. Watch out for the threshold."

He waited until the boy had managed to struggle inside the door of the wheelhouse before he turned back to look.

The girl and the little boy were gone, as if the wind had blown them into the void.

CHAPTER SIX

I

Tovah Nachtgeist had never felt close to her fellow passengers, or to anyone else for that matter, except David, and he didn't really count, as he was almost an extension of herself. The fuss about the warm clothing brought home to her once again how far removed she felt from the others.

As the ship approached Montevideo, the weather turned cold and everybody started to lament about the winter clothes they had lost in Hamburg. They talked about their lack of warm clothing as if it were an injustice which could be redressed by their making a fuss; yet the simple fact was that no one could be blamed for it except the Nazis. The crew had no winter coats to spare, and even if they had, why should they give them up?

Mrs. Feldschuh was the worst; she infected poor, addled Mrs. Schlachter, who began to rant about warm dresses for Lieschen, her grandchild; between them, they generated a wail of complaints that soon grew into a clamor. Mrs. Feldschuh got the others to the point of drawing up an ultimatum to the captain; but before they could submit their ridiculous demands, old Goldstein intervened and prevailed upon the captain to direct a telegram to the Uruguayan Red Cross alerting them to the situation and asking for help; the message would be sent the moment they were in range of Montevideo.

Her action had been like the lancing of a boil. The protestations died down the moment the telegram was decided upon; the whole issue was buried and forgotten. Nobody knew in the end whether the captain actually sent that telegram and nobody cared. It was yet another proof of old Goldstein's shrewdness. Tovah herself did not care for the bossy old woman, especially after she had interfered in her relationship with *Herr Doktor,* or "Hendrik," as Tovah called him boldly in her daydreams. There was no doubt at all that he had been very taken with her. He had been about to lift her into the lifeboat the night of the carnival, and Tovah was certain he would have kissed her; then old Goldstein's interference had changed him from a sweet, attentive man who had made her feel surrounded by tenderness into a distant stranger who seemed hardly aware of her existence. Heaven knew what Goldstein had said to him; it must have been pretty final to make him behave thereafter as if they had never sneaked into the lifeboat to do blood pressures, as if he had never gazed into her eyes with that unnerving, probing gentleness. Damn old Goldstein! A nearly eighteen-year-old was a grown woman, certainly after what she had gone through.

For more than three years, Tovah had lived on her own with David. She had no relatives left other than Yakov; when he departed for Palestine, she was thrown back onto her own resources. She survived, managed to keep David under control, clothed him, fed him, was mother, father and housemaid to him —if anyone was entitled to be mistress of her own life, it was she. But here came old Goldstein and put her big foot in and—squash! There went not just an evening, not just a tryst in a lifeboat under the stars, but a whole life. With Hendrik's cold, almost hostile behavior, Tovah's daydream of the future had become ludicrous, but it turned out to have a life of its own. It seemed as if Hendrik's rejection mysteriously fueled it, made it more real, more haunting, until she felt unable to shake it. It took over all her waking hours, and her dreams as well.

It centered on a house: a bungalow surrounded by palm trees with a big veranda and green slatted shutters and a white gravel path leading to a road and by the gate a painted sign, HENDRIK

RICHTERS, M.D., GENERAL MEDICINE. There would be a tricycle in
the yard and a playpen in the shade of a big old tree and the
laughter of children indoors; then a car would come down the
long white road, raising a cloud of dust, and swing into the yard
and there he would be, calling, *"Tovah? Tovah, wo bist du?"* and
she would come running from the veranda.

She saw the interior of the bungalow down to the smallest
detail: the curtains, the potted plants on the window sills, the
furniture, the big fourposter bed with its tent of mosquito netting.
It was all based on a book she had read about life in the tropics,
but it had an overwhelming reality to her, more so than everyday
life in the holds. The daydream, ridiculous as it was, made the
prospect of life in South America exciting, full of promise.

She knew it was nonsense. The best she could hope for was
a menial job as a housemaid or, if she were lucky, a governess.
Most of the passengers had relatives in South America or the
United States who had promised to send them money; she had
no one other than Yakov, in a kibbutz in Palestine, who had
barely enough money to keep body and soul together. Her
chances of finding any work at all were small indeed; yet she
deliberately addicted herself to that vision of the bungalow with
the green shutters and the laughter of children, the car coming
down the road with that high plume of dust behind it. She took
part in Spanish lessons, she dutifully made notes about the econ-
omy of the state of Uruguay, she even participated in the silly
playlets Mrs. Hallmann made up as Spanish exercises. "Good
morning, Postmistress, how are you today?" "Thank you, Mrs.
Wolf, I am very well indeed. What can I do for you this morning?" "Postage stamps, postcards and a parcel, *por favor.*"

As they approached the coast of South America, Tovah
wanted to talk to Hendrik, for the tension between the dream and
encroaching reality became unbearable. Was he just pretending
to be indifferent because old Goldstein had her beady eyes on
them? Was he waiting for the ship to arrive in Montevideo before
getting back together with her and maybe kissing her in a café
ashore? Did he secretly feel the way she did, and was he just
waiting for a chance to be alone with her, without that horrible

woman looming over them like an ogre? She desperately needed to talk to him. She even got to the point where, despite an infuriating blush, she boldly accosted him. But he pretended he hadn't heard and brushed past her, suddenly on his way to something urgent.

The last day before their arrival was hectic. People were chatting and obstructing the narrow passages between the beds, children howled, angry mothers scolded them, Mrs. Schlachter was even more nervous about her unruly granddaughter than usual and little Lieschen more spoiled and destructive. Hendrik pretended to be busy whenever he spotted Tovah coming, but her determination to confront him grew. She had to know; she felt she would go crazy unless she spoke to him.

But she didn't get the chance. The morning of the day of their arrival, as dawn broke over a wide, silvery estuary with dark banks in the distance, all passengers were called out and requested to start lining up on deck ready for disembarkation. It seemed much too early, there was no harbor in sight as yet. But it turned out to have been a wise move on the part of the captain, for the lining up took forever. There were altercations on the ladders between those who wanted to go down and those on their way up; children were whining, their mothers' voices grew shrill with nerves. As the ship entered Montevideo harbor, people were still bickering and running back and forth, or trying to worm their way into the waiting line closer to the gangway. Hendrik was nowhere in sight; Tovah asked about him when she saw Mr. Himmelbaum come down the steps to the lower bridge. *Herr Doktor* was very busy, Mr. Himmelbaum said, packing his belongings in the captain's cabin. It could mean only one thing: he was planning to make off the moment the passengers had left the ship.

They entered the harbor between two breakwaters; suddenly, there was the city. A big white passenger liner with yellow funnels was moored right inside the entrance; as they passed it, Tovah spotted a Dutch flag and recognized the ship from Le Havre.

For some reason, the sight of the liner made her realize it had to be now, it *had* to be; she would never see him again. She had to know if she meant anything to him, she had to know it *now*.

Yet, she shilly-shallied. She fussed over David, fiddled with his rucksack and was angry when he wouldn't stand still. She said, "Oh, I *beg* your pardon" with exaggerated politeness when Mrs. Schlachter bumped into her while trying to catch Lieschen, who was running up and down the deck, hitting people with her teddy bear. She found all kinds of small errands to do for the older women, her mind alternating between determination and despair. Finally, the ship moored alongside a dock with a white terminal building at the far end; the captain called through a megaphone, "Attention! Attention, everybody! All passengers proceed to the gangway! Before disembarking, please be sure to collect your passports from Mr. Wybrands, who will be standing at the head of the gangway. Proceed down the gangway in an orderly fashion, and hold on to the rail, as it is very steep. Captain and crew wish you luck in your new homeland, and Godspeed!"

She watched the gangway being swung out; that was the moment she finally managed to tear herself free from her lethal inertia. Saying to David, "Stay here! Don't move! I'll be right back," she ran up the stairs to the captain's cabin.

She arrived in the doorway panting, out of breath, and saw that Mr. Himmelbaum had been right: Hendrik was packing to leave. The table was heaped with clothes, as were the chairs; the settee was open; Hendrik was standing in the middle of the cabin, fitting Henky with a tropical helmet.

"Gosh, Doc," the boy said, "thank you! Terrific! Maybe a bit on the large side?"

"That's easy." Hendrik took the helmet, turned it upside down and said, "You adjust it by this string here. First undo this knot—"

She could stand it no longer. "Hendrik!" she said, louder and much more desperate than she had planned.

He looked up. She suddenly saw herself through his eyes: a gangling adolescent, blue rucksack on her back, babushka covering her hair, childish face pouting. She felt like fleeing.

"Oh, hello," he said. "Shouldn't you be disembarking?"

"I—I came to say goodbye . . . "

He seemed about to say, "Okay, goodbye," but the anguish in her eyes must have changed his mind. "Come in," he said. "You too, David."

She had not realized that David had followed her. She felt like telling him to beat it, but what with the cabin boy peering at her from under that helmet and Hendrik's obvious irritation, all she could say was, "I . . . I . . . " and there came the tears.

Outside, the roar of the foghorn throbbed. Mr. Meyer's voice shouted, "All passengers leave the ship! Please proceed in an orderly manner! *Don't push!*"

Hendrik said, "Scram, Henky."

"Yes, Doc . . . " The boy left.

"Well, I wish you all the best, Tovah, and you too, David. I hope you'll have a good life here. I'm sure you will." It was as though they had been just casual acquaintances.

The awareness that this was the decisive moment for her future made her say, "But I can't leave just like that! I—my God . . . " Oh, those idiotic tears! They ruined everything.

"Tovah, come on," Hendrik said, still smiling but with an edge of exasperation, "I understand you're nervous and apprehensive, but, really, there's nothing to worry about. You made it. You're free now, with a whole life ahead of you . . . " While speaking, he backed away from her, and was stopped by the desk. He turned, pretending to look for something in a drawer.

"Oh, please!" she heard herself call, her voice thick with those foul tears that ruined everything, everything. "We can't part like this! Not after that night . . . "

He opened a drawer, but pulled it out too far. It tipped over and spilled its contents on the floor. With a curse, he knelt to pick them up; she made a dash to help him. Among the junk on the floor was an old pistol; when she picked it up to put it back in the drawer, he wrenched it out of her grip and cried, "Are you crazy? That thing's loaded!" As if he thought she was planning to shoot him.

"I was just—" She knew now all was lost, and sobbed aloud.

"For God's sake! Tovah, listen, I—"

"Hello there," a woman's voice called from the doorway.

He looked up; Tovah saw his face change from an angry mask into that of the man who had once looked at her with such tenderness. "Susan!" he cried.

Tovah turned and saw two nurses in blue uniform standing in the doorway. Hendrik jumped to his feet, stuffed the pistol into his waistband and ran to embrace them.

The moment had passed. The dream was dead.

2

Susan Foster was startled when Hendrik lifted her over the threshold, kissed her passionately and cried, "Angel!" It should have been flattering, and she was prepared to accept it as exuberance until she happened to see the face of the girl who rose behind the table. It was wet with tears, the face of all betrayed maidens personified.

It needed no course in Psych. II to read the situation. Lecherous Hendrik had been seducing minors during the crossing, and now embraced her, *dea ex machina,* to get out of what had obviously been a showdown. He babbled on nervously; the girl gazed at them with desperation, then, with a stifled sob, ran out the door.

"Tovah . . . !" Hendrik cried half-heartedly.

The little boy with the rucksack came up to him, stuck out his tongue and said, *"Du kannst mir den Buckel hinauf steigen!"* Then he too darted out the door.

"Well, now!" Hendrik cried with false jocularity. "What a glorious surprise! Where do *you* come from?"

Susan looked at the handsome face, the wayward eyes and asked, "What was that he said? The little boy?"

"Oh, nothing," Hendrik replied casually. "He invited me to climb his hunchback, whatever that may mean."

"Didn't you see the ship when you came in?" Myrtle asked him. "We're just inside the breakwater, at the Muelle de Escala. You *must* have seen us!"

"I didn't get a chance to look, I was in here, packing. Well, this calls for a celebration!" He stuck his head out the door and called, "Henky!" Then, grinning, he looked her up and down with those bedroom eyes and said, "I can't tell you what a sight you are for sore eyes!"

"Yes," she said wryly. "Seems our arrival was very timely."

He didn't catch the irony. That must be how he went through life: evading all conflict or confrontation, hopping from one easy lay to the next, like a goddam butterfly.

"Where are you off to?" Myrtle asked in her British voice, picking up the slack in the conversation.

"Thank heavens, my days of shacking up with His Nibs are over; I'll be transferring to a liner in a day or two. I may even move onto your tub. But first I have to finish packing while the skipper's out. Ah! There you are." A grimy boy wearing a tropical helmet several sizes too big for him had appeared in the doorway. "What'll it be, girls? Dutch gin?"

"Susan, what about you?" Myrtle asked, gamely ignoring the atmosphere of tension.

"I couldn't care less."

"Oh, well," Myrtle said, "I'll have anything too, as long as it's on the rocks."

"No ice on this ship, love," Hendrik said. "Whatever booze you order, it'll be warm. How about an English beer?"

"In that case, Dutch gin, please."

"Okay, Henky," Hendrik said, "three Dutch gins. On the double."

"Yes, Doc . . . " The urchin disappeared.

"Well, what shall we do tonight? This deserves a celebration. I've loads to tell you . . . " He looked brightly from one to the other; but as far as Susan was concerned, the whole thing had soured. Why was it that always when you happened to meet a man who seemed a nice guy as well as a good lover, he did something that turned you off? Look at the slick manipulator! Quick as a flash, he turned the beam of his boyish charm on Myrtle, for all the good it would do him. She might look like the picture on an English cookie tin, rosy and blonde and blue-eyed; in reality, she was as bloody-minded as a Navy N.C.O., which indeed she had been before she joined the transatlantic run. What was more, he was wasting his time, for she had set her sights a lot higher than a lowly G.P.

There was a knock on the doorpost. Hendrik cried, "Come in, Henky!"

Instead of the urchin with the helmet, a military officer stood in the doorway. His shoulders were covered with stars, the visor of his peaked cap was resplendent with gold filigree. He saluted with a slow flourish and asked, "Are you the master of thees vessel?"

"No, sir," Hendrik replied, impressed. "I'm the ship's doctor. What can I do for you?"

The officer looked annoyed at having to discourse with a lower form of human life. "I have an urgent message for the master of thees vessel. Where do I find your *capitán?*"

"I wouldn't know, sir. He went ashore, to the agent's. He's due back any moment. Won't you sit down? Have a seat . . . " He started to clear a chair.

The officer looked at him as if he had made an indecent suggestion. "No waiting," he said sharply. "We must do eet without warning." He repeated his florid salute, gave Susan and Myrtle an appraising look and disappeared. The urchin with the tropical helmet came in, eyes bright with curiosity, carrying a tray with three small glasses; he put it on the table and dashed out again.

"What did he mean?" Hendrik asked nobody in particular. "Do what without warning? Arrest somebody?"

"They don't use military police for that over here," Myrtle said.

"That was an M.P.? With all that gold?"

"Colonel of the military police. They're the ones who check the passports of incoming passengers."

"Oh, do they?" He handed them their glasses. "Here's to our happy reunion! Cheers!"

He lifted his glass and knocked back his drink in one gulp. "Well, let me finish packing, and we'll begin the beguine!"

"Hadn't you better wait?" Myrtle asked.

"For what?"

"What the military are up to. I wouldn't trust them, you know. Tricky, these Latins."

"Why? What the hell could they be up to?"

"What's your cargo, except for these immigrants?"

"Nothing. Just the bodies."

"They may be planning a raiding party, looking for drugs or contraband. An informer may have given them a tip, don't you know. Last year, when I was in Valparaiso in H.M.S. *Hastings*—you know, one of the class '28 frigates with the big forefoot . . . "

As Myrtle's voice drawled on, Susan wondered what the hell she had seen in him in Le Havre. It made her feel bitter, and old.

3

The passengers, off the ship now and waiting in a double file on the quayside, had been standing still for almost half an hour.

"I wonder what the hold-up is," Mrs. Feldschuh said querulously. "There seems to be no movement at all; I've been standing by this selfsame pole for *hours.*"

"It's called a dolphin," Mr. Brandeis corrected. "And it can't have been more than twenty minutes."

"Nonsense," Mrs. Feldschuh snapped. "I have an excellent sense of time and—" Lieschen bumped into her, swinging her teddy bear as she ran down the row of waiting people. It stretched all the way from the bottom of the gangway to the terminal in the distance. "Oh, for mercy's sake, Mrs. Schlachter! *Please* control that grandchild of yours!"

Mrs. Schlachter had withdrawn into her private world and did not respond; Tovah too heard Mrs. Feldschuh's grating voice only on the periphery of her awareness. Her mood reflected the weather; it was a gray, dismal day. A thin drizzle blew over the ranks of shivering passengers in billowing gusts. The South American officer in gaudy uniform who had gone on board a while ago now came back and headed for the terminal, his face set in a disapproving scowl.

"I wonder what he's been up to," Mrs. Feldschuh ventured.

"I suppose he was looking for the captain," Mr. Brandeis said, "and I could have told him that the captain wasn't there. I wonder what was so important for him to go ashore at this moment of all moments. He could at least have waited until we were off the quay."

"He was a big boy," Mrs. Schlachter said, "but she was very little. He had a deep chest, yet he had never been an athlete."

Mrs. Feldschuh rolled her eyes; Mr. Brandeis looked away, not wanting to get involved. Because old Mrs. Schlachter had taken a liking to her, making her feel vaguely responsible, Tovah smiled politely at her.

Mrs. Feldschuh said, "I wonder what is wrong. Why are we being kept waiting in the rain? I thought South America would be different. Didn't you?"

Tovah, called back from her private world of misery, realized she was being addressed. Before she had been able to think of an answer, there was the sound of an argument at the head of the column: a man's voice raised in anger, a woman shouting something in Spanish, the man's voice responding furiously. Necks were craned, people tried to see what was going on by standing on their toes; some were breaking ranks. The voices became louder; Tovah recognized Mrs. Goldstein's; then there was the sound of a whistle, a hoarse command and Lieschen Schlachter came streaking down the row of waiting people from the direction of the terminal, shouting, "Soldiers! Soldiers! They're going to attack us!" It was obvious to Tovah that the child was exaggerating, this dramatic warning was no more than a sample of her usual mischief; but others, who had not had daily dealings with the brat, took the childish shrieks of alarm seriously. The commotion grew when there was the sound of tramping boots; rifles glinted in the drizzle as a platoon of soldiers came marching onto the quay. Someone shouted, "Back! They want us to go back on board! Back, back! Quick!"

It was not clear to Tovah what exactly happened after that, but the shout caused an explosion of pent-up fear, not only in the others but in herself, much stronger than on the quayside in Hamburg. That time, part of her had remained an objective observer. This time, she was swamped by an animal terror which made her rush toward the gangway in blind panic, kicking, beating, screaming when she fought her way back onto the ship among a mass of fighting people in the same blind panic as she. She didn't know what got into her, there was no objective observer this time; fear, panic made her kick and claw and scream; she only came to her senses when she heard a child shriek underfoot. A child—a child was being trampled! She tried to hold back the stampede of those behind her, but was unable to do so. Then she realized the child was Lieschen.

She managed to get hold of a little arm and fought her way out of the throng, dragging the child, who was screaming, "Teddy! Teddy! Help Teddy!"

Teddy. The child's toy must be underfoot in that crowd. Tovah pressed the sobbing child against her and watched, trembling with outrage and disgust, the inhuman fight at the bottom of the gangway. She saw women being shoved aside by panicking men. She saw one woman bite a hand that tried to hold her back. She saw David swept on board by one of the men. Suddenly, the crowd thinned out, those who climbed the gangway seemed to run faster, stumbling as they went, then Lieschen cried, "There! There he is! There! Oh, please, *please* get him for me!"

Tovah spotted a brown blur between the train rails on the dock. She pushed Lieschen in the direction of the gangway, crying, "I'll get it! Get up there, quick, *quick!*" She ran to collect the toy. Then she saw the soldiers.

They came, three of them, running toward her. Someone shouted at her in Spanish. She hesitated, then she made a final dash, picked it up, stumbled; as she looked up, she saw looming over her an angry boy's face, a raised gun. She managed to duck, ran for the gangway, tripped over something and crashed headlong on the cobbles, hitting her head on the edge of the gangway. Fear made her bounce back onto her feet; she raced up the gangway, away from that gun, that face of lunacy and violence; she arrived on deck sobbing, her eyes blurred with tears.

"That's a nasty cut, child," someone said. "You should have that seen to."

She wiped her eyes with her sleeve and saw it wasn't tears that blinded her, but blood. "I'm all right," she said. "I'm looking for Lieschen Schlachter."

The woman wandered off. Tovah sat down on a bollard, feeling no pain, just the wetness running into her eyes. She pressed Lieschen's teddy bear against her forehead, and suddenly found herself praying, "God, God, please help, God . . ."

There was no answer, just emptiness. A red, smoky emptiness. She felt giddy.

Whatever happened, she should not faint. She sat quite still, waiting for the giddiness to pass, wondering what had happened to them all.

4

The first inkling Kuiper had that anything out of the ordinary was taking place was when the taxi which took him from the agent's office back to the pier where his ship was moored was held up on the boulevard that skirted the harbor. Traffic was backed up for blocks; when they approached the gate to the dock, he discovered why. Armored personnel carriers were parked across the street, forming a barrier; every car had its papers checked by an M.P. supported by a platoon of armed soldiers.

He had to show his passport and his muster book; when the M.P. saw the name of the ship he said, "Starrapees! *Avanti! Pronto! Pronto!*" There was no mistaking the man's urgency; as to why he should be addressed in Italian, Kuiper had no idea. Maybe there was some trouble on board an Italian ship.

But when the taxi entered the gate to the pier, his heart sank. He could only see part of his ship from the gate, but enough to make him realize that was where the trouble was. The passengers were back on deck, he saw soldiers at the rail; there was a lot of commotion; even from this distance, he could hear shouts and wails. Impatiently, he handed his papers to the sentry on duty. The man perused them carefully, then turned and disappeared with them into the office behind him. Almost immediately, he returned and opened the door of the taxi. "Colonel Monteiro wants to see you, *Señor*. In here, please."

His heart sinking, Kuiper paid off the driver and hurried inside. A group of Army officers stood talking with customs agents in the vast, empty hall; as he approached, one of them came to meet him, a topheavy staff officer, his cap and shoulders gold-encrusted, his chest covered with ribbons. He was waving a passport. "Forgery!" he cried accusingly. "These visas are forgeries, all of them! And no wonder! They tried to send us their scum, their criminals! Look! Look here!" He held the passport, open, under Kuiper's nose. "See that? 'Keeper of a whorehouse!' Never in all my years have I seen such brazen admission of a criminal occupation!"

"What happened?" Kuiper asked. "Why are my passengers—"

"I sent them back on board! Entry into Uruguay denied because of lack of entry visa! All of them! In all my years— Look at it! *Look!*" He slapped the open passport angrily. "Whorehouse keeper indeed! If you have crooks or swindlers or prostitutes to get rid of, ship them to Montevideo! Dump them in Uruguay, garbage can of the world!"

To give himself time to find his bearings, Kuiper said with a show of calm, "May I see that, please?"

The officer pushed the passport at him and continued his monologue about those Germans taking Uruguay to be the garbage can of the world.

The passport was Mrs. Goldstein's. It did indeed list as her profession 'Manager of a whore-house,' *Managerin eines Bordellos.*

"What's more, the visa is a forgery! We have telephoned the Ministry, there's no record of any of these visas being issued in Hamburg!"

"But—but—look at this!" By some heavenly inspiration, Kuiper had put the official letter from the Uruguayan Consulate in his pocket before leaving the ship earlier that morning. He handed it to the irate officer. "There you are: the official confirmation from your own people in Hamburg."

The officer frowned. "Who gave you this?"

"The agent in Hamburg, at my specific request. As you'll see, it confirms the validity of their visas."

The colonel seemed taken aback. He grunted, read the letter; then he held it up to the light and his face changed. "I knew it!" he cried. "Forgery! This letter too is a forgery! An *insulting* forgery! What do they take us for? Children?!"

"But—but it's been stamped—legalized—"

"Look for yourself!" The colonel pushed the letter under Kuiper's nose. "See? See the pinpoint? The perforation in the center? That stamp has been drawn, not stamped! Have you ever seen such a crude imitation? I tell you, it's an insult! They must think we live still in the Dark Ages! Who on earth gave this to you? Worthless! A worthless swindle! Insult!" He tossed it back at Kuiper, who managed to catch it before it dropped to the floor. He followed the colonel's example and held it up to the light.

The stamp did indeed have a pinpoint perforation in the center, where, presumably, the leg of a pair of compasses had been placed to draw the concentric circles of which it was made up.

"Within twenty-four hours!" the colonel cried. "Before tomorrow noon, your ship must be out of this harbor! Our Navy will escort you into international waters! Go make your arrangements and get out, before our government takes official action. Only as an act of compassion do we allow you—"

"May I use your phone, please?"

"Why?" The colonel frowned at the interruption.

"I want to call my Consulate."

"Even if you called a thousand consulates, Captain: by tomorrow noon, out! Outside our territorial waters! Only by way of exception—"

"Where is it?"

The colonel looked at him, nostrils flaring. "There," he said, pointing. "But you can change nothing! It is time Germany learned that—"

The telephone rang a number of times before a woman's voice answered, "*Consulado General de Olanda, buenos días. Consulaat Generaal der Nederlanden, goeden morgen.*"

"Er—good morning. My name is Kuiper. I'm master of the Dutch freighter *Star of Peace,* docked in the River Basin. I have a cargo—a contingent—of two hundred and fifty passengers from Hamburg, Germany. They all have entry visas for Uruguay, but the authorities say they are forgeries, and—"

"*Momento.* I give you Mr. Spankenbrink."

There was a series of buzzes, then a man's voice said, "Spankenbrink."

"Good morning. My name is Kuiper, I am master of the Dutch freighter *Star of Peace,* moored in the River Basin. I have two hundred and fifty passengers, immigrants, on board who all have entrance visas for Uruguay, but now the authorities refuse to admit them because they say those visas—"

"What nationality?"

"Excuse me?"

"What's the nationality of those immigrants?"

"German."

"Jewish?"

"Excuse me?"

"Are they *Jews?*"

"Yes, but—"

"Call the Embassy."

"Excuse me?"

"This is a diplomatic matter. The Consulate does not handle those cases. Call the Embassy, ask for the chancellor's office. Here's the number . . . "

The Embassy's phone was busy. Kuiper wanted desperately to get to his ship, but this was important. His only protection, his only hope for help in this crisis was the Embassy. He dialed four times, becoming more and more desperate; finally, he got through. "Dutch Embassy?"

"*Si.*"

"Could you give me the chancellor's office, please?"

"Could you tell me your business?"

"Excuse me?"

"What is the nature of your call?"

"My name is Kuiper, I'm master of the Dutch freighter *Star of Peace,* moored in the River Basin; I arrived this morning with a complement of two hundred and fifty passengers—"

"All matters concerning shipping are handled by the Consular Service. Let me give you the number."

"But I just spoke to them! They told me to call *you!* The visas my passengers were given in Hamburg seem to be forgeries! They have been turned back by Immigration! I need help!"

"Hold on, please. I'll give you Mr. Pufmans."

Buzz. Buzz buzz. "Pufmans speaking."

"Mr. Pufmans, my name is Kuiper . . . "

This time he was allowed to tell the whole story without interruption. "So, Mr. Pufmans, that's how matters stand as of this moment. What do I do next?"

Silence.

"Mr. Pufmans?"

Silence.

"Mr. Pufmans! Are you *there?*"

Silence.

Kuiper looked around, with a beginning of panic. The officers and customs agents stood watching him—all except the colonel, who sat at a table, writing, his back to him. Kuiper was about to put the phone down when a metallic voice in the receiver quacked, "*Allo? Allo?*"

"Yes! This is Captain Kuiper! I was talking to Mr. Pufmans, but I lost the connection. Could you . . . "

"*Momento.* I'll connect you with Miss Vesters. *Momento, por favor.*"

Silence. Then another buzz. "Miss Vesters here."

"Look, ma'am! I'm trying to get through to the *chancellor.* This is an emergency! Ny name is—"

"I know, Captain. I'm the legal attaché, the chancellor referred you to me. Now calm down, please. First question: what is the name of the officer in charge?"

"Excuse me?"

"You are dealing with the military police in the River Basin Terminal, I gather. What is the name of the officer who refused your passengers entry?"

"Er—Mon—Montenegro, or something. A colonel."

"Colonel Monteiro?"

"Yes! Yes, that's him."

"All right, put him on."

"Yes, ma'am. One moment." He called, "Colonel!"

The fat man did not budge, nor turn around. He behaved as if he had not heard.

"Colonel Monteiro! The Dutch Embassy is on the telephone!"

No reaction. One of the customs officers put a finger to his lips and pointed at the colonel. Kuiper said into the phone, "One second, I'll get him," put the receiver down and went over to the writing officer. "Colonel? Excuse me: Colonel Monteiro?"

"H'm."

"Telephone for you."

"For me? No. For *you.*" He continued writing.

"Please, Colonel! It's Miss Vesters, the legal attaché. She'd like to talk to you. She's on the phone now."

"Ah," the colonel said, putting down his pen. "*Señorita* Vesters. I have something to say to *her.*" He rose with a creaking of leather and marched to the telephone. A brisk and unfriendly conversation ensued; the colonel slammed down the receiver and marched back to where Kuiper was waiting. "No one," he said, "*no one* can talk forged visas into valid ones. No one can change a brothel keeper into a chaste woman. Not even your Miss Vesters! Tomorrow! Noon!" He sat down and picked up his pen. "Go on board, Captain. She's coming, for all the good it will do you. Go and look after your passengers. Women!" He snorted. "Go. Go now! We have nothing more to say to each other. *Nada.*" He resumed his writing.

Kuiper stood staring at the man's back; then he braced himself and walked toward the door to the pier. The moment he stepped outside into the gray, cold drizzle, his first impulse was to run to his ship, but he became conscious of the eyes of the passengers watching him from the decks and walked with a measured stride as if the whole thing were under his control. He stepped across the rails, walked along the water's edge to the gangway. It was like Hamburg: torn paper bags, suitcases, hats and parcels; the dock was strewn with scattered objects. An upturned perambulator. A doll. A sinister object which he took to be a scalp but which turned out to be a woman's wig. He climbed the gangway; as he arrived on deck, he caught a first glimpse of the condition of the passengers. Indeed it was like Hamburg all over again: they were stunned, disoriented, some even injured. Two uniformed nurses he did not know and the doctor were occupying themselves with them. Children shrieked and howled, women sobbed, groups of old men clustered together by the ladders that led down into the holds, staring at him with the fixedness of shock. It was a wretched and infuriating spectacle; by the time he reached the lower bridge, he was filled with anger. He was the master of this ship; violence and brutality had been committed against his passengers, for whom he was responsible until they were safely ashore. As he approached his cabin, he was accosted by a bevy of people: Meyer, Henky, Chief Davelaar, Wybrands, the cook; he waved them all aside—"Not now, later. I'll see you all in a minute. Not now." He entered his cabin, shut and bolted the door and leaned against it, suddenly crumpling at the sight of the unexpected chaos in the room: the furniture heaped with stacks of clothing, the doors of the wardrobe open, the seat of the settee upended, clothes and shoes piled on the table, the drawers of his desk pulled out. Despair and panic reared behind him, a towering wave. He turned his back on the room, pressed his face against the door and prayed, "Oh God, God, Christ, God, help me! God, I cannot hold out, I cannot handle this. Please, God. Please, God, for the sake of Thy only begotten Son, help me . . . "

With breathtaking suddenness, peace and tranquillity descended upon him. He had the sense of a presence behind him, so real that he swung around to see who was standing there. But there was no one. There was nothing but the doctor's chaos spread all over his cabin, the flies buzzing against the portholes, the desk, the open settee. Yet, there was that sense of a presence, as there had been that night in the mission three years ago when he handed over his life to Christ. Then, it had felt like an arm around his shoulder; this time, it was as if the presence were standing behind him, a bodyguard, a guardian angel.

He jumped as there was a bang on the door against which he was leaning.

"Yes!"

The doorknob rattled; he remembered he had shot the bolt and opened it. It was the doctor.

"Yes?"

"Skipper, we have a serious problem. Can I speak to you for a moment?"

"Come in." He was amazed at his own calm, his inward peace, his sense of security. It seemed unreal, he expected it to collapse any moment and leave him trembling, weak-kneed, tearful, the way he had been when he cried out to God for help. God, he thought, help Thou my little faith.

"Yes, Doctor, what is it?"

"We have one serious case, Skipper. An emergency. It's old Mrs. Hallmann. She either fell or was hit over the head on the quayside. I don't know, I didn't see it. She was brought on board with a severe nosebleed, now she's in a coma, her pupils are dilated, her blood pressure is critically low. She must be taken to an emergency room as quickly as possible, we cannot handle this on board. We don't have the equipment, and Vinkemans and the nurses off *Tubantia* who are helping out are far too busy. I—I—really don't know what to do, Skipper."

Normally, this would have spooked him, the seriousness of it, the human life in his hands. Now, with that presence behind him, he said quietly, "All right, go to your patient, prepare her for transport. I'll go back to the gate and order an ambulance."

"But, Skipper, chances are they won't admit her! You haven't heard—"

"I have heard, Doctor. I had a meeting with Colonel Monteiro, I know exactly what the situation is and who I'm dealing with. You go back to your patient. I'll arrange it."

The man looked at him with relief. He really believed that the captain was in control. He said, "Yes, Skipper," and went to the door. There he turned around and said, "Thank you."

Kuiper was tempted to say, 'Don't thank me, thank God,' but

he put his cap back on, squared his shoulders and went out onto the lower bridge. There they were, the suppliants, all the people who wanted to see him, clamoring for his attention, but he said, "Sorry, men. This is an emergency. One of the passengers was badly hurt and has to go to a hospital. I'll see you when I get back." They made way for him as he headed for the stairs. He went down to the quayside, back to the hall where Colonel Monteiro still sat at the desk, chatting with a group of officers. At the sight of Kuiper, everyone backed off, leaving him to the martial figure behind the desk, who was suddenly busy sorting papers.

"Colonel Monteiro, we have a patient on board who's in critical condition and must be taken to a hospital at once. It's a matter of life and death. Would you please assist me in calling an ambulance?"

The colonel looked up through narrowed eyes, a leer of suspicion. "I'm sorry, Captain, but I cannot admit anyone without a valid visa. You'll have to look after your patient yourself."

"Colonel Monteiro, now you listen to me." It was not he who spoke, it was that power, that presence behind him. The colonel's face went blank with amazement. "I respect your rules, I respect the law, but this is a case beyond the law. This is an old woman who is dying. She *will* die unless she is taken to a hospital emergency room now. If she dies, Colonel Monteiro, her death will be your responsibility."

For a moment, the colonel's eyes and his battled it out. Then the colonel said a few words in Spanish. One of his officers saluted and went to the phone.

"The ambulance will be there," the colonel said, "but I will not allow that person to leave the pier without your signing a declaration that you are responsible for her return on board your ship after treatment."

"You draw up whatever declaration you deem necessary, Colonel. I'll sign it. Please have the ambulance drive up to the gangway and the attendants come on board with their stretcher."

"And she shall go alone! No one else will be allowed to leave this quay, understood?"

Kuiper said, "Thank you," and left.

He went back on board ship, where he was welcomed at the gangway by the doctor, Vinkemans and the two uniformed nurses.

"Well?" the doctor asked. "Are they coming?"

"Yes." He turned to the two nurses. "I want to thank you for your help. May I ask who you are?"

"Oh—yes . . . " the doctor said. "Allow me to present Nurse Foster, Nurse—er—Myrtle . . . "

"Sedgwick-Jones, Captain. A pleasure, I'm sure."

He shook hands with the nurses; then he said to the doctor, "Is there anything else you need to discuss with me at this point? If it can wait, I'd prefer to see you later in my cabin."

"Yes—er—yes, Skipper—of course."

"I've told the military to allow the attendants with their stretcher to come on board. All right?"

"Yes, Skipper, yes—that will be fine. Thank you."

He made his way through the silent throng of passengers, who all seemed to look to him for some reassurance, some sign of hope. He had nothing to tell them and, averting his eyes, proceeded to the lower bridge, where the others still waited.

"Before I see any of you: Henky, go in there and clear up the mess. There are clothes all over the place, they belong to the doctor. Stuff them back into the wardrobe and under the settee. Now."

"Yes, Captain. Straightaway, Captain . . . " The boy slipped inside.

"Yes, Meyer?"

"It's about the victuals, Joris. Cook says he doesn't have enough for even one more meal. How are we going to feed these people? We can't go ashore, they won't let us."

"Go down to the customs shed. You'll see some officers there. Tell them what your business is, that there is no food on board, that it must be ordered from the chandlers, and ask to use the telephone."

"I tried that before, but they threw me out."

"They won't this time. Take your muster book, show it to them as proof that you are the first officer, tell them I ordered you to use the telephone. If you have any problems, call me. You have the number of the chandlers?"

"I still think—"

"Don't think. If it doesn't work, come back and I'll face them down. Yes, Davelaar?"

The chief was angry, as usual. "What the hell is going on? These people are not allowed on shore here! What the hell are you going to do? What are *we* going to do? What the hell *is* all this?"

"Chief, keep your shirt on. I'm in the process of straightening it all out. The legal attaché from the Embassy is on her way here. Within the hour, we'll come up with a solution. Now, don't you spread any more alarm and despondency among the crew . . ."

"I ain't spreading nothing! *I* didn't take those Jews on board! I told you right at the beginning—"

"And that's enough!" He had rarely addressed the old man like that. Davelaar had been his father's friend, his confidant. In the past, whenever he had confronted the old man, he had felt the shadow of his father upon him. Now it was different. The days of insecurity and vacillation were over. He could not believe it, not quite.

Neither could Davelaar, by the look of him. "You wait, young man!" he growled. "You and I are in for a serious talk!"

"Once all this has been sorted out, I'll be delighted. At the moment, we're in an emergency, so do as I tell you. Go and calm down the crew, tell them the Dutch government has been informed and things are in the process of being taken care of."

Davelaar made off without further protest, which was unlike him.

The boy came out of the cabin and said, "It's all cleaned up, Captain. You can go in now."

"Thank you, Henky. I'm expecting a lady from the Embassy. When she comes, bring her straight up, okay?"

"Yes, Captain."

He went inside, followed by Wybrands, the second mate; but before the young man had been able to open his mouth, there was a knock on the door and in came Henky, saying, "Captain, here's the lady from the government."

"Show her in."

"Yes, Captain."

"Wybrands, we'll have to continue this some other time. Right now— Come in, ma'am."

After speaking with her on the phone, he had been expecting a mannish, middle-aged spinster; the young woman who stepped over the threshold could not be any older than thirty. She was dressed entirely in black, but looked anything but funereal. She wore a black beret at a rakish angle, a black suit and black rain boots, and she carried a black leather attaché case. Her lips were scarlet, her eyebrows two thin, painted lines over dark brown eyes, and her hair was bobbed in the latest fashion. His sense of insecurity returned. This could not be the legal attaché of the Embassy on whom he had pinned his hopes . . .

She held out a black-gloved hand and said, "Captain, I am Cynthia Vesters."

So it was she. "Okay, Wybrands: close the door when you leave. Sit down, ma'am."

"Thank you." She sat down on one of the chairs by the table, opened her briefcase on her lap, took out a pad and pencil and a pair of outsize glasses. "Captain, you're in a mess," she said cheerfully.

"So I gather."

"I stopped to see Colonel Monteiro just now; he showed me one of your passengers' passports. He insists that the visas were forged. He also mentioned a letter from a Uruguayan consul you showed him, on which even the official seal was crudely forged. To start with, could I have a look at that letter, please?"

He handed it to her; she went through the colonel's routine: holding it up against the light, shaking her head. "Crude is indeed the word," she said finally. "Who gave this to you? The Consulate?"

"No, the agent who arranged for the passage."

"I see." She put on her glasses and flicked the pages of a steno-pad. "Tell me what happened as from the moment of your first contact with the local authorities. In detail, please."

"Well, I entered port without any problems. I had a visit from a customs officer, who came on board with the pilot. I told him about the passengers, showed him the passports. He looked at one or two of them and everything seemed in order. After we were moored, the passengers started to disembark, and I went off to the agent's. While I was gone, the passengers went to the customs shed, were stopped by the military and ordered back on board."

She had been making notes. "Was there any shooting?"

"Not that I know of. As far as I can gather, the soldiers simply ordered them to turn around and go back on board."

"Then what caused the panic? They didn't stampede merely at the sight of soldiers?"

"Those people have memories of soldiers, ma'am."

"I see." She started to make notes again. "Jews, are they?"

"Yes."

"German?"

"Yes."

"Two hundred and fifty?"

"Yes."

"Last port of call?"

"Le Havre."

"Is that where you took them on?"

"No, Hamburg."

"Who arranged the transport?"

"A German brokerage firm."

"Name?"

"World Tours Incorporated."

"Head office? Is it in Hamburg?"

"Yes."

"Did you visit them in their office?"

"No, a representative came on board ship."

"Anyone else visit you? Any officials, I mean?"

"Yes. An officer."

"A military officer?"

"S.A., I believe—whatever that means." He remembered the pale young man with the jackboots. "He was pretty unpleasant."

She took off her glasses. "It sounds as though the forgeries were officially known to the Germans, if not sanctioned. Why was the stamp on that letter so crudely done, I wonder? With their resources they could afford a stamp, wouldn't you think? Why was it drawn by hand? There must be a reason."

"I wouldn't know, ma'am."

"It must be part of some cat-and-mouse game. Charming." She put her glasses back on. "Did you inform the Dutch Consulate in Hamburg of your arrangements?"

"No."

"You did not ask for any official assistance or advice?"

"No."

She sighed. "You're an innocent, Captain. You were the perfect foil. They must have loved you."

"You seem to know a lot about those people," he said, frowning.

"Of course I do, it's my business; my field is international law. The Nazis are deliberately corrupting international law. They stop at nothing: misrepresentation, forgeries, phony documents, perjured witnesses. This case is typical: a few hundred Jews, women, children, old men, of no value to them as slave labor, so they confiscate all their possessions, then 'allow' them to leave with something like ten dollars apiece and furnish them with phony visas for Uruguay. But that crude forgery is a new twist I don't understand—not yet. Why a clumsily drawn stamp that any immigration officer would spot at once? Why the deliberately specified criminal occupation in the passport I saw? You know the one I mean?"

"Was it a Mrs. Goldstein's?"

" 'Manager of a brothel,' it said."

"Yes. Mrs. Goldstein."

"Who's she?"

"The passengers' representative."

"Does she run a brothel?"

"She told me she ran a hotel."

Miss Vesters thought, tapping her teeth with her glasses. "Well, suppose she did indeed run a house of ill repute. Have you ever seen that stated in a passport, officially?"

"No."

She became aware of his discomfort at her professional excitement. Her eyes lost their faraway look, she put her glasses back on and resumed, pencil poised, "How were you paid? Cash?"

"That was the agreement; but he turned up with a check in German marks. I had quite a problem cashing that in Le Havre."

"For how much?"

He hesitated. "I don't see what that has to do with the situation," he said, tired of her questioning.

"They accepted your bid in the Amsterdam Exchange?"

"Yes."

"Well, then, it's a matter of public record, isn't it?"

"Twenty-four thousand dollars."

"U.S.?"

"Yes. But I don't see . . . "

She lifted a hand. "Just a minute, Captain. Did you arrange for the same amount to be put in escrow in Hamburg?"

"No. Why?"

"As a guarantee for their return passage, in case they were refused entry."

"Should I have? The thought did not occur to me."

She removed her glasses. The look she gave him was one of compassion. "Captain, you *are* a fool. Was there anyone else bidding in the exchange for this transport?"

"The Lloyd. But they backed off."

"And you did not ask them why?"

"No. I presumed it was because I underbid them. Why?"

"All transports of German Jewish immigrants to Latin America have run into problems. The U.S., the British Commonwealth, the European countries won't touch them any more. And after this, my guess is that Uruguay won't either. You own this ship?"

"Yes."

"In that case, I'm afraid this is going to cost you a lot of money, Captain. Why, for heaven's sake, did you get into this? You appear to me to be a decent man who wouldn't get mixed up in this slave trade."

"Slave trade?"

"To haul shiploads of terrified German Jews across the ocean at an exorbitant price, with accommodations that don't meet elementary standards, is—"

His pent-up anger could no longer be held in check. "You haven't seen the accommodations! I've carried on a decent trade with this vessel for three years, my father for thirty years before me! When I received the offer of two hundred and fifty passengers from Hamburg to Montevideo, I didn't ask if they were Christians or Jews. I fitted out my forward hold for the men, my aft hold for the women and children, complete with washrooms, toilets—you go down into my holds and look at the accommodations yourself—"

"All right, Captain," she said, raising her hand to calm him. "All I wanted to say—"

"And as for the exorbitant price, the Lloyd would have charged them double the amount!"

"The Lloyd didn't want to touch it, Captain."

"That's the Lloyd's business! I—" There was a knock on the door. "Yes!"

It was Mrs. Goldstein and the Rabbi. He wanted to see her, but right now was impossible.

"Captain," she said, "we want a word with you."

"Not now, Mrs. Goldstein. I'm busy."

The Rabbi cried, "But we represent the passengers! They are desperate, Captain!" He sounded close to tears.

"Not now, Rabbi. In half an hour's time."

"But, Captain," the old man persisted, "what am I to *say* to them? I must *say* something! The situation—"

"I'll know more in half an hour, not before. Please, Mrs. Goldstein."

Mrs. Goldstein put an arm around the old man's shoulders. "Come, Rebbe. We'll be back. Come." She managed to coax him out the door, which she closed behind her.

When they were gone, he said to Miss Vesters, "There you are. What *do* I say? That they'll be admitted, in the end?"

"Not a hope."

"You're sure?"

"Absolutely. The best we can hope for is that I may be able to postpone your departure a day or two. That's all."

He paced up and down, thinking it over. Then he said, "All right. In that case, I want to get under way as soon as possible. No point in adding more expense than is absolutely necessary.

Every day I hang around here will cost me money. What's the nearest port that will accept them, provided they get visas?"

She looked at him with a puzzled frown. "Come now, Captain —you aren't serious!"

He had no idea what she was talking about. "Excuse me?"

"This country was the last one in Latin America to accept Jewish refugees! Didn't you *know* that?"

"You—you mean—I won't be able to get rid of them anywhere?"

"No, Captain."

"Not even with valid visas?"

"No more immigration visas are being issued right now by any Latin American country to German Jewish refugees."

"But what about the Argentine?"

"No, sir."

"Brazil?"

"No."

"But—but Chile, surely?"

"Captain, as I said, Uruguay was the last haven for these people."

"But I can't sail all the way to the Galápagos Islands just to put them ashore!"

"You wouldn't be able to put them ashore, Captain, even on the Galápagos Islands."

"But then *where?*" It was a cry of desperation.

"Nowhere, Captain. There's only one solution: take them back to Hamburg."

He gazed at her, stunned.

5

———————————

Cynthia Vesters watched with a feeling of sympathy but at the same time a growing irritation as the seriousness of the predicament in which the poor man found himself finally penetrated to him. There was something touching in his disarray which aroused a motherly response in her, but as a lawyer she felt a growing exasperation with his criminal innocence. It was ludicrous to take on a load of Jews from Germany for South America without surrounding yourself with safeguards until you bristled with legal defenses; this pathetic innocent had walked straight into the Nazis' trap. The more she thought about it, the more convinced she became that the whole thing had been meticulously planned by some sadistic mind in Berlin to the smallest revolting detail. The crudely forged stamp, the taunting inscription in the passport—it all came under the heading of pulling the wings off a fly. And here was this unsophisticated soul, this unsuspecting victim; what she was watching, with pity and anger, was the dawning of the realization of what he had done to himself with his Dutchman's idea of a good business deal. Then, suddenly, she saw him set his jaw. "Back to Hamburg," he said grimly. "And you dare to suggest that to me—you, who talked about 'decency' a moment ago?"

This was becoming unreal. "Captain, let's leave ethical considerations out of our discussion for a moment, for you're on very thin ice there. I'm suggesting nothing, it's not my function to suggest anything. My function is to give you all the information at my disposal and then, should you ask for it, the best legal advice I can give in the circumstances. In your circumstances, the only advice I can give is for you to take your passengers back to Hamburg. It's not even advice, it's simply the only possibility left open to you."

"Madam," he said, voice trembling, "I must tell you that I deeply abhor your suggestion."

Maybe it was normal for someone in his situation to take it out on the messenger, but while she had for a moment sympathized with him, she now began to lose interest. "My dear man, all I'm trying to do is make you see reason."

"I don't reason, ma'am!" he cried. "I have a heart that feels, a conscience that must answer to God, a soul that is immortal! And so have you, even if you don't give a damn!"

This was becoming ridiculous. "Captain, let's stay with the facts. To start with—"

"The facts are, ma'am, that until three years ago I lived without God or His commandments; I brawled, I drank, I made such a mess of my life that my father turned his back on me; then God grabbed me by the scruff of my neck and flung me on my knees—"

"For heaven's sake, Captain! That's beside the point!"

"It's right *to* the point! Three years ago, by an act of grace, I came to Christ! Ever since, I have lived in peace with my conscience, abided by the laws of God and the world, grown in the awareness of Christ's presence, like a tree! Do you think I'd let myself be felled by the first gale God blows at me to test my roots?" He stood over her, blue eyes blazing. "I'll bend, ma'am, if God wills it! I'll let my branches be chopped off, if God wills it! I'll let myself be split and splintered, if God wills it! But I *won't* take those people back!"

Maybe for someone susceptible to religious fervor his outburst would have had some objective validity; to her, who detested all emotional religion, it was offensive. She felt like leaving him to rant to his heart's content in the privacy of his cabin; but it was her duty to help the poor brute past the rapids of his emotional outburst to his final acceptance of the inevitable; if that meant an argument, so be it. "I wouldn't care to believe in a God who forced me into an act of insanity, Captain," she said calmly.

"A person doesn't *care* to believe, ma'am, he *must!*"

"Let's try to talk common sense, Captain, shall we? What could you possibly do, other than take your passengers back to Germany, considering that no other country will admit them? You have no other option. The Germans have to readmit them for the simple reason that they are German nationals. So you might as well settle for the inevitable, and discuss in a rational manner—"

"I can put them ashore somewhere else!"

"Where?"

"Somewhere other than Germany! In a civilized country!"

"How, Captain, considering that no civilized country will allow you to do so?"

The blue eyes took on a look of childlike cunning. "If

needs be, I'll turn off my lights and put them ashore under cover of darkness."

For her even to discuss that would mean to involve the Embassy in an illegal operation. She snapped her attaché case shut and rose. "Captain, please take note that I, as an official representative of your government, advised you to take these people back to Germany without delay. Anything you might undertake contrary to that advice will be without the legal backing of your government. Good day, Captain." She went to the door; then, her hand on the knob, she turned back to him. She didn't know what it was—his sincerity, his innocence, his guts, the odd mixture of righteousness and elemental maleness—but he moved her. "Captain," she said, "listen to me. Listen for a moment to someone who can foresee the consequences of your decision, noble as it may be, because she's familiar with the political reality of today. Let's assume for a moment that you'd manage to smuggle your passengers ashore, somewhere in Latin America, under cover of darkness. Then what? You think they would be admitted into that country *force majeure?* No, Captain. By doing so, you would merely hand them over to the military of the country concerned, who would round them up and return them to Germany without delay. In effect, all you'd be doing would be to leave their execution to someone else."

"You mean they would not be interned?"

"No, Captain. They would be sent back to Germany, without mercy."

"But what about public opinion in those countries? Surely there would be an outcry!"

"Not in Latin America, Captain. Most countries here have a military dictatorship, public opinion is powerless. The only country in this hemisphere where public opinion has some clout is the United States, but—"

"Then I'll take them to the United States!"

"But my dear, good man! You're talking nonsense! To start with, the U.S. Coast Guard would intercept you—"

"Not me! I'll find a stretch of coast somewhere that's not patrolled by the Coast Guard!"

"All right, just for the sake of argument, let's say you were to put them ashore in the swamps of the Carolinas, or on some uninhabited island in Maine. They would wander about for a few days in misery, only to be rounded up and shipped back to Germany."

"But you said yourself that the only country—"

"If public opinion were alerted, Captain! But how will you go about alerting public opinion without alerting the Coast Guard? *Now* do you see that what you suggest is impossible?"

"It may be impossible," he said stubbornly, "but that makes no difference."

"But, my dear man!" she cried, exasperated. "You can't disregard *reason!*"

"It's not a question of reason, ma'am, but of faith. If God has taken the trouble to make His will known to me, He will provide me with the means to obey it." His face was at peace now. He seemed to have withdrawn into some inner sanctuary. She tried to think of something to say that might penetrate to him, but no one could stop a man from keeping his appointment in Samarra. "In that case, Captain," she said, "I have nothing further to say. Goodbye."

She opened the door, hesitated, took out a business card, put it on the table, said, "In case you change your mind," and left him alone with his dark and incomprehensible God.

6

Chief Davelaar had overheard the whole thing. Standing outside, on the river side of the lower bridge where there were no people, he had listened to the voices coming from the porthole. The crazy, God-smitten boy was planning to challenge the U.S. Coast Guard! It came to him, with a chill of apprehension, what this meant to the future of *Star*. *Star* was his home, his world, his life —now the boy was about to risk all that for a bunch of complaining, cantankerous, stuck-up bitches with airs, old kikes with delusions of High Life. Not in a thousand years, not in all eternity would he allow the crazy kid to sacrifice *Star* for that bunch of good-for-nothing Jews! Every extra mile they sailed before the unavoidable return voyage to goddam Hamburg was a threat to *Star,* for it would cost money, and her debt already was crushing.

The moment the female with the riding boots had left, Davelaar came around to the starboard side, tore open the door and barged straight in, shouting, "And now *I'm* going to have a word with you, young fella!"

Young Joris rose from his knees behind the table, where he had been drinking God again, and said, "Next time, knock! What do you want?"

Davelaar stepped across the threshold, slammed the door shut behind him and said, "What's all this about taking *Star* to the United States?"

"You've been eavesdropping again!"

"Yes!" he shouted. "And don't you dare start on me! I sailed with your father until the day he had his stroke! I nursed him! I carried him in my own arms to your wife's house! He was my friend! I knew him better than my own brother!" He suddenly found himself near tears, his voice hoarse with rage, confusion. This was not at all what he had planned to say; he had wanted to be rational and calm and fatherly. "Let me tell you this: if your Dad were alive today, he'd take you across his knee and spank the bejesus out of you! That's not religion you were talking to that woman, that was bullshit!"

That really got him. Young Joris puffed himself up like a frog and shouted, "Get out!"

But by now Davelaar was in control of himself again. He no longer had that quavering feeling of disintegration, of losing hold. "No, boy," he said calmly, "you can't get rid of me that easily. You may be the captain now, and make everybody believe you're as good as the Old Man was, but don't try that joke on me. I know you better than anyone else on board this ship. I taught you knots and splices when you were still in your britches—"

The boy turned away and asked, as if this discussion weren't taking place at all, "How much coal have we left?"

"What? Oh. Sixty tons. Now listen. I knew your Dad better than you ever did. He was a religious man all right, but he put the interest of the ship ahead of everything else, ahead of his soul and his salvation he put it! Sure, he was pious. He sang hymns and read the Bible and said prayers at every meal, but if the Lord Himself had as much as pointed a finger at old *Star,* your Dad would have bitten it off! So let me tell you—"

"Then I'll order five hundred tons today." There he sat, doing sums on a piece of paper, pretending he hadn't heard a word.

"Five hundred?! We'll be down over the mark!"

"We have two ballast tanks left to blow."

"All right, all right!" He was not about to be sidetracked. "Now you listen to me: for all I care, you may be as religious as —as the devil, but the moment you put *Star* in danger, you'll have to reckon with *me.* Hear that? Do you *hear* me, boy? As far as I'm concerned, you may gamble your eternal soul for those Jews, and your feeling heart into the bargain, but hands off this ship! Your Dad—"

The boy exploded. That's what Davelaar had wanted: to blast him out of that Skipper-next-to-God act. "You know as little about my father as you know about the Ten Commandments!" he shouted. "You judge everybody by your own miserable standards! My father was a saint!"

"Ha! That's the joke of the century! Let me tell you—"

"I'll *show* you!" The boy went to the bunk, took his Bible off the shelf, opened it and held it out to him. "Read that."

"What?"

"Read it!"

"I can't. Haven't got my glasses."

"All right, this is what my father wrote on the flyleaf when he gave me this Bible, two weeks before he passed away:

For my son Joris, as he takes over command of my ship. Son, in this book you will find your true north. If you get the devil on board, hoist the flag of the cross that you will find in the drawer with the ship's papers, and I will be standing behind you on the bridge. Never despair, even when facing the forces of hell, for one thing I know from experience, after a long life in the service of the Lord: once God makes His will known to you, He will provide you with the means to obey it. Father."

"*He* wrote that?"

"Who else?" The boy closed the Bible and put it back in his bunk.

"The flag of the cross?" Davelaar burst out laughing. "Now I've heard everything!"

There was a knock on the door. Good thing too, for Joris looked as if he was about to go for him. It was the messroom boy.

"Captain, someone to see you."

"Who?"

"I don't know, Captain—I believe an admiral . . . " Behind the boy, a tall figure appeared, a man in his sixties in a blue uniform coat with commodore's epaulets, the visor of his cap full of gold.

"Good afternoon, gentlemen. My name is Bruinsma, master of *Tubantia* moored a couple of piers away from you. I heard what happened and I have come to see if there's anything I can do to help."

"That's very kind of you, sir," Joris said, impressed by the resplendent presence. Then he took on his Skipper-next-to-God act again and said, "Beat it, Davelaar. Prepare for bunkering. We sail as soon as the coal's on board."

Davelaar knew he should have said something to put the boy in his place, but he was still laughing. The flag of the cross! Snickering, he stepped across the threshold onto the lower bridge and closed the door. And there they were, God damn them: Jews. Jews, Jews, wherever you looked, the ship was overrun by Jews as by a plague of roaches. Whatever else happened, he'd see to it that they were taken back to the country where they belonged. If it was the last thing he did, he'd get his ship back, fresh and clean and free of free-loading kikes. Back to Hamburg on a straight course. Three more weeks of jammed toilets, whining complaints, stuck-up airs and old men pissing in the bilges at dead of night. After that: freedom. Back to the best life any man could wish for himself: alone with his ship, in the vast, clean emptiness of the sea.

<hr />

7

"There isn't much you could do for us, Captain," Kuiper said, impressed by the grizzled commodore, who exuded authority. "I've been ordered to leave port, and I'll be escorted outside the three-mile limit by their Navy. A woman from the Embassy said she'll play for time, but if I have to leave, the sooner the better. Won't you sit down?"

"Thank you." The commodore took off his cap and sat down, calm, composed, secure in the confidence of unchallenged power. Kuiper was overcome by envy; he wondered how his visitor would have handled cantankerous old Davelaar.

"I sympathize with you," the commodore said, giving the cabin a look that appeared casual but registered everything. "These Jewish refugees are a pain in the neck. I've never had any dealings with them myself, but six months ago I came across a Greek freighter full of those wretches, anchored off Alexandria. Same story: no admittance. Seemed they had been turned down in five different ports, so now they had reached the stage where they offered themselves for sale at a dollar a head, for lifelong service, to anyone who wanted them, just to get ashore. But buyers? No, sir. People would sooner have bought a leper." He smiled, but his eyes remained aloof. They were the eyes of an old sea wolf who had seen it all. "You're going to take them back, then?" The eyes watched him unblinkingly, waiting.

Now was the time for the passion to settle and the voice of reason to carry the day; but Kuiper found that, even under the eyes of this intimidating observer, his resolve did not waver. Part of him wanted to be accepted by this man, be admitted to this club of Masters, Merchant Marine, but the other part, the crucial part, had sworn fealty to the Lord, Whose presence he had evoked with his desperate prayer for help. He was no longer alone with himself; he was, though tremulous with doubt, guided by an irresistible force, partner in a mission that scared him out of his wits, but to which he was now irrevocably committed. "No," he said, "I don't think I will."

There was a moment of silence, as if judgment were being passed. "Then what? Dump them somewhere on the sly?"

"No. Put them ashore in a civilized country, in the full light of public opinion."

The gaze of the sea-green eyes remained impersonal, observant. "And where are you planning to do that, friend?"

"I don't know yet . . . " Indeed he didn't. He had not had a chance to give it any thought, other than that it would have to be the United States of America. "I was thinking of the United States."

"The United States? Don't be silly. Brazil, man, or the Guianas. Somewhere in the rain forest where there are no roads. Put them in the boats and let them fend for themselves. Someone will pick 'em up soon enough. Send a signal once you're back in international waters."

"No, that wouldn't work."

"Why not?"

"According to the woman from the Embassy, that would mean the local military would round them up and ship them back to Germany."

"So what?"

"I want to set those people free, not leave their murder to someone else."

The unblinking eyes had seen enough; Kuiper was not going to be admitted to the club. "I see. You're an idealist."

"You mean: a fool."

"Maybe. You own this ship?"

"Yes."

"Mortgaged?"

"Up to the hilt."

"So you want to idealize with someone else's money? In that case, you're certainly not a fool, but probably a Christian. Right?"

Kuiper bristled. "Thank you for your interest, Captain, but—"

"Yes, young man: a naked girl is nice, but the truth is prettier with clothes on." The commodore rose, put on his cap; his blue bulk, epaulets glinting, seemed to fill the cabin. Then, surprisingly, he patted Kuiper on the shoulder and walked to the door. As he reached for the knob, he saw the photograph. "Nice couple of kids. Yours?"

"Yes."

"The wife looks like a pretty nice woman too. If I were you, I'd have a good look at that picture before sailing for the United States. Jesus had no children; that makes a difference."

"How did you know—?"

"That Jesus had no children?"

"Why I won't take these people back."

"Knowledge of human nature. You've got the head of a choleric and behave like a phlegmatic. Such a sin against nature can only be the result of a religious conversion."

"Thank you. Now, if you'll excuse me—"

"It's for me to thank *you,* young man. People like you give an old sinner hope again. A month from now, I'll be on the New York run. I'll look out for you. Who knows, maybe I can be of assistance."

"A month from now, I should be done with it."

The commodore smiled. It was not a reassuring smile. "Make no mistake, friend. You'll be just beginning. If a month from now you are still a Christian, then I, a confirmed agnostic, will be ready to accept that as a proof of the existence of God."

"You gave that proof yourself, a moment ago."

"Excuse me?"

"Your story about the ship full of Jews anchored off Alexandria who offered themselves for sale for a dollar a head, but no one would buy them."

"I don't understand."

Kuiper went to his bunk, got the Bible and looked up the chapter. "Deuteronomy twenty-eight, I think it's verse sixty-five. No, sixty-eight. What God will do to the Jews if they do not honor the Covenant. *And the Lord shall bring thee into Egypt again with ships . . . and there ye shall be sold unto your enemies for bondmen and bondwomen, and no man shall buy you.* A promise made two thousand years ago, fulfilled six months ago."

The commodore took a pair of glasses out of his breast pocket and held out his hand for the Bible.

8

Yes, there it was: exactly as the young man had read it. Remarkable! Well—that was an understatement. It was haunting. Bouke Bruinsma saw the ship again, outlined against the deep blue Mediterranean sky: a rusty old bucket, filthy and decrepit. He heard again the wail of a Jewish lament, oddly Levantine in that Arabian Nights setting of sunset and evening star. Even at the time, the scene had struck him as larger than life, heavy with the tragedy of ancient myth; now he understood why. He was not a man easily impressed, but this was eerie: *into Egypt again with ships . . . and there ye shall be sold for bondmen and bondwomen, and no man shall buy you . . .*

There was a knock on the door; the young captain called, "Come in!"

Two pathetic characters entered; a nervous old man with a Hasidic hat and a fat woman with hennaed hair. They both were in such a state of anguish that they did not notice him; they had eyes only for young Kuiper. "Well? Well, Captain?" the old man asked breathlessly. "What's happening? Are we going to be allowed to land?"

Kuiper looked uncomfortable. "It's too early to say, Rabbi. The Embassy has not officially informed me yet of the final decision of the authorities."

There was a short silence; then the woman said calmly, "No need for you to handle us gently, Captain. We'd rather know the truth and prepare ourselves to face it."

Kuiper hesitated, then he said, "All right: I'm afraid there's no hope that you will be permitted to land in Uruguay. Or in any other Latin American country, for that matter."

The Rabbi sat down at the table as if his knees were giving way. But when the woman spoke, her voice was almost casual. "The visas were forged, I take it?"

"So it seems."

"We should have known," the Rabbi said. "Everything they do to the Jews, even supposedly to help us, is a form of torture."

The woman put her hand on his shoulder. "We'd better go and tell them, Rebbe. Don't let's keep them waiting any longer than necessary." The old man rose, tired and beaten.

"Wish us luck, Captain," she said, with a smile.

They were on their way to the door when Kuiper said, "I'm not going to take you back to Germany, if that's what you understood."

They stood still, their backs to him; after a moment, both slowly turned around. The Rabbi stared at Kuiper in a way as if he had prepared himself for pain. "*Verzeihung?*"

"I will not take you people back to Hamburg. I'm going to try to put you ashore in the United States of America. I haven't worked out the details yet, but I am sure there is a way to give you and your people freedom with dignity. At least, I'll try. The rest is up to God."

The Rabbi didn't quite grasp it; the woman looked at Kuiper with an odd expression in her eyes. Then she asked, her voice shaky for the first time, "You—you *mean* that?"

"Yes, ma'am," Kuiper said simply.

Suddenly, she went toward him and put her arms around him and kissed him on both cheeks. "God bless you," she said, "God bless you, boy—dear boy."

Embarrassed, he mumbled, "Don't thank me, Mrs. Goldstein, I—"

"Come, Rebbe!"

The two hurried off, forgetting to close the door.

Bouke Bruinsma handed young Kuiper back his Bible. "I'll be in port for another twenty-four hours. If there's anything I can do to help, let me know. Any stores you need, medications—just send someone over with a list and I'll have it delivered."

"Thank you."

"Good luck, friend."

He wanted to say more, express respect, envy. Maybe that was why he remained silent: for some obscure reason, he felt envy. He reflected upon it as he descended the stairs to the deck and made his way through the throng of doomed creatures to the gangway. What was there to be envious about in the young man's suicidal decision? Possessing that amount of certainty? Obeying a moral imperative so recklessly? Was it an enviable state, to be following a pipe dream that could only end in disaster?

He walked down the quayside toward the gate, a resplendent figure in blue, gold braid shimmering in the sun. At the gate, the sentry sprang to attention; he absent-mindedly returned the salute. He walked through the cold shadow and emerged into the sunlight of the boulevard. There, he hailed a taxi and had himself driven to his ship, gazing absent-mindedly out the window at the crowds and the flags at the gates to the piers.

Here he was: at the pinnacle of power as a sailor, commodore of the most important shipping line of his nation; and there was that befuddled young man: about to set out on a hare-brained, headlong rush toward the Biblical tragedy he had witnessed off Alexandria. As a rational, intelligent man, he wouldn't be in that boy's shoes for a million. It was a prospect to give you the shivers: desperation, sickness, suicides, mutiny and, inevitably, in the end the gruesome hangman's voyage back to Germany. No, envy made no sense—unless, underneath it all, he was envious of the boy's youth.

Stuff and nonsense! What he needed was a good, strenuous workout in the ship's gym, a massage, a brisk swim in the pool and a tall, ice-cold drink in his quarters. Who was it that had said the worry about growing old was a young man's worry?

By the time he arrived at the gangway of the liner, he had decided to stop pussyfooting and to respond to the blatant challenge of that young British nurse. He would invite her for cocktails in his cabin, and let nature take its course.

Grotesque, that the boy's moral challenge should lead to the

decision on his part to commit adultery, but there it was. Ours
not to reason why.

9

Susan Foster was about to collapse in the suture chair and have
a cigarette after what must have been more than twenty bandaged
heads, hands, knees and elbows, when she discovered there was
one more patient waiting in the passage: a little boy with a torn
rucksack. He appeared hesitantly in the doorway.

"What's the matter with you, kid?"

"My sister . . . " The boy pointed down the corridor.

"Where is she?"

"Lying down."

"Where?"

"On the deck."

"What's the matter with her, honey? Is she sick? Wounded?"

"She hurt her head. She's bleeding."

"Can she walk?"

"I guess so."

"Tell her to come here and I'll take care of her."

The little boy obeyed; a white sock with a colored border
dangled from a rip in his rucksack as he walked away.

Susan sighed and started to unwrap yet another suture tray,
wondering where Hendrik, Myrtle and the medic were. They
must have their hands full, down in the holds; the cabin boy had
turned up at a given moment, asking for splints.

"Here she is."

She turned around and saw a red-haired girl standing in the
doorway, her face covered with blood from a good-sized cut in
her forehead.

"Come in, honey. Sit down there."

The girl came in and sat down in the chair. The little boy took
her place in the doorway, looking anxious.

"Why don't you go and play on deck for a while? Go and find some friends."

"I'm staying here," the boy said stubbornly.

"Well, I don't want you to. Off you go!" She went to close the door.

"You're going to hurt her," the boy said. "I want to stay here."

"Come on, honey, beat it. She'll be with you in a minute." She pushed him out, closed the door and inspected the wound. "That's quite a cut, honey. How did you manage to do that?"

"Lieschen Schlachter had dropped her teddy bear," the girl replied in a whisper. "It was lying between the rails on the quayside below. I went to get it for her. As I was picking it up, soldiers came for me and I— *Ouch!*"

"Yes, I know it stings. But I have to clean it first before I can do anything about it. Tell me, who's Lieschen Schlachter?"

"A little—" The girl winced; tears started to run down her face.

"Close your eyes, dear. We don't want this stuff to get into them. Here—bend your head over this basin and I'll squirt some of it in the wound."

She was rinsing out the laceration when the door opened and Myrtle and Hendrik came in. His coat and Myrtle's uniform were smeared with blood. "Looks as if you've been busy down there," Susan said.

"You can say that again," Hendrik replied. "I thought you'd be through by now."

"This is the last one, I think. Laceration, five centimeters. Here, take a look." She lifted the girl's face. "Keep your eyes closed, honey."

Hendrik, who had seemed in high spirits, said, "Oh my God." Only then did Susan realize who the girl was: the one who had come to say goodbye.

"That'll need stitches," he said impersonally.

"Stitches? She's not one of your sailors! If you suture that wound, it'll leave a scar."

Hendrik looked at her with a lop-sided smile. "Okay. What do you suggest, love?"

"I'd put on a butterfly."

"Good," Hendrik said, "be my guest." He turned to the girl. "She'll do a fine job, Tovah. She's first-rate. Come, Myrtle, let's leave her to it. Give us a whistle when you're through here; we thought we'd go and have a bite to eat together. But I must change first. Okay?" Without waiting for her answer, he fled; there was no other word for it.

The girl was now crying openly. Susan felt so angry that she was tempted to open the door and call him back, but common sense prevailed. She tore the envelope off a butterfly bandage, put it on the tray, gave it a dollop of Peruvian balsam and pulled on a pair of fresh gloves. "Okay, honey, I'm going to put the bandage on now. It'll sting, just for a moment. Ready?"

"Yes . . . "

"Okay, here goes."

It needed dexterity and concentration to pull the edges of the wound evenly together without wrinkling or shifting. The girl squirmed.

"Hold still, we're nearly there. Let me do a good job; if you keep still, I guarantee it'll just leave a hairline scar. You'll barely be able to see it. That's right. Hold it like that. One more second . . . there we are. You're all set. Sit still for a while, don't get up! Give the bandage a chance to settle." That was a bit of nonsense, but she wanted to talk with the girl. Despite her concentration on what she was doing, fury had been mounting inside her. The rat! What a miserable weakling he was! She took off her gloves. "Tell me what happened," she said, and went to the basin in the corner to wash her hands.

"I told you. Lieschen Schlachter—"

"That doctor fellow: he didn't knock you up, did he?"

"Pardon . . . ?"

"Had your period since you went into the clinch with him?"

The girl gazed at her, horrified, blushed to the roots of her hair and stammered, "I—I never . . . We never . . . "

"Okay," Susan said, drying her hands. She put the towel away and sat down on the stool next to the girl. "Turn around, honey. Face the light, so I can see."

The girl turned her head obediently and gazed at her. She had lovely eyes.

"How old are you?"

"Seventeen . . . " There came the tears again.

"Take it easy, sweetheart," she said matter-of-factly. "The world hasn't come to an end, you know."

The girl cried, surprisingly, "It has!"

"No, it hasn't. That's the way the cookie crumbles. It's a good thing to find that out early in the game: all men are hunters. That's the way they're made. Be glad you didn't get hung up on the pocket Don Juan. Know the saying? *Don Juan, done 'em all.* Don't worry, there's a whole bullpen full of them waiting for you out there."

The girl had closed her eyes. "I didn't mean him," she whispered.

For a moment, Susan was confused, then she realized. Of course the girl's world had come to an end. What was to happen to her, to all of them? They were all being shipped back to Germany. "Sorry. I didn't think." She got up from her stool and cleared away the tray with the wrappers and the basin.

As she stood with her back to the girl, emptying the tray into the trash can in the corner, it suddenly got to her: the outrage committed on these people, the horror that awaited them. Until now, she had been too busy looking after the casualties to give the overall picture much thought; now she was hit by the full impact of the monstrousness, and felt overcome by a feeling of powerlessness, of guilt. In a minute or so, she would leave this ship, go back to her own clean, comfortable cabin on *Tubantia*, shower and change, and go out on the town to have dinner with Myrtle and Hendrik and Frans Willemse. There would be some talk about the sensations of the day, Myrtle would have gory stories, Hendrik would be leery of her, she would act cold and disinterested—they would all carry on with their own lives, and the monstrousness they had witnessed would recede into the background, a story to be told at other dinner tables, to other men. But what about these poor wretches, who must have pinned all their hopes on being admitted into Uruguay? What about the girl behind her, who had in effect received her death sentence? What good would a hairline scar be to her? It was like combing a pony's mane before selling it to a butcher. My God . . . what could she *do*, other than bind up their wounds and act tough and then wash her hands of them and send them on their way? Yet, it almost made her feel like an accomplice of the sadists who tormented them.

But what could anyone do, other than protest and join anti-Nazi organizations? What power had she to make any difference to their fate, however small? All she could do was turn around now, say a few meaningless words, go down the gangway to the gate, show her pass to the sentry, head out into the street . . .

Suddenly, the idea struck her. The sentry. The pass. Salute, smile and out into the street.

She turned around and said, "Take off your dress."

The girl looked at her, startled.

Susan took off her uniform jacket. "Do as I tell you. Get out of your dress."

The girl could have no idea what the purpose was, but she must have been conditioned by years of obeying without question. She got up, unbuttoned her dress, stepped out of it and put it on the chair.

"Here you go," Susan said, holding out her uniform jacket. "Put this on."

"Why?"

Susan took off her uniform hat and put it on the girl's head. "Keep it tilted forward, like this, so they won't see the bandage. Okay! Looks good too."

"But *why?*" the girl asked nervously. "What do you want of me?"

"I want you to put on my uniform," Susan said, "go down the gangway, walk through the gate with a snappy salute for the sentry, like this." She demonstrated it. "Show him your pass, smile, salute again if he does and keep walking."

"But—"

"Once you're out of the gate, turn right. Walk down the

boulevard one block to the next gate. There, repeat the performance: smile, salute the sentry, show your pass, salute again and
walk on. *Tubantia* is first in line, you can't miss her: three yellow
stacks, blue sleeves, big white ship. Take the aft gangway, go to
the First Class infirmary on A deck, starboard. There wait for
me."

"But—"

"I know a guy here who's with Immigration. I don't know
him all that well, but he's ripe to be picked, so leave him to me.
It's going to be a labor of love, but I'll see to it that you get a
permit to stay in this country. So bring your passport. By the
way, here's the pass I'm talking about. Don't be nervous about it,
just show it. He won't read it if you salute and smile. They love
salutes. They love girls who smile at them. He may wink. But
don't you; give him a dead-fish look and march off. Swagger a bit.
All they ever really look at is your behind. You'll see: if you keep
your cool, it'll be as easy as falling off a log."

"But—but you—"

"Don't worry about me. My colleague will get me another
uniform. In the meantime, I'll just take a nap on this gyn table
here. I could do with a snooze after all this drama. Enough is
enough. Here. Take it."

10

Tovah looked at the piece of paper, confused by the momentous
choice so unexpectedly forced upon her. She visualized, with
hallucinatory clarity, the sentry, the salute, the smile, the walk
through the shadow of the gate into the sunlight, into freedom.
The moment was one of incredible promise. But what about
David? She could not leave him behind—or could she? Old Goldstein would look after him—everyone would . . .

"Come on, honey!" The nurse sounded impatient. "We
haven't got hours, you know."

Life, freedom—all she had dreamed about was handed to her,

waiting for her to take it. But was it the right choice? She wished she could talk it over with someone, someone she would trust with her life, someone her own age—Yakov. Yakov would have known at once what to do. But he was in Palestine, on the other side of the globe. What would he have said to her now, at this moment? She tried to evoke his presence, his face, his fierce blue eyes, his fervent passion: Israel . . .

Suddenly, as if he had come bodily to her aid, she heard his voice in her memory: *The curse of God is our selfishness. Every Jew is only out for himself. "I, I, I." We won't return home, the Diaspora will not end until we accept that we are a people, and act upon it.* She had no idea what it implied, but the choice was made. It was scary, it was the choice between freedom and total darkness, a life full of fear and uncertainty. Yet, somehow, the choice had been made. "No, thank you," she said. "It's very kind of you, but I can't."

The nurse frowned. "What do you mean, you can't? I don't make a habit of acting the Good Samaritan, you know; so you'd better grab it. This is your only chance, sweetheart."

The decision was total now. The darkness, the fog began to lift. She took off the hat and handed it to the nurse. "Thank you very much, but I can't."

"Hell!" the nurse cried, angry now. "Don't you realize what's ahead for you, child? No country in the whole world is going to admit you!"

"Thank you," Tovah said, with a feeling of strength. "You're very kind."

The nurse's dark eyes seemed to search hers for the answer. "Don't tell me you do this because of *him?*"

"I do it because of my people." For the first time in her life, she used those words. It gave her a shiver of excitement, joy, she did not know what, something she had never felt before, something totally unknown to her; yet it felt like something she had missed all her life, not knowing where to search for it. Now, suddenly, there it was.

"Your people? You're no people! You're German citizens who've been declared fair game by a madman called Hitler. A people needs a country, honey, and all the country you have right now is your own sweet ass. Save it while the going's good."

She had found a word now for that feeling, that new feeling of something lost and found. It was 'pride.' She said, "You're very kind, but I don't want to."

"Then what *do* you want, child? Don't you want to live?"

It was too new, she didn't know how to explain it to this woman. Then the name came back to her—the name Yakov had used when someone asked him what he would do, with all the world against him and the small band of settlers. 'Masada.' *No one can understand Israel who doesn't understand Masada.* She said, "I'm sorry. I don't believe you'd understand. You're very kind, but—I'm sorry."

The nurse's face hardened. "Don't feel sorry for *me*. It's your life, not mine." She took back her uniform jacket and stood for a moment looking into Tovah's eyes, not understanding, hurt. "I never believed those stories about you people acting like sheep driven to slaughter. You're mad, do you know that? Right this minute, you're committing suicide."

Before Tovah could answer, the door opened and David appeared in the doorway. "Tov . . . ?" he asked plaintively.

"Yes, David. I'm coming."

He looked at the bandage on her forehead. "Gosh," he said. "Did you cry?"

"Yes," she said. "I cried."

The nurse put on her hat and tapped it into place. Then she put on her jacket, buttoned it and said, "Okay, then, ta-ta. You can't say I didn't try." Briskly, she stepped across the threshold and was gone.

"What's the matter with her?" David asked suspiciously.

"Nothing. She was very kind."

"She's weird!" He came in and grabbed her arm. "Tov, listen! Do you know what they're saying? The captain's going to take us to some other place where—"

Suddenly she was overcome by fear, sheer terror at what she had done. She pressed him against her tightly, a gesture of protection, but at the same time looking for shelter from the fateful decision she had made.

"What's the matter with you?" he asked, bewildered.

Holding him, she whispered, "Hush . . . " Then she bent over and kissed his hair. It smelled of rope.

"Don't worry, Tov," he said, grown up and tough. "We'll be all right. You'll see."

"Yes," she said, "we will."

CHAPTER SEVEN

I

Bouke Bruinsma tried and tried—but despite the supple young body squirming under him, her chortlings of mounting pleasure, he felt his ardor slacken. It infuriated him. Whatever vainglorious fellow-members of his class might say, old age was a descent into impotence, a loss of virility, a mounting flood of tears rising in the back of a man's awareness like a merciless *tsunami* that would eventually, soon, too soon, wipe all before it: youth, passion, virility, the joy of the strong, fierce wind in one's hair, the salty taste of the spindrift on one's face, all that went with the joy of manhood, the boy in the boat to Skye.

But maybe it wasn't old age, not yet. It certainly wasn't the girl; she was spirited and knowledgeable, an excellent, gung-ho partner in this invigorating, no-holds-barred game of erotic tennis. No, it was the knowledge that young Kuiper and his freighter were leaving. Right now, while he lay here tangled in the sheets, grunting, snorting, old bull mounting a young heifer, there went the Knight in Shining Armor, the fool of God, the dream of all sailors: a ship of his own, a noble cause, risking it all, tattered old flag flying, bow pushing a creaming wave.

Abruptly, he dislodged himself from the undulating young body, mumbled, "Sorry, I just remembered; I have to check on something . . . " Pulling a sheet off the bed and wrapping it around him, he strode half-naked and hairy through his sitting room to the starboard window which overlooked the river.

There was no freighter to be seen. No tattered old flag. No creaming bow-wave. Either Sir Galahad had left, or he was held up by the drones of bureaucracy.

He felt her warm breath on his shoulder, an arm around his waist. He caught a whiff of her scent, animal, viscous, crudely exciting. "What's up, ducks?" she asked, a breast brushing his arm.

"I just wanted to see if *Star of Peace* was leaving."

"Oh, that one," she said, bored. She obviously did not consider young Sir Galahad and his crusade a worthy competition for her charms. "If you ask me, he's a bloody fool."

For some reason, it made him angry. "I'd hardly call him that."

"Well, what the hell does he think he'll achieve? All he'll do is make those people sick with hope, then turn around and take them to the butchers."

"That's unnecessarily harsh, I'd say."

"*You* say so—I've seen them. Lying on those bunks in those holds, bruised and bleeding. No, you just don't play around with people in that condition. You lay it on the line, and take them home. I don't believe in romantic compassion. As a matter of fact, I don't believe in selfless love." Boldly, she fondled him.

"I didn't think you would," he said. Seagulls swooped past the window, mewing. It brought back an image from the distant past: the sunlit bridge of the old *Maria,* the young mate he had been, old Captain Bosman saying, "It's one of those days when the seagulls do most of the work." He saw old Bosman's ghostly face, drooping mustache, melancholy eyes, bulbous nose, mirrored in the oil-slick water of the River Plate, glinting in the setting sun. "I don't think any man could put one over you."

"Oh, it has happened," she said, caressing him. "There was a man in North Africa once who asked me out to dinner. An ordinary sort of chap—all right, but no spark. We had dinner, wine, conversation, big tip. Then he asked if I'd care to have a look at the beach. There was no romance, just a way to end the evening. 'There's a moon out, let's take a walk on the beach.' So we went. It was sort of a hard beach to walk on—big pebbles, you know. We were only, well, I don't know, maybe fifty yards away from that restaurant, still in the light of its windows, when he just grabbed hold of me, threw me on my back and raped me. Can you believe that? I suppose he thought of it as the price for his dinner."

It was an unsavory story. He resented it; it seemed heinous and obscene while looking at the river, waiting for the old freighter with its cargo of lost souls and its young Knight in Shining Armor to pass in front of his eyes. What he resented most was that it excited him, obscenely, viciously. The vision of her hard, young body thrown on its back on those hard, round pebbles—he turned around and put his arms around her and ground his mouth on her young, soft lips and felt her supple, tempting willingness and said, "Come." He lifted her and carried her, playfully struggling, back to the bedroom, where he threw her on her back and mounted her the way that guy must have done that night, with the lights of the restaurant upon them, in his business suit, tearing her clothes, raping her, thrusting inside her cruelly, selfishly, oblivious of her cries, her angry struggling. And, my God!, that did it. Imagining himself in the tawdry role of that business-suited brute, visualizing her lying not on his soft, springy bed but on those hard, round pebbles, he reached his climax. Panting, heart pounding, he collapsed on top of her. For a moment, giddiness overcame him, a sickening sense of faintness, of spleen, that wave of tears, that dark, swelling *tsunami* bearing down on him. Then he felt her hand stroking his back. It was not a caress; it was not the hand of a lover, it was the hand of a nurse. "God damn you," he muttered in the pillow.

The hand stopped. "That wasn't a very nice thing to say, was it, now?"

"I didn't mean you," he said, stopping himself from adding the word 'child.'

"Then who did you mean, ducks?"

"Myself. And don't call me ducks."

"Oh, hoity-toity," she mocked. "Now we've had our little way, we're the commodore again, are we?"

He felt like beating the hell out of her. Maybe that's what she wanted. Maybe she was one of those who wanted to be beaten; maybe that would turn her on but good. Oh, my God . . . what was happening to him? Never before had he felt this sudden surge of violence within him; never before had he been turned on by brutality, hurting a woman. "Sorry," he said. "I—"

"Hush!" She slapped his buttock.

"What the hell—"

"Hush! There she goes!"

"Who, for Christ's sake?" He rose on his elbows.

"You want to see her leave, don't you? Well, if you ask me, that's *Star of Peace.* I heard that old steam horn in Le Havre."

He turned his head to one side and listened. Indeed, there sounded, far away, the deep-throated, throbbing '*brooon!*' of an old-fashioned foghorn.

"Go and have a look." She pushed him off her.

He stepped out of bed and, without a sheet this time, crossed the soft carpet of his sitting room to the window overlooking the river. And, indeed, there she came; but not the way he had visualized. She was surrounded by warships: two M.T.B.'s, a destroyer, a mine-sweeper; she looked like a derelict being taken to jail.

"Cor—" she said, behind him. "Looks as if the whole bloody Uruguayan Navy is taking him out to sea!"

Suddenly, he was overwhelmed by shame. There he stood, stark naked, wet with sweat, reeking of the juices of love, a lecherous blonde clinging to him with the suction of a mollusk, and there went that boy, that dreamer, escorted out by the gold-braided harlequins of their music-hall navy. He should be on the bridge; *Tubantia* should be hauling down her flag, saluting. "Excuse me." He pushed her aside, went to the telephone and dialed the bridge.

The telephone rang five times before finally the receiver was taken off the hook up there and a pompous young voice answered, "Bridge. Petersen."

"Where the hell were you, Petersen?"

"Sorry, sir, I was watching—"

"Stop watching, you idiot, attend to your duties! Have you hauled down the flag?"

"No, sir."

"Do so at once! Haul it down, wait for the salute to be returned, then haul it back up. On the double!"

"Yes, sir!" The telephone was thrown back onto the hook.

"That was a sweet idea, ducks."

He turned around. There she stood, on one of his white armchairs: British Venus on the half-shell. She was daring him; he felt like slapping her smirking face.

"What are you doing on that chair?"

"I want to see."

"See what?"

"See you forget him."

It was outrageous in its coarse, obscene negation of all that was noble, selfless, manly. "Come off that chair!" he cried, taut with fury.

She stuck out her tongue. And then it happened.

The old steam horn roared right outside: three throbbing bellows that set the ashtray on the glass coffee table trembling. Its mournful wail was drowned out by a scream of pleasure as he hit her, hit her, hit the hell out of her and lost himself, sobbing with tearful ecstasy, in the crashing crescent of the *tsunami*.

2

"Hey! What are *you* mooning about?"

Susan Foster looked around from her deck chair with a feeling of irritation and saw Myrtle standing behind her, creamy and blonde in a white terrycloth bathrobe.

"Mind if I join you, or are you composing poetry?"

"Meow," Susan said wearily.

Myrtle pulled up another deck chair and lay down beside her.

"Did you see old *Star* leave, by the way?"

"Yes, I did."

"Can you still see her?"

"No."

The shimmering expanse of the River Plate, red and orange in the setting sun, fused with the horizon behind the plate-glass windows of the heated promenade deck.

"Were you watching too?" Susan asked.

Myrtle giggled. "Hardly."

"Why not?"

"Well, to be absolutely candid; I was being beaten up."

Just like Myrtle—taunting, especially in that genteel British voice. "You don't say. Who did it this time?"

"Who do you think?"

"I see." So Myrtle had finally got herself the prize. It had taken her long enough. Maybe it was because of Hendrik, but Susan was sick of men, love, clumsy fumblings, the pointless, meaningless waste of some priceless substance, something she had sensed, inarticulately, when the Jewish girl refused freedom with that proud look in her eyes.

"Odd, isn't it, that old men are turned on by violence?" Myrtle mused, beside her. "He really hurt me, you know."

"You don't sound as if you were hurting."

"God, no. It was delicious. But it's odd, all the same. Do you know what set him off?"

"I can't wait."

"I told him, just off the top of my head without any particular reason, the story of that guy in North Africa, remember? The one who raped me on the beach in exchange for dinner? Well, what do you know: suddenly, all the guns came rolling out. Boy! Did he ever deliver a broadside, the old Horatio Nelson! You know; once you get them going, old men can be—"

"Oh, for God's sake!" Susan's angry cry was torn out of her before she knew it.

"Oh, excuse *me*, I'm sure," Myrtle said, exaggeratedly miffed.

"Would you do me a favor? Just shut up. Grant the guy at least the courtesy of discretion."

"Well now, isn't that a nice sentiment?" Myrtle purred. "What's this in honor of, may I ask?"

Suddenly, Susan could stand no more. She rose, left the crew's section of the promenade and climbed the stairs to the radio deck. There, leaning over the aft rail, she gazed at the dark horizon, across the turquoise rectangle of the swimming pool with its scattered dashes of orange deck chairs. What had she seen in the child that suddenly made her feel jealous? Innocence? Youth? Her foolish dream? If ever anyone had sacrificed freedom for a delusion, it was the girl. 'My people'! But how marvelous, how utterly terrific to *be* that mad, to really believe in something that was bigger than yourself, to stand there, all of seventeen years old, hand back that pass to freedom and say, "You're very kind, but no, thank you." Compared to cold, calculating manipulators like Myrtle, like herself . . .

She took out a cigarette, turned her back on the sea breeze to light it, glanced up and saw, on the port wing of the bridge, a lonely figure gazing out to sea, just as she had been doing. It was the commodore.

For some reason, it moved her to see him there like that. She had never cared for the man, never thought about him as human, but something about the solitary figure against the vast, flaming sky gave her a sense of kinship with him. He must be gazing at the horizon, trying to discern what she had been looking for: the small black dot of a ship heading out to sea.

'What a waste,' she found herself thinking. But maybe the waste was she: idle on the radio deck, smoking a cigarette, safe and comfortable and uninvolved, while out there, on the darkening ocean, a shipful of frightened people sailed into nowhere. Maybe that's where she belonged: with them, nursing the sick, helping mothers give birth, caring for their babies, watching over the lonely and the frightened at dead of night in those horrible holds stacked full of humanity. And here she was, catering to the whims of rich old women decked in diamonds who wanted back-rubs at three in the morning.

She turned back to the rail and stared at the empty ocean. Was that the problem? Was she fed up with herself because she was dissatisfied with the life she was leading? No, it wasn't that. And it had nothing to do with miserable Hendrik, either.

It had to do with the ship now sailing into the night, and with a red-haired girl, no more than a child, who had refused freedom for the sake of a dream.

3

After *Star of Peace* had been escorted outside the three-mile limit, the pilot left and the Navy vessels headed back for home. Only when the passengers saw the warships leave did they show their excitement; everywhere, small groups started talking, gesticulating, arguing. The mood at the officers' table after the meal, as they hung back awhile for an extra cup of coffee, was one of gloom. Old Davelaar was more grouchy than usual; Palstra the second engineer, Wybrands and Vinkemans seemed pensive; Hendrik himself had not recovered yet from the shock of the riot and its bloody aftermath. He had barely had a chance to say goodbye to Susan and Myrtle. Now he awoke to reality: still on board this ship, now engaged upon the hare-brained crusade of a mad captain. My God! "What in the world is the matter with him?" he asked no one in particular. "Can't he see this is crazy? Where the hell is he going to find the money for this?"

It woke up Davelaar from his morose musings. "*Our* money," the old man growled. "*We* are the ones who'll foot the bill. You can kiss our wages goodbye for the duration. He's not going to pay us a cent. Yes, he's crazy. His father was crazy too. They're all crazy."

"Well, I don't know about that," Wybrands said, slurping his coffee. "At least, he's doing something to get back at those goddam Nazis. All we ever do is sit around and talk."

"We don't just talk. We pay," Davelaar persisted.

"So we pay. He stands to lose his shirt over this, all we lose is a few weeks' wages. I don't know what my missus is going to say, but my guess is she'll go along with it, once I tell her about those bastards back in Hamburg. It makes me feel a hell of a lot better, let me tell you."

Davelaar grunted something; to change the subject, Hendrik ventured, "Since when has the captain been a militant Christian? All his life?"

"Three years," Davelaar said. "Before that, he was something different."

Silence fell around the table; Hendrik realized they all must want to know more about the man in whose hands their fate now rested. Davelaar was the only one present who had known the captain since he was a boy. The other men around the table had never known Kuiper other than as a solemn Bible-thumper. But who was he? What motivated him to risk everything he had for the sake of a boatload of strangers? "Tell us about it, Chief."

Davelaar glared at him, then looked around the table at the attentive faces of the men. He took out of his pocket a worn little tobacco pouch and started to fill his pipe.

"Up to three years ago, he was a nail in his dad's coffin. Always picking fights with people bigger than him. Always chasing women. And drink? You never saw anything like it. He'd drink himself senseless night after night when ashore. He'd drink until he'd stand like a statue and if you pushed him he'd topple over and never know it. The times I've carried that boy on board! Me and Meyer, we always were the ones the Old Man would send after him. And then one day God struck him, just like that, and he turned into what he is now. All within the space of one hour."

Wybrands asked, "What happened?"

Davelaar lit his pipe. "It was the day his father had a stroke." He waved out the match. "We were in port. We carried the Old Man to the boy's house; the boy's wife, Anna, looked after him, and we went to look for Joris at the usual places: the saloons, the brothels, the police station. There, somebody said: 'Go have a look in the mission at the far end of Market Street.' So we went to look and there he was, on his knees, sobbing his heart out with a bunch of sky pilots praying and singing around him. He had found Jesus, they said. Or Jesus had found him, whatever. Well, I wish Jesus had kept him."

"But why then?" Wybrands asked. "How come he got converted at that particular moment?"

"Because he was scared shitless," Davelaar replied. "He didn't have the guts to step into the Old Man's boots and take over command of this ship without a dose of Dutch courage. Other men would've gone and drunk themselves senseless, but he did that every day. Something, someone put the bee in his bonnet to go and seek help by falling on his knees and yammering 'God help me' or whatever they holler. Maybe he passed a sky pilot in the street who smiled at him. I've seen that happen: there you go, miserable as sin, walking down the street, and there comes a sky pilot who smiles at you, and that's it. That's how little it takes. Anyhow, once he was through sobbing and yammering, he rose to his feet, clean as a whistle, stars in his eyes, and he stayed that way. No more bottles, no more whores, no more brawls with bouncers. From drunk's alley to bridge in one leap, with wings. All he ever does these days is read the Bible, pray, and eavesdrop with ears like ventilators for anybody using the Lord's name in vain. Now he's found something in the Bible that says: keep those Jews out of Germany, and so that's what he does. To please God, Jesus Christ, his father—who knows? By now, I think they're pretty well mixed up in his crazy mind."

"His father was a Christian too?" Palstra asked.

"Sure he was," Davelaar answered, puffing his pipe. "But a true one. He really spoke with God. I heard him do it myself. It wasn't like anything you hear in church, or like the subservient stuff I occasionally hear the boy mumble on his knees. The Old Man never went down on his knees. With all of us present, he'd tell God exactly what he thought of Him. I'm not a religious man myself, not one bit, but to hear the Old Man have it out with the Almighty gave you the shivers sometimes. He wouldn't take no for an answer. From God, I mean. He'd say, 'Now *listen!* Are you the Lord of Hosts or aren't you? Okay then: get that customs officer off my back!' And would you believe it: it worked. I think because God really loved the Old Man, the way we all did. He was a cantankerous old cuss, and as mean as a stoat, but, Jesus! You could be as mad as hell with him, yet we all would go through fire for him . . . Well, never mind." He rose. "Let's get cracking. Palstra, get yourself below. It's your watch coming up."

"I suppose I'd better mosey along too," Wybrands said. "*Mahlzeit,* gentlemen."

Hendrik and Vinkemans muttered "*Mahlzeit,*" and watched Henky as he cleared the dishes off the table. When the boy was gone, Vinkemans said, "If you ask me, he does it to please his father."

"Who's that?"

Vinkemans gazed at him like a mournful old elk. "Maybe it's your living with him that made you fail to notice."

"What?"

"The portrait over his desk. It's new. I saw it for the first time today when I came in to have the orders list signed. An old man with a beard. If you ask me, it's Pop."

"So what?"

"A man putting up his father's picture at a moment like this proves he's insecure. It's like putting up joss sticks in front of the statue of a tribal god. Ancestor worship, that's what it is. Lucky Mrs. Hallmann."

Hendrik realized, with a shock of shame, that he had forgotten all about Mrs. Hallmann. "My God, that's true! They kept her! Didn't you follow it up?"

"No. I apologize," Vinkemans said smugly. "I thought: 'As long as I don't mention her, she may be forgotten in the scuffle.' That makes at least one soul saved out of two hundred and fifty. Not much, but better than none. For the next two or three weeks, we'll have two hundred forty-nine. Then, thanks to Mrs. Spiegel, we'll have two fifty again. Or, who knows, two fifty-one. She may have twins."

"Have you had a look at her today?"

"About an hour ago. My guess is: within the next two weeks. I'd even pare it down to ten days."

"We'd better clear the consulting room for her."

"I don't think that's necessary. Why not screen off bed number one in the infirmary, the one by the porthole?"

"But it's going to be an unholy racket. What about the other patients?"

"They're all old women," Vinkemans said. "It'll give them a bit of excitement. Women love to be in on births. Anyhow, it's a long way off."

There was a silence, then Hendrik said, "Well, I suppose I'd better turn in. I want to sort out my stuff before His Nibs comes off watch."

"Right you are. Good night, Doctor."

" 'Night, Vinkemans. Let me know if there's anything up. You know where to find me: back on the damn settee."

Vinkemans laughed mournfully. "I sympathize," he said.

Hendrik made his way through the arguing groups of passengers and the playing children to the lower bridge. The first thing he did after entering the cabin was to go and have a look. Indeed, there it was: the sepia-colored photograph of an old man with a beard, leering from under a peaked cap. Not a prepossessing ancestor to worship. Could Vinkemans' reading of the captain be right? Was the sudden appearance of this picture a sign of Kuiper's insecurity? As he turned away, his eye was caught by a note on the desk, in Kuiper's handwriting. *Tell Davelaar to knock it off.* Knock off what? Complaining? Expectorating? Bullying the women about his toilets? Whatever it was, it was not the memo of an insecure man.

When finally he lay on the settee, uncomfortable as hell, rueing the loss of a private cabin on board *Tubantia* which had seemed tantalizingly within reach, he heard the captain come in and pretended to be asleep.

Within minutes, he was.

4

In her bunk, staring into the darkness, Tovah Nachtgeist wondered what on earth had possessed her to refuse the nurse's incredible offer. To think of Yakov of all people, and his feverish talk about Masada, while the door to freedom was being opened to her! She must have been mad.

The euphoria of the emotional decision had worn off; now she was left with nagging regret. 'My people'! Mrs. Goldstein, Mrs. Schlachter, Mrs. Feldschuh, the Rabbi? Not much of a people. Not even if you counted Hannelore Weisbrot, Anna Feldschuh, Lieschen Schlachter and the rest of the kids. Only David was 'her people.' Together, they inhabited a country of shared memories, a never-never land, population two. Was he the true reason she had refused to pass through the door to freedom that had briefly opened in front of her? Had she sacrificed a new life in a new land because she would have had to leave him behind? Well, be that as it may: what was her future now?

Mrs. Hoflein and Mrs. Adler, whom she had overheard as they were making the beds in the infirmary, did not believe the captain could succeed in putting them ashore in America. Nobody believed in it, except the kids and Mr. Vinkemans, but he was so nice and patient that he was prepared to believe anything if it would make someone happy. She did not believe in it herself tonight, staring into the darkness, wracked by regret and a growing sense of approaching disaster. But there was Yakov's voice, even in his absence, even after all these months—almost a year now: *'Jews are cursed by the death wish of looking after themselves first. Don't you see that only as a people can we hope to survive? Without Israel, we are doomed to extinction.'*

The passion, the conviction, the power of the voice! *No one can understand Israel who doesn't understand Masada.*

Masada. What had the suicide of nine hundred fanatics, two thousand years ago, to do with her? Israel. Who knows: it might come about one day. But what had that to do with *her,* here, now, this minute, this night? By the time it came about, she and all the people asleep around her would be long dead.

Hendrik. The mere thought of him made her furious. Not at him, but at herself, her propensity to dream, dream reality away until in the end there was nothing except bitterness, disgust, hatred for herself. She was a stupid, rudderless schmo, helpless prey to anyone who pretended, however briefly, that he cared about her, like Hendrik. Like Yakov.

She was suddenly stricken with loneliness. The thought occurred to her to pray. She had prayed many times before, but never really believed there was a God who was aware of her. He was aware of every falling sparrow, counted the hairs on everybody's head, except hers, it seemed. It would be wonderful if she could indeed talk to Him, like Job. Like Yakov.

"God . . . ?"

Of course nothing happened. The ship slowly heeled over, with a creaking of the scaffolding of the bunks, a secretive wave of sound, swelling and receding.

She listened to the creaking start in the distance, come slowly closer; then her own bunk creaked, and the creaking drew away into the distance. A short silence, and it came back again from the other side. It was like lying in a cradle, slowly rocking from side to side.

Before she fell asleep, her last thought was a wordless prayer to Yakov's God. It ended in a dream that someone—vast, allpowerful, all-knowing, all-loving—was slowly rocking her to sleep.

5

In his captain's bed in the dark, Joris Kuiper went through the midnight of the soul.

The euphoria of the decision had worn off; the reality of his situation began to take hold. Both the woman from the Embassy and the commodore of *Tubantia* had called him a fool. At the time, he had shrugged it off, almost reveled in it; for wasn't it a great and glorious thing to be called a fool of God? But now, open-eyed in the darkness, listening to the familiar sounds of sea and ship, the concept lost its luster. Not every fool could be called a fool of God. Only very rarely a saintly soul would be honored with that name, after a true sacrifice, usually of his very life. Did he fall in that category? Not at all.

To smuggle two hundred and fifty people ashore in the full light of public opinion was indeed a foolish notion. You could not perform a secret act of that magnitude in the glare of publicity. The only realistic solution would be to put these people ashore on a stretch of coastline with seagulls as the only observers; then, before anyone had had a chance to round them up, he should steam full speed to the nearest port, call the newspapers, the wire services and tell them what he had done so they could send reporters and photographers and put the landing in the glare of publicity. So it had to be a two-pronged operation: first, put them ashore in total secrecy, then head for the nearest port at full speed and, once there, bang the drum.

But how long would this take? Three weeks or so, during which he would use all his stores to feed passengers and crew, burn hundreds of tons of coal, pay the men's wages—it would take all the profit he had made on this voyage, and more. As he totaled it up in his mind, he came to the conclusion that after he had completed the operation he would not have the money left to pay the crew or buy any more fuel and provisions. His stores were enough for a little over three weeks. He would have to ration the food; but he could not cut the coal consumption. Sailing at half-speed would make his coal last longer, but he did not have sufficient provisions to cover the time lost. So he would have to burn up coal at maximum speed, which would just about take him to Boston approaches. Should he make an intermediary stop in some backwater like Antigua or St. Maarten? Bunker there without raising any hares? But where would he get the money? Could Anna arrange another loan? Or a return cargo for which he could ask an advance? He had not written to her yet; as far as she knew, he was disembarking his passengers in Montevideo and shopping around for a return cargo. He should have written her. He should have thought all this through much earlier; now it was too late. And all because he had sensed a presence behind him. Maybe the word 'fool' wasn't strong enough.

But there was the Bible. There was what his father had written in it: *Once God makes His will known to you, He will provide you with the means to obey it.* But had this been God's will? Was there a justification in Scripture for this reckless act of bravado? There was such a thing as the devil, starting with the serpent in

Paradise. What guarantee had he that the presence he had sensed behind him was indeed God, or one of His angels? How did he know it had not been a delusion cast by the devil? Maybe he should pray and open his soul to the Lord and ask for a clear commandment.

He folded his hands and prayed, "Lord, I love thee, make me Thy servant, make me Thy instrument. Whatever Thou desirest of me I will do. Even should it seem impossible, I truly believe that if Thou makest Thy will known to me, Thou wilt provide me with the means to obey it. So, make Thy will known to me, oh Lord. Dear Lord, beloved Lord, command me, Thy servant."

He lay waiting in silence, his mind a blank, but no voice came. The only sound was the creaking of the ship, laboring with the long, slow swell of the South Atlantic. Then there emerged in the darkness of his unseeing eyes an image: an old man on the gangway, carrying his cross, his forehead covered with blood, his eyes looking up at him in mute supplication. And the answer formed itself in his thoughts not as a voice, not as a vision, but as knowledge. *Verily I say unto you, inasmuch as ye have done it unto one of the least of these my brethren, ye have done it unto me.*

And he knew: here is my command. Even if my ship carried only one of the least of these His brethren, I shall take him to freedom, if it costs me all I have. Without Him, my life was dark, putrid, drenched in blood, violence, sin. Now I am asked: will you repay Me for the grace I bestowed on you?

There was a knock on the door.

He called, "Yes?"

Wybrands stuck his head in and whispered, so as not to wake the doctor, "Captain: quarter-hour."

"Thank you, Wybrands," he said. "I'll be there."

Part Two

WANDERINGS

CHAPTER ONE

The striking thing about Kuiper, Hendrik discovered to his surprise, was the man's intelligence. There he was, cast out into limbo with two hundred and forty-nine almost hysterical passengers, and after no more than a few hours of musing, doing sums on bits of paper, scanning charts and reading coastal pilots, he came up with a plan that would have been remarkable had it been the outcome of a week's preparation.

The plan was presented to the officers, the passengers' representatives and Hendrik himself on the morning after their departure from Montevideo. Kuiper called them all together in his cabin, which made for a tight squeeze and an overpowering body odor. Goldstein and the Rabbi were in a high old state after receiving the call for an important meeting in the captain's quarters; they were convinced that Kuiper had had second thoughts overnight and decided he would take the ship back to Hamburg after all. Chief Davelaar seemed to have come to the same conclusion, for he was virtually beaming as he came in, accompanied by his sidekick, the bovine Palstra.

Kuiper put them straight in short order. He unrolled a chart on the table and announced that he had decided to put the passengers into the boats about three weeks from today, off Folly Island near Charleston, South Carolina. "Here," he said, and he pointed at a spot on the chart. It looked innocuous: a wide river mouth, colored a pleasant blue, full of reassuring numbers that seemed to indicate a thorough knowledge of the location on the part of the captain.

"All passengers will take to the boats and rafts at first light on August twentieth, a Sunday, so the beaches of the island should be quiet. Depending on tide and wind, I will anchor either off the island in the open, or inside Stono Inlet, here. The operation will have to be very fast; the moment the last raft is in the water, I'll back off and head for Charleston full speed. As you can see on this chart, it's virtually around the corner. There, I'll alert the press, the wire services, all there is in the way of publicity within hours of the landing. But once you're ashore, Rabbi and Mrs. Goldstein, you'll have to guide your people as fast as you can down this road to this little community here, called Folly Beach. There's likely to be a large number of tourists at this time of year. Shout and yell as you enter the village, bang on doors and shutters, get them out of their beds so your presence is established and witnessed. The danger is that the government will round you up before anyone is any the wiser; the more of a commotion you create, the safer you'll be."

He rolled up the chart.

"As far as the landing is concerned, speed is what counts. We'll have to go through a series of boat drills on our way to the States, until every passenger knows exactly where to line up in the holds, how to climb the ladders quickly, where to line up on deck and which boat to board. The oldest passengers, the infirm, the sick, the pregnant will take to the boats, all others to the rafts. Those allotted to the rafts will have to practice going up and down the scramble nets and how to handle ropes, as the rafts are going to be tied together and towed to the shore by the boats. We'll start this afternoon with the first drill: line up in the holds, climb the ladders, line up on deck, get on board the boats; and as for the scramble nets, I'll suspend one of them from the lower bridge athwartships, and we'll cover the deck with mattresses. Groups of twenty people at a time will be practicing climbing up and down those nets."

"Up?" Wybrands asked. "Why up? Once they're gone, they're gone, aren't they?"

"We may be intercepted," Kuiper said casually, "in which case the Coast Guard, or whoever it is, will certainly order all passengers back on board. We might as well be prepared." He looked around the circle of worried faces. "So, as I said: daily exercises. Not just boat drill and scramble nets, but Wybrands and the bo'sun will teach knots and boat-handling to selected passengers so the towlines between the rafts and the boats will be belayed in the proper manner. Those passengers, once they have acquired a thorough knowledge of the ropes, will teach others. I want every single passenger on board this ship to know exactly what to do in case he or she is faced with the responsibility for a raft. I want those rafts manned with sailors, not helpless people depending on others for their salvation. Is that understood?"

"You're crazy," Davelaar stated calmly.

Kuiper ignored him. His determination was impressive, and it appeared to be founded on knowledge and seamanship. Hendrik didn't know how far this performance was put on just for psychological reasons, but it all sounded reasonable and intelligent.

"Mrs. Goldstein, and you, Rabbi," Kuiper continued, "I want you to take this chart along and show it to the passengers. I want everybody to know exactly what is happening, exactly what we are planning and exactly where we stand every hour of the day. The moment there is ignorance there is fear, and the moment there is fear there is the danger of panic. *That* is the danger, Mrs. Goldstein, Rabbi; remember that. Panic is the enemy, not the United States Coast Guard." Both the Rabbi and Mrs. Goldstein nodded obediently. "It's going to take us, God willing, twenty-one days to reach Folly Island. That may seem like a lot of time to you, but we'll need every hour of those twenty-one days to be well prepared when we arrive for our landing. For don't forget, this whole business I just described has to be done in the dark; the convoy of boats and rafts will have to be heading for the shore at first light. So we'll start with daylight rehearsals and shift to night rehearsals as soon as possible."

Hendrik began to get an inkling of the reality of what Kuiper was planning. The mere concept of having two hundred and forty-nine women, children, elderly, sick, pregnant women and mentally disturbed people climb those ladders in the dark was hair-raising, not to mention the scramble nets, which so far he had only seen rolled up on deck: coarse nets made of rope with a core of steel for people to climb down to the water. To ask old men like the Rabbi and Mr. Himmelbaum to clamber down those nets with the surging waves of the sea below them was like asking them to perform a circus act on the high trapeze. It was ridiculous. Maybe Davelaar was right and the whole thing *was* crazy.

"To merely have dry runs on deck is not going to be sufficient," the captain continued, unrolling another chart. "We should have at least two or three full drills, up to and including the towing away of the rafts by the boats. Now, there are a few inlets and river estuaries on our route where we can go through such an exercise. There's one here, in central Brazil; there's one here, higher up; and there are the Windward Islands; we could go through the drill in the lee of one of them."

"Joris," Davelaar said calmly, "you're plumb crazy."

This time, the captain met the challenge. "Tell me why."

"You're going to kill people, Joris. You've got it all worked out in your mind, but you haven't been thinking about *real* people. I see those real people every day in the holds. I see women, I see children, I see old dotards that piss in the bilges at night. They don't know whether they're coming or going. You couldn't even ask those people to pick up an egg off the deck, they'd break it. You're going to kill them, Joris. They're going to break their goddam necks. You'll kill half of them before you're through. So, the hell with it. Take them back."

"Thank you," Kuiper said. "Now, as I was saying—"

"I'm not going to listen to any more of this crap," Davelaar said. He started to work his way through the tight little crowd toward the door. "You kill 'em if you must, I'm not going to be your accomplice." He opened the door and slammed himself out.

Usually, Hendrik discounted old Davelaar's grumblings and curses as being those of a cantankerous old bastard, but this time he had spoken calmly and with convincing realism. Kuiper had

sounded convincing too; but the moment you gave his proposi-
tion some sober thought, you realized Davelaar was right: there
were going to be accidents, however well you trained the passengers. Then he realized, with a start, that he was being addressed.

"Doctor? Is that possible?"

"Er—I'm sorry, Skipper. I was thinking of something else.
What was that you said?"

"I want you to make up a list of people who should be put
in the boats because they can't manage the scramble nets. I also
want you to discuss with your medic what to do about any
patients you may have. I want that list and a report on how you
propose to handle your patients by tomorrow night. Does that
give you enough time?"

"Er—yes, Skipper, yes—I suppose it does." It didn't bear
thinking about, not really. He couldn't wait to get out of here and
discuss it with Vinkemans.

"Well, that'll be all for today," the captain said, rolling up the
chart. "We'll meet again in a few days. Rabbi and Mrs. Goldstein,
I want you to stay so we can talk this through more thoroughly.
Thank you, gentlemen."

With a sense of relief, Hendrik made his way out of the cabin
with the other members of the staff. They gathered, a small
stunned group, in the starboard corner of the lower bridge, out
of earshot of the cabin: Meyer, Wybrands, Palstra the second
engineer, the bo'sun, the cook and himself. They were silent until
Meyer said, to no one in particular, "Jesus."

"Do you suppose he wants everyone to take a packed lunch?"
the cook asked. It gave a surrealist touch to the whole thing: Mrs.
Spiegel, nine months pregnant, going down a scramble net with
a packed lunch. But then, she probably would be one of the élite
who would take to the boats.

"Do you think this rail would support the weight of a scramble net and twenty people?" Wybrands queried, peering down
the twenty-foot drop to the deck.

"I'll tell you what we'll do," said Palstra, "we'll anchor the top
of that net further back: to the davits. I'll weld you a couple of

eyes to the side of the engine-room hatch over there and if need be—"

"Jesus," Meyer said, still in shock. "It's not just him in there. It's all of you. You're all crazy." He walked off, presumably to join the only other sane person on board, his crony Davelaar.

"He may be right, you know," Hendrik ventured.

But Wybrands, Palstra, the cook and even the bo'sun, normally a level-headed, unimaginative man, seemed to be caught in the web of the captain's fantasy. Hendrik listened to them as they continued discussing how to anchor the scramble net on the lower bridge so that it wouldn't be just the rail that had to support it. They sounded like a bunch of kids discussing how to build a tree house. Was he the one who was crazy? There was only one man on board whose answer to that question he would trust: Vinkemans.

He found him in the main infirmary, exercising his peculiar brand of bedside manner over Mr. Brandeis, a prostatic hypertrophy combined with acute prostatitis who needed daily catheterization. "I'd like a word with you, Vinkemans," Hendrik said. "Good morning, Mr. Brandeis, how are we this morning?"

"Poorly," the old man breathed, with a natural talent for the drama. "Very poorly, *Herr Doktor,* very poorly."

"I'll be right back and we'll talk some more," Vinkemans said, patting the old man's veined hand lying on the bedcover like a detached little animal, some wrinkled member of the turtle family.

In the passage, Hendrik said, "This is going to take some time, and I need to talk to you in private. Let's go to the forecastle. All right?"

"Whatever you say, Doctor," Vinkemans intoned, back in his role of the mournful elk. "You're the boss."

"Oh, cut it out," Hendrik said amicably; after three weeks, he and Vinkemans had really come to know each other. Now, more than ever, they would have to depend on one another psychologically as well as professionally. This was going to be one hell of a challenge.

The forecastle was windy and cool. There was a light drizzle, more like a heavy fog, which surrounded them with a luminous haze. Right overhead, the sky must be blue and cloudless; it was as if winter were slowly evaporating under their very eyes. Soon they would be back in the subtropics, then the tropics and the murderous heat of the equator.

"His Nibs has come up with a game plan," Hendrik started, "and it's a dilly. It sounds quite reasonable at first hearing, but when you give it a little thought . . . Well, you tell me what you think."

Vinkemans listened attentively to the Rabbi and Mr. Himmelbaum clawing their way up ladders at dead of night, Mrs. Schlachter being taught knots and splices and how to tow the rafts with lifeboats, and the pregnant Mrs. Spiegel going down the scramble net with her packed lunch. In the retelling, it sounded insane.

To Hendrik's surprise, the mournful old elk did not dismiss it out of hand. He even, after long, melancholy reflection, nodded his antlered head and said, "Quite a fella, the captain."

"You don't think it's crazy?"

The wet brown eyes gave him a somber look. "I think it's brilliant."

It came as a shock; Vinkemans was no fool. "Could you explain to me why?"

"Well . . . " Another period of mournful reflection. "You see, once he made up his mind that he was not going to take these people back to Germany, he had no other alternative than to put them into the boats at some point and beach them somewhere. Well, that's quite an operation. He might as well prepare them for it. Either that, or his noble decision was so much hot air—he would make a ritual gesture to assuage his own conscience, and then, a hundred miles north of here, just change course for Hamburg. But that he's not going to do. He may be heading for disaster, but he's not going to take them back."

"Why not?" It was the first time Hendrik put himself that question. So far, he had merely tried to adapt to events as they occurred.

"Because, Doctor, he is not a mystic like myself, he is an

Evangelical Christian. That means he does not rely on some religious experience; he has arrived at a theological conclusion. To him, the Bible says in effect, 'Thou shalt not take those people back,' and that's all there is to it. There's no arguing with him, there's no compromise; this is how Christians in Roman times ended up in the lion's den. And if I were the Jews, I'd be happier with a dogmatic like him than a mystic whose emotions may change somewhere down the road. He's not going to flinch, I can tell you that. He'll see this through to the bitter end. And bitter it will be. But I think it's a brilliant plan."

"But there are going to be accidents! Old men scrambling down those nets at dead of night . . . "

"Possibly. But believe me, Doctor: even if they drop dead by the score, he's going to sail on, right into the teeth of the American Coast Guard."

It didn't seem an encouraging prospect, but what intrigued Hendrik was why Vinkemans was so taken with the captain's plan. "I still don't understand why you call this idea of boat drills and midnight exercises brilliant. I think it's going to be a murderous mess."

Vinkemans gazed ruefully into the drizzle. "I think it's brilliant because it not only assures these people that he is serious, it gives them something to *do*. They're going to be busy every minute of the day. Knots and splicing classes, scrambling classes, boat-handling classes—who knows, he may even start to teach some of them navigation. Yes, I think it's brilliant."

"Well, I must say! You surprise me. Just visualize them, for one thing, scrambling up those perpendicular ladders at dead of night!"

"Doctor," Vinkemans said, in his most commiserating undertaker's voice, "just think of the alternative. Think of not rehearsing, not preparing these people. Think of what that would mean when they come to be beached in a hurry. Above all, think of them just sitting around these three weeks with nothing to do except nurse their fear. I'd plump for the scramble net and the ladders any time. Can't you see? He's turning them from victims into fighters. I don't know where he got it from; I've always thought of him as merely a stupid, bull-headed man. But if I'm right, he's going to transform a shipload of kids, pregnant women, invalids and elderly people into a regiment of commandoes. It may be all in the mind; as a matter of fact, it will be, but I think he's going to bring it off."

Hendrik looked at him with amazement. "You can't be serious, Vinkemans! Old Mr. Himmelbaum, incontinent Mr. Brandeis, pregnant Mrs. Spiegel, nutty Mrs. Schlachter—commandoes?"

Vinkemans smiled in resignation. "You forget one thing, Doctor: they are Jews."

"What the hell difference does that make?"

"They have endured as a people scattered over the earth for two thousand years. They may look and act like helpless victims, they may even believe they are, but they would not have survived as a people if that were the truth. You'll see."

Hendrik sighed, "All right, I'll see. We'll all see. What you and I have to do now is sit down somewhere and work out who should go into the boats, and who should be condemned to scramble down the net to the rafts."

"Let's do that," Vinkemans said, with a hint of his bedside manner. "Let's check on Mr. Brandeis and then go through the passenger list. Shall we?"

"You're an odd one, Vinkemans," Hendrik said, looking at him intently, "you really are."

Vinkemans smiled coyly, as if it had been a compliment. Then he fell back into his role and said gloomily, "Let's go."

They checked on Mr. Brandeis; then they sat down at the staff table in the starboard catwalk, where they worked through the passenger list until Henky came to lay the table for the first sitting of the noon meal.

2

Tovah, one among a silent group of women listening to Mrs. Goldstein, felt relief at first, then a growing excitement. It was true! The captain *was* going to do it! He *was* going to put them ashore in America! She only realized that everyone shared her excitement when suddenly someone started cheering. Everyone joined in. Hannelore Weisbrot threw her arms around Tovah's neck, hugging her, crying with joy. Then Gretchen Kahn did the same thing, and Lieschen Schlachter, little as she was, and together they danced around, holding on to each other. And so did everyone else: all the women had embraced those nearest to them, were hugging them, crying, dancing—it was a pandemonium of joy until old Goldstein's market-vendor voice called them to order and managed to achieve silence.

"Ladies!" she bellowed, standing on top of a footlocker. "The captain has ordered us to prepare ourselves for the landing. This means rehearsals, and lessons for everyone in things like boat-handling and ropes and—and—oars and such, and we're going to have constant lifeboat drills and evacuation practice. That means organization! We cannot go at it like a flock of geese, pushing each other out of the way at the bottom of those ladders. We must organize ourselves, military fashion, or the whole exercise will end in one holy mess. Agreed? Will all those who agree with this concept please say so?"

The women, who, like Tovah herself, were in a mood to agree with anything that promised action, cheered, even though on second thoughts it was ludicrous to suggest that old biddies like Mrs. Schlachter and Mrs. Feldschuh could be organized in any fashion, let alone a military one.

But as it turned out, that was not what Mrs. Goldstein had in mind. "I want you to appoint a leader," she bellowed. "The captain says we must be ready for a full-dress rehearsal of the landing one week from now. That means we have very little time for discussion. So appoint your leader *now!*"

"You!" Mrs. Hahnemann shouted, and everybody cheered and laughed.

Mrs. Goldstein was not troubled by false modesty. "*Schon gut,*" she shouted, "on condition we do this Army-fashion! I'll accept only if I am given total authority; that means I will appoint officers to serve under me, and no arguing, ladies! This is not going to be a joyride, this is *war*. It is us, Jewish women of the *Star of Peace*, against the powers of the world!"

"And what about the men?" someone shouted.

"They're doing exactly the same: electing a leader who will appoint officers. Agreed?"

"Yes, *Frau General!*" Mrs. Adler joked. Everyone laughed and cheered and it ended in a burst of sustained applause.

"Very well," Mrs. Goldstein shouted, "I appoint *you* my second in command!"

It was a good choice, Tovah had come to know Mrs. Adler in the hospital work they did together; she was a powerhouse.

"Tovah Nachtgeist!" Mrs. Goldstein bellowed, making Tovah's heart miss a beat. "You are appointed leader of the teenagers! I want to see both you and Mrs. Adler—*now.*"

Obediently, Tovah worked her way through the crowd to where Mrs. Goldstein, now sitting on the footlocker, awaited the arrival of her subordinates. The other women, obligingly, left an open space around her so as to enable her and her officers to confer in peace. It was amazing how quickly, without any arguing or protest, the hundred-odd women, who so far had rarely agreed on anything at all, accepted Mrs. Goldstein's leadership without question.

Tovah could understand why Mrs. Adler was chosen, but not why she herself should be given command of the teenagers. Mrs. Goldstein lost no time explaining it to her. "You are the oldest, you have some notion of nursing and looking after helpless people. I want you to organize all the girls from age ten up, and younger ones if you think they're responsible enough, and give each of them a job. When we start practicing the evacuation, there are going to be problems with the older people, with cripples like Mrs. Schmidt, blind Mrs. Kohnstamm, our few pregnant ladies, and confused women like Mrs. Schlachter who may become disoriented under pressure. Each one of you young people will be responsible for one particular person who needs supervision and help. Including the boys, how many are you altogether? I mean, the ones over ten?"

Tovah had no idea. "I wouldn't know, Mrs. Goldstein. I suppose we must be—well—at least twenty—no, more like thirty."

"Very well, appoint two other girls, so that you'll each have ten kids under your direct command. That means three of you and three boys. Agreed?"

"Yes, Mrs. Goldstein."

"All right. Now go and see what the boys are up to. Find out who your opposite number is."

Tovah's friends had been observing the conference from a distance and were dying to hear what was happening. She took Hannelore Weisbrot aside and explained to her what was going on; together they decided that Anna Feldschuh should be the third in their group. The three of them went to find out who the boys had chosen.

At the top of the ladder they were met by David, who obviously had been waiting for Tovah. He was not allowed in the women's hold but always hanging around the ladder waiting for his sister. "Tov!" he cried, the moment he saw her. "Tov, I'm a sergeant, in charge of five soldiers!"

"Well, that's terrific, Dave. How old are they?"

"Oh, all of them are over three."

"Think you can handle them?"

"Of course I can! I'll have a stick!"

"I don't think that's the answer, David," she said patiently. "Come, we have to go. I'll talk to you later."

There were few people on deck; obviously, everybody was gathering in groups in the holds, organizing themselves. Tovah and her two friends set out to look for the boys; when they reached the foredeck, which was the men's section, they found Yitzhak Stuhlmacher, Philip Roth and Josef Wartenberg deep in discussion. As it was raining, they decided to have their meeting at one of the dining tables amidships, which was sheltered by the boat deck.

"Well," Yitzhak began when they were seated, "who of you is in command?"

"I am," Tovah said.

He looked at her, sizing her up. He was a surly, handsome fifteen-year-old whose mother doted on him. Tovah wondered why he had been chosen to lead the boys; she would have preferred Philip, who seemed less moody; but then, she didn't know any of them well, just by sight and the occasional game during the crossing.

However, it soon became apparent that Yitzhak had a very methodical mind and a natural authority, whereas Philip and the others, good as their suggestions were, showed some unsureness and seemed happy to be led. They agreed that Yitzhak and Tovah would be their representatives on the central committee now being organized, of which Mrs. Goldstein and Mr. Jablonski were the leaders. Tovah knew Mr. Jablonski: short, swarthy, he had always seemed abrupt and unfriendly to her, but he had been the only one who had dared argue with the angry officer in Montevideo. She was told that Mr. Jablonski was a cobbler from Königsberg in East Prussia, the part of Germany that was separated from the rest by the Polish Corridor. It seemed he had been the president of the Zionist Committee in East Prussia until the Nazis disbanded it under the Nuremberg Laws.

After a while, the others left Yitzhak and Tovah alone. It was interesting to see how quickly everyone adjusted to the chain of command; it was generally assumed that the two of them had things to discuss that did not concern the others at this point. The table suddenly seemed large and empty; the drizzle had turned into rain which blew into the drafty passage in billowing gusts. "Let's find someplace else to talk," Yitzhak suggested. "How about the forecastle, where the doctor goes?"

"But it's going to be even worse out there!"

"Not behind the anchor winch. And I have an umbrella."

They went out there; it was indeed wet and windy, and the ship seemed to pitch much more than in the midships. They sat down in the shelter of the winch; when he put up the umbrella, she recognized it as his mother's: large with blue and white sections, like a beach umbrella.

"Well," he said, "it's going to be tough. You know that." It was a statement, not a question.

"Yes," she said.

"As I see it," he continued, "our main problem is going to be discipline. Today, everyone is ready to do what they're told, but once the novelty wears off, they're going to hate being ordered about."

"But this is serious! It's not a game."

"I know—but they don't. They're kids; you can't suddenly turn them into grown-ups."

"So what do you suggest?"

"I think we should accept them for what they are, and play it their way."

"I don't understand."

"By making it a game. By playing at being a Jewish legion in history, in Roman times."

She hesitated. "Masada?" She wondered if he even knew of it.

He looked at the rain, then he said, "Let's hope not. I'm not ready for that."

"It's a game, you said."

He gave her a searching look. "All right: Masada. Let's tell them about Masada. Make *it* the game. You tell your kids about it, I'll tell mine."

"What, exactly?"

"Well—how the troops behaved. What they went through. How they obeyed their commanders and those who didn't were punished. How they met every day in council of war, the way we do. The roles the men played, and the women."

"Do you know about that?" she asked, astounded. "I thought nobody knew. I thought there were no records."

He gave her a sly smile. It changed his face from that of a surly, handsome boy into an impish cherub. "You know that, and I know that, but I don't think anyone else does. We'll have to make up our own history as we go along. And we may well be right too. It must have been a situation rather like this, in Masada. They can't have organized themselves in any other way than we're doing now."

"You mean, invent everything?"

"Yes."

"I don't think we can do that," she said. "It would mean we'd be telling them a bunch of lies."

"They're not going to find that out while they're on board this ship. And who cares what happens after? We have three weeks. After that, the game is up one way or the other. It *is* like Masada. And because we're Jews, we carry within us the same temperament, the same concept of God."

She looked at him, startled. It was an extraordinary thing for a boy to say, certainly a boy like him. He had never struck her as in any way religious or traditional. During services, he had always seemed to be bored and rather sneering about the old men and their Wailing Wall prayers. The Cantor, Mr. Vorzug, could really lay it on, once he got going. Yitzhak had always looked as if it gave him a toothache. Now here he sat, under his beach umbrella with the rain dripping around them, and talked about God as if he really meant it. "I didn't know," she said.

"Shall I tell you a secret?" There was that impish smile again. "Neither did I, until—well, just recently."

"Montevideo?"

She thought he was not going to answer; he looked at her with those strange, gold-flecked eyes, then he said, "Yes, in Montevideo. You too?"

It gave her a chill of discomfort. It seemed so intimate, so personal; yet the temptation to tell him was stronger than her reticence. "I was given the chance to borrow someone's uniform and go ashore disguised as a nurse," she blurted out. "The person in question promised she'd get me a permit to live in Uruguay."

"And you refused?"

She nodded.

They were silent for a while, each with their own thoughts. She was sorry now she had told him. It was strange, but it felt almost as if she had lost something. Then he said, "That should make you carry a lot of conviction, once you start telling them. Do your parents know about this, by the way?"

"My parents?"

"Aren't they on board?"

"They're dead."

"Oh?" His eyes asked the question.

"My father was killed by the brownshirts. My mother died.

They said it was a heart ailment. But she died of loneliness and fright."

"I understand," he said after a moment.

"Understand what?" she asked with a sudden flare-up of hostility.

"Why you didn't accept that offer in Montevideo. You can't have that happen to your parents and walk away."

She had never thought of it in those terms. She wasn't sure she wanted to think about it at all. She had wanted to forget her parents and what had happened to them, and she had succeeded. Life had to go on. It had not occurred to her—her parents had died because they were Jews; if she had accepted that nurse's offer, she would have walked away from something she now knew she must do: give a meaning to their deaths, a meaning to her Jewishness. Then, suddenly, there was Yakov. This was exactly up his street. Again, without her being aware of it, her cousin in Palestine had her under his spell.

CHAPTER TWO

I

Vinkemans was proven right once again: the difference in the attitude of the passengers after Montevideo was so striking that Hendrik found it hard to believe. With amazement, he watched old ladies clambering up and down the ladder not once, but three or four times in a row in strenuous boat drills, and elderly hypochondriacs like Mr. Himmelbaum climbing in and out of the lifeboats without a single mention of arthritic joints, slipped disks or *Hexenschuss.*

The most hazardous exercise of all was the scramble net. It had been suspended from the lower bridge and anchored as Palstra, the second engineer, had suggested. The boats could take a hundred and eighty passengers; the rafts would be the lot of the rest. To see not just teenagers but men and women old enough to be their grandparents claw their way up and down the net made Hendrik's hair stand on end; he pleaded with Kuiper in a moment of privacy to think of an alternative. "Believe me, Skipper, there are going to be accidents. I don't care how keen those people are, you can't turn city-bred, mush-muscled creatures like them into marines by simply waving a magic wand. I have serious reservations about the ladders, but Jesus! When it comes to those goddam nets . . . " Judging by his reaction, Kuiper was more concerned about the blasphemy than about the prospect of having *Frau* Hoflein and *Herr* Vorzug plummet down thirty feet onto the rafts at dead of night off Fools' Beach, South Carolina, or whatever the damn place was called. The elderly themselves didn't seem to be concerned either, maybe because they were too busy or simply too exhausted. Apart from the boat and scramble-net drill, there were classes in boat-handling given by Wybrands, knots and splices taught by the bo'sun; even Vinkemans had let himself be shanghaied into teaching first aid and artificial respiration. It took a fair amount of his time, which meant that Hendrik often found himself in sole charge of the infirmary; but that did not really matter much, as there had been a marked drop in the number of patients. Regular customers like Himmelbaum and Brandeis came less often to have their blood pressure taken, bladder catheterized, hemorrhoids checked, mysterious cricks in the neck diagnosed; just a few diabetics turned up for their daily shots of insulin, and isolated cases like a boil to be lanced or a sty to be seen to.

The change that had come over the adolescents was even more striking. For one thing, they showed a sudden concern for the old people. Hendrik had little contact with Tovah, but he understood that she had a leading position among the teenagers; he saw her frequently in a huddle with a boy called Stuhlmacher who seemed to be the leader of the pack. She too appeared transformed: no longer a shy young girl haunted by the shadow of her little brother, but, judging by the way she ordered the others about and the alacrity with which she was obeyed, she was turning into his pet aversion: a bossy woman, a second Mrs. Goldstein in the making.

It was not until the evening of the fourth day that he discovered the source of the new spirit among the teenagers. He had gone down into the women's hold to have a look at Mrs. Spiegel, now so close to confinement that she should no longer climb the ladder to come to his office, who had complained of "contractions." He greeted her with a hearty *"Guten Abend, Frau Spiegel! Wie geht's denn?"* as he appeared beside her bunk in the glare of the naked lightbulb in the aisle.

Mrs. Spiegel, who normally was so shy that she hardly dared blink, put a finger as delicate as a clay pipe stem to her lips and whispered, "Sh! *Instruktion!*"

"Where?"

She pointed toward a group of kids in the aisle beyond the adjoining row of bunks. Hendrik could not see them clearly because of the scaffolding of the intervening beds, but there seemed to be quite a crowd listening to someone, a woman.

He checked Mrs. Spiegel's condition, found that the uterus had descended somewhat and the cervix had begun to dilate, but there was no immediacy. As always, she was as passive as a hypnotized subject. During his examination, he half listened to the woman's voice nearby and caught isolated words: "Romans," "Zealots," "Palace."

When he left Mrs. Spiegel, he turned a corner and peeked into the next aisle. Unobserved, he had a good view of the gathering and discovered to his surprise that the lecturer was Tovah. She was telling the story of the last battle of the Jews with the Romans before the Diaspora and how more than nine hundred Jewish defenders of the Palace of Herod had committed suicide rather than surrender to the Romans who had laid siege to them. Only two women and a few children who had hidden in an aqueduct survived this blood bath and reported what had happened. She told the story colorfully and with passion; the kids were listening to her with extraordinary concentration and even Hendrik himself was brought under her spell. He was so absorbed in the story and the way in which Tovah was telling it that he was startled out of his wits by the silhouette of a child suddenly dangling upside-down in front of his nose. "Boo," she said.

He recognized the pigtails. Lieschen Schlachter was the tomboy of the women's holds; an angelic child with huge blue eyes, tripping about in a dainty Victorian dress like a little shepherdess off a mantelpiece, she was the terror of her section, disastrously spoiled by her doting grandmother. "Lieschen," he whispered, "you ought to be in bed. Stop hanging upside-down in front of people's noses and scaring them half to death. Go away."

"I am Jesus," she said, "singing under water with long hair."

As she was not about to budge, he had no choice but to mumble, "It's time for Jesus to go to bed," and make his way back to the ladder.

When he entered the men's hold that night to have a look at a patient who was running a high fever, he discovered that a similar meeting for teenage boys was being held, led by the Stuhlmacher boy. He listened in on that gathering too and discovered that the boy was talking about the same incident: the last defense of the Jews against the Romans in a place called Masada. The details the Stuhlmacher boy related, he discovered to his amusement, conflicted with the ones Tovah had dished out next door. The two of them must be a pair of gifted liars.

2

Kuiper ordained that the first dress rehearsal for the landing in America was to take place in Brazil on the night of the seventh day. The sheltered inlet where they would actually practice getting into the boats and rafts was behind a promontory in the rain forest called Ponta do Muta. There was no human habitation nearby and Kuiper seemed confident that they could go through their paces undisturbed; but as it was going to take place at night, there was to be a boat drill in the dark as part of their preparation. It seemed a scary undertaking: to have the elderly and infirm scramble up the ladders in broad daylight was bad enough; to have them do so in pitch darkness seemed crazy. But the passengers did not appear to be daunted by the prospect; and the organization of the whole thing in the men's holds, as Hendrik and Vinkemans observed it from the deck, was remarkable. Life jackets were handed out, every section of the ladder was lit up by flashlight by one of the teenagers; at the command of a man called Jablonski who seemed to be their commander-in-chief, the elderly started their hazardous ascent. It turned out that each one of them was led by a youngster who seemed to be responsible for him; when they reached the deck, they were taken by the arm and guided to their lifeboat by the familiar route they had taken many times during daylight exercises. It was impressive, but when it came to the scramble net, there were hold-ups and confusion and two near-accidents; at a given moment, Jablonski called the whole thing off and told everybody to go back into the holds. The descent down the ladder was less organized than the ascent had been.

An hour later, after Hendrik had gone to bed for the night on his settee and Kuiper was about to climb into his bunk in his underwear, there was a knock on the door.

"Yes?" Kuiper called.

In came Mrs. Goldstein, the Rabbi and Mr. Jablonski.

"Oh—I'm sorry," Mrs. Goldstein said, seeing the captain standing there in his ill-closing B.V.D.'s with the gesture of Adam in Paradise on medieval paintings. "We'll come back . . ."

"No," Kuiper said, "just give me a moment and I'll—"

Hendrik wondered what he was planning; to his knowledge, Kuiper did not possess a robe. But the captain found a solution by climbing into his bunk and conducting the audience from there. "Right," he said when he was installed. "What's on your mind?"

"Well," Mr. Jablonski started, "as you know, we went through a pre-dress rehearsal tonight, and although we've all been working very hard, hours and hours of practice, we find that we are just not ready yet."

"It's those nets," Mrs. Goldstein said. The Rabbi seemed to be there just for decoration; he stood quietly, hatted and shawled, in the foreground like the *Anschnitt* in an art photograph. "To-night two people fell onto the deck," she continued. "If it hadn't been for the mattresses, they would have been badly hurt, if not killed."

"In reality, there will be water," Kuiper said, aloft in his bunk.

"But there are other things," Mr. Jablonski continued. "In the women's holds, there was a serious incident with Mrs. Schlachter—"

"That was *not* serious," Mrs. Goldstein corrected. "Mrs. Schlachter just wanted to turn around halfway because she heard her granddaughter below her. She is a little confused at times, and it has since been decided that she will be the last to go up. Tovah Nachtgeist will be there to look after her. So that's no argument. But—"

"We shall not be ready," the Rabbi said, in a gentle, singsong voice. He sounded almost like a dreamer talking in his sleep, but to the others it seemed to settle the argument.

"Well . . . " Kuiper shrugged. "If that's the way you feel . . . But you must realize what this means: we'll have to go through the whole exercise under much less favorable circumstances. I'm not in a position right now to show it to you on the chart, but the next location suitable for a full-scale drill is north of one of the islands in the Amazon estuary. That's virtually on the equator. It will be very much hotter there, and we can expect thunderstorms at night with high winds. Also, we'll run the risk of being spotted by the Brazilian Navy or their customs."

But old Goldstein stuck to her guns. "That's too bad," she said, "but we are responsible for our people. We cannot risk accidents. They simply are not ready, as the Rebbe said. We need more practice."

"As you wish," Kuiper said crisply. "Good night."

"Good night, Captain . . . " They filed out. In the doorway, Jablonski, who was the last to leave, turned around and said, "And thank you, Captain, for all you are doing for us."

"My pleasure," Kuiper said from his bunk. The whole thing was rather ludicrous, more like a French bedroom farce than the Greek tragedy it probably was.

"Well," Kuiper said morosely, after Jablonski had closed the door behind him, "that's unfortunate. I'm sure that nobody would have bothered us, day after tomorrow. Now we are likely to run into trouble."

"But they weren't ready for it, Skipper. Vinkemans and I watched them go through their paces and it *was* a mess. Older people don't function well in the dark. They can't see, they get frightened, they become confused. Why don't you hold your exercise in that inlet during the day?"

Kuiper grunted. Then he said, "It has to be nighttime. In

broad daylight, there are going to be fishermen, there'll be people observing us from the shore. I don't want to risk the Americans being forewarned when we turn up. They must go through that drill at night."

"Well, they are simply not ready, Skipper. Anyway, you can't force them to do what they don't want to do. That's where it stops, doesn't it?"

Kuiper said nothing. He folded his hands and closed his eyes.

To give him privacy in his consultation with the Almighty, Hendrik turned over with his face to the wall and soon fell asleep.

CHAPTER THREE

I

Eight days later, in the early dawn of the thirteenth day after leaving Montevideo, *Star of Peace* nosed into the channel between Bailique Island and the north shore of the Amazon estuary.

The passengers were ready for the dress rehearsal. They had practiced the orderly evacuation of the holds, the lining up for boats and rafts every night. The scramble nets had, after a few more near-accidents, been abandoned; after long discussions with Meyer, the bo'sun, the second engineer and Wybrands, Kuiper had decided, as the sea would be calm, to lower both port and starboard gangways to the waterline and to let the passengers board the rafts that way. This meant that the landing off Folly Beach in South Carolina had to be scrapped; they would now have to enter Stono Inlet to avoid the Atlantic swell which would make the ship roll even under the best weather conditions. To lower the gangways meant they needed still water; it also meant some sort of dock or platform from which the passengers could step into the rafts without making it a hazardous operation, especially for the older ones. The bo'sun and Palstra constructed two floating platforms, supported by empty oil drums, which would be lowered into the water by the forward derricks and serve as landing docks. The rafts would be floated alongside and teenagers would assist the older passengers getting into them. Six boats, each containing thirty people, were to be lowered in unison; each boat was then to proceed to pick up two rafts; then the whole flotilla was to proceed to the spot selected for the landing. There would of course be no actual landing this time; Kuiper had set as a goal twenty minutes maximum from the first boat being lowered until the convoy reached the shore; anything over that limit would mean a rapidly diminishing margin of surprise.

The night before the landing, nobody slept much. The holds were restless with last-minute rehearsals of details of the evacuation; the bo'sun fussed over the boats, the pulleys, the davits like a mother hen; Hendrik and Vinkemans went through the procedure of evacuating the infirmary and putting the patients in the boats so frequently that Kuiper had to shout from the bridge an order to douse those flashlights because they were approaching the shore. Kuiper himself spent an hour with Meyer in the chartroom discussing the navigational part of the operation. The channel north of Bailique Island was shallow and shoaled, so he had scheduled the evacuation for the last hour of the incoming tide. The current of the river at this time of year was fast and he could not risk the whole tangle of boats and rafts floating out to sea. It was new moon; most of the operation would take place in total darkness. It suited Kuiper from the point of view of secrecy; but to have old people, women and small children go through the evacuation in the dark without lights on deck was risky. Yet the landing had to be rehearsed. They *had* to go through the whole operation from beginning to end, leaving nothing to chance when they got to the United States; once there, it would turn into a battle of wits between Kuiper and the Coast Guard.

So, at three o'clock in the morning, with the bo'sun singing out the depth in a Gregorian chant in the bow as he swung and hauled the lead, *Star of Peace,* all lights extinguished, nosed, dead slow, into the narrow channel. There were thunderstorms about; sheet lightning shivered all around them on the horizon; it was helpful, as it gave Kuiper momentary glimpses of the shore, but the last thing he needed at this point was one of those tropical downpours with cyclonic high winds. Wybrands and Palstra

were responsible for the towlines; he called down to them to
make sure that everything was secure and no rafts could break
away in a squall and be swept out to sea into the night.

He did not have much time to keep track of the passengers,
as his mind was on the ship; but he frequently glanced fore and
aft from both wings of the bridge during his nervous pacing,
while listening to the depths chanted by the bo'sun. In the twitch-
ing glare of the world-large ferns of lightning, he saw that the
boats were manned and ready to go and that, on deck, orderly
lines of people waited to go down the gangways to the rafts; there
were no signs of agitation or nervousness. There still was too
much current running, despite the incoming tide, so he had better
drop anchor, his second option. Better to hold the ship heading
into the current than risk having her bow swing out in the darkness and sideswipe the rafts.

At the command of his whistle, the anchor chain thundered
out through the hawse hole, setting the whole ship a-shudder; it
seemed to be echoed by a roll of thunder over the forest. 'Dear
God,' Kuiper prayed, 'don't let there be a squall, not now!' For
he was committed; the gangways were lowered, the floating
docks brought into position; the passengers were so conditioned
by now that they didn't waste any time. The lines started to move
down the gangways to the platforms, with only here and there
the glowworm glimmer of a blacked-out flashlight. Now was the
moment. He had gone through it at least twenty times in rehearsal and fifty times in his mind; still, he had his heart in his
mouth as he blew his whistle and shouted, "Lower starboard
boats! Let go starboard rafts!"

There was the squealing of pulleys, and loud splashes as the
rafts hit the water.

"Lower port boats! Let go port rafts!"

He couldn't see what anyone was doing. All he heard was
splashes, squealing pulleys, shouts from his crew. The passengers
themselves were silent. Not a child whined. They moved steadily
down the catwalks in single file, down the gangways; boatloads
of them plummeted down into the night at a speed which, seen
from the bridge as lightning flashed, seemed that of a falling

stone. It flashed closer and closer, on all sides; the whole of the jungle twitched and shivered in blinding blue flashes; thunder rolled upriver. But there went the first boat, towing two rafts; Kuiper ran to the other wing of the bridge and saw that at the same moment the second boat had taken off. It was now rapidly falling behind the ship in the current, joining the first and its rafts; the whole thing moved like clockwork. And that without a sound from the passengers.

Then he heard the rain: a terrifying sound, as of an approaching train. He knew there would be wind in it and shouted through his megaphone, "Belay boats! Belay boats!" He ran to the other wing and shouted the same command into the darkness. The rain hit him like the surf; the wind nearly ripped the megaphone from his hands. Everywhere around him was the sound of a torrent of water hitting the deck, the funnel, the wheelhouse, the rail. He was drenched in seconds; lightning flashing in the squall lit up what looked like a caldron of steam. Then, with the suddenness of a curtain swept aside, there were the river, the shore, the island floodlit by continuous lightning; behind him were the boats, emerging from a cloud of steam, the rafts in tow: one—two—three—all six boats attached to the ship by straining lines. He wanted to shout through his megaphone, but a gulp of water from the mouthpiece choked him. He shook the thing dry, then he bellowed, "Starboard One! Everyone accounted for?"

A shout from the cloud answered, "Yes!"

"Starboard Two! Everybody there?"

"Yes . . . !" It sounded faraway, as if echoing in a cave.

"Starboard Three—"

He hailed all six boats; everyone was accounted for. He was soaked to the skin, blinded by water running from his cap; he dared not imagine the condition those poor people in the boats must be in, the old people, the women, the children; not to mention the younger ones in the rafts, up to their waists in the river. The rest of the exercise would have to be abandoned; there was no point in tormenting them any longer than was necessary. The getting into the boats and the rafts had been accomplished, the flotilla formed; that was enough for now. He blew his whistle and shouted, "End of exercise! Everybody back on board! Starboard One! Unload your passengers!"

Someone tugged his sleeve; he could not see who it was until a flash of lightning showed Palstra's rain-soaked head, beaming from ear to ear. "Seven minutes, Captain! Seven fucking minutes! It's a goddam miracle!"

"Palstra, watch your language!" It helped him overcome the impulse to embrace the man out of sheer gratitude. He went to the port wing, blew his whistle and shouted, "Port One! Unload your passengers! Watch out for those stanchions!"

The rain had stopped as suddenly as it had started. Presently, the first of the occupants of Starboard One stepped onto the deck from the gangway. "Can we turn the floodlights on now, Captain?" Palstra asked behind him.

"No." He said it without hesitation. Then he added almost apologetically, "We must not attract attention, no one must get wind of what we're doing. We have to get out of here unseen. Be back at sea by daybreak."

"Aye, aye, Captain."

Down on deck, he heard the first sound from his passengers since the exercise began: singing. They were singing!

Awed by their courage, their sheer guts, he leaned over the rail and called to no one in particular down there, "Well done! Seven minutes! Top-notch!"

"Thank you!" someone shouted back.

Singing sounded all over the ship as they came back on board, one by one, soaked to the skin. The boats were being hoisted back into the davits and the empty rafts hauled back on deck. Thunder rolled, lightning flashed, but now it seemed festive, like fireworks. The whole ship was bathed in its sheen; then, at the height of the rejoicing, just as the last boat was swung back into the davits, a piercing scream plummeted down into silence. The whole ship fell silent, holding its breath in shock.

"Oh my God . . . " Palstra said.

It took Kuiper a moment to gather the courage; then he said, "Lights."

Palstra shouted the order into the darkness.

2

The floodlights flashed on and set the decks and the caves of the holds in a garish white glare. Tovah saw Mrs. Schlachter dash toward the ladder, shrieking, "*Lieschen!*" The old woman tried to clamber over the bulkhead of the hold onto the ladder; people, shaken out of the paralysis of shock by her mad act, grabbed her, tried to hold her back; she started to scream.

Tovah's first impulse was to go down into the hold herself, but Mrs. Schlachter was her responsibility. She pushed her way through the crowd until she reached the struggling old woman; she put an arm around her shoulders and tried to calm her with soothing words, but Mrs. Schlachter was totally irrational with grief and horror. She went on screaming, screaming; Tovah held her tightly until the screams turned into sobs and the old woman collapsed in her arms. Tovah sat down on the deck with her, stroking her hair, still numb with shock. What had happened? Lieschen had fallen, that's all she knew; but how? What had happened? Hendrik ran past her, followed by Mr. Vinkemans; at the sight of the doctor, Mrs. Schlachter started to scream again and shriek, "*Lieschen! Herr Doktor! Lieschen! Lieschen! Lieschen ist tot!*" She heard Mr. Vinkemans say, "Go ahead, Doctor, I'll see to her." Hendrik vanished down the ladder. Mr. Vinkemans knelt beside them, opened his little bag and brought out a syringe. Mrs. Schlachter went on struggling and screaming; Tovah clung to her desperately while Mr. Vinkemans gave her an injection; gradually, the old woman gave up the struggle and went limp in her arms. Mr. Vinkemans stayed with them for a while, looking at Mrs. Schlachter with such tenderness and concern that Tovah only then fully realized the horror of what had happened: Lieschen Schlachter had fallen down the ladder into the hold. She didn't dare visualize how the child must be lying there, three storeys below. How could it have happened? All had gone so well; despite the fact that everybody was soaked, they had all been in such high spirits . . .

The captain came, made his way through the silent crowd that was forming around the entrance to the hold, and looked down. He stood quite still for a while, then he turned around and called Mr. Vinkemans. "Do you want us to lower a stretcher?" he asked.

"Yes, please," Mr. Vinkemans said.

The captain shouted orders; a loading boom was swung over the hold, someone brought a stretcher, it was lowered into the hold. Mrs. Schlachter lay quite still now in Tovah's arms, her head on her shoulder. Although she knew the old lady would no longer notice it, Tovah went on stroking her hair soothingly as the portent of what had happened penetrated to her. Death had struck and suddenly changed it all, turning an exciting adventure into a terrible, frightening reality. As she sat there, slowly stroking the sleeping old woman's hair, she felt as if she were waking up from a dream, a daydream of courage and purpose. Wrong. It was all going wrong. Suddenly, it was as if a shadow, a chill had come over her and the ship. Then someone squatted beside her and asked, "How is she?" It was Yitzhak.

"All right," she replied.

He gave her one of those searching looks. "And you?"

"All right."

"As soon as you're free, let's get together."

"All right."

He patted her shoulder and left; there was a puddle of sea water on the deck beside her after he was gone. She herself must be soaking; she had not felt it. It was unbearably hot; steam seemed to rise from the ship itself, swirling in the harsh white beams of the floodlights. Then everyone fell silent.

In the silence, pulleys squealed. And suddenly there was the stretcher rising from the hold, small and insubstantial, covered with a sheet. The loading boom swung over the deck, the stretcher was lowered; although Mrs. Schlachter was asleep, Tovah pressed her head against her shoulder to prevent the old woman from looking. Two men carried the stretcher away. Hendrik came out of the hold.

"Dead?" the captain asked, his voice low, but close enough for Tovah to hear.

Hendrik's face was very white in the harsh light. "Yes," he replied.

Together, the captain, Mr. Vinkemans and Hendrik walked away, following the stretcher.

The crowd quietly dispersed and Mrs. Hoflein came over to Tovah, who still sat cradling Mrs. Schlachter in her arms. "What are we going to do with her, Tovah?"

"Well . . . I don't know . . . Maybe she should be taken to the infirmary?"

"That's where Lieschen is. We don't want her to wake up there. I'll see if I can arrange something else." She vanished.

After a while, she returned with Mr. Vinkemans and two sailors who carried a stretcher.

"We're going to put her in her own bed," Mrs. Hoflein said. "Mr. Vinkemans and these gentlemen will put her on the stretcher and lower her into the hold. Maybe you'd better come along in case she wakes up. You have a way with her."

"All right," Tovah said.

Mrs. Schlachter was put on the stretcher, gently, so as not to wake her up. But she was so fast asleep that she was lost to the world. She was tied down, then the stretcher was lifted, swung over the hold by the boom and lowered out of sight. Tovah followed down the ladder, more careful now than she had been for a long time. How could it have happened? Had Lieschen slipped? She was such a tomboy . . . Or was it because she had been wet, like the others? Tovah didn't want to think about it. She didn't want to visualize how the child must have lain there at the bottom of the ladder.

As she reached the lower level, someone said, "Just a moment." She waited, holding on to the ladder; then the voice said, "All right, you can step down now."

It was Mrs. Adler, with a bucket and a mop.

Tovah did not look at the floor, but walked, staring straight ahead, to the aisle where Mrs. Schlachter's bunk was. As she entered the narrow corridor and walked past rows of silent women, she wondered if this was how people had looked two thousand years ago after the first death in Masada.

3

It was most embarrassing, but just as Hendrik was telling Kuiper about the nature of the child's trauma, Chief Davelaar came barging into the cabin and shouted, "Murderer! You murderer! Goddammit, I *told* you there would be an accident! Why, for Christ's sake, didn't you listen to me?"

"Davelaar, that's enough! I've told you—"

But the old man shouted, "You've told me! You have killed a child with that Christian crap of yours! Why the hell don't you take those people back to Germany? Why the hell don't you—"

Then Kuiper roared, with spine-chilling fury, *"Get out!!"* When the chief ignored his order, the captain grabbed him by the scruff of his neck, opened the door and threw him out. It was such an alarming explosion of violence that Hendrik felt his skin contract. Never before had he seen Kuiper lose his cool; the incident seemed to reveal a pent-up rage that was terrifying, totally destructive and irrational. But the captain calmly closed the door, confronted Hendrik with perfect composure and said in a relaxed, conversational tone, "Sorry about that. You were saying?"

"I . . . er . . . Death must have been instantaneous the moment she hit the ground . . . "

"You mean the ceiling."

"I beg your pardon?"

"That's what we call the plank floor that covers the bilges. Carry on."

It seemed a callous remark. Maybe it was intended to demonstrate control of the situation. If that was the purpose, it failed. "I have no more to say, Skipper. What's the next step?"

"I'll need a death certificate from you. I'll enter the incident in the log, but we need a proper form for the authorities."

Hendrik wondered which authorities. Who would be interested in the death of a child that no country was prepared to admit? The Germans certainly wouldn't. "Very well, Skipper. I'll see to it. We'll have a burial at sea, I presume?"

"Of course. Preferably later today or, at the latest, tomorrow. The sooner the better, in these temperatures."

"I believe that, according to Jewish custom, burial must take place within twenty-four hours."

"Well, then, don't let's delay. I'll schedule it for—" he glanced at the clock—"eighteen hundred hours. Anything else?"

"No."

"Very well. Go and make your arrangements, I'll make mine."

Hendrik left the cabin and stepped onto the lower bridge. The sun was rising, the dark and menacing coast of the jungle receding; *Star of Peace* was headed back to sea. He was deeply upset by the death of the child; Davelaar's outrage had struck a responsive chord. What if their effort to land these people in the United States were to fail? The outcome seemed inevitable. It was a worthy effort; but something in the captain's stolid determination didn't sound right. That sudden outburst of violence seemed to reveal a totally different kind of person behind the unbending, principled Christian following his conscience.

He discussed it with Vinkemans an hour later, after they had viewed the little body and made out the death certificate. They strolled over to the forecastle, where, mercifully, this time no kids were loafing by the anchor winch.

"All this is getting to the captain," he said, leaning against the rail.

"Ah?"

"I was reporting on the accident when the chief came in and started to bawl him out. And suddenly it was as if the man—the captain—went through a sort of transformation. It was a Jekyll-and-Hyde situation: all of a sudden he turned from a stolid, unemotional character into a raving maniac. He picked old Davelaar up and threw him bodily out of the cabin. It was all over in seconds. It shook me to the core."

"Why?"

"Well, the man clearly has a split personality. Let me tell you,

I was scared out of my wits. If he ever cuts loose . . . "

"Well, his nerves are fraying, and no wonder. People control their tempers most of the time. That's the hallmark of civilization, I'd think."

There were times when Vinkemans became insufferably pedantic. "This was not just a case of a man losing his temper, old boy: this was someone showing his true colors. I live with him, so I have a continuous observation post. In my estimation, the man pretends to be the reverse of what he actually is. Today I saw the true Kuiper. Some revelation, I must say."

Vinkemans gave it some earnest thought, then he said, "I think it is merely a revelation of his sense of insecurity. I told you before: my guess is that he's trying to live up to a behavioral model, his father. People who are insecure in positions of authority often try to assume characteristics of some older person they admire; of course, never characteristics that are theirs by nature."

"That seems a fairly shaky basis for the man's authority, wouldn't you say?"

"Oh, I don't know. It has worked pretty well for others. As long as the image of the emulated model retains its integrity, it's a perfectly workable arrangement."

Hendrik smiled. "Sometimes, Vinkemans, you sound like a lecturing professor. Where did you pick up all that psychiatric jargon?"

"Oh," Vinkemans said vaguely, "the subject has always interested me. What makes people tick, you know. And in the captain's case it's fairly important that we see him clearly. Sooner or later, he's going to need our help."

"I've never met a man less likely to need anybody's help."

Vinkemans gazed at the receding jungle with an expression of mourning. "Not for his sake so much as for the sake of the passengers. We must go on believing that there is an alternative to handing them back to the Germans. And he's the key figure. It's his ship, his decision. On board *Star of Peace,* he's God. Rather than analyze his weakness, we should shore him up. He's the only hope they've got. *We've* got. If we are in this for their sake, that is."

Downstairs on the deck sounded a heart-rending, alien chant.

Despite its unfamiliar cadenzas, it expressed the sadness and the grief for the child who died.

"What's that?" Hendrik asked.

"The *Kaddish*," Vinkemans replied.

4

Was the death of the child his fault? Should he have allowed the floodlights to be turned on earlier?

As he paced to and fro in his cabin in growing confusion, Kuiper realized that this was not the true question. His faith in the outcome had been secure, unshakable; there was no rational reason why this accident should suddenly have undermined his belief in the truth of what his father had written in his Bible. If it *was* God's will that he should not take these people back to Germany, God would provide him with the means to obey it. But was it God's will?

The exercise had gone well. The rapid landing of two hundred and forty-nine people had proven to be a practical possibility. The death of the child had been a minor incident in what amounted to a major victory for all concerned. Then why should this minor incident suddenly have undermined his faith in his accurate reading of God's will?

Davelaar's interruption had been no new development. The old man had maintained all along that the expedition was merely a delay of those people's execution. Then why had his words provoked him so this time? Why had the old man managed to unleash the beast within, however briefly?

Maybe that in itself was the reason. His doubt had nothing to do with what God wanted of him; it had to do with the frightening fragility of his reborn self as it had suddenly been revealed. These last three years, he had been marching about pigeonchested in the conviction that the old Joris, the brawler, the drunk, the womanizer, the foul-mouthed bellowing goon, was gone forever, eradicated by the mystical act of his giving his life to Christ, the miracle of salvation. And yet for one split second there he had been again: the old Joris who had picked up Davelaar and flung him bodily out the door—the beast that had laid low bouncers, wrecked saloons, slapped women until they stopped screaming . . .

He covered his face with his hands and sank onto his knees, praying, "God, God, have mercy! Oh, have mercy on my soul, oh God, have mercy, have mercy . . ."

Miraculously, there came stillness, inner tranquillity, that awesome sense of a presence behind him. There were no words, no images; all he sensed was its reality. It fundamentally changed his point of view.

The death of the little girl meant that now he must be more committed than ever, or her death would have been in vain. As he knelt there, sensing the presence behind him, he had a first inkling of the lengths to which this decision might take him, irrevocable now after the death of the child. It was very brief, a qualm, a moment of formless fear; then there was a knock on the door.

He rose. "Come in!"

In came two kids: a fair-haired boy and the red-headed girl. "Yes?"

"Captain," the boy said, in a voice that betrayed shaky resolve, "we came to tell you that Lieschen's death was our fault. We were responsible for her. We failed in our responsibility. We want to apologize and thank you for—for what you have done for us and for—for everything."

Kuiper looked from one to the other, then he said, "Don't thank me. Thank our God, Who is the same."

The boy said, in a whisper, "Yes, Captain," and they left.

5
_____

That evening, before sunset, Lieschen Schlachter was buried at sea. The Rabbi had ordained that there be no outward signs of grief, no rending of clothes, no wailing: Mrs. Schlachter was still sedated because of her fragile state, she was the only close relative of the dead child, there was no cause for anyone else to go in for excessive demonstrations of sorrow.

At the suggestion of Mrs. Goldstein, the eight young people who were to carry Lieschen to her grave went through a rehearsal under the guidance of the bo'sun so that no clumsy bumbling would mar the ceremony. The eight—four girls, Hannelore Weisbrot, Gretchen Kahn, Anna Feldschuh and Tovah—and four boys, Yitzhak Stuhlmacher, Philip Roth, Fritz Stahl and Josef Wartenberg—carried the empty bier, rested the end of it on the rail and stood facing one another across it.

The bo'sun said, "And here, I suppose, there's going to be some sort of service? I don't know about Jews, but usually somebody says something at this point. After that, you wait for the captain's command, then you raise the end of the plank, the body slides off it and drops into the sea. Let me see you do that now, after I say 'In God's name.' Here goes: one, two, three, in God's name—yes!"

They raised the end of the plank, which was very light. Yitzhak asked, "Is this high enough?"

"Don't worry about that," the bo'sun said, "play it by ear. Just raise it steadily until the body starts to slide. Considering the weight of the person, it may have to be a little higher than you have it now. When it's gone, lay the plank down on the deck, fold the sheet and leave it all where it is; we'll take care of the rest. You know about the sheet, don't you? It's usually a flag, but your people didn't want the Dutch one, so she'll be covered with a sheet instead. You two at the far end of the plank—" he indicated Yitzhak and Tovah—"you'll have to hang on to the end of it so that the body just slips from under, and that'll be all. Now are there any questions?"

"Will the ship be stopped?" Gretchen Kahn asked, her voice thick with tears.

"Of course it will," the bo'sun said, "and it will stay stopped until the end of the service; then we move on. It'll all be done in a proper and respectful manner, don't you worry. All right, do you want to go through it once more?"

They shook their heads.

"Right then, that's all for now."

When the moment came, everyone was on deck. The Rabbi and the ten men of the *minyan* were grouped together near the spot where the bier would rest. The pallbearers were ready when the cargo boom brought the plank with the white sheet down from the lower bridge and swung it slowly to where the eight youngsters were waiting. When it was lowered for them to raise and carry, Tovah saw that someone had painted a black Star of David on it. The bo'sun took off the sling and whispered, "Go!"

While Mr. Vorzug chanted the special *Kaddish* for the graveside, the eight carefully carried the plank to the appointed spot and rested it on the rail, Tovah and Yitzhak holding the end of the sheet. They stood at attention throughout the service, then the Rabbi nodded at the captain. The captain said, "One—two—three, in God's name!" They lifted the end of the plank as the bo'sun had taught them; much sooner than they expected there was a slithering sound, frightening because it sounded alive, and while everyone present spoke in unison "May she come to her place in peace," the small burden slipped from under the sheet and dropped. Nobody watched it fall; nobody heard the splash; the heart-breaking wail of Mr. Vorzug starting the memorial prayer overwhelmed it. The eight teenagers, taking the place of the relatives of the deceased, joined in: "El Moleh Rachamim"— O Lord full of Mercy . . .

To Tovah it was an experience the like of which she had never had before—it was as if, while chanting the ancient words of sorrow and mourning, she had contact with Lieschen, wherever she might be; as if for those few moments their fingers touched across the dark void that now divided them.

When the service was over, everyone dispersed so silently that the ringing of the engine-room telegraph bell could be heard as the captain signaled for the ship to resume speed. Nobody spoke, yet no one went back into the holds; the decks were crowded with silent people watching the sunset, a huge conflagration over the distant jungle with black silhouettes of birds winging through it in arrowhead formation. They stayed on deck until darkness fell and the crests of the bow-waves began to shimmer in the night with luminous phosphorescence.

6

There was no meal that night. Tovah went to bed early and fell asleep almost at once. She was wakened in what she thought must be the middle of the night by anguished screams close by. She knew it was Mrs. Schlachter even before someone shook her and said, "Tovah! You'd better come, she's in bad shape! She's crying for you!"

She hurried in her nightgown through the semi-darkness of the night-lights to Mrs. Schlachter's bunk. Someone whispered, "They've gone to fetch the doctor—try to keep her quiet until he comes."

Mrs. Schlachter was half propped up in her bunk, clutching Lieschen's teddy bear, jabbering nonsense. Tovah tried to calm her, but it appeared she was convinced she had seen Lieschen and knew now that Lieschen was not dead after all. She had seen her just now, wearing a white dress, crying and lost; she desperately needed someone to help her. But where *was* she? In any case, Lieschen was not dead, she was alive! Alive!

By the time Hendrik turned up, Mrs. Schlachter was clinging to Tovah so tightly that when the injection finally took effect Tovah's arms hurt.

"Poor soul," Hendrik said. "Was she hallucinating?"

"Yes."

"She may have more episodes like this. They'll pass with time, but until they do I'd better keep her sedated. It's all about the child, I suppose?"

"She thought she saw Lieschen, in a white dress, looking lost."

"Poor soul," he said again. "Well—thanks for your help. Sleep well."

As she stood up to leave, her foot hit something soft: the teddy bear. She picked it up and put it in bed beside the old woman, then went back to her bunk.

CHAPTER FOUR

Something had to be done, Hendrik decided the following night, to relieve the gloom that had settled over the ship since the death of the child. It seemed the accident had brought about a fundamental change in the passengers' concept of the future. Until that time, everyone had been convinced that Kuiper's audacious scheme to smuggle them ashore in America in the full light of public opinion was sure to succeed. The general optimism had been so infectious that Hendrik himself had come to consider they had a fair chance of success. Now the prevailing mood of despondency got to him too. They had been living in a fool's paradise; of course Kuiper's plan was nonsense. Davelaar was right: in the end, they would have to take the poor souls back to Hamburg. He now wondered how he could have been so gullible.

The atmosphere of defeat became so oppressive that Hendrik took it up with Vinkemans. "How about another carnival? It worked wonders last time."

Vinkemans looked somberly at the leaden sea. They were in the doldrums now: the windless, murderously hot latitude that brought sweltering heat, a hazy sky and a sea that looked dead. "No," he replied, "that wouldn't work a second time—it would be too contrived. Who knows, maybe Mrs. Spiegel will help us out."

Mrs. Spiegel's confinement was indeed very near. Despite numerous false alarms, it simply was biologically impossible that the uterus could descend any further or the cervix dilate any wider without the child dropping on the floor. So the expectant mother had been put to bed in the infirmary; sterile conditions had been established; now there she lay: shy, almost secretive in her self-effacing humility, with a Gioconda smile which looked full of mystery, but might well be mere embarrassment at her failure to perform.

Two days after the burial at sea, there at last came the first wavering squeal of the next link in the chain of immortality of the people of Israel: Moshe Spiegel, seven pounds, bow-legged, purple-faced, with an enormous shock of pitch-black hair.

The effect of Moshe Spiegel's arrival on the gloom-ridden passengers was all Vinkemans had hoped for, and more. The outburst of joy was such that it set the ship a-quiver with foot-stomping, hand-clapping, chorus-chanting exuberance. The celebration turned into another carnival; Palstra, tapping memories of a rural childhood in Holland, arranged sack and egg races for the children; Meyer provided the sacks and Cook was coaxed into giving them the eggs, only nobody had told him to hard-boil them first.

Conspicuously not taking part in the festival of joy was Mrs. Schlachter, who until then had had the distinction of being the recipient of the *shivah*, the seven-day mourning period during which a procession of passengers visited with her to present their condolences. It was her right to be the center of attention during that time, and the psychological benefit had been considerable; it was a grave injustice that Moshe Spiegel took it all away from her with his first squeal. No wonder she reacted with a sense of outrage which expressed itself by an intensification of her delusion that her granddaughter was not dead but still around in the holds, looking for some mysterious exit. Hendrik was brought down at dead of night by Mrs. Goldstein herself, who, with uncharacteristic urgency, begged him to sedate old Mrs. Schlachter and, possibly, take her under his care in the hospital. He went down into the women's hold, but even before he reached the lower level he could hear the screams of the deranged woman in the ghostly dusk of the night-lights in the aisles. He found her cowering in her bunk, clutching the teddy bear, eyes wide with terror in the beam of his flashlight. "She's here!" she raved. "She came to see me! She doesn't know where to go, she's terrified, she's here! I *told* you I saw her! She came, she came!"

"But how did you know it was she, Mrs. Schlachter?" Hendrik asked soothingly, pulling out the plunger of the syringe. "It's pretty dark in here. Couldn't it have been some other child?"

"Oh, no," she said, "oh, no, I *know* it was she. I saw her just like last time: in a garden or a park smelling of flowers, of fresh-cut grass."

"And which garden would that be, Mrs. Schlachter?" He squirted the air out of the syringe against the light.

"I don't know! I don't know! Maybe it's the garden at home —she loved the garden, you know, she always played there, when it was summer she was always in the garden. And now, there she is again, and she comes and says, 'Granny, Granny, I don't know where to *go*. Please, Granny, help me.' She's lost, I tell you. She's too little. She needs help!"

"Well, maybe we can help her. But first, let's have some rest . . . " He rubbed the area on her arm with alcohol. "You'll just feel a slight pinprick . . . "

"It won't make any difference," she said, close to tears. "You can put me under, *Herr Doktor,* but you cannot make her go away. She'll be here, she'll go on being here, I have to help her. I have to, I have to . . . "

"Yes, Mrs. Schlachter," he said, "and you will. But first, try to have some rest now . . . " He took her hand in an effort to calm her, stroked it gently and said, "Tell me about her. Tell me what she was like."

"What she *is* like," Mrs. Schlachter said stubbornly, eyes closed.

"Yes, right: what she is like. She must love you very much."

"Oh, I don't know about that. You never know with children. Do they ever love anyone except themselves . . . ?" She began to sound drowsy.

"She seemed a happy little girl, very imaginative," Hendrik ventured, observing her.

"Yes . . . Yes . . . But someone must help her . . . I must help her! I must get up and . . . and find her . . . "

"Hush, Mrs. Schlachter, hush." The stroking hand had its hypnotic effect. "Just rest awhile, we'll talk later. We should talk, don't you think?"

Mrs. Schlachter did not reply.

After a few minutes, Mrs. Goldstein whispered, "Thank you, Doctor."

"Any time," Hendrik said, snapping his bag shut. "Whenever she gets into a state like this, just call me. The delusion will wear off with time."

"Let's hope so," Mrs. Goldstein said.

CHAPTER FIVE

I

The first seaplane with U.S. Navy markings circled over *Star of Peace* the morning she rounded Barbuda Island and set course for Stono Inlet, South Carolina. They had just left Sombrero lighthouse to the leeward and were crossing Anegada Passage. Kuiper, hearing the drone of engines overhead, ran out onto the lower bridge and saw the plane banking on the starboard side of the ship; then it doubled back and headed west-southwestward for either St. Thomas or Puerto Rico. It might not mean anything; possibly, the plane had just happened to be in the area and had taken a look at the old freighter with its decks full of people, out of sheer curiosity.

But two days later, east of Caicos Island, another U.S. Navy seaplane approached from the southwest, circled over the ship and headed back in the direction from which it had come, obviously Guantanamo airbase in Cuba. Kuiper became worried. Maybe it was coincidence, maybe the Americans just liked to keep track of international shipping so close to their overseas possessions. But that seemed farfetched: the Bahamas were British.

As the weather was perfect, the passengers and the crew were happy, the ship was on schedule, he had time to worry. What if their progress was being tracked by the U.S. Navy? What if the element of surprise, the key to his plan, was lost and the Americans were waiting for him in Stono Inlet?

He gave it a lot of thought, weighing all alternatives; then, forty-eight hours later, the day before they were due to arrive, they were buzzed again, this time by an amphibian two-propeller biplane with the letters USCG under both wings and on the fuselage *U.S. Coast Guard 126.*

At this, Kuiper sat down at his desk and took out a sheet of stationery, together with the business card of the legal attaché from the Embassy in Montevideo.

> *Dear Miss Vesters. You may remember me. I am master of the Dutch freighter Star of Peace which docked in Montevideo with immigrants who were not admitted. You were helpful in clarifying the situation for me; I remember specifically your saying that the United States of America was the only country in this hemisphere where public opinion might exert enough influence on the authorities to bring about admission of my passengers as political refugees.*
>
> *It is my intention to put these people ashore in Stono Inlet, South Carolina, tomorrow (Sunday, August 20) at dawn. Immediately thereafter, I intend to head full speed for nearby Charleston, where I shall alert newspapers, radio stations, and anyone else who might spread the word of their arrival so as to make it a newsworthy event.*
>
> *It now appears that this plan may be known to the United States immigration authorities. I have reason to believe that the progress of my vessel has been tracked by the U.S. Navy, that they are aware of my intention, but (so far) not of my exact destination.*
>
> *Should they prevent me from landing my passengers on U.S. territory, I will mail this letter at the earliest opportunity, in the hope that you may be able and willing to comply with the following request.*
>
> *Your receiving this letter will indicate that my first effort to land my passengers on U.S. territory has failed and that, although I will persist, further efforts are unlikely to succeed. Therefore, would you please use any means at your disposal to alert public opinion in the United States so as to exert pressure from within the country for the admission of these people who, otherwise, must be returned to Germany? If you are right, if public opinion can make a crucial differ-*

ence in the United States, it is now up to you to beat the drum and make the existence of my passengers and their plight known to all American citizens.

Thanking you in advance for your efforts to that end, I remain, madam, yours truly, Joris Kuiper, Skipper next to God, S.S. Star of Peace.

On the envelope he wrote: *Miss Cynthia Vesters, Legal Attaché, Royal Netherlands Embassy, Montevideo, Uruguay,* and in the corner, in large letters: PRIVATE AND PERSONAL. He sealed the envelope, put it in a drawer of his desk and went to the bridge.

Night was falling; before the sun rose again, his mission would either have succeeded or failed. There was no sense of crisis or drama; he was at peace in the conviction that he had done all he could, that he had taken care of all eventualities; the outcome rested now with the Lord, Who had made His will known to him and Who would therefore provide him with the means to obey it.

"Wybrands," he said, "please call Mrs. Goldstein and Mr. Jablonski to the chartroom."

"Yes, Captain."

"Also get the doctor and Mate Meyer."

"Yes, Captain."

The two passengers turned up first; they were really on their toes down there. There had been rehearsals and boat drills every day, conducted with renewed zest and determination; as far as the passengers were concerned, the landing would take place without a hitch.

"Friends," Kuiper said when everyone was present in the small cubicle of the chartroom, "let's take a look at the situation so you'll know exactly what is ahead of you and what you're expected to do. Here . . . " He unrolled a chart on the table and weighted it down to keep it flat. It was marked *Stono and North Edisto Rivers.* "I've decided not to put you ashore on Folly Island," he continued, "as we've had persistent westerly winds, it's low tide, and the entrance to the Stono River is badly shoaled. I'm unfamiliar with the area and I don't want to risk running aground. So we're going in . . . here." He indicated a river estuary, well buoyed, marked *North Edisto River*. "The channel, as you can see, is nice and deep—and look at this . . . " He indicated a sandbank to the north with the ominous notation *Breakers*. "We don't want to mess with those in the open. So, here we go: upriver, nice and easy—" the compasses followed the course—"until we get to this buoy here, where we veer to starboard and enter this waterway . . . " It was a narrow tributary marked *Bohicket Creek*. "As you can see, I'll have plenty of water under the keel right up to here and room to maneuver. At this point, we lower the gangways and proceed as planned. To take you ashore in those sheltered waters is going to be a breeze. From here, you proceed on foot to this hamlet called Rockville, a distance of less than a mile. I'm sorry I can't offer you a road this time, it's swampland, but we'll put you on firm ground. Once you're in Rockville, you proceed as planned: arouse the town, while I sail for Charleston at flank speed to alert the newspapers and the radio stations. Now, Mrs. Goldstein, Mr. Jablonski—are your people ready?"

"Absolutely," Mr. Jablonski said.

"Doctor?"

"All I need is five minutes' notice. And, of course, Meyer's help."

"Meyer?" Kuiper asked. "Are the booms ready to bring up the stretchers from the hospital?"

"Yes."

"All right, then." Kuiper looked at his watch. "I make it twenty-three minutes past eight. God willing, we'll drop anchor in Bohicket Creek at about four-fifteen tomorrow morning. It will be dark, we'll show no lights, and this time we must avoid sounds as well. The key to success will be to get you ashore with nobody any the wiser. After that, it's up to you. Understood?"

They nodded and muttered agreement.

"Well, now let each of us go and plead with our God."

Silently, they trooped out of the chartroom.

2

Star of Peace approached the South Carolina coast at half-speed
under cover of darkness. It was a moonless night, ideal for the
operation. No wind, the sea as calm as a lake but for a low swell
heaving in from the northeast.

Everything and everyone was ready; this was what they had
rehearsed for all these weeks. The boat passengers were lined up
in single file on the boat deck, those headed for the rafts in the
catwalks on both port and starboard side; the gangways were
ready to be lowered, the rafts ready to be jettisoned.

Hendrik, who with Vinkemans was attending the sick on
their stretchers on the boat deck, saw a white buoy light flash in
the distance, once every four seconds, and behind it a red one. He
felt an incredulous elation. They had made it! There wasn't a soul
in sight; an inlet glinted in the dark between two low, dark
headlands. This seemed to be all there was to it: just take the ship
into sheltered waters an hour before daybreak on a Sunday morning while everyone was asleep, lower the gangways—

Suddenly, a siren howled, four whooping bleeps. A searchlight flashed on, flooding the boat deck with a harsh glare. A
metallic voice bellowed, "Stop all engines! This is the United
States Coast Guard! Prepare to be boarded! Lower Jacob's ladder
over starboard!"

The engine-room telegraph rang out, the engine stopped, the
vibration ceased. An eerie silence fell over the ship. No panic, no
commotion—nobody said a word, everybody stayed exactly
where they were, motionless, speechless. Then the captain called
through the megaphone, "Passengers! Return to your quarters in
an orderly fashion! We will not be landing this morning! I will
keep you informed as soon as I have more information! Now
please return to your quarters! Thank you!" After a short pause,
he added, "I'm sorry."

The passengers responded with admirable composure. The
single files that had been waiting on the boat deck and catwalks

turned around and headed for the holds. Hendrik and Vinkemans saw to the safe lowering of the stretchers. Then Hendrik heard the splashing of oars and saw, in the eerie glare of the searchlight, a rowboat with seven or eight men approach the ship. The light glinted on rifles.

A few minutes later, a surprisingly young officer climbed over the rail on starboard. He was dressed in white shirt and shorts; the top of his cap was protected by a waterproof cover; around his waist he wore a belt with a pistol in a holster. He saluted, and addressed Hendrik among the silent group watching his arrival. "Are you the captain, sir?"

"No, I'm the ship's surgeon. I'll take you to the captain."

"Thank you, much obliged." He sounded apologetic and rather insecure.

Hendrik guided him up the stairs to the lower bridge. The ship was silent, everybody seemed to be holding their breath; the only sound in the stillness of the morning was the hiss of steam from the safety valve, a white plume in front of the stack, blown landward, dissolving in the blue of the dawn.

The captain was awaiting their arrival. The officer saluted again. "Lieutenant Junior Grade Higgins, U.S. Coast Guard, sir. I'm executive officer of the cutter *Trygona*. My orders are to stop you, as you are in the three-mile zone. You are requested to remain in international waters. My orders are to inform you that you will be under constant observation, day and night, and that each time you enter the three-mile zone you will be ordered to return to international waters." He sounded as if he had learned the speech by heart and was relieved to have brought it off without hitches.

Kuiper received it with equanimity. "Thank you, Lieutenant," he said. "I'll take note of that. Are you returning to the shore, may I ask?"

"No, sir. We have orders to stay with you. Why?" The lieutenant, obviously relieved that it had all gone so smoothly, sounded pleasant enough.

"I have a letter to be mailed. Could someone do that for me? I don't have a stamp for it."

"Oh, that we'll be happy to provide," the lieutenant said eagerly. "I'll see to it that it's mailed at our earliest opportunity."

"Thank you. It's for South America. If you'd send it airmail?"

"Oh, certainly. By all means." The officer took the letter, put it in his breast pocket, saluted and said, "Captain, it was a pleasure. Now if you would kindly double back and stay in international waters, everything will be hunky-dory."

As the lieutenant turned to go, Kuiper said, "May I ask you for one more service? Would you send that letter special delivery? I'll be happy to pay for it."

"Captain, no need; of course the Coast Guard will be delighted. I mean, we all regret this, Captain. I mean, personally, I do. So, please. I'll be delighted. Airmail, special delivery. It will probably be tomorrow or the day after. Any other mail I can take?"

"Not for me," Kuiper said. "But thank you for the offer. I'll ask around. Should there be some mail next time—"

The lieutenant gave him a hard look. "Better not, Captain. Take my advice: don't play games. We're not looking for any trouble, but we don't kid around. *Trygona* is used to this kind of work, she used to hunt bootleggers during Prohibition. You may lose sight of us, Captain, we'll never lose sight of you. So . . . " He looked as if he wanted to say something else, thought better of it, saluted smartly, made an about-turn and marched back to the Jacob's ladder.

It seemed a dispiriting anti-climax. The whole thing was so bland. No dramatic confrontation between right and wrong; not a word about the passengers and the tragic fate now awaiting them; just the ready smile of the relieved young lieutenant, the letter in the breast pocket, the promise of an airmail stamp. Hendrik watched him as he nimbly descended the ladder, jumped into the launch and was rowed away by his boarding party toward the Coast Guard cutter, a long white ghost in the daybreak.

Kuiper called through his megaphone, "Mrs. Goldstein! Mr. Jablonski! Doctor! Meyer! To my cabin, please!"

The engine-room telegraph rang; the ship began to vibrate

again; black smoke belched from the stack. *Star of Peace* slowly gathered speed, swung around and headed for the sunrise.

3

They gathered in the cabin, a dejected little group. The only one seemingly unaffected by what had happened was the captain.

He reported the officer's message to the passengers; after allowing it to sink in, he continued, "I'm not prepared to take this development as final. I have written a letter to the legal attaché of the Embassy in Montevideo, in which I ask her to alert American public opinion. No doubt she will do so at once. In the meantime, we are going to be tracked by the Coast Guard day and night. I'll stay outside the three-mile limit, but just, while slowly making my way north. I'll go for occasional dashes inland to keep the pot boiling; so, be prepared for us to be stopped and boarded a few more times. My bet is that the Americans will become so used to the game that they'll get over-confident. Further north, New England way, there'll be morning fog this time of year. That may give us a chance to slip through and effect a landing. By then, the American public will be alerted to your presence by the Embassy. So, take heart. All is not lost."

"What happens if the American public is alerted but not aroused, Captain?" Mrs. Goldstein asked calmly.

Kuiper looked at her thoughtfully. "Mrs. Goldstein, as it is clearly God's will that you shall be given your freedom with dignity, we must believe that He'll provide us with the means to obey it. If we can't do that, we might as well head back to Hamburg now."

She looked at him for a moment in a way that to Hendrik seemed oddly like pity, then she said, "Yes, Captain."

They left. Hendrik hesitated, then left with them; he could not face staying alone with Kuiper at that moment. Overcome by dejection, he wandered over to the port wing of the lower bridge to watch the receding coastline, the end of their hopes.

"Doctor, could I speak to you for a moment?"

It was Vinkemans. He sounded oddly formal. "Yes, Vinkemans. What is it?"

"I suggest you ask Mrs. Goldstein for more nursing volunteers."

The way in which the man said it gave Hendrik the feeling that something was wrong. Vinkemans stood there, prim and professional as always in his crisp, clean whites, but there was a change. "Why?"

"It's obvious that the captain may go through the motions for a while, but ultimately he's going to have to take the passengers back to Germany."

"So?"

"I cannot handle a return voyage to Germany with these people. I couldn't possibly face it. I wish to inform you that if the captain decides to return to Hamburg, I shall leave the ship."

"Leave the ship? How?"

"I'll take one of the rafts and make my way to the coast."

Hendrik gazed at the man in disbelief. "You can't be serious, Vinkemans! That's crazy! And if these people have to go back, that will be when they'll need you most of all!"

"I cannot face it. I'm sorry. We all have our limitations. I cannot face taking these people back to Germany. I simply can't. I wanted you to know that, so you can make your arrangements before—before the moment comes."

"But you can't just toss a raft overboard and jump after it! You'd drown!"

The man's cavernous face took on an expression Hendrik had never seen on it before. "I'd rather drown, Doctor, than accompany these people to their death."

Hendrik shook his head. "Vinkemans, you're nuts. You can't walk out on me just like that! The patients—"

Someone came running, it was Mrs. Hoflein. "*Doktor! Herr Doktor! Frau Schlachter* . . . Quick, come quick . . . !"

"What's the matter? Hallucinating again?"

"Oh, yes, oh, yes! But it's very bad this time. She *sees* her, she *sees* the little child. She's running up and down the aisles, calling her name. *Herr Doktor,* please come!"

"Very well, Mrs. Hoflein. I'll be right there." The woman ran back toward the hold. "You see, Vinkemans," he said, "what you'd be leaving me with? If the message comes down from the bridge that we're headed back for Hamburg, there'll be a hell of a lot more people running up and down those aisles. You can't leave me to face that alone. Sorry—you simply can't." With that, he turned away and went to the infirmary to collect his bag.

Vinkemans, of all people! If he'd had to make a guess as to who'd be the last to crack up under the strain, it would have been his melancholy medic. Of course it was nonsense, of course he would stay; but somehow Vinkemans' little speech had been more alarming than the young lieutenant's.

4

Little Hansi Kramer turned up just as Tovah was trying to put Mrs. Schlachter to bed after Hendrik had given her an injection. Poor, addled woman, she was in such a pitiful state that Tovah did not want to make her a spectacle for gawking five-year-olds. "Go away, Hansi," she said. "Go and play. Gretchen is organizing a game in the children's corner."

The little girl eyed her solemnly, then suddenly stuffed a small ball of paper into her hand. "Yitzhak said I had to give it to you *quietly,*" she whispered with the penetrating whisper of the unschooled conspirator; then she skipped off down the aisle toward the children's corner.

"What did she mean?" asked Mrs. Schlachter suspiciously. "What are you keeping from me? What are they *doing* to Lieschen?" There was nothing for it, Tovah had to open the crumpled paper in the presence of the old woman and read the words aloud. *We must meet as soon as possible, usual place, Yitzhak.* She did not read the rest: *Keep this to yourself—important.* But Mrs. Schlachter said, "Give it here! Show it to me! I want to *see* what it says!"

"You didn't show your love letters around when you were my age, did you?" Tovah countered.

"Ah—" Either old Mrs. Schlachter became sentimental or the injection was taking hold; in any case, she acquiesced and lay down on her bunk.

Tovah covered her with the blanket. "Now—isn't that better? Aren't you more comfortable now?"

"Love . . . " Mrs. Schlachter said; her voice, which had been strident, was now soft and sad. "Love letters . . . " She closed her eyes; tears trickled down her cheeks and ran into her ears, but she seemed unaware of them.

Tovah stayed with her a short while; the urgency of Yitzhak's note was so compelling that she left the sleeping old woman sooner than she would otherwise have done. She climbed the ladder to the deck and emerged into the wind and the sunlight of a radiant summer day.

There were few people on deck; on her way to the forecastle, she glanced at the distant shore and the white man-o'-war with the gun on the foredeck sailing between them and the coast. Only now, as she hurried along the deck to their meeting place, did the magnitude of the calamity penetrate to her. How many ships did the American Navy have? There must be hundreds! Even if the captain managed to outwit this one and shake it off, there would be a fleet of others ready to bar their way next time they tried to sneak ashore. If there was a next time.

Yitzhak was waiting for her, squatting beside the anchor winch, his curly hair whisked by the wind. "Hello," he said. "What kept you?"

"Mrs. Schlachter," she replied, sitting down next to him on the cold deck.

"Don't do that," he said. "You'll get cystitis. Sit on your heels like I do."

"What do you know about things like cystitis?"

"I plan to be a doctor," he said. "And I have a hypochondriac mother."

"Well? What's up?"

He looked at her thoughtfully. She could not read his gold-flecked eyes. Then he said, "Philip has been kicked."

"Kicked? By whom?"

"By one of the sailors. The one with the beard."

"When?"

"As we were being 'directed' back into the hold."

"But *why?*"

"To make him hurry up. 'Move along, you little Jew bastard.' That's what the man said, according to Philip. In other words, the epidemic has started. It's surprising that it took so long."

"But why should one man, who may have just been upset or angry—"

"Tovah . . . " He put a hand on hers. "Don't do what we all did in Mannheim after the night of the broken glass: try to find excuses for them because we couldn't face the truth. Now that we have been turned back by the Americans, anti-Semitism is going to be rampant among the crew. You've seen plenty of early signs yourself."

"But just because one sailor, in a moment of stress—and old Mr. Davelaar . . . "

"Tovah," he said patiently, "it's not just one sailor. It's not just old Mr. Davelaar. Haven't you seen it happen in Germany? Kicking and shoving and cursing us and calling us Jew bastards and stinking Yids will be normal behavior from now on."

"But I don't understand! Why now?"

"Because there is no hope left. No way out. They start kicking and cursing us because they see no way out. And they hate *us* for it. They want to be rid of us. And now they have decided that, they want to get it over with. 'Let's take the Jew bastards back to Germany, where they belong.' Where we should have been taken in the first place, if Mr. Davelaar had had his way in Montevideo."

She looked away and gazed at the sea. Then she decided to say it. "There is another solution."

He remained silent for a while, then he said, "Don't be silly."

"We might prevail on the captain to take us to Palestine."

"To where?"

"It's the only place in the world where people will welcome us."

He shook his head. "Even if he were prepared to do it, Palestine is in the hands of the British. They're as determined to keep Jews out as the Americans and the rest are. They have trouble enough with the local Arabs because of the Zionists; they're not about to admit a few hundred more of us."

"The British don't matter; the Jews do. When we land, we'll get help from people ashore. I have a cousin called Yakov who is in Palestine. He's the one who told me about Masada. The moment he knows that a ship with Jews is heading for Palestine, he'll find a way to get us ashore. He and his friends will take care of the British. He'll tell us where to go, he'll arrange it all . . . "

Again, he put his hand on hers. "Tovah," he said, "even if all you say is true, it can never happen."

"Why not?"

"Do you think old Davelaar or the sailor who kicked Philip will be ready to sail this ship to Palestine, with all the risks involved, without getting paid a cent? That's where the rub is. We're costing them money. The captain must have counted on delivering us in Montevideo and then getting another cargo. Now he's messing about, trying to put us ashore; finally, he'll have to take us back to Germany, and all that without the crew earning a cent." He shook his head. "No. All we can do is look after ourselves. Form some kind of defense league against more beatings."

"And then?" she asked, angry with him because he was right.

"Then—Masada. Fight to the death." He smiled. "I know what you're going to ask: fight with what?"

She saw it in her mind's eye: the drawer Hendrik had pulled out of the desk in Montevideo, spilling its contents on the floor.

She turned toward him. "Are you serious about Masada?"

"Why?"

"I know where there's a gun."

CHAPTER SIX

I

Cynthia Vesters squealed in a toe-tingling spasm of ecstasy which started the slow-pulsing spiral to delicious disintegration. Then the doorbell rang. Dan cursed with a vehemence and an inventiveness that surprised her; he had seemed such a controlled young lawyer. The bell went on ringing; someone must be leaning with his finger on the button. "You'd better go and see who that is," she said. "I'm hardly in a condition to answer doorbells."

He cursed again, withdrew rather brusquely and strode to the door, suddenly looking frail and insecure in his nakedness. "*Quien es?*" he asked, before opening it.

A voice shouted something in the passage.

"An express letter for you, registered," Dan said. "Want me to sign for it?"

She giggled. "You're the one with the pen."

He gave vent to another juicy American cussword and grabbed his pants off the chair. After pulling them on, hopping about, he took a pen from his jacket and went to open the door. He signed something, slammed the door shut, brought the letter to her and tossed it onto her stomach. "Don't keep him waiting," he said.

"Who do you mean?"

"Whoever it is you laid in the U.S. Coast Guard."

Indeed the letter bore the stamp of the American Coast Guard. She turned it over and said, "My God."

"That must have been an interesting experience."

Quickly, she tore open the letter and read.

"Well?"

"He wants me to alert American public opinion," she said.

"Is it a proposal?"

"Don't be a bloody ass! This is serious. As a Jew, you should be sensitive to this."

"I should?"

She looked at him over the edge of the letter. He had taken off his pants again and stood, angry and frail, in the slanting light of the winter sun that streamed in through the bay window. He was the most interesting, most exciting lover; maybe the anger went with the frailty. "Don't be childish," she said. "The man who wrote this is risking his ship, all he has in the world to keep two hundred and fifty Jews from being taken back to Germany. The U.S. Coast Guard intercepted him when he tried to smuggle them ashore."

"Where?"

She looked at the postmark. "Charleston, South Carolina. Now he wants me to alert U.S. public opinion."

"Why you?"

"It's a Dutch vessel. He tried to disembark his immigrants here in Montevideo, but their visas were forgeries and they were expelled. All except one: a sick old woman who was taken to a hospital; she was later put on a plane by Monteiro and returned to Germany. I was sent to investigate. In our conversation, I happened to mention that, theoretically, American public opinion was the only hope his passengers had in this hemisphere."

"That was pretty irresponsible of you, dear girl," he said. "I'd keep that from your ambassador, if I were you. You might find yourself out on your ear." He went to get his cigarettes and lit one with her lighter; his hand was shaking.

She stared at him, frowning. "What are you so mad about, all of a sudden? Is it because I mentioned you're a Jew?"

He angrily tossed the lighter back onto the glass table with a clatter. "I am *not* a Jew! I'm an American! That's what makes me so goddam mad! When it comes to the crunch, when there's anything really serious to discuss, the first thing you hear is 'Ah, you're a Jew, so you'll understand,' or 'As a Jew, you should know.' I'm sick of it! My parents were Jewish, sure; but in America everybody's parents have been something else—Yugoslav, Dutch, Norwegian, Spanish . . . Why the hell must I be pursued for the rest of my life by the very word 'Jew' the moment I'm called on to become involved in something? So can it, will you? I don't care what goddam letters you get, I don't care what kind of a plot you're involved in: let's fuck!"

"That, dear love, is hardly the way to rekindle the flame of ardor," she said good-naturedly. "Toss me a cigarette, there's a dear."

He threw her the pack. "Sorry if I sound pissed off, but I *am*. It's not your fault, I know you don't mean it, but by God! It drives me up the wall! *That's* why the whole miserable comedy continues!" He retrieved the lighter and snapped it on to light her cigarette.

"Thank you, darling," she said soothingly. "Tell me, what comedy?"

"The scandal! The cancer!" He paced up and down. "That's why I'm not admitted to clubs, hotels! And I don't *give* a damn, I don't *care* about religion, about Israel, about—about my parents being Jews! I'm an American, I act like an American, I think like an American, and I'll be goddamned if I'll carry the curse of my parents for the rest of my days! I'll be damned! How did you find out, by the way, that I was a Jew? Do I look that Jewish? Why not an Italian? Who told you?"

She blew a plume of smoke in his direction and said with a smile, "Nobody. But Italian men weigh about half an ounce more than you do, sweetheart."

"Oh, for God's sake! Every other American man has been circumcised for hygienic reasons! Haven't you noticed? Am I your first lover?"

She sat up in bed and pulled up the sheet to cover her nakedness in an unconscious gesture. "Let's talk about the man's passengers, shall we? I'm not appealing to you as a Jew, I'm appealing to you as a lawyer. So calm down, stop taking the whole thing as a personal insult and try to concentrate professionally for a moment on the problem of a ship out there with two hundred and fifty German Jews on board, expelled from their homeland, who were slipped forged visas for Uruguay and were turned back as a result. Now they can't find any other country to admit them, except, of course, Germany. The captain of the ship is reluctant to take them back, as well he might be."

"And so you suggested the United States."

"I told him, merely as a legal hypothesis, that in order to get them admitted into the United States he would have to smuggle them ashore in the full light of public opinion. Of course that is nonsense, and I told him so."

"Did you also tell him it was illegal?"

"Of course. Chapter and verse. But somehow he got to me. It may be quixotic, but you have to admire the man. He's hell-bent on finding sanctuary for those people, because his faith won't allow him to take them back to Germany. I must say it was refreshing to come across someone, of whichever faith, prepared to practice it instead of just preaching. The least I could do was give him my best advice, whether it would make me popular with the ambassador or not. Compared to his, my risk was so small as to be embarrassing."

"Very noble and romantic, but cruel and stupid."

"Be that as it may: I have a certain responsibility in this and I want to help him if I can. Now that he's been stopped by the Coast Guard, I think indeed the only help I can give is by getting his story into the American papers. Make a real scandal of it. Put pressure on the government, on U.S. Immigration."

"No. That's not the way."

"You have a better suggestion?"

"Let me think." He went and stood in front of the window, smoking, a slender silhouette against the wintry trees, their branches glinting with rain.

"Maybe not quite that close to the window, if you don't mind."

"Sorry." He turned and came back into the room. "Don't

tackle this from the publicity angle." He ground out his cigarette in the ashtray. "If you do that, you'll only put the politicians' backs up. The way to go about it would be to put on pressure through the lobby."

"Which one?"

"The Jewish one. If you were to alert some key people in the Anti-Defamation League, you might get some action. If you bring in the newspapers and start a public stink, all you'd do is box in the members of Congress by arousing their constituency with all its prejudices, and limit their political options."

"Okay. How do I go about it? Or we, rather."

He thought it over, drawing deeply on a new cigarette. Then he looked straight at her and said, "Let's get one thing straight: I won't touch it."

She couldn't believe her ears. "Dan, you're kidding! You mean—you refuse to be involved?"

"I refuse to be identified with it in Washington. It's your baby, you handle it. I'll give you my advice, but I will *not* have my name mentioned in connection with this at all. Is that clear?"

"Yes," she said. "Quite clear."

He sensed her contempt. "I know what this must seem like to you, but it's not as crass as it sounds. There's a lot of unspoken anti-Semitism in the diplomatic service. If I felt I could really help those people, I might say the hell with it, but I don't think the guy has a ghost of a chance of putting those people ashore. And as to his doing so in the full light of public opinion, well, the less said about that, the better. All right, I'll give you a few names and addresses. But I forbid you to mention my name. Is that understood?"

She felt like telling him to get the hell out. She had the feeling she suddenly did not know this man at all. She needed time to think it over, to overcome her sudden sense of revulsion. He had seemed so original, sensitive . . . But she mustn't let the young captain, that blue-eyed innocent, become the victim of her personal emotions. The man needed help, and Dan was bright enough and influential enough to help, if only she could prevail on him to do so. "Come on, darling," she said, with an effort, "you don't mean that! You're not going to let me flummox around when you have all the information right at your fingertips!"

"I'll give you names, I'll give you addresses, tomorrow. That's all I *have* to give. That, and the warning that you're flogging a dead horse. No lobby, however powerful, will be able to force the government to recognize those people as political refugees and give them asylum."

"But, darling—"

"This is 1939, darling. We are into appeasement of Hitler and the Nazis, since Munich. And now the Germans are acting up again over the Polish Corridor, everyone is walking on eggs. Anyhow, nobody is going to believe that those Jews would suffer a worse fate back in Germany than the Negro in the South. The campaign you're planning doesn't stand a chance because you have no case. The worst crime that can be said to have been perpetrated on those people is that they were sold visas for Uruguay which turned out to be forgeries. Tough. No, my dear. You tell your captain to stop messing around and take them back to Germany. I'll give you those names if you still want them, but if you follow my advice, tell him to go back."

"But *you*, Dan? What do *you* believe? Don't *you* know what's going to happen to those people when they get back to Germany?"

"Yes, I do. They'll be forced to live in ghettos. They won't be allowed to use public transportation. They won't be admitted to restaurants, hotels, cinemas, theaters, concert halls. And because they don't have black faces to set them apart, they'll have to wear yellow stars on their coats. You try and raise a stink about that in the United States, and wait for the N.A.A.C.P. to start screaming: 'Why get upset about the Jews of Germany suffering the same fate as the Negro in the South?' What gave you the idea, by the way, that these people will be lynched the moment they arrive back in Germany? Do you know something I don't know?"

She looked at him glowering at her. Maybe he was just neurotic about the whole Jewish situation, but it seemed incredible that he had not even read the information all embassies received on conditions in Germany. She decided not to goad him any longer. "Oh, well, the usual stuff," she said. "We get regular reports from Berlin. There's an awful lot of brutality and organized violence against the Jews. And that's not likely to get any better."

"Well—" he ground out his cigarette—"I'll send you that list of names tomorrow. Now, will that get the Ancient Mariner out of our bed? Or is it a young mariner?"

"Dan," she said, getting up with the sheet held in front of her, "I don't think I can, not right now. You haven't seen those sad creatures. I have."

He smiled. "I said you were a sensitive girl."

"Do you want to shower first or shall I?"

"Be my guest," he said, and returned to the window to look at the trees.

In the shower, she thought about the Jewish lobby and the list of names Dan would be sending the following day. God, it would all take forever. And meanwhile that gallant young skipper and his cargo of refugees were sailing north along the American coast, waiting for her to perform a miracle. There had to be something she could do. Someone, somewhere. Wait a minute! She stopped, staring at her reflection in the mirror. What about that naval attaché who'd left for Washington four months ago? What was his name? Van der Kamp. Frans. Was it Frans or Fritz? Frans. She should get him on the phone, or send him a note by pouch. As the U.S. Coast Guard was involved, they would undoubtedly have notified the Dutch Embassy, which would mean Frans van der Kamp. Come to think of it, he'd been very attentive at the time and quite unwilling to accept that she and Dan were serious about each other. He'd be very much cheered to hear from her after all this time.

She wrote the letter after Dan had left, sitting at the glass table in her robe. Frans . . . Now, was she sure it was Frans? Yes, sure. Blond, little mustache, pale blue eyes . . . 'Princess,' he had called her, which hadn't helped. She would have to ladle on the schmaltz. But why not? She had been unable to help those poor

people as a lawyer; who knows, she might be able to help them
as a woman.

*Dear Frans, I've thought so much about you since we last met.
These past four months seem a long time now I look back on them.
Is there any hope of your coming back to Montevideo? I may—just
may!—be transferred to Washington. (But please don't mention this
to anyone, I'm telling you in the strictest confidence!)*

*The reason why I am writing this particular letter is that I
received an appeal from a certain Captain Kuiper, Joris, of the Dutch
freighter "Star of Peace," now off the coast of North America . . .*

She summarized the situation, assuming that by the time the
letter reached him he would have been put into the picture by the
Coast Guard; then she settled down with determination to the
rather repulsive but necessary job of seduction.

For it to be successful, she should have a fairly clear picture
of the guy in mind. Was he a heroic, romantic character at heart?
Was he a man of principle? As she remembered him, he was
rather a stick-in-the-mud, a bit of a martinet. There might be no
point in appealing to his humanity if it would involve breaking
rules or 'the tradition of the Navy.' And what *could* he do, after
all? Nothing, other than convince the young captain that he
should take his passengers back to Germany without delay, that
all further efforts to land them illegally would in essence be cruel.

But as she sat there, trying to picture the tall, blond, rather
vacuous man she had known briefly in what now seemed gray
antiquity, his very blandness enabled her to create a 'Frans van
der Kamp' who became the antithesis of Dan: solid, reliable,
unemotional and—above all!—no chip on his shoulder. Quite the
reverse: in her experience, a lack of inner security was as rare in
the Navy as a lack of the sense of smell in a dog. Well, let's give
it a whirl.

*I know it sounds absolutely silly and feminine and rather like "a
princess" who is long on emotions and short on brains, but I can't
be at peace with myself without telling you how deeply moved I was
by those people and their miserable fate, and by the man who set out
on this idiotic but heroic expedition. I wouldn't know how to help him*

from here, as he asks me to do; I have some contacts in the American Embassy . . . On second thoughts, she crossed that out. *In my fantasies (which admittedly are totally silly and unrealistic) I see you helping the man and those poor wretches condemned to be returned to Germany. Silly, isn't it? I know that you aren't in a position to help even if you wished to, which I'm sure you do. What could the Naval Attaché with the Dutch Embassy in Washington do to prevail upon the Americans to grant them political asylum? Despite the noble phrases which may be uttered by the politicians, political reality will force the guy to return his passengers to Germany. It's his own ship, he bears the cost of the operation himself, it'll probably cost him all he has.*

Dear Frans, I'm sorry! I suddenly feel I shouldn't have written to you at all. I should have written to you, of course, but not this irresponsible, thoughtless letter. But, quite frankly, you might as well know exactly which kind of person you're dealing with. Anyhow, just for—may I say "the hell of it"? I usually don't use these terms . . .

This she crossed out also. To ladle on the schmaltz was all right, but now she was turning it into a parody. With all these crossings out, she would have to rewrite the letter; that might not be a bad idea anyhow. On second thoughts, why write at all? Why put herself under an obligation toward that pale-eyed, mustachioed martinet, without a rational hope that it would make any difference to the fate of those people? It occurred to her that the real impulse for her writing might be anger at Dan. If Frans only knew—and she hoped his name was Frans—the letter was written literally on the rebound. Or was it? She was sincerely concerned about those poor people, but for her to write to the Dutch naval attaché in Washington asking for help was ludicrous.

Even so, she rewrote the letter, made it more factual; when she was through, she decided it still was impetuous, emotional and pointless. She was about to throw it into the wastebasket when she decided to toss a coin for it. Heads, send it; tails, tear it up.

It was tails; even so, the next morning she stuck it into an envelope without rereading it, marked it PERSONAL and sent it by airmail, not by diplomatic pouch. After all, there were limits.

2

During the rest of August 1939, *Star of Peace* sailed northward, dead slow, along the eastern seaboard of the United States, small black smudge in the dazzling vastness of sea and sky. The weather was radiant, cloudless, with no more than a gentle breeze from the west during daylight hours, from the east at night. But the long Atlantic swell was always there, like the somnolent breathing of a colossal body, slowly swelling hills of transparent water marbled by foam, making the old ship plunge her blunt bow into their slopes, rise ponderously, reach for the sky and plunge back with a laboring corkscrew motion that set the tables in the catwalks scraping and sent a wave of groans, creakings, squeaks and moans through the innards of the vessel. The passengers had improvised their awnings again with bedsheets and the tarpaulins the bo'sun had lent them; seen from the bridge, it looked like a village market once more. To the occasional Coast Guard plane circling overhead, *Star of Peace* must have looked like a covered wagon slowly rolling and pitching its stubborn way across the trackless sea.

Kuiper was waiting for an opportunity to dash inland, but, throughout the sun-blazed days and star-bright nights, the low white Coast Guard cutter *Trygona* with her two buff stacks and cannon on the foredeck hovered nearby, trundling along at *Star*'s pace but full of poised power that could whisk her up to forty knots at a moment's notice. To outsail or outwit that seasoned hunter, Kuiper knew, was impossible. He would have to wait for the weather to help him. But day after day it looked as if there had never been a cloud in the sky over the Atlantic Ocean and never would be one. His only hope, under these conditions, was fog.

Early one morning in late August, off Manasquan, New Jersey, there came a sudden patch of it. Wybrands was on watch; he rushed to call the captain. During the past days, there had been more rehearsals to keep the passengers on their toes and their spirits up; now those hours of practice stood them in good stead.

Kuiper was out of his bunk in a flash; the passengers were alerted; within minutes and in total silence, they were lined up for disembarkation. Kuiper extinguished the running lights and headed *Star* toward the shore.

The fog was thick; he could barely see a ship's length ahead of him. But the beach was a mere three miles away, twenty minutes' sailing time; the tide was low, so even if he ran *Star* aground, he need only wait for high water to free the ship.

As they made for the shore, the fog cleared briefly for a moment. Glancing quickly behind him, Kuiper saw with a sense of elation that *Trygona* was nowhere in sight. For the first time, he had managed to shake the white ghost that had haunted them. The tension on board rose as they moved through the swirls of mist; he took the megaphone to order the gangways to be lowered. Then, as he drew breath to speak, there came the howl of the siren, the bright moon of a searchlight in the fog. The metallic voice bawled over the starboard, "Stop engines! This is the United States Coast Guard! Prepare to be boarded! Lower Jacob's ladder over starboard!"

The passengers wailed in dismay. The engine-room telegraph rang out; the vibration stopped; *Star of Peace* stopped dead in the water. From the cotton-wool world of the fog came the rhythmic splashing of oars; the silhouette of the rowboat and its gun-toting crew emerged into the two-dimensional world. How on earth could the captain of the cutter have spotted them when Kuiper himself had been unable to see one ship's length ahead of his bow? Well, Lieutenant Higgins had said it during his first visit off the North Edisto River: 'You may lose sight of us, Captain, we'll never lose sight of you.'

The lieutenant, spruce, trim and as full of poised power as *Trygona* herself, climbed the Jacob's ladder, stepped onto the deck, answered Kuiper's greeting with a smart salute and, in the privacy of the cabin, reeled off his little litany once more. "My orders are to inform you that you find yourself within the three-mile zone. You are requested to withdraw and remain in international waters . . . " After that he had a Dutch gin, asked politely if there was any more mail for him to collect; then he said casually, "By the way, Captain, the Coast Guard has been advised of the formation of a Jewish committee ashore which will press for admission of your passengers as political refugees. Under the circumstances, it seems a sensible idea for you to stand off the three-mile zone without further trying to effect a landing, and just wait for the outcome of the committee's efforts. This is off the record—I just thought you'd like to know."

It came as a total surprise. Kuiper had decided long ago that his letter to Miss Vesters had been a futile gesture, if, indeed, it had been mailed at all. "Will they contact me by wireless?" he asked.

"I'm sure they will, in due course," Lieutenant Higgins said amiably. "And if they should have difficulty raising you, we'll be happy to pass the message on. We keep a twenty-four-hour radio watch."

By the time Higgins left, the sun had burned off the haze and there was the glorious summer day again, radiant, peaceable, the sea shimmering, pristine, smooth and bland. As the ship headed back out to sea, Kuiper called all passengers together on the foredeck; he stood above them on the bridge, the crowd of faces peered up at him as it had in Hamburg. The long, low ghost of *Trygona* hovered nearby; binoculars were probably being trained on him and the sound of his voice could be picked up in the still morning air. Better not use the megaphone.

"I am sorry," he said. "I realize this has been a tough setback for you, so I'm happy to tell you that I received word this morning that a Jewish committee has been formed ashore which will vigorously pursue all possible avenues to bring about your admission as political refugees—"

The passengers cheered. He was less optimistic about the outcome of the committee's intervention than they were, but it helped; any news that cheered them was a bonus.

"However," he continued, "we must not rely on any quick action by any group, no matter how sympathetic. For reasons which I'm sure you'll understand, we cannot remain at sea indefinitely. Fortunately, we have two other possibilities. First, I'll go on cruising north along the coast at our present speed, and if an opportunity to effect a landing presents itself, I'll try again. The opportunities will become more frequent as we get further north, where long periods of fog are common at this time of year. However, by the time we have passed Nantucket, both our fuel and our provisions will be virtually exhausted. At that moment, this ship will be dead in the water. When we're drifting helpless in the open sea, the American authorities will have no choice but to send a tugboat and tow us into port. Once that happens, I'll alert all shore stations within reach of my radio and make your presence known. So don't lose heart. Thank you."

For a moment, he thought he had failed to convince them; then somebody started to applaud and everyone else joined in.

It made him feel like an impostor, for, although he had no idea which solution the Americans might come up with, *Trygona* and her unblinking vigil, even innocuous Lieutenant Higgins and his boyish charm had brought home to him that the odds were not in his favor. But then, anyone witnessing the agony on the cross of a frail young Jewish prophet two thousand years ago would not have placed any bets on His one day changing the face of the world. And here He was once again: frail, helpless, surrounded by Caesar's legions. Ah, yes, He *was* here, right on board *Star of Peace,* for had He not said so Himself, two thousand years ago? *Where two or three are gathered together in My name, there will I be, in the midst of them.*

In that faith, *Star* would sail on.

CHAPTER SEVEN

I

Commander Frans van der Kamp, naval attaché of the Dutch Embassy in Washington, was called in by the ambassador early on August 28. His Excellency was in a foul mood, and no wonder: the Germans were at it again, for the fourth time in as many years. First it had been the Rhineland they grabbed, then Austria, then Czechoslovakia and now they demanded the Danzig Corridor, the part of Poland that had been German up to 1919. Of course the battle of wills between Hitler and Chamberlain would end the same way it had last time, with the English and their allies giving in and granting the bully all he demanded; but while the game of bluff and bluster was going on, it was a trying time for ambassadors. His Excellency's secretary looked apprehensive as she backed toward the door, giving the commander a faint smile of either encouragement or warning, he could not determine which. "Good morning, Your Excellency," he said.

The ambassador grunted, looked at him over the half-moons of his reading glasses with an expression of dyspepsia and said, "That triple goddamned freighter captain is about to create a diplomatic incident, and I want you to forestall him."

"Er—who's that, sir?" As if he didn't know. But this was going to be a prickly one.

233

"Don't act stupid, van der Kamp," the ambassador snapped. "You know damn well who I mean, and I want you to get on to it right now, this minute. Drop everything. I don't give a damn what you're doing, drop it, get on to this and organize—well—something! Surely we can do something to stop that idiot fouling up our relations with the Americans! He . . . Well, don't let me start the day with obscenities. You take care of it, take care of him, and report to me in full when you've done it."

"Done what, Your Excellency?" van der Kamp asked blandly.

"Stopped him, goddammit, you damned ass!" The old man really had steam up this morning; it could not be just the hapless freighter captain. It must have been something in those dispatches he'd been stuffing into a desk drawer as his naval attaché was being ushered into his presence. "I don't want to know how you're going to do it, just *do* it!"

"Very good, sir." There was little else he could say at this point. "Can I bring in the U.S. Coast Guard?"

"The Coast Guard? Why? What would you bring them in for?"

"Well, sir, I thought I might need to go there myself, and unless we use the Navy, the Coast Guard would obviously be the ones to—"

"Use anyone you like! Damn it all, that's *your* job! Don't bother me with the details. Go and get that captain; have him arrested, have him certified insane, I don't care how you do it, but stop him! Do you hear me? *Stop him!*"

"Very good, sir." If there was one thing van der Kamp hated in his job, it was to be the butt of the old man's foul temper. He turned to leave.

The shrill voice stopped him on his way out. "Do it, just do it, but leave me out of it! Is that understood?"

"Indeed, sir. Once the necessary documents have been drawn up, I will bring them to you for signing."

"Don't bring me anything!" the ambassador cried furiously. "You draw up your own orders, use the authority you have, don't bother me with anything!"

"Yessir." Van der Kamp opened the door.

"If you need anybody's signature, get the consul general's!"

"Very good, sir. Would you instruct him, sir?"

"Get out!" the ambassador yelled. "Don't tell me how to run my office, get out!" Obviously, shrieking at one's subordinates had some therapeutic effect.

"Very well, sir." This time, van der Kamp was allowed to leave the room. Pity that by the time Foreign Office personnel reached ambassadorial rank, most of them were decrepit. Or, at the very least, subject to senile rages.

Back in his office, van der Kamp studied the latest reports on the movements of *Star of Peace*, furnished by the U.S. Coast Guard, District Commander New York. *At eighteen hundred EST vessel passed three miles south of Ocean Beach, Fire Island, heading east. Weather stable. No signals exchanged. Estimated fuel hours remaining: eighty-six.* Clearly, the ambassador was right. It was time for a showdown one way or the other. Van der Kamp pressed the buzzer on his desk; Havering, his A.D.C., appeared in the doorway. "Good morning, sir."

"Havering, sit down." The ensign complied, respectfully. He was young, ambitious, clear-eyed, and the hair on the crown of his head had trouble lying down. It varied with the weather; this morning, a small tuft stood bolt upright on the top of his head, giving him the look of an alert woodpecker.

"We had better start organizing a visit to *Star of Peace*," van der Kamp began. "And the time has come to activate the insanity option. For that, we need two licensed physicians; *Star*'s own ship's surgeon is not going to be enough. Have you worked out the positions of Dutch liners relative to the vessel?"

"Yessir. I have determined that as of nine hundred hours this morning—"

"I'm not interested in nine hundred hours this morning, Havering. I need to know which passenger liner with a doctor on board is closest to *Star of Peace* at, say, around noon tomorrow."

Havering wrote it in his little book. He was very proud of his little book. He brought it in each time he entered the office, like an eager dog bringing a stick. "Relative to which coordinates, sir?"

Van der Kamp swiveled his chair around to face the window. The sill was full of sparrows even at this hour, greedy little blighters, waiting for the crumbled half-doughnut due at eleven. "Well, let's work that out, Havering. The man was sighted south of Fire Island at six o'clock last night; at the speed he's been making lately, he should be somewhere off Martha's Vineyard by the same time tonight. I intend to board him tomorrow morning around six hundred at the latest. That should put him somewhere off the northern tip of Nantucket Island; there I'll tell him to double back to New York. If the Coast Guard's estimate of his remaining fuel hours is correct, he should make that comfortably. So you tell me which liner will be closest to him at twelve hundred hours August thirty-first."

Havering wrote busily in his little book. "And what would the exact position be, sir?"

"My God, man! Work it out for yourself! You know his speed. Give me the coordinates and the name of the liner and the telephone number of her New York office. I want the works, including who to contact."

"Yessir. Very good, sir." Havering wrote. "Which department would you wish to contact, sir?"

"The boss man, whoever it might be. I'll have to throw some weight around."

"Very good, sir." Havering wrote, van der Kamp asked himself what. Did he write 'Contact boss man'? He treated orders like marbles dropped on a hard floor, skittering away from him.

"When you're through, get me Commander Boswell, U.S. Coast Guard."

"Yessir." Havering wrote it down. "Anything else, sir?"

"No, you may go."

"Very well, sir. Thank you, sir."

When van der Kamp stopped him as he reached for the doorknob, he realized in a moment of double vision that he was behaving like the ambassador. "By the way, Havering: before you do anything else, get me my coffee and my doughnut."

The ensign looked at him, thunderstruck. "Right now, sir?" He sounded as if the order constituted a breach of security.

"Yes, right now. I can't stand the racket on my window sill."

Havering's face was a study. Then he said, "Yessir. Very good, sir." The way he closed the door behind him, careful not to make it click, spoke for itself.

Thoughtfully, van der Kamp gazed at the closed door; then with his key he opened the EYES ONLY drawer in his desk and took out Cynthia's letter. He read the well-known phrases again, this time without getting hung up on the personal stuff. Now, where was it? Ah, yes:

When I met the captain, I was impressed by his integrity as well as his conservativism. He is definitely not a rebel, but an earnest member of his church (probably Dutch Reformed) who has reached a point where he must either put his faith into practice or suffer a collapse of whatever being a member of a church means to a religious man.

He locked the letter away, looked up a name in the Embassy directory, dialed a number and, swinging his chair back to face the window, gazed at the sparrows. The call was answered after three rings. "Yes?" The female voice was unctuous.

"Mrs. Haldeman?"

"This is she."

"Good morning, Mrs. Haldeman. This is Commander van der Kamp speaking, naval attaché to the Embassy. Is your husband in?"

"He is in, Commander, but he's in bed. He's not feeling well. Can I take the message?"

"I'm afraid it's fairly complicated, Mrs. Haldeman. Is there any way in which I could speak to Mr. Haldeman direct?"

There was a silence during which something was decided. Then the unctuous voice said, with a chill of sharpness, "If you persist, Commander, I'll take the phone to him."

"Mrs. Ha—" Too late. There was a click and then the dial tone. Van der Kamp muttered a curse, waited awhile and dialed the number again. This time, a hoarse male voice answered.

"Pastor Haldeman?"

"Yes . . . " He did indeed sound sick, poor guy.

"This is Commander van der Kamp. I called a few moments ago . . . "

"Yes, I know. My wife pulled the phone out. She has no idea of anything mechanical. Ask her to draw a bicycle and she wonders how many wheels. What can I do for you?"

"Well, it's a situation I'd like to discuss with you in person if I may, Pastor Haldeman. It concerns a—well, don't let me try to tell you on the phone. Could I come and see you in about an hour's time? It's urgent."

"Well, certainly. Come whenever you like. I'm in bed, but there's nothing really wrong with me, quite frankly. It's my wife, you know. So you just come. I'll be glad for a bit of company. Are you going to give me a ship again?"

"Not quite, sir. But I'd like to take you out to sea for a brief sortie tomorrow morning, if that's agreeable."

"Tomorrow morning?" The old voice sounded delighted. "Well, certainly! I— Don't tell my wife, I'll tell her."

"Very well, sir. I'll see you anon."

"Yes, yes, delighted, delighted!"

Well, that was one down and about ten to go. Van der Kamp bellowed at the closed door, "Where's my coffee?"

The door sprang open and there was Havering of the anxious face. "It's brewing, sir, it's brewing!"

"And what about my call to Commander Boswell?"

"Coming, sir, coming . . . "

Ah, what it was to be young and in the Navy. The telephone rang.

"Yes? Ah, Boswell, yes. How are you this morning?"

Boswell expressed his outrage at the Krauts and their shenanigans, which put everyone on edge once again.

"Yes, I do agree. But here's a question I'd like to ask you. I'd like to board *Star of Peace* around daybreak tomorrow morning. Could you organize it? I'll probably be in the company of one other person. If I can get myself to Woods Hole or wherever by, say, suppertime, would that suit?"

Havering brought in the coffee. The sparrows chirped outside the window at the sight of the doughnut.

"Splendid! I'll wait for your call. Thanks very much."

He took a sip of his coffee; it was too hot. He swung back his chair and dialed another number.

"Rabbi Shine, please. Commander van der Kamp, Netherlands Embassy." He waited. "Ah, Rabbi Shine! Good morning. This is Commander van der Kamp. I'm about to pay a visit to *Star of Peace* and I wonder: is there anything you wish me to relay to the passengers?"

The gentle, cultured voice at the other end of the line explained at length and with audible frustration how, so far, all efforts to communicate with either the State Department or the Legislature on any meaningful level had been futile. However, there was another avenue that they were now exploring; as soon as there was anything to impart to the master of *Star of Peace* and her unfortunate passengers, he would do so by wireless.

Van der Kamp inquired politely about the new avenue; while the gentle voice explained at some length, Havering came in with a sheaf of papers, which he deposited on the desk. After concluding the conversation with some polite words of commiseration, van der Kamp picked up the papers and saw they were the *Notices to Mariners* for the current week. For some reason known only to bureaucrats, copies of this document meant for sea captains were mailed to the naval attachés of all embassies in town, to end up invariably in their wastebaskets. Being about to put to sea himself this time, however briefly, he looked through them, munching his half of the doughnut with the sparrows clamoring on the window sill. On page three, an item caught his eye.

He gazed at the page for a long while, then he swiveled his chair, faced the window and, oblivious of the rioting sparrows, finished the doughnut, lost in thought.

2

Around daybreak on August 29, the solid fog Kuiper had been waiting for came down with a vengeance. It came none too soon; they had reached Nantucket Island. The moment of truth was upon them.

There was another reason why he was glad this chance presented itself to break the spell of monotony and growing dissatisfaction. Something had changed on board; he could not put his finger on it, but there was a change, and he did not care for it. Maybe it was just a general mood of boredom and growing disillusion among the passengers; the crew quite clearly had had enough, they wanted this to be over and done with, they wanted to go home. But there was something else: an elusive disturbing element.

What could it be? Was something brewing among the crew? He had never known a mutiny, but this was probably how it must feel just before it exploded. Well, he welcomed this opportunity for action with a distinct sense of relief.

The fog was heavy and cloying, ideal for the operation he had in mind. Only, it came too late in the morning for his liking. It was so thick that, despite the hour, it was barely tinged with the blue of the dawn; but the sun, once it rose, still had a lot of power, it might burn off even this heavy cloud within the hour. In any event, he had finally shaken *Trygona,* the Coast Guard cutter. He was almost sure he had seen her sneak off at dead of night, for the first time since she had attached herself to *Star.* Had she gone to bunker? If he had been sure of that, he'd have effected this landing overnight. Be that as it may, now he must act fast before she spotted him again in this fog. She had lost him momentarily, of that he was certain; he listened for the sound of her engine in the thick, cloying cloud, but there was not a whisper. She might be lying somewhere not far away, listening too. So they should execute the coming maneuver in total silence.

In a whisper, he sent Wybrands to order the passengers into the boats and to call the two representatives, the doctor, Meyer and the bo'sun to the chartroom. They arrived silently, secretly; he spoke only when the door was closed. "All right, Mrs. Goldstein, Mr. Jablonski," he said, "this is it; let's hope, third time lucky. We're right here, off the east coast of this island, close to this little township here, called Siasconset. It's not as sheltered a landing as I would've liked, but we must profit from this fog while it lasts. You won't be able to see the coast, but the men in the boats have compasses; they'll put you ashore well before the fog lifts."

"Is the drill going to be the same as before?" Mr. Jablonski asked.

"Yes. Only, we must maintain total silence. Siasconset is a seaside resort like Folly Beach. At present, it's crowded with people. Once you manage to alert the village, make everybody run out of their houses, you're safe. I have decided not to put you on the beach of the township proper, where there's a high cliff, but somewhat to the north, here, near this lighthouse. To get to the village, don't follow the beach—you'd run the risk of being spotted by the Coast Guard. Cross these low dunes here until you hit this road. There you turn left, follow the road—not slap in the middle, but on the shoulders in case of spotter planes. Then—" There was a knock on the door. He opened it to a crack.

It was Johansen in oilskins and sou'wester. "Four fathom at the lead, Captain," he whispered.

"Boats ready to go?"

"Yes."

"All right. Wybrands, you take the bridge, stop the engine, keep the lead going."

"Aye, aye, Captain." Wybrands left; Kuiper closed the door.

"Well, Mr. Jablonski, Mrs. Goldstein, here you go." He handed Jablonski the strongbox with the passports. "Remember: total silence. Not a sound. God be with us." He let the others go out first, then he followed them and tiptoed up the steps to the bridge.

The fog had turned into drizzle; he was going to need oilskins. He saw the messroom boy hovering at the bottom of the steps and whispered, "Henky! Get my foul-weather gear! It's hanging inside the door to my cabin!"

The boy scurried off.

Seen from the bridge, the preparations appeared to go smoothly. The raft passengers were lining up in the catwalks, the gangways ready to be lowered, the boats crowded with shadowy figures.

"Johansen!" He barely raised his voice.

"Aye, Captain!" The muffled voice came from the forecastle, hidden in the fog.

"Speed?"

"Dead in the water, Captain."

"Depth?"

"Five fathom three."

"Meyer!"

"Yes, Captain."

"Lower all boats."

"Aye, aye . . . "

Pulleys squealed loudly in the fog. Looking down from the port wing to check when the gangways could be lowered without endangering the descending boats, he felt a slight breath of wind. He looked up, saw the fog disperse briefly; suddenly, everything happened at once: a siren bleeped four times, a flash, a boom, the splash of a shell hitting the water.

"Captain!" Johansen shouted. "Shot across the bow!"

The effect of the warning shot, harmless in itself, was as if the ship had received a direct hit. Women screamed, children's voices streaked down the deck in the fog, transforming the ship from an orderly self-contained little world into a chaotic blur of running bodies, wailing voices, children's shrieks, shouted commands—a panic like the ones that had stricken the passengers in Hamburg and in Montevideo, reducing them to terrified cattle in pointless flight from an overwhelming malevolent force.

Kuiper ran to the wheelhouse, pulled the line of the foghorn; four hoarse bellows resounded, dulled by the fog. "Haul up boats!" he shouted.

The metallic voice barked across the water. "*Star of Peace!* Stay where you are! You'll be boarded on starboard!"

"Wybrands," Kuiper said, "let's receive them in style. Lower the starboard gangway."

"Aye, aye, Captain."

The whistle of the engine-room speaking tube squealed in the wheelhouse. Kuiper went inside, pulled the whistle out. "Yes, captain here." He put his ear to the mouthpiece.

"What the hell is going on?" Davelaar's distorted voice quacked.

"Steady as you are," Kuiper replied, "we're being boarded by the Coast Guard."

He went back onto the bridge. The sounds of panic had died down, but a wailing of women on the aft deck persisted. He was about to shout a command in that direction, a reassurance, anything to put an end to that eerie, unnerving lament; then he saw a black form standing at the top of the stairs. "Yes, Mr. Jablonski?"

"Do you wish the passengers to return to the holds, Captain?"

"If you please," he replied. "I'm sorry, Mr. Jablonski."

"Yes, Captain. I understand. Thank you for trying." The man sounded calm and composed; it must be just the women and children.

"All right, Wybrands. Let's have some light on deck."

"Aye, aye."

Wybrands switched on the lights; Kuiper saw Jablonski's wet, glistening shape pass to starboard. Where was that boy with his oilskins? He was getting soaked. "Henky!" he shouted. There was no reply.

"I'll go and have a look, Skipper," a voice said behind him. He had not heard the doctor come up.

"Thank you, I'd appreciate that."

From the starboard side came the sound of the approaching rowboat.

3

When Hendrik entered the cabin, he found it empty. He was about to go back to the bridge and watch the arrival of the Coast Guard when he heard a woman muttering close by. For a moment, he thought Mrs. Schlachter had wandered onto the lower bridge, but as he looked around, he saw no one. Then he realized the sound came from inside the cabin, and there, huddled under the table where he must have dived for cover when the shot was fired, was Henky.

Hendrik knelt beside the boy and caught a string of jumbled

words: "Mr. Davelaar's glass bowl, the kids' toys, the mate's knife, the cook's cigarette holder. Make them stop, make them stop shooting, oh Lord, oh beautiful Lord who art in heaven, and Mr. Wybrands' cufflinks, and Mr. Palstra's hair lotion . . . "

"Hey, Henky!" Hendrik shook him by the shoulder. "Stop that! Come out of there!"

But the boy went on jabbering. "I promise, I promise, but make me stop praying, oh Lord, come on, make me say amen, I beg you, make me stop this, please, please—"

"Come on! Up you get!"

Hendrik dragged him from under the table and boxed his ears. The boy cried, *"Amen!"* and burst into tears.

He was obviously hysterical, so he had better steer clear of the captain for the time being. Hendrik was due to go down into the hold to check on Mrs. Schlachter, who had taken off again; Henky could carry his bag. He took it off the table, gave it to the boy and said, "Take this, go on down into the women's hold and wait for me at the bottom of the ladder."

"No, no . . . " the boy whimpered.

"Come *on,* Henky! Get going!"

"No, no, not in the hold!" the boy cried in a panic. "Please, Doc! Not in the hold, *please!*"

"What's the matter with the hold?"

Henky burst into tears again. "You beat them!" he cried, sobbing. "You beat them Jews!"

Hendrik had been about to push him out the door; now he froze and he asked, with a cold feeling in the nape of his neck, "What are you talking about? Who is beating the Jews?"

"You!" Henky cried. "The bo'sun and Mr. Davelaar and Mr. Meyer and—and Mr. Wybrands and Mr. Davelaar and—and the bo'sun, everyone!"

"You're crazy!"

"We've been thrown back two times now! Now Cook will do it!"

"Cook?"

"Cook said so!"

"What? Come on, Henky, speak up!"

His voice thick with tears, the boy replied, "Cook said, 'As we sailed,' he said, 'my heart was like jelly,' he said, 'so sorry I was for them poor Jews, but now,' he said, 'now I agree with anyone who says they should be sent back to Germany, for they crucified Jesus,' he said, 'and they find fault with my grub on top of it, and so I'll feed them rat poison, the lot of them, if we're thrown back once more . . .'"

The door was thrown open and Meyer hurried in, followed by Davelaar, whose coverall was splotched with rain. "And what kind of ship was it?" Davelaar asked. "Same cutter?"

"Don't ask me!" Meyer replied, heading for the table. "A gun with a boat under it. Now leave me alone!" He started to roll up the chart, roughly.

"Let me tell you, it was a narrow escape!" Davelaar said. "God help me, I felt my whole shop shudder! Are those Yankees on board yet?"

"What are you pestering me for?" Meyer cried. "Go and look for yourself!" He went to the captain's bunk with his rolled-up chart and lifted the mattress.

"What are you doing with that?" Davelaar asked.

"He told me to hide it! It's scribbled all over with notes for landing places. I've to get rid of it before those Yankees arrive."

"Give it to me," Hendrik said. He took the chart from Meyer's hands and went to the settee.

"How many of them are there, anyway?" Davelaar asked.

"Six and a civilian," Meyer answered. "Hell, Doc! What are you doing with that chart?"

Hendrik lifted the seat of the settee. "Putting it in here."

"Civilian? What do you mean?" Davelaar persisted.

"But you're crumpling it all up, Doc!" Meyer cried. "We won't be able to use it any more!"

Davelaar tugged at Meyer's sleeve. "Speak up, man! Are they going to tow us into port? What civilian?"

"Oh, damn you! Whiskers and a bowler hat, that's all I know!"

Hendrik lowered the seat of the settee and said to Henky, who stood listening as if mesmerized, "Go ahead! Take that bag to the top of the ladder of the women's hold and wait for me there, quick!"

"Yes, Doc." Henky slunk out.

The moment the boy had closed the door, Hendrik said, "I want a word with you two. Have you been manhandling the passengers?"

Meyer gave him a shifty look, then his eyes slid away and he said, "If they were planning to tow us in, they'd have brought along a pilot."

"What about the civilian?" Davelaar asked. "Could he be the pilot?"

"So you admit it," Hendrik said.

"What do we admit?" Meyer shouted. "We admit nothing!" Then he continued to Davelaar, "If they intended to escort—"

He was interrupted by the door being opened. Kuiper came in, his cap and tunic soaked with rain, followed by two naval officers in oilskins, their caps protected by waterproof covers. One of them Hendrik recognized as Lieutenant Higgins off the *Trygona*. The other was obviously his superior: tall, blond, pale blue eyes, mouth set in a thin scowl. To Hendrik's surprise, the man came straight for him, held out his hand and said, "Van der Kamp!" After they had shaken hands, he did the same to Davelaar and Meyer. Kuiper said in the uncomfortable silence that followed, "Commander van der Kamp is naval attaché with our Embassy in Washington. We have another Dutchman on board, I didn't catch his name."

"Pastor Haldeman," the commander said. "Netherlands Navy chaplain, retired."

"And what's *he* supposed to do?" Davelaar asked aggressively.

"That will become clear in due course," the commander answered. "Now, gentlemen, if you'd be so kind, we'd like a word with your captain. In private."

Hendrik gestured to Meyer and Davelaar, who were spellbound by the situation; they left reluctantly. Hendrik closed the door of the cabin behind them; on his way to the stairs, he heard Meyer's voice, "Hey, Doc! Listen to me a moment, will you?" But he ignored it and headed for the women's hold.

Halfway there, at the far end of the starboard catwalk, he was hit by the eerie wailing which had been rising and falling in the background from the moment the shot was fired.

He stood still, his back to the hold, and stared over the rail at the boat below, the flank of the ship, the gray, featureless world of the fogbound sea. He was overcome by the overwhelming impulse to abscond. During a few moments of near-panic, he felt the way Vinkemans must have felt when he decided to jump ship: give up, escape from what suddenly had become a threatening world full of evil. Beatings, cruelty, disintegration . . .

He knew it was a momentary reaction. He did not take Vinkemans' threat seriously, but now he could identify with the state of mind that had driven the man to think in those terms: throwing a raft overboard, diving after it, finding himself adrift at sea five miles offshore, wind and current taking him out into the ocean . . .

After a moment, he sighed and braced himself. Wearing the fixed smile of benevolent authority, he headed for the women's hold, where mad Mrs. Schlachter and her grandchild's ghost awaited *Herr Doktor*'s arrival.

4

"Captain," Lieutenant Higgins said, the moment they were alone, "I'm disappointed in you. I thought we had agreed that you would not try to land those people but wait outside the three-mile limit for word from the Jewish committee."

"I can't remember giving you my word," Kuiper said. "Would you like a drink?"

The young man glanced at the Dutch commander and shook his head. "No, thank you, sir." He had accepted last time, so he must be impressed by his dour companion. Kuiper had realized the moment he set eyes on the man that he would have a harder time with him than with the American Coast Guard, who had been reasonably understanding and cooperative. Higgins obviously hated the orders he was compelled to carry out; the Dutch naval attaché did not give the impression that he was suffering from any conflict of conscience.

"Captain," Higgins said, "I think I'm going to let you have a word with the representative of your government. Would you care to take over, sir?"

"Thank you." Commander van der Kamp took off his cap, his oilskins, opened a wet briefcase and brought out some papers.

"Shall I leave you to it, sir?"

"No, Lieutenant. I'd like you to be in on this." He added, as an afterthought, "If you don't mind."

"No, sir. Very good, sir." The lieutenant retreated to a corner of the cabin.

Van der Kamp sat down at the table and sorted out his papers.

"Captain," he said, his pale blue eyes expressionless, "you've made a good try, but you're up against impossible odds. There's only one rational way out, and that's for you to accept the inevitable. The Americans will not allow you to land your illegal immigrants, and they have proven to possess the means of preventing your doing so. What they are prepared to do, for humanitarian reasons, is refuel you, provide drinking water and restock your provisions. But this only on condition you cease your endeavors; so you have no other choice but to take your passengers back to Hamburg. The restocking and coaling will take place September second, off Sandy Hook if the swell permits, otherwise just inside. Neither you nor any of your crew or passengers will be allowed to land. I have here—" he picked up one of the papers on the table —"a document drawn up by the Embassy setting out these conditions. Before we go any further, I'll ask you to read and sign it."

The information shook Kuiper to the core. He had not counted on the Americans refueling and restocking him without towing him into port. Maybe he could still bring that about by simply refusing to stick his head into the noose at their convenience. "I'm not going to sign anything at this point," he said.

Van der Kamp remained unfazed. "If you refuse to sign this document, Captain, you thereby effectively forfeit any assistance your government might still be able to give you."

"All right, leave it with me, I'll read it later."

Van der Kamp looked at him thoughtfully; then he said, "In that case, there is nothing left for us to discuss. I will now call in Pastor Haldeman." He gathered up his papers, put them back into his briefcase and rose. As he picked up his oilskins, Kuiper asked, "Who is this Pastor Haldeman?"

"You are motivated by considerations of a religious nature, are you not?"

"What's that got to do with it?"

"You are a member of the Dutch Reformed Church, I gather?" Higgins helped him into his oilskins; van der Kamp turned his head and said, "Thank you."

"I don't understand what any of this—"

"Pastor Haldeman is a Navy chaplain, minister of your church. He has great experience with sailors, he's a knowledgeable and understanding man. As the ambassador wished to leave no stone unturned to arrive at a constructive resolution of this—er—controversy, he thought it would be helpful—"

"I don't want to see any pastor!" Kuiper cried angrily. The very idea of a clergyman trying to talk him into taking his passengers back to Germany revolted him. "I don't want any so-called man of God telling me to send my passengers to their death!"

Unmoved, van der Kamp went to the door, opened it and said, "Would you come in, Padre?"

Almost immediately, a black-caped shape loomed in the doorway. It turned out to be an old man with a bowler hat. When the officers had left and closed the door, he held out his hand. "Brother, good morning."

"We're not brothers!"

"Are you a Christian?"

"Yes!"

Without warning, the old man's hand flew up and slapped his face, hard. With a shout, Kuiper raised his fist, but his arm was grabbed with surprising strength and forced down. The old man said, "Sermon on the Mount, Matthew five, verse thirty-nine. *Whosoever shall smite thee on thy right cheek, turn to him the other also.* So you are not a Christian. You're trying to become one, like myself. Sit down."

Stunned, Kuiper watched as the old man sat down, put his hat on the table and started to wring out the water-logged edges of his cape. He wandered over to the picture of Anna and the children beside the door, seeking help. As he stood gazing at them, he sensed that something had changed: he no longer felt the presence of the angel behind him. He gazed at Anna in total desolation, unnerved by doubt for the first time since his vision of Christ stumbling up his gangway that morning in Hamburg, an eternity ago.

"But—how *can* it be wrong, what I'm trying to do?" he asked.

5

Pastor Haldeman received the question with satisfaction. Many times in his long ministry he had used the same device to deflate the puffed-up bluster of pacifists, protesters, self-righteous interpreters of the Bible. All of them, like this one, young. All of them misguided, all of them usurping the inner certainty of the truly humble disciple of Christ.

God had been right to send him here last night, despite Agatha's angry insistence that he stay in bed and nurse his cold, that he had no business at his age traipsing around in small boats at dead of night, ambassador or no ambassador. The young captain, like the others before him, was shaken to the core, his bluster gone, his defiance deflated, asking himself how what he was doing *could* be wrong, as if that were an impossible thought.

"What are you trying to do?" Haldeman asked. Gently now, no challenges, no hint of confrontation, all sweet reasonableness and pastoral love: gentle shepherd and lost lamb.

"Trying to save my passengers . . . "

"By taking them back weary and exhausted, instead of well rested and strong?"

"I won't take them back!"

"Not today, perhaps; then in a couple of weeks."

"I *will* put them ashore!"

"How can you be so sure? Has God told you? Have you seen a sign?"

"No . . . "

"Then you won't put them ashore, for *I* have seen a sign: Coast Guard cutters, forty miles per hour. Planes, shadowing you day and night. All the money, all the power of the world against —you."

It bewildered the young captain. He walked up and down, then he cried, "But I can't have been misreading the Bible all these years!"

Haldeman smiled. "The Bible is a mysterious book, God's word appears to contradict itself in many places. That's why we need the guidance of the church and its ministers. I have been a theologian for thirty-five years; when I was a student, I thought I could interpret the Bible all on my own. I no longer think so."

The captain paced up and down again, his hands clasping and unclasping behind his back. Suddenly, he seemed to come to a decision. "Sir," he said, a note of finality in his voice, "answer me, not as the representative of my government or my church, but as yourself: a man of God. In all honesty, do you really think that it *could* be God's will for me to take those people back? Knowing what awaits them?"

"I think it's God's will that you try to become a Christian. You won't by torturing two hundred and forty-nine people for the sake of your own salvation. If you can't accept the orders of the authorities, there is only one way out for you: resign. Hand over the command of your ship to your first mate and leave the sea. *Then* you'll have made a sacrifice for your faith, but in private, as Christ teaches. Not with trumpets on the corner of the street, but in darkness. Then you'll be as good a Christian as the poor fellow who won't take a job on the railroad because he will not work on the Sabbath."

"But that man has only got himself and his family to consider! I hold the fate of all those helpless people in my hands!"

"If I could believe for only one second that you could indeed save those people, I'd say you were right."

"Why shouldn't I? If God has taken the trouble to make His will known to me, He'll give me the means to obey it!"

"The only one, dear boy, who has as yet been able to interpret God's will flawlessly was Jesus. And you'll forgive me if I cannot see you as the second coming."

"See me as you see yourself! A servant of the Lord!"

"Saint Matthew twelve, verse nineteen: *Behold my servant: he shall not strive nor cry, neither shall any man hear his voice in the streets.*"

"The same Matthew, I don't know the verse: *What I tell ye in darkness, that speak ye in light, and what ye hear in the ear, that preach ye upon the housetops!*"

Haldeman sighed. "Dear boy, there's no point in our entering into a discussion on the interpretation of the Scriptures. You have erred. You have overstepped the boundaries of free interpretation of the Scriptures set for every member of the church. In the name of the synod of the Reformed Church of the Netherlands, I must charge you to cease your endeavors."

"And the Jews?" the captain cried. "What does the synod say about the Jews? Am I to murder them?"

His sincerity was beyond question. He stood there, defiant, despairing, yet with a certain grandeur. Was it the grandeur of delusion? Had he seen things others had not seen? Even if he had, no man was a law unto himself. "Leave them to God. You have done too much already."

"And if I should think I have not done enough?"

"If you should persist in your endeavors to put those people ashore illegally, you would act against the explicit command of your church."

The captain looked at him warily. "Maybe you too have a statement for me to sign?"

Haldeman took the by now somewhat soggy paper from his inside pocket. "Not a statement, exactly. I just jotted down the standpoint of the church. You'd oblige me if you'd sign this, so as to prevent any misunderstanding with the ambassador." He put it on the table for the captain to read and sign; incredibly, the man took it and tore it up, dropping the pieces on the floor.

Haldeman rose and said, his voice shaking, "You have just torn up the principles that have guided our church for three hundred years!"

"And what have they guided it *to?*" the captain cried. He pointed at the door. "Listen!"

In the silence sounded the distant wailing that had continued unremittingly all the time.

Haldeman took his hat and went toward the door. "I will pray for you," he said. "I can do no more."

"Thank you," the captain said. "My passengers and I will pray for you, and for the Reformed Church of the Netherlands."

Haldeman put on his soaked hat, feeling like a judge passing sentence of death. He opened the door to leave, and found two people standing outside in the rain, a man and a woman. The man carried a box.

"Excuse me," the woman said, "I didn't mean to disturb . . . "

"You have arrived at exactly the right moment, Mrs. Goldstein," the captain said. "Come in, please."

It was still raining. Haldeman went down the stairs from the lower bridge to the deck. Everywhere were people watching him, anxious, silent. The rising sun was a haloed orb in the drizzle. "This way, Padre," a voice said. It was the naval attaché. "Let's have a word, here."

He was taken to the gangway, where the young American Coast Guard officer was waiting for them. On the platform to the gangway, out of earshot of those silent people, the attaché asked, "Well? Any success?"

"I'm afraid not. He is determined to go ahead. He will not listen to reason, to any authority other than his own conscience, based on his personal interpretation of the Bible. I'm afraid you have no other option than to execute your plan."

"Thank you," the attaché said neutrally. "Come, Lieutenant, let's go and find the doctor. You go back to the boat, Padre. Sit down for a while."

Haldeman slowly went down the long, steep incline of the gangway, feeling old and ill. He had done what they had asked of him. It could have been asked of any Christian minister who accepted that a man, all by himself, was a lost soul in a dark valley full of demons. But he felt no satisfaction, not even a sense of rightness. All he felt was exhaustion, and a terrible sadness.

Sitting in the back of the rowboat, observed by curious oarsmen, he felt close to tears. Agatha had been right: he should have stayed home in bed. He should have said to the commander—what? That he wasn't feeling well? Was retired? Wasn't knowledgeable enough about Germans, Jews, man's inhumanity to man? Was a citizen of Holland, a peaceable country that had not known war for over a hundred years? A priest of a church that had not faced the dark midnight of the soul for over three hundred?

It was all too much, too much. He slumped on his seat among the oarsmen like Pliny the Elder among the soaring columns of ancient Rome, weeping as he realized that he was too old for the evil of his times.

6

Jablonski handed Kuiper the box with the passports. "Sorry, Captain, I'm afraid it got rather wet."

"All of us are very grateful, Captain," Mrs. Goldstein said, "but I suppose—I suppose now you will . . . or is there still some hope left? Please be honest with us."

Kuiper did not know what to answer. The visit by the clergyman had disoriented him. What could he tell her? That he no longer saw any way out, but still put their lives on one card, God? A God that now had turned out to be his alone? Could he ask her, 'Help me believe, or I will fail. Hold me up as Aaron did Moses during the battle of Rephidim, or all will be lost'?

"It's for the sake of the others, Captain," Jablonski said. "They're beginning to lose heart. Is there anything we can tell them? Anything at all?"

After a moment, Kuiper said, "All right, I'll level with you.

I have not had any news from the committee ashore. They must be doing all they can. At least, you can tell your people that the committee ashore is active. Tell them that I'm expecting a radiogram from them at any moment. I think that's honest. Apart from—"

The door was opened without knocking; it was the doctor, in what appeared to be a state of agitation. "Skipper! I *must* talk to you!"

"What is it?" Kuiper asked tersely.

The doctor took a deep breath and said, "The crew is molesting the Jew—" he corrected himself—"the passengers. I—"

"Molesting? Who is?"

"The officers, the bo'sun, the sailors, everybody! While they were lining up for the gangways, there was pushing and beating, and as they were getting into the boats, belts were used to speed them up."

Kuiper turned to Mrs. Goldstein. "Is that true?"

She looked him in the eye and said, "Yes, Captain." She said it as if it were the most normal thing in the world.

"You—you mean there has been *violence?*"

"Captain, what did you expect? This voyage has been like raising a culture of anti-Semitism under laboratory conditions. Economic distress among the crew because of Jews, an outside threat, helplessness on the part of the Jews . . . "

The doctor virtually jumped on her. "But how did you expect us to prevent this—this outrage if you kept your mouths shut? For the past two weeks, I've treated wounds, bruises, which the patients said were the result of knocking into something or falling down, and now they turn out to be—"

Kuiper held up his hand. "One moment!" He turned to Mrs. Goldstein. "I'd like you to come and see me later, and you too, Mr. Jablonski. I'll look into this matter at once. Now, please, go down into the holds, reassure your people and, if you can, please, *please* put an end to that wailing!"

Mrs. Goldstein said calmly, "We'll try." Then she smiled at Kuiper and the doctor, and said to Jablonski, "Let's go."

As the door closed behind them, Kuiper turned to the doctor.

"Where did you pick up that rumor?"

"It's not a rumor, Skipper! It's true! The boy Henky blurted it out in a moment of hysteria. I checked with passengers I treated for cuts and bruises. They gave me names. The cook is one of the ringleaders, setting the crew against the Jews. It seems somebody complained about the food."

"But when we left South America, the crew cheered! What's happened to the men? What got into them?!"

"After the setbacks we had trying to put these people ashore, they lost heart. They no longer believe it can be done. They see their money being gambled away by a religious fanatic for people who no longer believe in their rescue themselves. That's another thing I must warn you about: if we are intercepted once more as we were today, there may be an epidemic of suicides below."

"Come, come, Doctor, don't dramatize! These people have behaved in an exemplary manner so far. I see no reason—"

"Read my reports!" the doctor cried. "Look for yourself, from the bridge! Half of them are camping on deck now because the cramped room below is driving them nuts: claustrophobia is spreading like a contagious disease. I'm diluting my bromide one to seventy now, otherwise my stock won't last. Psychosomatic complaints are the order of the day. One more emotional trauma like the one they just lived through, and all those cases may end up as suicides. And if *that's* to be the result of your errand of mercy—"

"That'll do!" Kuiper could take no more. "Go below and see what you can do."

"There's one more thing, Skipper—"

"No! Not now. Later."

The doctor looked at him, shrugged his shoulders, said, "Okeydoke" and left.

The moment he was alone, Kuiper knelt by the chair, folded his hands and prayed, "God! Dear God! . . . Dear God . . . "

He groped for words and found none. But there was the angel, right behind him, and it was as if he heard the soft, slick hiss of the drawing of a sword.

7

When Hendrik emerged on the lower bridge, a voice said, "Doctor!"

Two yellow figures loomed in the drizzle, now a luminous haze. "We'd like a word with you in private, Doctor. It's important."

They were the Dutch commander and the Coast Guard lieutenant.

"Oh," Hendrik said, "yes . . ."

"Where can we go?" the commander asked. "We need ten minutes, somewhere private where we won't be disturbed."

"There's no such place on board this ship. If we don't want to be disturbed, we'll have to go on board your rowboat."

"That, I'm afraid, is not a good idea." The man sounded matter-of-fact, not at all impressed by the circumstances. The women below were giving free rein now to their fear and desperation. In spite of the captain's request, the wailing from the aft hold continued unabated.

"Why not?"

"For a number of reasons, I'd feel more comfortable broaching this particular subject on board this ship. So where do we go?"

"In that case, we might as well stay right where we are. But I may be called for at any minute."

"Isn't this fairly close to the master's cabin? What we have to discuss concerns the captain. Can't we go to your cabin?"

Hendrik smiled. "I share the captain's cabin." Obviously, this character had no concept of conditions on board the ship. It was going to be a pleasure to enlighten him.

"All right," van der Kamp said, "let's go into the corner, over there."

They did. Van der Kamp positioned himself so he could keep an eye on the stairs to the lower bridge and the door of the captain's cabin. Then he said in the bland tone of a traffic cop writing out a ticket, "We want to discuss with you the necessity of putting a stop to all this."

Hendrik looked away at the luminous void of the fog. The Greek chorus wailed in the background. Somewhere, unseen, a seagull mewed. "Before you go any further," he said, "let me tell you that if you're going to ask me to convince the captain, or reason with him, you'll be wasting your time. He'll never give up, unless God tells him to."

"Well, God had a go at it in the person of Pastor Haldeman," van der Kamp said blandly, "with a singular lack of success. So, there's only one way out—eliminate him. That's where you come in."

For one mad moment, Hendrik thought the man was suggesting he give the captain a lethal injection.

"How, for Christ's sake?"

"By certifying him insane."

Hendrik looked at the blank face, the toothbrush mustache, the pale eyes devoid of emotion. "You can't be serious!"

"Why not?"

"Because your suggestion is insane! Not the captain!"

"The government does not agree. Neither do the psychiatric experts ashore."

"Well, screw the experts! The captain is a Christian! He may not be the most charming of Christians, but at least he has a conscience, and he acts upon it!"

"Doctor," van der Kamp said, with the patience of the cop, "your Captain Kuiper happens to be causing a series of international incidents. He has tried three times to land illegal immigrants in the United States. By virtue of the fact that his vessel flies the Netherlands flag, your government is involved."

"The hell with my government," Hendrik said with feeling. "I'll see you all in hell first, before I collaborate in your neat little scheme. Insane? He's not insane, he's putting his faith into practice! And the fact that you consider that to be insane tells me more about you and my government than I care to know!"

If he had hoped to make an impression on the traffic cop, he was mistaken. "Doctor," van der Kamp said calmly, "as a physician, you must be familiar with the disaster syndrome. Are you not?"

"What the hell has that got to do with it?"

"If I am correctly informed, symptoms include loss of perspective, warped sense of reality, coping with immediate emergencies with any means at hand, abandoning accepted standards."

"So?"

"You are showing those symptoms, Doctor. You are, I'm sure, doing an excellent job under conditions that are not acceptable by civilized standards, but you have lost your sense of perspective. Your captain can no longer hope to land his passengers clandestinely. He is being tracked around the clock by sea and air. Even you must admit that the mere idea of trying once again to land those people is irrational. It alone should be sufficient to relieve him of his responsibility as master. All we ask of you, as the ship's doctor, is to agree with us that what the captain is trying to do is insane, and declare so in writing. That will be enough to empower us to instruct the first officer to assume command and take the vessel back to Germany."

"I could not possibly do that! I—"

"To make your task easier, the ambassador has contacted the liner *Tubantia* on her way from Amsterdam to New York. She's due to pass you at fourteen hundred hours today. Your opposite number will be requested to be present at a formal hearing and sign the certificate with you. I'm sure he will comply. Anyone not subject to the disaster syndrome will agree that this situation is untenable and must be terminated."

Tubantia . . . Willemse, Susan, Myrtle . . . It gave a sudden perspective to his present situation: alone, lost in this eerie fog with his patients . . . God—the mere thought of *Tubantia* approaching made his eyes fill with idiotic tears. Emotionally, he realized, he was hanging on by his nails. God, dear God . . . Suddenly the whole thing became unbearable—insane, indeed. "But what about the committee?" he asked. "The committee is trying to gain admission for them. Shouldn't we at least hang on and wait for what they come up with?"

"Doctor," van der Kamp said patiently, "whatever the committee may come up with, it is not going to affect the attitude of the United States government. Nothing is going to happen to these people when they return to their country of origin. They had permission to emigrate, they were victimized by some unscrupulous crook who furnished forged visas—"

"That crook was the German government itself!"

"How do you know that? Do you have proof? To our knowledge and that of U.S. Intelligence, the German government was in no way involved in this swindle. It was a private company with whom the captain made a private deal; no doubt it will be prosecuted by the German authorities."

Hendrik gazed at the man with an astonishment that changed into loathing. To say calmly that the German government had nothing to do with the forged visas was not just ludicrous, it was criminal. "How, for God's sake, could a private company profit from forged visas?"

"The passengers were prepared to pay outrageous sums of money for them; some unscrupulous manipulator got into the act and sold them forgeries. These people are the victims of a swindle, not of political persecution. All there is left for them to do is to cut their losses and go home."

"Mr. van der Kamp," Hendrik said with a show of calm, "I don't know if you are representative of my government, but if you are, it's made up of callous, conniving cowards who turn their backs on human suffering and despair with some cock-and-bull story that is too laughable to even consider. You may be able to satisfy your conscience with that crap, I cannot. These people cannot return to Germany. I've been with them for seven weeks now and know them well. I've heard their stories. I've treated their injuries, and not just the physical ones: the psychological ones also. They have gone through hell, and for you to stand there and tell me that it's just a matter of their going home and cutting their losses—sir, at this moment I'm ashamed of my government." Ah! That was good! That was wonderful! That gave him the most tremendous lift!

"Doctor," the traffic cop said, unimpressed, "your government and the United States government want your captain to stop trying to land illegal immigrants on United States territory. Now, we can send a warship, we can take over command by force, but the humane thing to do would be to quietly replace the captain with the first officer. The ship's doctor of *Tubantia* will be here in a matter of hours; he will join you at the hearing; you will jointly declare the captain unfit to command his vessel because of irrational behavior, and that'll be all."

"Apart from the small detail that it will seal the passengers' fate, as Meyer will take them back to Germany."

"Correct."

Hendrik had to admit it was a clean, antiseptic solution. Had this proposal been made to him in Montevideo, he would probably have agreed; now he felt compelled by some imperative he could not define to say, "Sir, to put it simply: no. I'm a physician, not a politician. Good day." With that he strode off, nearly came a cropper at the top of the steps, but managed to make a dignified exit.

To go down onto the deck was like descending into Dante's Inferno. There were the wails of the damned, and vague shapes in the fog closed in on him the moment they realized who he was. He fled to the infirmary, where, with a relief that expressed itself nearly in a sob, he found Vinkemans. "Well, thank God you're here!" he said. "Let's go next door, I have something to discuss with you." He took the man by the shoulder; it was thin and brittle like a bird's. He had not realized Vinkemans was so frail. "In here." He closed the door of the consulting room behind them. "Do you know what that character asked me to do—the naval attaché? He wants me to certify His Nibs insane!"

Vinkemans said nothing. His eyes were dark pools into which Hendrik gazed; he slowly realized that he was looking at pure panic. Vinkemans was not only on the brink of cracking up, he was incapable of rational judgment. "I warned you, Doctor," he said in a voice that sounded strained. "I told you what I would do if this ship were to go back to Germany. All I can say, Doctor, is: I was serious. The moment this ship heads back to Hamburg, I leave."

Hendrik looked at the dark pools, his professional training

reasserting itself. At the time, he had taken Vinkemans' threat to be a momentary loss of control; it had sounded so unlike the man who had shown himself to be a conscientious, caring nurse in the untiring service of his patients. Now he realized it was not the captain who was insane, it was Vinkemans. He would have to handle this with circumspection.

"Of course, Vinkemans, if that's how you feel, that's what you must do," he said. "But you and I should talk it over first. You mustn't take any unnecessary risks. If you want to leave, we'll have to make sensible arrangements."

"How?" The calm with which Vinkemans put the question was somehow ominous.

"Well, for instance, *Tubantia* is on her way here. She'll be alongside some time this afternoon and send Dr. Willemse over in a launch. So think it over and consider going back with him. It would be preferable to swimming to a raft, or whatever it was you were planning. Don't you agree?"

The eyes remained dark, unfathomable, filled with inchoate panic. "Where is she going?" Vinkemans asked in that strained voice.

"New York. So why don't you go back with Dr. Willemse, have yourself taken to New York, enjoy a few days on the town . . . "

Vinkemans did not reply. He just stared. My God, the man really was over the edge. Hendrik asked himself how it was possible that he hadn't noticed. He had been too wrapped up in emergencies to register Vinkemans' emotional disintegration.

"Tell you what: why don't you lie down for a while? You must be worn out. Take a Seconal, have a few hours' sleep and then let's talk again. Maybe the whole thing will take on a different aspect."

"Doctor, I'm sorry," Vinkemans said slowly, "you must face the facts. You will not have me to help you when this ship returns to Germany. I told you to ask Mrs. Goldstein for more nurses. You did not believe me. Now, I'm sorry, you're left in the lurch. I feel bad about it, but there is not a chance that I'll stay on board this ship if it returns to Germany. Is that clear, Doctor? Have I finally got through to you?" He sounded as if his next move would be to grab a scalpel and run amuck.

"Of course, Vinkemans," he said, smiling. "I'm not going to stop you. All I want is to work out the most sensible plan with you. And it would seem that this is a perfect opportunity. On *Tubantia,* you'll have a cabin to yourself, all the luxuries of a big ocean liner—I wish I had the chance!"

"I must get through to you, Doctor, I want you to *really* believe me. *Really.* "

"Of course I believe you, Vinkemans." Hendrik wondered if he should pat the man's shoulder, but that might unleash the panic. "I think I'd better go and have a look at those women," he said. He left Vinkemans standing, somehow terribly alone, in the dingy little consulting room where they had gone through so many crises together.

As he re-emerged into the morning haze, now scented with the smell of beached kelp, it penetrated to him: Vinkemans was leaving. He would have to face the rest of the voyage alone.

The realization filled him with the instant and overwhelming urge to flee. Throughout the voyage, Vinkemans had been the more experienced, the more caring of the two of them. Maybe he himself should return to *Tubantia* with Willemse, after doing whatever the government wanted him to do. His bravado of a few moments ago, when he told van der Kamp what he thought of him, had without substance, a puff of smoke. To stay behind alone on this ship full of people on the brink of hysteria . . . He would never be able to handle it, not in a thousand years. He was not supposed to have this kind of challenge thrown at him. He had made the decision early in life: he was not going to be tested, he was going to be comfortable. He had better be true to himself and beat it. He was not cut out for heroics, he was not going to stay on the sinking *Titanic* and sing *Nearer, My God, to Thee.* Let the Jews take care of themselves. He had done what he could, what he had contracted to do, and more. He was going to go back to *Tubantia* with Vinkemans and whoop it up with Susan. Ah! A woman in his arms!

But it didn't work. Something had changed. He had changed.

God only knew what had happened to him, but he would be unable to do it. Maybe it was just cowardice; maybe he simply couldn't confront the disapproval of his peers for abandoning his patients in their hour of need.

Who cared? Whatever his motivation, noble or otherwise, Vinkemans would go to *Tubantia* without him.

8

Kuiper was still on his knees by the chair, oblivious of the time he had spent in prayer, when there was a sharp knock on the door and it was opened without his acknowledgment.

He stood up and was about to reprimand the intruder when he saw it was the two officers in their foul-weather gear. They each carried a briefcase and looked as if they meant business. "All right, Captain," Lieutenant Higgins said, "let's wrap this up. The padre has told us the outcome of your discussion, so let's not waste any more words. He's all yours, sir."

"Thank you," the naval attaché said. He put his briefcase on the table, opened it and pulled out his papers. Then he said to Higgins, "You have your copy?"

"Yeah, got it right here. Fire away, sir."

Van der Kamp looked Kuiper over with expressionless eyes and said, "By the way: in case you feel like tearing up this document too, we have four copies. I'll read it to you." He cleared his throat.

"I, the undersigned, Kuiper, Joris, born, etc., skipper next to God of the vessel 'Star of Peace' of Netherlands registry, home port den Helder, number etc., affirm by signing this document that I agree to the following arrangement. I will proceed at suitable speed to Ambrose Lightship to arrive there at dawn on September second, 1939. On that date and in that location I will be instructed by the U.S. Coast Guard where to anchor for the purpose of coaling, provisioning and taking on drinking water. Neither I nor any member of my staff, crew or passengers will attempt to land while the foregoing is in

progress. After completion of the coaling, etc., I will set course for Hamburg, Germany, and not attempt at any time to illegally land any of my passengers on U.S. territory. I have been fully informed by Commander F. W. C. van der Kamp, who witnesses my signature, of the grave consequences that would result from said illegal act(s). Read and signed on board the vessel etc., in the presence of Commander etc. . . . "

He turned the document around, put his finger at the bottom and said, "Sign here, please. All four copies, if you will."

"Why should I?"

"Come on, Captain, time's getting short. Sign, please."

"What are those 'grave consequences'?"

Lieutenant Higgins cursed, stuffed his papers into his briefcase and said, "Dammit, I'm not a lawyer, I'm a sailor! Let's take him to the bridge, sir. It's time we moved him out."

Van der Kamp said calmly, "Why don't you signal that we'll be under way presently? Let me have a word with him in private."

"Yessir," Higgins said. "But better make it snappy." He saluted. "Sir."

After he had left and closed the door behind him, van der Kamp seemed to relax. "Okay, Captain," he said in a tone that was almost human, "I think the time has come to put our cards on the table so we don't blunder into a situation that neither of us wants to bring about."

"I don't understand."

"The Americans want us to pull the coals out of the fire for them. That's why I'm here. We realized you might not be willing to accept the agreement. A Dutch tugboat is standing by in Sheepshead Bay. The moment you go dead in the water, she'll pick you up and tow you to Bermuda. The British are a different kettle of fish from the Yankees, let me tell you. No committee of Jews there, no bleeding hearts. British hearts never bleed, Captain, not even for themselves."

"But what—"

"They'll bunker you up, replenish your stores, pack you off back to sea—and then let things on board your ship take care of themselves. If I were you, I'd heed the writing on the wall and accept the agreement." He pulled a pen from his pocket, held it out to Kuiper and said, "Sign, please."

Kuiper looked at the silver pen, the face without expression, and said, "I don't understand you."

"What?"

"The American is embarrassed by what he has to do. You sound as if you act out of conviction."

The face did not change. "I do."

"You do?"

"I'm a Dutchman, not an American. The Germans are massed on our border, armed to the teeth. There's no point in our provoking them. You're messing with dynamite, Captain. Get the hell out of here or you may cause an explosion that'll blow us all to smithereens. Sign!"

Kuiper stubbornly shook his head. "Sorry. I won't."

"As you wish." It did not seem to faze the man at all. He calmly collected his papers, put them back in his briefcase and pocketed the pen. At the door, he said, "By the way, before I forget: after we've left, make sure you keep a lookout as from, say, midnight today."

"Why?"

"So you haven't kept up on your *Notices to Mariners,* have you? All right, I happen to have the cutting with me . . . " He opened his briefcase again, looked through the contents and brought out a printed piece of paper. "Here, have a look."

It was a page from the current *Notices to Mariners:*

All shipping is advised that from August 29th through September 1st 1939 a Boston/New York sailboat race will be in progress, which will terminate near Ambrose Lightship. Appr. 70 yachts are expected to participate, caution is advised for all vessels between Boston approaches and Nantucket Lightship as from five hundred hrs. EST Aug. 29th, and between Nantucket Lightship and Ambrose ditto as from zero hrs. EST Sept. 1st. through appr. twelve hundred hrs EST. In the vicinity of Ambrose Lightship extreme caution is indicated throughout the early morning hours up to midday, as a number of motorized pleasure craft and sightseeing vessels are expected, some of which will be carrying film crews and reporters, and may be changing course suddenly and erratically. Pilot service off Ambrose is expected to proceed normally, but the possibility of delay must be taken into account.

Kuiper handed him back the piece of paper. "Thank you."

"You'd better hang on to that, Captain; you may want to refer to it later. It depends how serious you are."

"Why?"

Van der Kamp glanced at the door; then he asked, keeping his voice low, "How serious *are* you about wanting to land these people on U.S. territory in the full light of public opinion? Are you prepared to do so whatever the cost to you personally?"

"Why?"

This time, van der Kamp went to open the door to see if anyone was eavesdropping, then came back and whispered, "I'm going to ask you two questions, which I want you to repeat after me. In case of an inquiry, I want to be able to declare under oath that you put these questions to me and that I had no choice, in my position, other than to answer them truthfully. Understand?"

Kuiper did not; all he understood was that the man in some obscure way was taking a personal risk.

"Number one. Ask me: 'Are the yachts taking part in this regatta all of American registry?' " When Kuiper hesitated, he urged, "Ask me! But keep your voice down."

"Are all those yachts of American registry?"

"The answer is yes. Number two: 'Are these American yachts legally United States territory?' . . . Go ahead, ask me."

"Are they?"

"Ask the question. Quietly, please."

"Are these American yachts legally United States territory?"

"The answer is yes. So it's up to you now."

Kuiper realized there was a message here of vital importance; what was it? "But there's no way I can get my passengers on board those yachts! Or do you mean they'll be obliged to pick up my passengers if I put them in the boats and set them adrift?"

Van der Kamp gave him an odd look. "If you put your

passengers in the boats and set them adrift, nobody would be obliged to pick them up, Captain, unless they were the survivors of a shipwreck. Now let's go to the bridge." He went to the door. "By the way—in view of what we just discussed, how about signing that declaration of intent after all? That way, you wouldn't be arousing any sleeping dogs."

Kuiper shook his head.

Van der Kamp sighed. "Ah, well, I'll just tell the Coast Guard you refuse to sign anything, but will be heading for New York all the same. Now let's get cracking; I can't let you hang around here any longer."

"I—I would like to be alone for a moment, please," Kuiper said.

"Then please order your mate to take over and head due south."

Kuiper went to the door, called for Meyer; when the mate turned up, he gave the order. Then he closed the door, leaned against it and whispered, "God, not that. Please, not that!"

He went to his chair and knelt and rested his head on his hands. "God, God . . . please, please let this cup pass from me . . . "

There was no answer, only the awareness of the presence behind him.

CHAPTER EIGHT

I

Chief Davelaar, down in the engine room, obeyed the ring of the telegraph and set the old lady in motion: half-speed ahead. The whistle of the speaking tube squealed; Palstra, filling his oil can at the workbench, was about to answer, but Davelaar yelled, "I'll get it," over the hissing and swishing of the engine. He swung toward the tube from behind the plunging pistons with an agility that belied his age, pulled the whistle out and spoke into the tube, "Engine room." He pressed his ear to the mouthpiece to hear the answer, expecting Joris' voice. But it was Meyer's.

"Chief, the Navy wants to talk to us in private. Can we meet in your cabin?"

"When?"

"Now. It's urgent."

Davelaar stuffed the whistle back into the tube. "Palstra!" he yelled. "Take over for a while! I've got to take care of something overhead!"

"Aye, aye!"

Davelaar climbed the iron stairs to the deck, emerged into the deafening silence of the corridor and, wiping his hands on his wad of cotton waste, went to his cabin.

When he entered, he found Meyer sitting in the armchair, looking shifty.

"Where's the Navy?" Davelaar asked.

"They aren't coming."

"What do you mean, they aren't coming? That's what you called me up for!"

"They had to stay on the bridge, so they asked me to tell you."

"Tell me what? Goddammit, man, get on with it! It's my watch, I can't keep on asking Palstra to fill in for me. What the hell's the matter?"

"They're going to certify Joris insane," Meyer said slowly and precisely, as if he didn't quite understand what he was saying.

"Who is?"

"The Navy is."

"The Navy can't certify him insane. That needs a doctor."

"Well, we have a doctor. And they're going to get another one from *Tubantia*, who's bearing down on us and will be here during the afternoon watch."

"Then what?"

"Then they'll declare him incompetent, relieve him of his command and make me temporary captain."

"Jesus!" Davelaar was about to say, 'You can't accept that! You aren't competent!' But he thought better of it. "Joris insane? They're not going to bring that off. You know and I know, everybody on board knows that the boy's not insane. He's a nut, but not an out-and-out lunatic."

"The doctors will do what the Navy tells them. At least, that's what the Navy says."

"Then what are *you* supposed to do?"

Meyer gave him a sliding look. "I'm supposed to take the ship to New York, where we'll be coaled and provisioned in the lee of Sandy Hook. Then I'm supposed to take the Jews back to Hamburg."

"Hallelujah," Davelaar said. He pulled out his chewing to-bacco, took a quid and stuffed it into his cheek. As he savored the bittersweet taste, he pictured the scene: Joris, certified insane, told to get into a boat? Not in a thousand years. The boy might think of himself as a cheek-turning Christian now, but he couldn't have changed his spots. Davelaar remembered his visits to jail cells all over the world, with the Old Man's money in his pocket, to bail the young bastard out. "Meyer," he said, "that's not going to work."

"Why not?" There was defiance in Meyer's voice.

"Joris is not going to take it lying down. Unless they brain him or jump him, he'll tear the place apart."

"Oh . . . Yes . . . " Meyer's brief moment of self-assurance was over.

"Remember the fight in New Orleans, that barroom he demolished? Half a dozen American deputies it took. You think a bunch of boys off a Coast Guard cutter can handle him? Or that pasty-faced goldfinch from the Embassy? He'll make mincemeat of the lot of them."

"The crew will help," Meyer said, "if I explain it to them."

"Explain what?"

"That it means we're going home."

They might. And if not the crew, his own stokers. The black choir hardly knew Joris; their world was as separate from the bridge as the moon. If they were told that all that was standing between them and going home was that the captain had gone crazy and had to be subdued, they would tackle him all right. They were a ruthless bunch.

He visualized their jumping Joris and trussing him up. To his surprise, it saddened him, like the capturing of a proud wild animal. But then, what was the alternative? They were almost out of fuel, food was getting short, the Jews had lost their cockiness and self-assurance; there was no other solution but to take the ship back to Germany. And Joris would never do it. He was like his father: once he had made up his mind about something, boy, he was going to see it through.

"Did the Navy say there was a chance the Jews might be admitted?" he asked.

"They didn't say. They said, 'Stay outside a six-mile limit on your way to New York, and there wait for a response from the committee.' "

"Why six?"

"I don't know. Some sailboat race or something."

Davelaar squirted a jet of juice; the cuspidor rang out. "How long can we keep that up? I'm out of fuel, almost. Today we can still make New York, tomorrow it will have to be Boston. We may find ourself dead in the water."

"In that case, they'll tow us away, they say."

"Tow us where?"

"Hamilton."

So it would have to be done. The moment had come. "Looks like I've got to do it," he said, not realizing he was saying it aloud.

"Huh?"

"I can rip his guts out without laying a finger on him."

"How?"

"The story of the coconuts."

Meyer's eyes opened wide. "But that's like throwing a lantern into a haystack!"

"No, it'll gut him. It'll take his goddam God away, that's what it'll do."

As Meyer stared at him, there was a timid knock on the door. He called, "Come in!" Nothing happened. He went to open it.

It was Henky, weeping, carrying something small.

"What do you want?"

The boy gave him the object he held in his hand. "I've come to give this back, Chief, I stole it . . . "

It was the glass ball with the Eiffel Tower in the snowstorm. "You goddam little sneak!" Davelaar yelled. "I'm going to get you, you sneaky bastard!" He went for the child, but Henky was too smart a rat for an old tomcat. He streaked down the passage and was gone from sight by the time Davelaar got to the end and yelled, "Where are you? Where are you, you sneaky little shit!? Wait till I get my hands on you!"

The child, like all sea-urchins he had ever known, had vanished into thin air.

2

"So," Hendrik said to the group of women on the forecastle, "we'll all have to pull our weight, and if you could find me some more volunteers, that would be a great help."

They were huddled together, their hair whisked about by the wind: Tovah, Mrs. Adler, Mrs. Hoflein and Hendrik. He had called them out there for 'a conference'; Tovah, like everyone else, had feared he was going to tell them that they were about to be taken back to Germany. But all he wanted to tell them was that Mr. Vinkemans had fallen ill and would be leaving the ship that afternoon, and that from now on the responsibility for the care of the patients would be theirs.

"But what's the matter with him?" Mrs. Adler asked. "Why must he leave?"

"Er, pneumonia," Hendrik replied. "He has to be transferred to *Tubantia,* where they are equipped to handle him during the few hours it will take them to get him to a hospital in New York."

Tovah knew, as she supposed did the two others, that it was not true: Mr. Vinkemans had had a nervous breakdown, the symptoms had been obvious for days. What they really wanted to know, and what Mrs. Adler had tried to get out of Hendrik with her question, was whether they were going to be taken back to Hamburg. The rumor was that Mr. Vinkemans had demanded to leave because a number of older people had announced that rather than return to Hamburg they would do away with themselves. Tovah decided to put the question bluntly. "Tell us honestly: are we about to be taken back to Germany?"

"Oh, no. No, no, no! No question of it!" Had he just said 'no' and looked her in the eye, she might have believed him.

"I see."

He realized that he had failed to convince her, or the two others, who looked at him somberly. "I promise you that is not the case," he asserted. "I would tell you if it were so, and you would be the first to know because you would have to deal with the effects of such an announcement. So why should I fool you? To the best of my knowledge, at this point we are waiting for the outcome of the deliberations between the committee and the authorities. They've promised they'll send us a telegram as soon as they have something to report, whatever it may be. That should be any moment now."

There was an uncomfortable silence. Then Mrs. Hoflein said, "Very well. Thank you, *Herr Doktor.* Come, ladies."

"And see what you can do about more volunteers, please," Hendrik urged, as they turned to go.

"We will," Mrs. Adler said.

On their way to the hold, they did not speak, each preoccupied with her own thoughts. What Tovah wanted above all was to contact Yitzhak as soon as she could. They must talk this over, the time had come for a council of war.

She found him near the ladder into the women's hold, which was as far as the men were allowed to go. Obviously, he was waiting for her, informed by their intelligence network of the conference with the doctor on the forecastle.

"Well?" he asked, making it sound casual, almost bored. "Had a nice talk?"

She looked around to see if they were being watched, then she said, her voice low, "We must talk. Let's meet by the winch." She did not wait for his answer, but sidled off to make her way gradually to the forecastle, where she found him already installed in their usual meeting place. She glanced around and ducked out of sight to squat beside him. "The time has come," she said. "I think the decision has been made."

"Are you certain?"

"Virtually. He assured us that nobody was even *thinking* of taking us back. There was the usual yak about the committee and how they'd keep us informed, but I know he was lying. They have a plan; it hasn't fallen into place yet, but they're going to take us back. They're working out the details."

"Any idea what they involve?"

"No. Do you have any information?"

"Philip picked up, through Josef Wartenberg, who overheard

them talking about it, that the Navy officers want to contact the liner *Tubantia*, which is on its way, and ask for a doctor to join ours in 'a hearing' later today. We don't know what that means. It may have to do with Vinkemans."

"What do we do when they announce we're going back?"

"That we must talk over with the others. I have called for a meeting; I took the liberty of calling up your girls too. They should be waiting for us now."

"Where?"

"At the table."

"But we'll be overheard!"

"We have young kids covering the approaches. They'll let us know if someone tries to listen in. Shall we go?"

"Okay. Are we going to do it?"

He looked at her with that cherubic smile which made him look so young and innocent, and said, "Yes." He got to his feet. "Let's go separately. You first."

"Well, God be with us," she said, realizing how melodramatic she sounded.

When she arrived at the usual table, they were all there: Hannelore Weisbrot, Gretchen Kahn, Anna Feldschuh, Philip Roth, Fritz Stahl and Josef Wartenberg. She had not spotted any young kids on her way to the table and she didn't spot them now, but, knowing Yitzhak, all approaches must be guarded.

She had just sat down and the paper cup with the usual lemonade was being passed around when Yitzhak turned up and said, "Can I have some of that, please?"

After he had been handed the cup, he said, without the slightest hint of drama, "Well, this seems to be it. We must prepare for takeover at a moment's notice. Any more news, Josef?"

"Yes. Arnold overheard Meyer and Wybrands talking. We know now why they wanted that doctor from the *Tubantia* to come over: they wanted to certify the captain insane. But our doctor refuses to cooperate, so they can't."

"The *captain?*" Hannelore asked, shocked.

Josef nodded.

"All right," Yitzhak said, "it has been suggested we execute our plan of taking over the ship, keeping the captain hostage and forcing the first mate to take us to Palestine. But there's little point in our talking about the details of the operation until we have the gun. In other words, the moment has come for Tovah to tell us exactly where it is; then we'll discuss how to go for it with the best chance of success. Tovah?"

She could not suppress a shiver. Until that moment, they had not been involved in any real action. With this decision, they'd set something in motion that would turn the game of Masada into reality. But her voice was steady when she replied, "It's in the middle drawer of the desk in the captain's cabin. There's also a box of ammunition marked 'Soft Centers.' And a pair of hand-cuffs, if we want it."

"All right," Yitzhak said, "let's discuss who'll go for the gun, and when. Someone will have to sneak into that cabin while it's empty. First: should it be one or two? A gun, a box of ammunition and a pair of handcuffs is a lot of stuff for one person to hide."

"One," Philip said firmly. "Two kids in a cabin means they're up to something. One kid can say he came to look for the doctor."

"Why?" Gretchen Kahn asked. "He should have a reason."

"That's easy," Anna Feldschuh said, "an emergency in one of the holds."

"Are you planning to have somebody break a leg? It had better be a real emergency."

"I know," Tovah said. "Let whoever it is say that Mrs. Schlachter is raving again and that she needs an injection."

"What if she's not raving?" Fritz Stahl asked.

"Don't worry," Anna Feldschuh said, "she will."

"How do you know? Can you make her?"

"All it takes is for someone to mention that they have seen Lieschen."

"No," Tovah said. "We can't do that. It's not right. Let whoever it is just say that Mrs. Schlachter has had one of her turns; by the time the doctor turns up, she has calmed down. I'll make sure to be there, I'll say she had trouble but that it's blown over."

"All right," Yitzhak said, "let's settle for that. Now the decision: who's going to do it? If we're going to use Mrs. Schlachter, it will have to be one of the girls. Tovah, if Mrs. Schlachter were to start up again and need an injection, who would you send for the doctor?"

Tovah thought it over. "I suppose I'd go myself. No . . . I would stay with her; I'm the only one who can control her under those circumstances. I think I'd send David, if he was around."

"Very well," Yitzhak concluded. "Let's settle on David. Do you think he can handle it, Tovah?"

She visualized David slipping into the cabin, opening the drawer, getting the gun, the box of ammunition. "Do we want the handcuffs?"

Yitzhak looked around the table.

"We might need them," Josef said. "Presumably, we take the captain prisoner, with one of us holding the gun . . . "

"All right," Yitzhak said. "Let's say David has got hold of the pistol, the ammunition and handcuffs; he'll deliver them to—who? Tovah?"

"That seems to be the best," Josef said. "Let her wait for him on deck. We don't want him wandering around with that gun any longer than necessary."

"All right," Yitzhak said, "now we get to the operation itself. It's unrealistic to think that we can take this ship to Palestine. But a ship that's been taken over by a bunch of teenagers who are keeping the captain hostage and state that they'd rather be shot and die than be sent back to Germany—that's news. That will get into the newspapers. It means we'll have to make a real show of it. We'll have to haul down the Dutch flag and replace it with the Star of David . . . "

"Was it you who painted that star on Lieschen's shroud?" Philip asked.

"No. But let me finish! So we must abandon the concept of forcing the crew to sail the ship to Palestine. That's a pipe dream. We must plan a last stand. A—well, a present-day Masada. And *mean* it. In other words, unlikely as it may be, we must be ready to die."

A silence fell, in which Tovah sensed for the first time that they were no longer living in a half-world of dreams and hopes and shoring one another up with big talk. But if this was for real, was she ready to die? She knew the answer, without hesitation: she'd rather die like the Jews in Masada than let herself be taken back to Germany. But what about David? He was so little; had she the right to decide for him? Maybe it would never come to this . . .

Hannelore broke the silence. "But what about the others?"

"Who?"

"The rest, the old ones. Will they go along, once we have taken over the ship?"

Josef snorted. "Of course they will. They're just a bunch of cowards. We'll be holding the gun; if they want to be taken back to Germany, we'll turn it on them."

"Of course they don't want to be taken back!" Anna cried.

"Some of them want just that," Yitzhak stated calmly. "I know Jablonski and the Rabbi are discussing that option if the committee fails."

There was a shocked silence; this time it was Philip who broke it. "Well, Yitzhak, my friend, there's your answer: the moment for us to take over the ship is when the old ones decide to ask to be taken back. Then we might as well stand up and be shot. If only to save the honor of the Jewish race."

"People," Anna corrected. "We're a nation, not a race."

"Friends," Yitzhak urged, "let's stick with the subject. So far, we have decided three—"

He was interrupted by a soft, urgent whistle.

"Hush!" Josef said. "Somebody coming!"

They started a meaningless conversation, passing the paper cup around, wondering who was about to show up.

It was Henky, the cabin boy. He came toward their table, carrying something in a tee shirt. "Here," he said, "I've come to give these back."

They watched incredulously as he put on the table three pocket knives, a fountain pen and a watch. "God almighty, that's mine!" Fritz Stahl cried, furious.

Henky dumped the rest of the loot on the table and fled.

"Hey! Stop!" But by the time Fritz had jumped to his feet to go after him, the boy had disappeared.

3

Henky could not understand what was the matter with God. He had done exactly what he had promised to do when he crouched praying under the captain's table, but all he got in return was that people got mad at him. Chief Davelaar, mad as hell; those kids, after his skin; and now Cook, hitting the ceiling at the sight of his little brass pelican from Florida.

"Where the smoking whorehouse did *that* come from, you little bucket of tepid piss?"

Cook only went in for complicated cuss-names when he was fit to be tied, so Henky chickened out despite his promise to God to confess his sins, and said, "I—I found it as I turned over your mattress, sir. It was underneath."

"Turned my mattress? When? Why?" Cook stood, narrow-eyed, ready to give him the back of his hand, while behind him on the galley stove the lids of pots and pans clappered with hisses of steam.

"I wanted to get rid of that hollow for you, sir. I thought if I turned it over . . . "

Cook looked at the little pelican, then he shook his head and said, "Well, I'll be darned."

No cussword, so he had bought the story. That mattress had better be turned pretty quick, before Cook went to his cabin. Henky was on his way out of the galley when Cook called him back. "Hold it! I've got a tray for the bridge!" He slammed a bunch of mugs onto a tray, muttering, "Captain, Mate Meyer, watch at the wheel, those two Navy guys—who else is there?"

"Mr. Wybrands is standing by in the radio room, sir."

"Okay, that makes six." Cook poured coffee into the mugs from the kettle that had been among the clappers, put on the sugar bowl and pierced the lid of a can of condensed milk. "There you go. Don't spill any. Put that tray on your fingertips, shoulder height, and keep your eyes off it! Hop to it!" Henky escaped, balancing the tray on his fingers at shoulder height, obediently keeping his eyes off it until he was out of sight. Cook had this superstition that if you carried it that way, you wouldn't spill anything. Well, Henky had news for him. He climbed the stairs to the lower bridge and was about to swing onto the steps to the bridge itself when he spotted a kid outside the captain's cabin. He must be waiting for the doctor, as passengers were not allowed on the lower bridge. The boy was wearing a raincoat.

Upstairs, a lot of people were standing about, unusually silent. The ship was on the move. Over starboard lay a white beach. There were fluffy clouds in the sky, it had turned into a lovely day, but the people on the bridge looked dour.

He served the captain first, who barely noticed him. Then the Dutch Navy officer, who said, "Thank you," without looking at him. Then the American officer, who said, "Hey, that's a welcome sight! Guess I'll have some cream, please. And three lumps. Any spoons?"

"No, sir. No spoons. People on the bridge use pencils, or if they have a comb—"

"Get on with it, boy!" Mate Meyer snapped.

"Yessir . . . " He served Mate Meyer next, who glowered at the tray and said, "Look at the mess! Will you ever learn not to spill the damn coffee? This mug's dripping all over my clothes!"

"Yessir." He slipped into the wheelhouse.

The bo'sun at the wheel gave him a wink and said, "Tell Cook to put less in. There's no way you can stop it from spilling if they're that full."

"Yessir."

The bo'sun was the only one in a good mood; when Henky got to the radio room, Mr. Wybrands, cursing and swearing, sat at his desk with the usual collection of screws, nuts and little objects scattered in front of the radio, the lid of which was open. "Put it down, put it down!" Mr. Wybrands snarled without looking up. "Don't touch anything!"

"No, sir. There you are, sir."

"Okay, now beat it. *Beat it!*"

Henky flashed out the door, swung the tray to dry it and headed for the steps. He'd return to the galley as slowly he could, enjoying the sunlight and the sea while he had the chance. As he started down to the lower bridge, he saw out of the corner of his eye the boy in the raincoat slip into the captain's cabin. Suddenly, the penny dropped: the raincoat didn't make sense, the weather was warm. Henky himself had worn a raincoat in toy shops and department stores. The boy was a thief!

On an impulse, he turned around and climbed back up to the bridge. He headed for Mate Meyer; then the captain happened to turn around and spot him, so Henky changed course and went for him. "Somebody to see you in the cabin, sir."

"Who is it?"

"Don't know, sir. It's a kid."

"Go and ask him what he wants."

"Yessir . . . "

That had not been the idea, but now he couldn't get out of it. So he took a deep breath, went down the steps again and crossed over to the cabin. After a short hesitation, he knocked and instantly opened the door. At first, he thought the boy had left; then he saw him standing by the desk, looking mean. He recognized him now: the little brother of the red-haired girl. "The captain wants to know what you want."

Yes, dammit, he *had* been stealing, for he closed a drawer by leaning against it as he replied, "I'm not waiting for the captain. I'm waiting for the doctor."

"Oh, I see." Henky was not about to let that boy stay in the cabin by himself. "Well, you can't stay here."

The boy looked as if he'd like to kick his shins, then he said, "Mrs. Schlachter's acting up again. She needs a shot."

"Okay, I'll tell him." Henky stood his ground, waiting for the boy to move. There was a battle of wills, then the boy moved toward the door.

Henky considered frisking him, but decided against it. After the boy had left, he went over to the desk, opened the drawer and looked inside. At the beginning of the voyage, he had gone through all drawers in all cabins; but he could not remember exactly what had been in this one. The boy might have been looking for money or cigarettes.

He went out onto the lower bridge with his tray, leaned over the rail and stared at the sea. Who could he tell? What could he say? Nothing at this point. He'd just have to keep his eyes peeled from now on.

The doctor was not in the infirmary; Henky was about to turn away when he heard voices behind the curtain that screened off Mr. Vinkemans' bed. "Doc?" he asked.

The curtain was pushed aside by the doctor. "What do you want?"

"They're asking for you in the women's hold, Doc. That queer old lady is having fits again."

"Mrs. Schlachter?"

"Yes, Doc."

"Okay. I'll be right there." The curtain was closed again.

Henky wandered back to the deck with his tray and leaned over the rail again. Should he tell the doctor?

"There you are, you lazy little stinker!"

Cook was leaning out the door of the galley, having a fit. "What do you think this is? A sanitarium? Go get those empty mugs, you slimy little snot-frog!"

Henky sprinted back to the bridge.

4

To Hendrik's surprise, Mrs. Schlachter welcomed him with a smile and a happy *"Guten Morgen, Herr Doktor!"* She was sitting up in bed, a blue ribbon in her hair, and seemed quite *compos mentis.*

"Mrs. Schlachter, I've come to have a look at you. Tell me, how are you? Any difficulties?"

"Oh, no, no, no, *Herr Doktor,*" she said, with the exaggerated stress of the unstable. "Your pills are doing wonders for me. I feel so calm, so happy, so—joyful. Really, I feel joyful." To prove it, she gave him a toothy smile, belied by the sadness in her eyes.

He hesitated to do this to the old lady, but he should find out whether she had indeed had an episode, in which case he would sedate her, or whether the whole thing had been a false alarm. "Any sign of your granddaughter lately, Mrs. Schlachter?"

The smile slowly died. She looked at him for the first time since the child's death as if she was aware of him as a person, not just as a menacing shadow in her demon-haunted universe. "You don't believe me," she said in a normal voice. "You think I'm a silly old woman imagining things."

"Why should I?" he asked. "Have you been imagining things?"

"I am *not, Herr Doktor. I do* see Lieschen at times."

"I'm sure you do, Mrs. Schlachter. But is she real?"

She thought it over; then she replied carefully, "She is real and yet not real. But she is around."

"How, Mrs. Schlachter? Exactly what do you see?"

"I see her in a white summer dress, just in from a garden. She looks frightened, lost, as if she's waiting for someone to help her. Help her do what? I can't understand."

Her sincerity was impressive in its calm, and suddenly he was intrigued by her story.

"How does she manifest herself? Do you suddenly see her? Do you hear her voice?"

"No," the old woman said quietly, "I never hear her. I wish I did. I'd love to. No, I only see her. In a white dress. Just in from the garden."

"How do you know that?"

"What?"

"That she's just in from the garden?"

"I smell it."

"You mean you smell something before she appears?"

"Flowers. Like our garden in Heidelberg. Lieschen loved the garden. She is lost in a garden, like the one at home. Home . . . " She gazed at him, her eyes unfocused and sad. "I think I want to rest now." She seemed to shrink in front of his eyes. She was wearing a pink bed jacket; it looked as if her body no longer filled it.

"Let me help you." He reached out to help her out of the jacket, but a voice beside him said, "Let me do that. That's my job." It was Tovah.

"Thank you," he said. "I'll leave her to you." He patted Mrs. Schlachter's hand. "Have a nice rest. If you need me, just call me. I'll be there."

She did not answer; her moment of lucidity had come and gone like a patch of sunlight on a clouded day.

"Did she have a crisis just now?" he asked in a whisper.

"Yes," Tovah said. "Poor woman."

"Yes," he said. He would have liked to ask more, but his relationship with the girl was still uncomfortable.

He managed to make his way to the ladder without being stopped by a patient, which was amazing. As he emerged on deck, he saw the rowboat of the Coast Guard cutter leave, heading for the low white vessel wallowing between them and Nantucket Island on the slow Atlantic swell. They must have crossed the three-mile limit and were now heading out to sea. The weather was gorgeous, the air pure and clean after the fug in the holds; he felt like climbing into his lifeboat. But he still had that telegram to send.

He found Wybrands in a foul mood, the desk in front of the radio set covered with screws, nuts and coils.

"My God," Hendrik said, "what are you doing?"

"One contact," Wybrands muttered without looking up. "One fucking little contact! Junk, that's what it is, junk! Booze in the cupboard up there." Without looking, he pointed at a door above the set.

Hendrik opened it and found an earthenware crock of Dutch gin and some glasses. "Want one?"

"No," Wybrands grunted. "Help yourself. Won't be a minute."

Hendrik helped himself to a stiff belt, then a second. Ah, that was better! He pulled up a stool and sat down at the desk beside Wybrands, reached for a telegram form and started to write:

Willemse, M.D. Tubantia. Will you take on . . . What should he call Vinkemans? 'Depressed crew member' did not sound urgent enough. 'Mental patient' was on the strong side. But it would cut out shilly-shallying.

"Okay," Wybrands said with a sigh of accomplishment. "Let's put all this rabbit shit back inside and see what happens." He proceeded to put the set back together with surprising dexterity for a man with hands that large; then he switched on the transmitter, put on his earphones, gave a short rat-tat on his Morse key and said, "Done it!" He took off his phone and said, "Now you can give me a drink. Let me have that telegram."

Hendrik handed him the form, brought out the booze and decided he might as well have a third. He wasn't going anywhere.

"Who's the mental patient?"

"Vinkemans. He's not insane by definition, but I have to put my opposite number and his commodore in the right mood to receive him. So let's call him that for the time being."

"Who are you going to use for a replacement?"

"Oh, I have a few women. I can handle it. Nothing to it. Here you go." He handed Wybrands a glass. "Cheers."

They both made short shrift of their drinks. Wybrands smacked his lips and said, "Well, let's see if we can get a word in edgeways. Boy, those guys are busy transmitting twenty-four hours a day; I'll have the devil of a time getting in there. But let's find out." He put on his earphones and started to work the key; there was a light flickering overhead; the small cubicle slowly filled with a smell of batteries. He seemed to be sending the same Morse signal time and time again; suddenly, he looked up with a grin and said, "Yes! Give me that sheet."

He transmitted the telegram, listened, then said, "They ask if he's violent."

"No, no, say comatose."

"How do you spell that?"

Hendrik spelled it for him. Only as the message was going out did he reflect that this might be pushing the diagnosis of poor Vinkemans' condition a little far; but after three snifters, who cared?

Wybrands listened and said, "They'll pass it on. Anything else?"

"Yes." It suddenly occurred to him that he would need a lot of sedatives before this trip was over: in suspension, not tablets, or he might end up with a shipful of potential suicides. "Ask for this . . . " He scribbled it on a pad: *Urgently need sedative for two hundred in suspension.*

"Two hundred what?"

"Just ask." He poured himself a fourth.

"What the hell is 'in suspension'?"

"Never mind."

Wybrands worked the key; the stench of acid was stifling.

"Tell you what: add 'T.I.D.' As in tiddlywinks. Stands for three times daily."

"Okay . . . " He signaled it, listened, and said, *"Will pass on message. Good luck. End."*

He signed off, took off his earphones, turned off the transmitter, raised the glass Hendrik had refilled for him and said, "To home and sanity."

"To a miracle," Hendrik said. For that was what it would take to keep this joint from exploding after Vinkemans had been shipped out, leaving him to face the bees in the bonnets alone. God help them all. He tossed back his fourth and grinned at the drunken thought that, if truth be told, it was he who should be shipped out as incompetent: into the launch, wave goodbye, and prrr-prrr across to *Tubantia,* straight into the arms and legs of bonny Susan with the light green hair.

"Let's keep going," Wybrands said, pouring. "Come hell or high water."

"Both," Hendrik said. As he drank, for some idiotic reason there was Mrs. What's-her-name in Amsterdam, with her orange tomcat spread-eagled on the ottoman. She had talked about high water. A barn keeling over in a flood. A brunette climbing the rafters; a smell of honeysuckle.

Ah, well, time for another. "Here's to a great lady," he said, "and her cat."

Generously, Wybrands joined in the toast.

CHAPTER NINE

I

Commodore Bouke Bruinsma lay stark naked on the massage table in the First Class gym, drowsily aware of having his shoulder muscles manipulated, when the blissful ministry of the masseur's hands suddenly ceased and his voice said respectfully, "Commodore? Here's the doctor to see you."

Bruinsma slowly spelled a hair-curling curse in his mind before opening one eye and saying coldly, "Yes, Doctor? What is it?"

"We have a message from *Star of Peace*, Commodore. They're requesting we take on a mental patient, comatose."

"Who's that? Her captain?"

"No, her medic."

Bruinsma closed the eye. Well, that explained the mysterious telegram from the agent in New York:

Netherlands Embassy requests you prepare for your surgeon to join in sanity bearing on board Dutch freighter Star of Peace off Long Island stop company authorizes ensuing delay.

One of those damned irritating telegrams that sounded efficient and on top of things but betrayed a dismal ignorance of the reality of stopping a transatlantic liner with twelve hundred passengers, getting a launch across, hauling it back on board, justifying the whole maneuver to the poker players in First Class who ran on schedules tighter than those of transcontinental trains.

"All right, Willemse," he said, "what's your reaction to the request?"

"I'm game, sir. I mean, it's all right with me. We can put the patient in isolation in the Cabin Class infirmary. Or in the prison cell on B deck if he's really violent."

"How far away is she now?"

"The bridge thinks forty-five miles."

The bridge thinks. 'The bridge' being young Petersen, Balaam's ass. "Did *Star* ask for a confirmation?"

"I—er—I think so . . . " Another thinker.

"All right, Doctor. Go to the radio room, tell them to confirm the arrangement and ask if nursing assistance is required."

"I beg your pardon?"

This time, Bruinsma opened both eyes. Willemse was standing there with his cap under his arm, like a headwaiter with the menu. "Do they need nurses to restrain that madman? Or is he supposed to remain obligingly comatose while being trussed like a pig and lowered aboard a launch in a sling?"

"A sling, sir?"

"How else do you propose they drop him into our launch? By parachute?"

"I see."

"And while you're up there, tell Petersen to ask the U.S. Coast Guard in Boston for the exact location of *Star* and report it to the bridge."

"Yes, Commodore."

Bruinsma closed his eyes. "And tell the bridge I'm on my way."

"Very well, Commodore."

The masseur did not resume his blissful ministry; Bruinsma opened his eyes again. Willemse had not moved. "Now what else have you got for me, Doctor? The wine list?"

"Er—should the passengers be advised?"

God help and protect us from nautical doctors. "Doctor," he

said, "let's make a deal: you distribute the horse pills, I sail the ship. Get on with it, Barend."

The masseur resumed his ministry. As his shoulders luxuriated in the sensuous squeezing, Bruinsma reflected that the mad medic would make a better message to broadcast to the passengers on the intercom than 'Our doctor's presence is required for a sanity hearing.' This much he had learned, the hard way: if a liner captain conveys the message to his passengers that the ship is going to be late arriving, he had better tell them why and it had better be the truth, or some financial wizard would slap a suit on the company for damages. Somebody in First Class with a couple of hundred thousand bucks riding on their arrival in New York on time might take a jaundiced view of 'assistance at a sanity hearing.' 'Assistance to subdue and transfer a violent mental patient' was better, as the Law of the Sea obliged masters of passing vessels to render that kind of assistance. It also made for a more pithy entertainment for the ghouls among his passengers.

Bruinsma had showered and was on his way down the passage to his cabin in his terrycloth robe when a girl's voice asked, "Sir?"

It was Nurse Foster.

"Yes, Foster?"

"May I have a word with you, sir?"

Had she been a man, he'd have sent her packing; but she was a pretty young woman and Myrtle's friend to boot. "Come in," he said.

He opened the door and let her enter, then pointed at one of the white armchairs and said, "Sit down, I'll be right with you. Or is it urgent?"

"Well, sort of, sir . . . " She did not sit down. She looked flustered and emotional. Various possibilities presented themselves; you never knew with women. It was probably old Lady Endersby again, complaining that she had rung her bell for the nurse for three-quarters of an hour before it was answered.

"All right, let's have it," he said.

"I—I ask permission to go to *Star of Peace*, sir."

"Why, of course. I told the doctor he'd need assistance." He turned away to go to his bedroom.

"I—I want to go for keeps, sir."

He turned around, slowly. "Say that again?"

"I ask permission to transfer to *Star of Peace* to replace the medic, sir."

He looked at her without sympathy, remembering she had a thing going with the young doctor over there. All women sailors, dammit, thought with their reproductive organs. "No," he said. "I'm not authorized to transfer members of my crew to other ships on the high seas unless it's a matter of life and death, clearly stated as such in a written request by the master of the vessel in question. You're permitted to go aboard and assist in bringing over the patient, but there can be no question of a transfer." This time, he turned his back on her and went into his bedroom. As he was dressing, he finally heard the door of his sitting room close —she had dithered for quite a while, trying to muster up the courage to plead with him. Thank God she hadn't. If there was one thing that set his teeth on edge it was whining, whether by crew members or grandchildren.

Before going up to the chartroom, he telephoned a telegram to the radio room, requesting confirmation that tugboats would be waiting for him despite the estimated two-hour delay.

As he arrived on the bridge, young Petersen was walking to and fro at high speed, hands clasped behind his back, every inch the officer in charge of a thirty-thousand-ton liner.

"Okay, Petersen," he said, "let's have a look at the chart. Have you got *Star*'s position?"

"Yessir. I marked it, sir."

"How very efficient of you."

Bent over *New York Approaches* in the green-shaded light of the chart lamp, Bruinsma saw that she was about forty miles away, just under two hours' sailing. He had better make that announcement now; if he waited longer, it would cause trouble with the crap-shooters of high finance. He pulled out a note-pad to scribble the message; impromptu announcements were a bad idea. As he was writing, Petersen turned up with a radio sheet and said, "Here's a notice to mariners, sir, that just came in."

Sighing, he looked up. "What is it?"

"Warning to all traffic, sir: a six-mile-deep coastal zone, Nantucket to Ambrose, requires extra vigilance because of a regatta, sir."

"As from when?"

"Oh—er—sorry, sir. Tomorrow, zero hundred hours, sir."

"And we will be in New York by then, won't we, Petersen?"

"Yessir. Sorry, sir."

"Well, should anything else urgent turn up, I'll be in the radio room."

"Yessir."

The radio room was in the usual pre-arrival bustle: with four operators, the Morse signals from the speakers made it sound like an aviary. Both the chief and the assistant radio officer were on duty; both rose as they saw him enter. "Good morning. What's the latest from *Star?*"

"A request for sedatives, sir," Chief Sparks replied. "Here it is, sir."

It was a terse message: *Urgently request sedative for 200 in suspension, TID.* They must be faced with massive depression, hysteria and even suicidal tendencies, to ask for the stuff in suspension. The picture it evoked was Alexandria all over again. Boy, he did not envy that doctor right now. "All right, Sparks, pass it on to the doctor. Now I have an announcement to make. Let me have the mike, please." He sat down at the microphone table.

"Yessir." The chief fiddled with knobs and switches, then called, "Silence, please!" A red light went on by the side of the microphone. "You're on now, sir."

"Now hear this, now hear this. This is Commodore Bruinsma speaking. I must advise you that our arrival in New York harbor will be delayed by approximately two hours, for the following reason. We have received an urgent request from the Netherlands freighter *Star of Peace* to send over a doctor and nurses in order to subdue a violent mental patient and take him on board this ship for transfer to Bellevue Hospital in New York City. We expect to be alongside the freighter in approximately two hours' time.

The port side of the boat deck will be declared out of bounds during the operation, until the patient has been securely confined to the appropriate quarters. For those of you interested in the technicalities of an operation like this, let me explain that we happen to be the vessel nearest to the freighter in question, which obliges us by law to respond to the request. Our approximate hour of arrival in New York harbor has now been modified to eight-thirty P.M. For those of you who may miss railroad or airplane connections due to this delay, arrangements will be made for an overnight stay in a hotel in New York, and our agent will assist you in making new reservations. Thank you." He nodded to the chief radio officer, who flicked a switch. "Thank you, Sparks. Have you received a reply yet from New York regarding the tugboats?"

"Yessir. Moran assures us he will have boats available at that time. They'll be waiting in the usual location."

"Very well. Should anything new turn up, I'll be in my cabin."

"Yessir."

The way back to his cabin led via the boat deck; already, the excitement among the passengers was evident. There was no one in the pool, they were clustered in groups, talking. Bruinsma wondered how many of them had any idea what conditions on board that freighter must be like. But why should they? All they knew was that there was a lunatic to be subdued and picked up. They knew nothing of the Jews on board that ship, they had never heard of whatever the name of the freighter in Alexandria had been. Somehow, that telegram about the sedatives had darkened the radiance of the glorious summer day. When he arrived in his cabin, it looked bleak and lonely. He had a good hour to kill. On an impulse, he picked up the telephone and dialed a number.

"Cabin Class infirmary. Nurse Sedgwick-Jones speaking."

"Okay," he said, "I have an hour or so. How about popping over?"

"Oh—oh, okay. Super. I won't be long. Ta-ta." There was a click, but she failed to put the horn back on properly, for he heard her voice say, "Sorry, ducks, I have to run. The Old Man finds he's got time on his hands, so he's requesting permission to lay alongside."

His first impulse was to whistle into the instrument to attract her attention and give her hell, but he put the receiver down. Who was 'ducks'? Must be that girl Foster. It was not the idea that Myrtle should start blabbing about their relationship to the crew. So far only to the girl Foster, probably; he doubted she would have been gossiping to anyone else, but he knew from bitter experience that gossip about captains could not be contained for long on board ship, so he'd better cut it off at the pass. After a few moments, he dialed another number.

"Commodore's office. Miss van Alkemade."

"Miss van Alkemade, I have a statement to dictate. Come over, please, and bring your steno-pad."

"Yessir. I'll be right there."

She turned up at once: cool, efficient, middle-aged and as devoid of sexual attraction as Mother Goose. She sat down in one of his armchairs, pad on lap, pencil poised.

"All right, this has to be typed on blank stationery, two copies for the company, one for the master in question, two for our files and one for the log."

"Yessir."

"We the undersigned: Commodore Bruinsma, Bouke, skipper next to God of the vessel *Tubantia,* and Kuiper (I don't know the guy's first name, leave it open), skipper next to God of the vessel *Star of Peace,* both of Dutch registry, declare that, consequent to the illness and subsequent removal of medic (don't know the guy's name, leave it open), a life-threatening situation exists among the passengers of *Star of Peace.* Captain Kuiper urgently requests that a substitute medic be dispatched to his vessel from *Tubantia.* Pursuant to article (I don't know the number, look it up) of the Law on Mutual Assistance among Ships on the High Seas, Commodore Bruinsma in response to that request has ordered the transfer of Nurse Foster (don't know her first name) to *Star of Peace,* where she will remain until such date as the passengers are disembarked, or a substitute medic or nurse has arrived to replace her. All costs of this transfer to be charged to the owners of *Star of Peace*. All right, Miss van Alkemade. Also, get out that girl's muster book for me and put it on my desk with those documents when you've done them. I'm not sure yet that the situation warrants the transfer, I'll go and find out for myself, but I want to have the paperwork done in case it proves necessary. Thank you."

She rose primly and marched out, stepping aside to let Myrtle enter as she opened the door.

"Hello. How jolly D of you to call me!"

It was Eve, not the serpent, who'd had the forked tongue in Paradise.

"Sorry," he said, "I'm afraid we have to scrub our little tête-à-tête."

"Oh, no! Why?" Look at that face; you'd think she'd just heard her favorite aunt had broken her hip. Permission to lay alongside, indeed.

"We don't have the time. I have to get ready."

"For what?"

"I'm going on board that ship," he said.

2

When *Tubantia* was alongside, huge and white, her decks lined with spectators, Kuiper watched her launch being lowered. It came darting across the sparkling sea; only when it was swinging in for mooring did he recognize the tall, burly figure in her bow. He went to the gangway to welcome him.

Commodore Bruinsma, white and gold, climbed the Jacob's ladder with surprising agility.

"Welcome, Captain," Kuiper said as he reached the deck. "Good afternoon. Kind of you to stop by."

But the commodore did not take the outstretched hand. "Let me have a look first," he said. He took Kuiper by the shoulders and turned him toward the sun. "How's the holy fire?" The sea-green eyes, shrewd and all-seeing, searched his. "Dimmed a bit, I'd say."

"Let's go to my cabin," Kuiper said, acutely conscious of the silent watchers surrounding them. "This way, please."

In the cabin, Bruinsma took off his cap. "I've brought with me the sedatives your doctor asked for. In suspension, not pills. Obviously, he's afraid of suicides." He wandered over to the porthole. "Quite a responsibility, young man. But, well, they'd be called God's will, I presume."

"Yes!"

Bruinsma turned around. The sea-green eyes snapped with anger. "I can understand that a Christian who finds his house burgled says, 'It was God's will I was burgled.' But that the thief says, 'It was God's will that I committed the burglary'?"

"When God spoke to me, the danger of suicides was over."

The eyes became hooded, watchful. "Spoke to you? How?"

"Through a naval officer."

"And what did the naval officer say?"

"Tomorrow all ships in this area will be on alert because of a regatta. Scores of yachts. American."

"So?"

"If I broadcast an S.O.S. and my passengers take to the boats, those yachts will be obliged to pick them up. Won't they?"

"If they are the vessels nearest to you, yes. But why the S.O.S.?"

"Boatloads of reporters will come out to record the finish of that race. There will be planes overhead with newsreel cameras, radio reporters. If I sail into that regatta and scuttle my ship, the yachts and the powerboats will have to pick up my passengers, who will thereby arrive on United States territory in the full light of public opinion."

After a short, motionless silence, Bruinsma said evenly, "If you scuttle your ship, the banks that mortgaged her will be after you like a pack of hounds. And their insurance company. My guess is you'll end up with a year in prison."

"So be it."

"And you're likely to lose your Master's Certificate for life.

You'll probably never be permitted to command a ship again."

"I know." He was surprised at his own equanimity. It was all still abstract, unreal. He felt like an impostor.

Bruinsma frowned. "You intend to go down with your ship?"

It surprised Kuiper; he would have thought the commodore to be more perspicacious than that. "Suicide? You know little about Christianity."

"Of course, forgive me. I forgot the attraction of martyrdom."

"I won't be a martyr if I do it."

"No. You'll only be a fool. They will be the martyrs." He pointed at the portrait of Anna and the children. "Does she know about this, by the way?"

"Not yet. I've written out a telegram, but I'd rather not give it to my operator to send; next thing, it would be all over the ship. I wonder: would you forward it through your radio room?"

"Of course."

He took the paper from his desk and handed it to Bruinsma, who put it in his pocket, unread. "You're waiting for her approval?"

"I hope for her support."

"And if she won't give it to you?"

He thought it over. What if Anna were to say 'If you do that, I'll leave you'? That, of course, was nonsense. Or was it?

He wandered over to the portrait and looked at her; her earnest face, honest eyes, the brooch Dad had given her. Suddenly, the whole idea seemed crazy, a dream.

He closed his eyes as the consequences of God's plan overwhelmed him.

3

Bruinsma watched him, and sensed his weakening. The whole idea was insane—clearly, the boy had buckled under the strain. To act on your principles was all very well, but when it became destructive, it turned into lunacy. The boy was obviously off his rocker by now. Pity, he had liked the idea of the young Knight in Shining Armor sailing to slay the dragon of governmental hypocrisy. He would have to shake him out of his destructive delusion. "So!" he said forcefully. "And now we close that Bible!"

Kuiper turned around and looked at him, bewildered.

"Yes! It's time you learned to distinguish between Christianity and simple human decency, young man!"

"I don't understand . . . "

"For five thousand years, we have been pestering our Lord; the moment has come to leave Him in peace for a while! What do you think *I* would have done in your place, two months ago in South America, if it had been my ship? Taken those Jews back to Germany?"

"I thought you made that quite clear at the time."

"No, my dear Christian! I would have done the same thing you did, not because I'm a Christian but because I'm a plain decent man. You Christians can't even be decent without the help of God. You'd murder, steal, lie, whore around the moment he let go of you! But am I a murderer? A thief? A liar? No. I'm a decent man without pestering God."

Kuiper looked at him for a long moment; then he said, "In that case, I hand over my command to you."

"I beg your pardon?"

"I ask you to take over command of my ship. You seem to have the zest left to carry on, I have not. If the cause of decency really means something to you, hand over your command to your first officer, inform your company, become a free man and take over my ship. I'll sign half of it over to you, right here and now. I'll make you my partner."

"Don't talk nonsense."

"Then stop throwing bull at me! I've been asked to nail myself to the cross! I'm not interested in word games!"

For a moment, Bruinsma visualized it: the radiogram to the company, goodbye pension, goodbye security, a half-share in this rusty old bucket filled with desperate people about to be handed back to their executioners. What he was in effect being asked was to take command of the ship he had seen off Alexandria. He realized with a sense of incredulous surprise that his own moment of truth had suddenly been thrust upon him. This was what he had contemplated as he stood watching the departure of *Star* through the window of his cabin, stark naked, reeking of lust, the luscious body of a young, willing blonde warm beside him. He remembered his sense of nostalgia, the facile wish that it could be he, old Knight in Buckled Armor, sailing that ship to her destiny.

The young man was watching him; it was a bitter moment when he had to answer, with a sense of farewell, "Thank you. Not this time."

Kuiper took it without comment, but with a curious lack of condemnation; to witness another man's moral defeat did not seem to give him a sense of superiority. He went to his desk for another sheet of paper. "I've drawn up a declaration stating that I assume full responsibility. It's meant to safeguard my staff from prosecution. Would you mind having a look at it to see if it serves that purpose?"

Bruinsma put on his glasses, took the paper and read it. Then he handed it back.

"Is it all right?" the boy asked.

Bruinsma folded his glasses, put them back in his breast pocket and said, "I wish I were your father."

"My father would have done exactly the same thing."

"But why? You're not a family of lunatics, are you?"

"My father was a Christian too," the boy said simply.

"Oh, for God's sake!" Bruinsma went toward the door, but halfway there he remembered the document Miss van Alkemade had typed. He hesitated; if Kuiper signed, it meant the girl would have to stay on board this ship. Should he reverse his decision, now he knew what the man was contemplating? No. Not only would she be needed if Kuiper carried out his crazy plan; she'd be able to rejoin *Tubantia* in New York in a few days' time. He took the paper from his pocket. "By the way, I have something here for you to sign. One of my nurses has volunteered to replace your medic; if you want her, we should do it formally, or she'll be considered a ship-jumper and lose her social benefits. So, if you'll sign here . . . "

"What is it?"

"The official request, by you, for assistance in this emergency. It *is* an emergency, isn't it? You can't let your doctor face two hundred potential suicides alone, once you've announced that you're going to have to take them back to Germany."

Kuiper stared at him for a moment. Then he took out his pen and signed.

It was an odd feeling to walk away from the boy without having been able to puncture his delusion. As he stood with his hand on the doorknob, Bruinsma turned and said, "I'll alert my radio room. If there's no S.O.S. signal from you, I'll treat myself and a young friend of mine to a bottle of champagne." He opened the door and added, "If there is, I hope that God of yours, if He exists, may one day save my soul too, if I've got such a thing."

He left, closing the door behind him. Outside on the lower bridge, he found Willemse waiting for him. "Is the patient ready?"

"Yes, Commodore. Any moment now."

"Well, get on with it. Every minute costs the company money." He marched to the Jacob's ladder, climbed down without his feet slipping on the rungs—quite a feat at his age—and was helped into the launch by respectful hands. It was Nurse Foster, her brown eyes huge and beautiful.

"Thank you," he said as he stepped down. "Have the medications been delivered?"

"Yes, Commodore."

"The captain signed the formal request, so you're free to go. But wait until the patient has been secured; we don't want a raving lunatic thrashing about in this launch on our way back."

"Yessir," she said in a small voice. He suddenly became aware that she was afraid; it made him feel vaguely guilty.

"Well, dammit, we haven't got all day! Every minute costs the company money! Hey, you there: get up that ladder and find out what's holding them up!"

"Yessir! Right away, sir!"

The junior officer climbed the rope ladder with depressing agility, swung himself over the rail and was gone.

4

"Doctor! Commodore Bruinsma says the patient must be transferred *now!*" It was a young, pink-cheeked deck officer in a natty
white uniform, as well scrubbed and polished as a French *pomme
de luxe.* As he saw Hendrik's reluctance and Vinkemans' hollow-
cheeked face, he added self-consciously, "Sorry about that, sir,
but the commodore says every minute costs the company
money."

It was not the most tactful remark to have made; old Vinkemans went into a rather effeminate crisis. "Oh! Doctor! I'm so
crushed with shame! I'm so horribly ashamed, so wretchedly
sorry to leave you with this . . . " He burst into sobs, clutched
Hendrik's arm and put his head on his shoulder, a rather unnerving gesture.

Hendrik said to the apple-cheeked subaltern, "We'll be right
there." The boy clicked his heels and saluted, Navy fashion, made
an about-turn and marched out of the infirmary, tripping on the
high threshold. Outside sounded voices, the banging of a heavy
object against the wall; obviously, crew members were on their
way in with a stretcher.

Vinkemans suddenly lifted his head, gazed at Hendrik with
feverish eyes and said, "Doctor! Now please, please remember
when Mrs. Scholle has to go onto the bedpan, it has to be warmed
first, and when Mr. Himmelbaum—"

"Vinkemans," Hendrik said, trying to assume a voice of calm
authority, "don't you worry about a thing. I'm grateful for the
way you've helped me out so far. You have a perfect right to crack
up, it simply means that you are a more sensitive soul than I am.
Yes! Come in!"

Two men turned up with the stretcher. Vinkemans started a
rather hysterical *vocalise;* it was a relief when, finally, they had
strapped him onto the stretcher and, bumping into doorposts and
stumbling over the threshold with low-grade curses, disappeared
down the passage.

Hendrik could not stand watching the man being lowered into the launch; again he was overcome by sheer panic at the prospect of facing the future alone. But he set his jaw, marched resolutely down the passage, up the steps to the lower bridge, into the cabin, across to the corner cupboard, yanked open the door and poured himself a triple gin. It went down like hellfire. He howled with heartburn when it hit his stomach lining. My God, he was crazy! Already, he was reeling after his session with Wybrands in the radio room; to pour gasoline onto the fire like this . . . He slammed the door of the corner cupboard shut, leaned his forehead against it and stood in a quandary as to whether to bawl or burst into schizophrenic laughter. Well, whichever: here he was, without a medic, without anyone to help him face the mounting horror of what lay ahead except a bunch of half-baked women. The only solution might be to sedate them all; rather a ship full of inert bodies doused with Nembutal than two hundred potential suicides. He hoped Willemse had sent over that medication.

As if in answer to his thoughts, there was a knock on the door and it was opened at once. It could only be a crew member, so he said, "Put it in the corner."

There were footsteps, then a woman's voice said, "Hello there."

He whipped around and there—God in heaven almighty!—was Susan. "Susan! Susan, Susan, blessed virgin!" he cried.

"Hardly," she said calmly. When he tried to kiss her, she added coldly, "Sorry. Let's get this straight at the outset: I came for the patients, not for you."

He heard himself say, with a drawl that seemed to belong to some non-existent species, "Well, that's remarkably civil of you. Be my guest, have a look at them by all means. How about a drink, before you drink in the sights and scurry back to dear old *Tub?*"

Her eyes were dark amber, two pools to choose from for a swan dive of the soul. Then she said, "Sorry, old thing. I'm here to stay."

"You're *what?*"

"I have permission from the company in the person of Com-

modore Bruinsma to transfer to *Star of Peace* because of the
emergency created by the collapse of your medic." Her gaze
shifted to his mouth. "But let's forget about our personal relationship. As far as I'm concerned, that's a thing of the past."

To his amazement, he didn't mind. "God," he said, "this sure
beats booze! You have your work cut out for you, sweetheart.
'Emergency' isn't the word. This is Code Blue, two hundred of
them. Let me have a look at you." He took her by the shoulders
and held her at arm's length. It made no difference. He didn't give
a damn about the fact that she was an attractive woman with
whom he had romped in the hay; that he could do without. What
he needed was a first-class nurse. She'd better come up to snuff;
old Vinkemans had been a hard act to follow.

5

When he looked at her with those wicked blue eyes that would
charm the ducks off a pond, she realized that something had
happened to him. He was no longer just a pretty boy without a
thought in his head other than who he'd lay tonight; he had, in
some way, become a man.

"Tell me," he said, "how the hell did you manage to swing
this?"

"Law of the Sea. When Willemse told me about your request
for us to take over a comatose mental patient and I found out it
was your medic, I went to see the Old Man and volunteered. At
first, he wouldn't let me go; then he looked it up in his law books
and realized he was obliged to. By the way, I have to hand your
captain my muster book, don't let me forget that. But first, fill me
in . . ."

"Well, I'm due in the infirmary in five minutes to deal with
the day's problems; join me and see for yourself."

"Do they know yet that they're probably going back to Germany?"

"No. They're hoping that the committee ashore will have an

effect. But, from what I hear, there isn't a chance they'll be given political asylum; so back they go. My medic couldn't face it. He cracked up."

"How come you didn't?"

He shrugged his shoulders. "Maybe I'm thicker-skinned than he was," he said. "Think you can take it?"

"I had better, hadn't I?"

He patted her shoulder and said with a grin, "Good sport. Well, let's go and face the music. I warn you, it's *Overture 1812*, with cannon."

The passage outside the infirmary, which she remembered from the day in Montevideo, was filled with waiting patients. When she entered the consulting room, she was startled to find the girl she had offered her uniform to and who had turned her down. "Oh, hello," she said. "How have you been doing?"

"All right, thank you," the girl replied with a marked lack of warmth. Then she asked, "Does this mean I'll no longer be needed?"

"Not at all," Hendrik replied. "But use this hour to get some rest. You'll all be needed very much indeed. Oh, hello, Mr. Himmelbaum. Come in." It was an elderly man, obviously in a highly nervous state. "Sit down. How are we today?"

While the old man told him in a quavering voice, Susan suddenly realized that she had passed beyond the horizon she had glimpsed in Montevideo, when she stood on the radio deck gazing at the black dot of a ship disappearing, envious of the girl, the courage of her choice. She wondered if the girl had felt then as she herself did right now: terrified to the point of tears by her own bravery.

6

Bouke Bruinsma found the telegram as he went through the pockets of his white suit while changing for cocktails in First Class.

Anna Kuiper, Haven Street 25, den Helder, Holland. I must choose between denying my Saviour and keeping everything or obeying Him and losing everything. Answer for you and the children. Joris.

It was an odd message. Was the woman fully informed? This telegram certainly gave her no clue as to what her husband was up to. No one reading it would realize that the man was asking his wife if it was okay if he scuttled his ship. One thing the telegram did, though. It proved Kuiper had not truly made up his mind: he wanted his wife to decide for him, without actually telling her what the decision was. It took a bit of the glow off the Young Knight in Shining Armor. So he'd go to the brink, but at the brink he'd fold and take those Jews back to Germany.

Bruinsma went to the telephone in his boxer shorts and dialed a number; the radio room answered. "Commodore here. I have a telegram for Holland, urgent. Have it picked up at once and sent Priority One, special delivery, twenty-four hours."

"Yessir."

He poured himself a drink. And what if the incredible happened? What if young Kuiper, negligible, anonymous, a two-bit freighter captain with a plain wife and two plain children, suddenly were to rise and say "NO," not only to Hitler but to all the gutless, cowardly, hypocritical governments of the world? But the age of heroism was past. That telegram was not the stuff of heroes. He'd end up taking the goddam Jews back to goddam Germany and join the club. Alexandria, here I come.

There was a knock on the door. He called, "Come in!" It was Florsheim, a pipsqueak from the radio room, who reeled back at the sight of his commodore in underwear.

"Oh! I'm so sorry, sir! I didn't realize . . . "

"Here," he said, holding out the telegram. "I told Sparks: urgent. Should have gone out an hour ago. Run, boy!"

"Yessir! Yes!" The boy sprinted out the door with such docile vigor that he forgot to close it.

Bruinsma poured himself another, suddenly sick of everything: the booze, that *tsunami* of violent lust building up without

his even thinking of her. He put on his dress uniform, and went
to join the poker players in the First Class library for cocktails;
but in the elevator he changed his mind. "Let me out on B deck,"
he said to the attendant.

In the Cabin Class infirmary, where he had ordered the medic
to be stacked, he found Myrtle mixing a green Jekyll-and-Hyde
concoction with smoke rising from it. "Good evening, Miss
Sedgwick-Jones," he said formally. "What are you pouring into
that poor guy?"

"Oh, good evening, sir. This is just to soothe our tummy. It'll
make us all woozy and woolly and soft, won't it, Robert?"

The hollow-cheeked man in the bed gazed at the glass of foul
green liquid she carried, as if it floated toward him in mid-air,
poltergeist cocktail with straw. "Is it all right if I wait a little?"
he asked in a small voice.

"No," Myrtle replied with a smile like a rictus. "We stopped
a liner on its way to New York, we were transferred to her at
great expense, now we decide we are not going to make any more
problems. Drink it, please."

The man, browbeaten into canine submission, drank the poltergeist cocktail in long, glucking gulps, Adam's apple bobbing,
and ended with a gasp and a green mustache.

"Good boy," Myrtle said briskly. She snatched the glass away,
put it on the bedside table, gave the man a sharp poke in his side
which made him collapse like a plank, tucked him in and said,
"There. Now we're going bye-byes." She was about to yank the
curtain shut, but Bruinsma stopped her.

"I'd like a word with him," he said.

"I've just given him a sleeping draft!"

"I don't give a damn what you gave him. Get out of here, I
want to talk to this man in private."

"Oh, hoity-toity," she muttered, put the empty glass on the
counter with a demonstrative clunk, marched out of the infirmary
with a display of pistoning buttocks and slammed the door.

"Well, Rinkelmans," he said, turning to the bed and pulling
up a chair. "How are you feeling?"

"Very well, sir. Thank you, sir. It's Vinkemans, sir."

"All right, Vinkemans, before we have our little chat, let's get a few things straight. I'm not a doctor. I've sailed with men for three-quarters of my life, and in my considered opinion, you're not a mental patient; I'd say the reverse. I had a look at that ship, I know what's in store for those passengers, and if I'd been you, I too would have moved heaven and earth to get out from under. In my book, you're a malingerer. But a malingerer with cause."

The man looked at him sullenly. "Whatever you say, sir."

It confirmed his diagnosis, which he had never doubted; he could spot a shirker at first sight. "No need to take it as a blot on your professional honor, Vinkemans. I won't advertise it. I never disagree with the experts; let *them* decide what's the matter with you. I'm just telling you this so you may understand why I'm going to say what I'm about to say. I want to pick your brains, Vinkemans. And I'm not inclined to pick the brains of a nut."

"Yessir." The man still acted a snit, but he was obviously intrigued. He looked like a fairy; that meant he'd kill for gossip —no point in asking him to keep this conversation between themselves. But by the time they got to New York and had whisked this character into Bellevue, Kuiper would have decided the issue one way or the other.

"Very well: it's about your captain. He has the opportunity to scuttle his ship in order to force American flag yachts to pick up his passengers, which would put them on U.S. territory with enough publicity to prevent their being shipped back to Germany. He'd not only lose his ship and his money, he'd lose his Master's Certificate and serve a prison term into the bargain. That's a lot to sacrifice for a bunch of refugees. You have sailed with him long enough to know what he's like; in your opinion, is he likely to use that opportunity? Does he care enough about his passengers to sink his damn ship for their freedom?"

The man's eyes took on a frightened look. "Oh my God . . . "

"What does that mean? Yes or no?"

"Oh my God! If I'd known that, I'd never have left!"

"Look, I'm not saying he's going to do it. All I know is that he has the opportunity. I'm asking you because if your captain scuttles his ship, he'll create an international incident, and I'd like to have my ducks in a row before I'm hauled on the carpet for not alerting the authorities. So tell me what you think: is he likely to sacrifice everything he has and go to prison just to get those Jews admitted into the U.S.?"

The man gazed at him unseeingly. Myrtle's poltergeist cocktail was obviously in the process of knocking him out. "It depends on his father."

"I don't get you."

"If his father should turn out to have been a counterfeit, like most fathers when it comes down to the line, he won't."

What a strange thing for him to say! Either he was as bright and observant as he looked to be, or Myrtle's cocktail had indeed got to him. "What do you mean by that?"

"He obviously judges everything he does by what his father would have done. He's not a born skipper next to God, he had it foisted on him. He struck me as being insecure. Quotes his father all the time, has the man's picture over his desk, bigger than that of his wife and kids. My answer would be: if his father would have scuttled the ship, or if Kuiper believes he would, he may do it. But what—"

Bruinsma cut him short; he was in no mood for a jaw session. He wanted to get the man's expertise, fast, and join the poker game upstairs. But the remark had dislodged the memory of something young Kuiper had said in his cabin on board *Star* that afternoon. 'My father would have done the same thing. Of that I'm certain.' So, according to this sharp-eyed character, it would depend on how certain. "He asked me to send a telegram to his wife this afternoon in which he asks for her decision. Does he really mean his father's? Does the old man live with them?"

"No, he's dead. I gather he's been dead for three years. But he's very much alive to Captain Kuiper. At times I thought . . . " He hesitated.

"Well?"

"It sounds ridiculous, but there were moments, while I was with him, when I felt—well—as if the Old Man was with us. It was like having a ghost on board." The man's eyes became unfocused. "A ghost . . . " Myrtle's cocktail was beginning its brutal work.

"Well, I'll let you get some rest," Bruinsma said, rising. "Thanks for the expertise." He was putting the chair away when he heard a stifled sound behind him; he turned around and saw the guy was crying.

He could not stand weeping men, but he went over to him and said, "It's all right. We'll take good care of you."

"But what's to become of me?" the man sobbed theatrically, like a rejected mistress in a Victorian drama. "I deserted them!"

"We'll see how you are when we arrive in New York, then we'll decide what is best: put you into a hospital, or take you to Amsterdam. I'll do whatever the doctors say. Now get some rest."

"I should have stayed! I betrayed him!"

"Who? Your captain?"

"No, no . . . !"

Bruinsma decided he'd had enough. He went to the door and called, "Nurse!"

Myrtle took her time appearing. She came mincing down the corridor as if modeling her uniform for a crowd of uncharmed buyers. "You called, Commodore?"

"Cut it out," he said, keeping his voice low. "The guy's going into hysterics. I'll call you later." Without waiting for one of her British answers, he marched off to the elevator and joined the game in the First Class library.

But he soon got bored; what was more, his place was on the bridge now they were approaching New York.

He went to his cabin and poured himself a glass of Drambuie, from which he sipped while changing into his bridge uniform. He mulled over the medic feeling the presence of the ghost of Kuiper's father and remembered, out of nowhere, a performance he had seen years ago in Durban, South Africa: *The Prince of Denmark* by William Shakespeare, in Afrikaans. God only knew how he had happened to be there; it had been with a woman. He remembered roaring with laughter, to her stern disapproval, at the line *'Omlet, I am your papa's spook.'*

Smiling at the memory, he sipped his Drambuie, and suddenly there it was, the true definition of Joris Kuiper: not a Christian crusader, not a Young Knight in Shining Armor, but a Hamlet of the sea.

Part Three

ARRIVALS

CHAPTER ONE

I

Anna Kuiper was dreaming about midgets and mice, but someone was shaking her shoulder, trying to wake her up, calling her
urgently. She tried to hang on to the dream in which she sat in
a railroad compartment with in one hand a white mouse, in the
other a tiny midget. She had to throw one of them out the
window, and if that person did not stop shaking her shoulder, she
might make the same mistake she had seen someone make when
she was a child sitting opposite an old gentleman in another
railroad compartment. Slowly and tantalizingly, he had peeled a
hard-boiled egg, tucking the bits of shell into the hollow of his
hand holding the naked egg. She was hungry and sat there slaver-
ing, gazing at that delicious egg; then he opened the window,
threw out the egg and was left with a handful of eggshell. She had
laughed; the astonishment, anger, fury on his face were directed
instantly at her: ill-mannered child shrieking with laughter. Then
it all became a jumble of images, memories, fears, laughter, and
she emerged from the no-man's-land of sleep. It was four-year-old
Jantje shaking her by the shoulder, calling, "Mother, Mother, Ma!
Please wake up, *please!* There's someone banging on the door!"

"What's the time?" she asked, confused, gathering to her the
daily person she had become.

313

"I don't know, Ma!" Jantje cried, on the verge of tears. "Nobody wants to wake up! Arnold won't wake up, you won't wake up—"

"Hush, hush," she said, swinging her legs out of bed and groping for her slippers with her toes. "Give me my robe, there's a sweetie. There, it's on the chair."

Now that she was awake, Jantje could safely burst into tears and did so.

"Hush, baby, hush. Don't you start carrying on now, all's well. I'll go and find out who it is. Now be quiet, there's a good boy." She pulled the robe around her, tied the belt and flip-flopped to the front door, switching on the light in the hall. She peered through the little spy hole and saw it was Mr. Horsting, the harbormaster. He always brought the messages of ships lost at sea.

She didn't feel anything, she didn't think anything, she just went numb. She opened the door and looked at him and said, "Yes?"

He stood there, benign and smiling, a telegram in his hand. Death. That's how death looked: not a skeleton, not a ghost in a black cloak, but Mr. Horsting, beaming, peaked cap on the back of his head, holding out a telegram, saying, "From your husband, Annie. We just picked it up from Scheveningen Radio. It said 'urgent,' so they channeled it through me; Mrs. Polder isn't awake yet. The post office doesn't open till eight o'clock."

"Is he dead?" she asked calmly. The catch in her throat was not emotion, just a frog.

"Dead? Hell, no! Ho, ho!" Mr. Horsting's laughter echoed in the narrow street red with the dawn. "He's alive and kicking! But —well—you'll see for yourself. It's a real puzzle, that one. You and he must have a code; that's the only thing I can think of. Nobody in the office could make head or tail of it. Anyhow, it's about Jesus."

She took the envelope and said, "Thank you, Mr. Horsting."

"You're welcome," Mr. Horsting said. "I'm on my way home anyway, it's been a long night. If it wasn't so early, I'd come in and have a cup of coffee with you, but you probably want to go back to bed. So, another time." He laughed again. "Dead!" Then he said soberly, "But you're right; he could have been, he could have been. It has been my task, quite often . . . " Shaking his head, he turned and wandered off down the street still talking. Like all men, he was so self-centered that, the older he got, the less he noticed nobody listened to him any more.

Ah, men. Shivering, she pulled her robe around her more tightly, turned her back on the dawn and said to whining Jantje, "Now you shut up, boy, or I'll give you something to *really* yell about. Now shut up! Be quiet! Go back to bed! There's nothing, nothing: just Mr. Horsting bringing a message from your dad. And he's okay, he's not dead, there's nothing wrong, so shut up and go back to sleep. Go on!" She pushed him off down the hall, and noticed too late that Flip, the cat, had managed to flash out the front door as she closed it. Well, so he'd get hit by a car; the hell with him.

Jantje obeyed, crying louder so as to make it last; she flip-flopped to the kitchen, turned on the light and sat down at the table to open the envelope. What an odd dream: to throw a midget out of a railroad carriage, or a white mouse. What in the world . . .

> *Anna Kuiper, Haven Street 25, den Helder, Holland. I must choose between denying my Saviour and keeping everything or obeying Him and losing everything. Answer for you and the children. Joris.*

Mr. Horsting was right: an incomprehensible telegram. About Jesus. She might as well chuck it into the trash can. Damn it, she wasn't going to reply to that. It was nonsense. She was through with nonsense. She was damned if she was going to be sucked back into his life. She was out of it now, she had children, a cat . . . Suddenly, she felt terribly angry with herself for letting Flip escape into the street. It gave her an eerie feeling of the whole thing coming apart: her tight little world, two little boys, a cat, a neat little house with everything in its proper place . . .

Angrily, she went to the sink, filled the kettle, slammed it onto the gas ring, took out the cocoa tin, the milk from the fly cup-board outside the back door, hoping that Flip might be waiting there, but he wasn't. Now, what had she taken out milk for, if she was boiling water? She should heat the milk, shouldn't she? Oh, the hell with it. She stuffed it all back: the kettle in the fly cupboard, the milk on the shelf—

Suddenly unnerved, she slumped onto the chair, her head in her hands, and moaned, just moaned, like a child wanting it all to stop, to go back to the way it had been just a few minutes earlier. She wanted to go back to bed, to her dream; she wanted to pick up that other problem, the real problem: how to keep herself from throwing out the midget and hanging on to the mouse.

"Mom?"

"Yes, Arnold," she said wearily, without looking up.

"What's the matter, Mom?"

She looked up, finding to her surprise that her eyes were blurred with tears. "Nothing," she said. "What are you doing up at this hour?"

"I want to have a pee."

"Then go and have a pee. And then go back to bed. It's too early."

"Okay." He went back into the hall in his bare feet, like a sleepwalker. In the doorway, he turned around. "Who was that banging on the door?"

"Flip," she said.

"Oh." He shuffled off; she waited for the door of the toilet to close; she heard the tinkle and then the flushing and he went shuffling back to his bedroom. 'Click' went the bedroom door.

I must choose between denying my Saviour and keeping everything or obeying Him and losing everything.

Now, what the hell did *that* mean? She looked at it out of the corner of her eye. How could she make that kind of decision? There he was: big, burly, strong; when he took you in his arms and made love to you, it was like being slammed by the surf and swept up the beach. And then you get a telegram like this. "Meow, meow, meow!" She read the question out loud, in mocking cat language. What the hell was going on with him? She'd had enough messages from him to last a lifetime. 'Mrs. Kuiper? Your husband is locked up in the police station and he asks if

you'd go and see his father.' And 'Mrs. Kuiper? Your husband is
in the emergency room of Citizens' Hospital after a fight, and asks
if you could bring some clothes and then go and see his father.'

But this was not like those other times. This was a telegram
about Jesus, as Mr. Horsting had said. *Deny Him and keep every-*
thing, obey Him and lose everything. Answer for you and the children.
It was like a rebus in the Sunday paper. 'Look at the picture and
find the constable.' Then you had to turn the picture upside down
and there, in the foliage of the tree, was the face with the mustache. Well, no face with mustache this time: Jesus, my Saviour.
Deny him and keep everything, obey Him and lose everything.

Suddenly she was overcome by unholy anger. The fury that
had been pent up for years, ever since his goddam conversion. He
had betrayed her. He had turned into someone else. She had
married a man; with all his faults—anger, violence, boozing disas-
ters—he had been a *man,* her man, and suddenly: bingo! Saint
Joris, smarming around her, praying at every turn. They went to
bed and he made love to her and the first thing you knew as you
lay helpless on the beach, hurled there by the surf, he was on his
knees beside the bed, asking Jesus for forgiveness. Bah! She flung
the telegram aside and went back to the sink and turned on the
tap full force. After a moment, she slowly turned it off. She must
calm down, she must look at this the way she had to look at
everything—the children, Flip, the neighbors, even her dream.
Always decisions, decisions. What do you throw out? The mouse
or the midget?

Presently, she made herself a cup of coffee, and the activity
of that small routine calmed her, smoothed out the fury, made her
look—quietly, rationally—at the fact that it was not he but she
who was being asked either to lose everything or to keep everything, so he might satisfy his Saviour.

She sat stirring her coffee at the kitchen table, staring into
space, her feet getting cold, feeling very young, as if her feet were
the last thing left of the child in the railroad compartment gazing
at the gentleman peeling the egg. He had taken away everything,
the bastard. Her youth, her innocence, her dreams—and now he
sent her a telegram like this.

It made no sense. She had no idea what it was about. But she knew him. She knew he was forever living on the brink of violence. He had almost destroyed both of them by drinking himself senseless and beating people up, demolishing things and then staggering through the night streets to bawl at his father's door: "Come out, you son of a bitch! Come out, you bastard! Come out, you sky pilot! Stand up for yourself, you holy shit!"

She covered her face with her hands. 'God,' she thought, 'Christ, anybody, anybody at all, give it back to me. Give me my life back, please, *please?*'

But this was nonsense. It didn't solve anything; all it did was postpone the inevitable: she had to make that decision.

She swallowed some coffee. It was too hot, she burned her mouth. Quickly, she poured herself a glass of water and drank it down; when she picked up the thread of her thoughts again, there was the Old Man standing over her, saying: 'Come on, forget the cub. You're not made for boys, you're made for men.' The memory made her rise and rinse her cup and rub her forehead and force herself to think. What next? If I reply: 'Why the hell can't you make up your own mind for once?' he'll go on a rampage. If I reply: 'Go ahead, follow your Saviour,' God knows what he's up to. Give all his money to the poor. Hand his ship to the lepers, like St. Francis. Kiss kiss, and the hell with *Star of Peace,* and who cares if your wife hates you, hates you for it?

Hates you for it.

Where had she read that? Recently? *If any man hate not his wife and children . . .*

"Mom?"

She asked calmly, "Yes, Arnold?"

"It can't have been Flip."

"What are you talking about, child?"

"Flip can't bang on the door. Who was it?"

She looked at him standing in the doorway, drowsy with sleep, like a drunk, like his father in diminutive, a midget. Ah, there it was! The surf had hit her and swept her up the beach and she was left with a midget in one hand and a white mouse in the other.

"Go back to bed, child. It was nothing. A telegram from your dad."

"What did it say?"

"That he's well and will be home soon. Now go back to bed. Go back to bed, please, *please*. Okay?"

"I knew it couldn't have been," the boy said, and shuffled off on his bare feet. She waited for the click of the bedroom door; then she decided she had better do what Joris asked and choose for him between his Saviour and her worldly possessions. If she didn't, he'd whore and gamble and booze and carouse them away anyhow. She had to do it like a good little Christian wife, in a gentle, loving manner. How could she tell him in a gentle manner, 'Go ahead, you bastard, blow it all, and God damn you for asking *me*'?

If any man come to me and hate not his wife and children.

It must have been the Bible, but how could it have been? It didn't sound like gentle Jesus meek and mild. Yet, where else could she have read it?

She had to stay in control now, not ham it up or else she would lose touch with reality altogether. The only way of handling this was to put it out of her mind for now, turn her back on it, make breakfast, get the boys off to school, make the beds, clear the kitchen, put the house in order, then go for a walk to the lookout, taking her Bible along. Then just sit and wait.

That was exactly what she did. She went back to the bedroom, which felt empty now Flip had taken off; she dressed, made the bed, prepared breakfast, got the boys up, made sure they washed behind their ears and that their partings were straight; then, at last, off they went and in came Flip, thank God. Then she took her Bible, put her shawl around her shoulders and set off down the street, smiling at all the peering faces in the neighboring windows, all of them knowing about the telegram because of Mr. Horsting. He was not a gossip, but to start yelling at daybreak in the empty street meant he might as well have made it a headline in the morning paper. Finally, she sat down on the windy bench at the lookout and gazed at the sea, the horizon and across the turbulent water of Hell's Gate at the island of Texel in the distance. The sun was warm, the gulls gackered overhead.

Just to stop the tears from reaching her eyes, she opened the Bible at the New Testament. Almost at once, there it was, as if it had lain in wait for her: *If any man come to me and hate not his wife and children, he cannot be my disciple.*

There it was, in black and white: either hate me and Arnold and Jantje and Flip, or gentle Jesus meek and mild will turn his back on you and consider you unworthy of him. It made her sick. She should have had herself burned, like the Vikings' widows, with the ribs and rags of flesh of the Old Man. But no—let the dead bury the dead. Her loyalty must be with the living.

An hour later, she rose and walked back the way she had come. Mrs. Polder, jolly and rotund behind her grille in the post office, said, "Good morning, Annie. What can I do for you, dear?"

"I have a telegram for my husband, on board *Star of Peace*. Would you send it for me, please?"

Mrs. Polder frowned curiously as she read the mysterious message. "What code is that, Annie? The operators in Schevenin-gen Radio are strict on codes."

"Tell Scheveningen Radio it's a quote from the Bible," she replied, and stopped herself from adding, 'How's that for a slap in the puss?'

"Oh, I see," Mrs. Polder said with a doubtful smile. "In that case, I suppose it'll be all right."

Anna Kuiper walked home; then, on an impulse, she put on the silver brooch with the whistle and went out again, feeling scared and on the verge of tears.

She went to the center of town, entered the chill cave of Maison Française and bought herself the extravagant hat she'd been looking at for weeks. It had two egret plumes and a fake emerald; the Old Man would have approved of it.

2

Twelve hours later, as *Star of Peace,* heading west at slow speed, was halfway to New York, a telegram arrived for the captain from his wife. Wybrands couldn't make head nor tail of it, but gave it to Palstra to deliver on his way down. Palstra went all the way down, to the chief engineer's cabin, where he found Meyer and Davelaar discussing the fuel situation. "Look what I've got here," he said.

Davelaar put on his glasses and read it. "What the hell does *that* mean?"

"I haven't the foggiest idea. Wybrands just handed it to me. It's obviously a quote from the Bible. Do you have one?"

Davelaar grunted, shook his head and read the mysterious message again. *"Luke fourteen, twenty-six hugs Annie, kiss Arnold, kiss kiss Jantje, meow Flip.* Either it's a code, or the woman is having us on."

He remembered the last time he had seen her: skinny, poker-faced, mousy hair and that telltale whistle brooch.

"Well, what do you think?" Meyer asked, sitting on the edge of the bunk, legs spread, belly resting on his thighs, breathing heavily from the exertion of carrying what must amount to a twenty-pound baby. "Think it means anything?"

"Sure it means something," Davelaar said angrily. "She's telling him something in code because she doesn't want us to know. Fourteen hugs, twenty-six kisses, meow. If you ask me, she's making us hopscotch down the deck and straight over the edge. Smart cookie, that one. My God, she had better be."

"But what are we going to *do?*" Meyer urged, panting.

"You do nothing," Davelaar said, folding the paper and putting it in his pocket. "To start with, we're not going to give it to him. Then, I think the moment has come for him and me to have a chat. This has gone on long enough; the shitty doctor refuses to certify him, it's up to us now. Leave him to me." He made for the door.

"Don't bring me into it!" Meyer cried nervously.

"Don't worry," Davelaar said with contempt. "We have enough of a mess on the floor as it is. Let me by, Palstra."

Palstra made room for him as he wormed his way past the bunk.

"Just stand by. This won't take long." Davelaar opened the door and found the boy Henky hanging around outside. By the

time he cried, "Scat!" the boy had already whizzed off to the end
of the passage and vanished from sight.

He made his way with grim determination up the stairs,
across the deck where the damn Jews were loitering, and up the
steps to the lower bridge. But outside the door to the captain's
cabin he hesitated. He had never expected it to come to this; in
spite of everything, Joris meant a lot to him. To have to do this
to him was worse than violence. Again he was struck by the
image of a proud wild animal about to be captured and trussed
and put in a cage. You simply didn't do what he was about to do
if you were an upstanding man. It had nothing to do with God
or religion, it had to do with tall ships and the men who sailed
them, with the tacit brotherhood of the sea. But he had no choice.
Without knocking, he opened the door and stepped over the
threshold.

Joris was on his knees by the chair at the table, praying. When
he heard the door, he looked up. Something in his eyes made
Davelaar almost change his mind: pain, desperation, a mute plea
for help. For a moment, he was tempted to say: 'Come on, boy,
knock it off; take the goddam Jews back and let's have done with
it.' But he knew it was hopeless. "I've come to tell you something," he said, closing the door behind him and leaning against
it. He was not going to be thrown out this time.

"Tell me what?"

"The truth about your father." Thank God it would not have
to be the whole truth, or he would never get out of this cabin
alive.

3

So now crazy old Davelaar was about to come up with some
'truth about his father'! As if anyone had known his father better,
soul to soul, than he himself!

"Go away," Kuiper said, getting to his feet. "Who's at the
engine? It's your watch!"

But Davelaar stood his ground. "The Old Man would have done the same thing you did, eh? Because of what he wrote in that goddam Bible? Well, let me tell you—"

Kuiper went for him, but Davelaar moved quickly aside, crying, "Do you know what that flag is? That flag of the cross he wants you to hoist in the foretop?"

"Get out!"

"The dirty shirt of the devil! The rag—"

"You—!"

Davelaar dodged around the table.

"Get out, you dirty old bastard! Get out, I say!" He cornered the old man by the washstand.

"No! Let me go! The truth! If the memory of your father is sacred to you, then you *listen to me!* Listen to the story of the flag of the cross! You don't know it!"

Kuiper had dragged him to the door; there, something in the old man's eyes made him let go of the scraggy neck. "If you say one word against my father . . . "

"If I say one word that isn't true, may I drop dead on the spot! So help me God!" He raised a dirty hand.

"Don't take His name in vain!" Kuiper slapped the hand down. "I warn you: one word—"

"New Guinea, twenty years ago. In debt to every chandler in the East. Three more days and the ship would've been chained by the sheriff. And no cargo, nowhere. Then two missionaries from up river came on board, to talk to your father about the Bible; but really what they came for was to offer him a deal. For over a year, they had been converting Papuans in the jungle, and what had they told those dumb buggers? 'Out of every two coconuts you cut down, put one aside for Jesus. We'll turn 'em into copra and arrange for transport to heaven.' Now they offered your dad Christ's copra at a bargain price, because he was a brother. Well, I thought it was a dandy deal, but by the mere looks of him I saw the Old Man was going to turn it down. And, sure enough: 'No, thank you, brothers,' he said, 'I think I'll pass this one up.' They left; the moment they had gone, he yelled as if to raise the dead: 'Make steam! Get ready to sail!' In no time at all, we cast off and sailed upriver with a weight on the safety valve."

"To go where?"

"I'll tell you! He got the bo'sun to make a flag: a white flag with a black cross, the thing he's telling you to hoist now. He got the mate's apprentice to put on a nightshirt and a beard made out of twine, and gave him a length of copper pipe bent like a shepherd's crook which I'd made up for him. The boy was put on the forecastle and told to sing *Bringing in the Sheaves*. Then your father rowed ashore in the work boat to tell the Papuans that Jesus had come for his coconuts."

The door was opened, hitting Davelaar in the back. He jumped aside; it was Henky carrying a piece of paper.

"A—another telegram, sir . . . Mr. Wybrands . . . "

"Give it here!" Davelaar ripped it out of his hand and cried, "Out!" The boy scurried; Davelaar put the paper on the table.

Kuiper slumped in a chair, staring at him in shock and disbelief. It couldn't be true! It was just a vicious story . . .

"The natives went mad," Davelaar continued. "They leaped up and down, yelled, threw their children up in the air; then the first dugout came paddling toward the ship, piled high with copra. When we weighed anchor at sunset, we were loaded down over the mark with Jesus' coconuts, for free."

"I—I don't believe it," Kuiper said.

"If you don't believe it, boy, ask Meyer. He's your proof. It was *him* your dad dressed up as Jesus!"

There was a silence in which Kuiper tried to hold on to something, some certainty, some fixed point in his life. If Meyer had been involved, it must be true. He wouldn't dare lie.

"I'm sorry, Joris." The old man touched his shoulder, the way he had done so many times in the past when he'd come to spring him with his father's money from police stations, jail cells, emergency rooms. "Come on, don't torture yourself any longer. Take those Jews back. Be your own man, boy. Stop trying to do what you think your dad would have done. He wasn't what you think he was. He was human, Joris, like the rest of us. When it came to choosing between the ship and his principles, he chose the ship.

Come, stop this nonsense. The *Star* is your life, my life, all our lives. Take those Jews back." The hand patted his shoulder. "Take them back."

Kuiper heard the steps go to the door, the door close, and was left alone in his father's cabin.

4

The moment Henky saw Chief Davelaar come out of the captain's cabin and walk off in the opposite direction, he slipped from behind the life-jacket chest and made a dash for the door. He knew that if he knocked, the chief would hear him, so he opened the door, stuck his head in, saw the captain sitting at the table and whispered urgently, "Captain! Captain, write it down! Write it down quickly! Luke . . . " A hand grabbed his neck and he was yanked back. It was Mr. Davelaar, furious, hissing, "Sneaky little shit! What were you doing there? What was that? What was it you said?"

"Nothing, Chief . . . "

The old man shook him violently; the next thing would be a back-hander. "Speak up! Speak up, you little sneak! *What* were you telling him?"

"N-nothing . . . Chief . . . "

"I'll nothing you, you—" Mr. Davelaar was about to hit him, but suddenly he dropped his hand, grinned and let go of him.

Out of the corner of his eye, Henky spotted the Rabbi coming up the steps; he saw his chance and ran.

"Come here!" Mr. Davelaar yelled. "Come back, I said!"

But once he was running, no one could catch up with him. He streaked down the boat deck, past the lifeboats; when he heard Mr. Davelaar's steps behind him, he darted behind the stack, leaped over the engine-room skylight, circled the cabin, dashed down the boat deck again on the other side; by that time, the chief had lost sight of him, but Henky could still hear him yelling. He clambered up the davit to number-three boat, pried open the cover and crawled inside.

5
———————————

Hendrik was in the women's hold looking after a hysterical patient, one of many, when he heard someone say excitedly that a telegram had just arrived from the committee in America.

The mood among the passengers was in a precarious balance. It could go either way: out-and-out hysteria or a collapse into lethargy. The telegram, if it had indeed arrived, was certain to tip the balance; it was imperative that he know what it said before it became general knowledge. So, as soon as he could get away, he headed for the midships.

As he arrived on the lower bridge, he saw the Rabbi hovering in front of the door to the cabin. The old man looked nervous and disoriented; obviously, he was trying to muster the courage to go in and confront the captain. Hendrik was about to address him when the old man knocked and went in.

On an impulse, Hendrik followed him. Kuiper was sitting behind the table, his head in his hands. Melancholy and defeatism hung in the enclosed little room like smog.

"Captain . . . ?" the Rabbi asked, in a whisper.

Kuiper lifted his head. He looked ghastly. Never before had Hendrik seen this expression on his face; he looked the way Vinkemans had, just before he came apart.

"I don't want to disturb you, Captain," the Rabbi said, "but we were told a telegram has arrived from the committee in America. My people have sent me to ask you what it says . . . Could you tell me, please?"

Kuiper looked at him with an odd indifference. "I've received no telegram," he said. His voice was hoarse.

"But . . . but excuse me . . . " The Rabbi pointed at a piece of paper that was lying on the table. "Isn't that it, Captain?"

Kuiper pulled the paper toward him and read. You could hear a pin drop in the cabin.

"What—what does it say?" the Rabbi asked, finally.

Kuiper pushed the paper in his direction.

The Rabbi picked it up, held it at arm's length and read, frowning. Then he lowered the paper. His face looked haggard. "Eight weeks . . . " he whispered.

Hendrik took the paper from him.

> *No decision nor meaningful contact made so far stop. We remain hopeful but be prepared for delay of at least eight weeks before any action owing to senate recess stop. Many urgent matters precede yours on official agenda for coming session stop. Our prayers go with you.*

It came as no surprise, after what van der Kamp had said; but to the passengers it would be shattering news. Hendrik tried to think of something to say, but the silence was so heavy that it inhibited him. The Rabbi stood with his eyes closed, either in prayer or in shock, he could not tell. Kuiper sat behind the table, his head in his hands. All Hendrik could do was put the paper back on the table, discreetly, and make his getaway. He must go and find Susan.

Then the Rabbi said, "Do you still not understand?" His voice was calm; it seemed as if he had acquired a sudden authority.

Kuiper raised his head and gave him a puzzled look.

"Captain," the Rabbi said, "it is time you saw the truth: you are putting yourself between us and our God."

It was such a bizarre thing to say that all Kuiper could do, and indeed Hendrik himself, was stare at the old man in total bewilderment.

"All these weeks, I have kept silent, Captain," the Rabbi continued, "because I too am human, and frail, and afraid of pain. But, whatever I might have hoped as a human being, as a man of God I knew."

"Knew what?" Hendrik asked, nonplused.

The Rabbi shifted his gaze onto him. His eyes looked unfocused; his face was serene. "What every Jew knows," he answered calmly. "The anathema of the Pentateuch is upon us."

"But what—"

"Listen! Listen to the voice of the Eternal." The old man closed his eyes, began to rock to and fro, and intoned in a singsong voice of quiet power, *"Cursed shalt thou be in the city and cursed shalt thou be in the field. Cursed shall be thy basket and thy store. Cursed shall be the fruit of thy body and the fruit of thy land. Cursed shalt thou be when thou comest in and cursed shalt thou be when thou goest out. Thou shalt betroth a wife and another man shall lie with her. Thou shalt build a house and another man shall dwell therein. Thou shalt plant a vineyard and another man shall garner the grapes thereof. Thy sons . . . "* His voice faltered, but he rallied. *"Thy sons and thy daughters shall be given to another people, and thine eyes shall look and fill with longing for them all the day long, but there shall be no might in thy hands. And thou shalt grope at noonday as the blind gropeth in darkness—an astonishment, a proverb, a byword among all nations."*

It was eerily impressive. The ancient words seemed to give the fate of the passengers an unexpected perspective. What, so far, had seemed to be an isolated incident took on the dark hue of an awesome retribution. But even as he sensed this, Hendrik knew that it was sheer melodrama. Worse: a dangerous aberration.

"Captain," the old man said quietly, but with that new authority, "you must now remove yourself from between us and our God. Take us back."

Kuiper stared at him with an expression of hurt and disbelief. "You—you *want* that?"

"God wills it." He turned away and went to the door. "Take us back." He opened the door and left.

Kuiper looked stunned, and no wonder. Hendrik felt sorry for him. All these weeks, he had been all alone. Not one member of the crew had really supported him. He had kept to himself and his God, bent on his Scripture-directed mission to save his passengers. And now the passengers themselves had lost faith in him and asked to be taken back to Germany—in God's name. He looked as if he needed help, but what could anyone say? The die had been cast; what the impact on the passengers would be was anybody's guess. Susan had better be told to prepare for the worst.

"Sorry, Skipper," he said. "I know it's rough. I'd love to stay and talk it over with you, but I'd better go and see to my patients." He went to the door. "Call me if you need me."

With a feeling of guilt, he turned his back on the poor man and left him to face his moment of truth, alone.

6

When they saw Hendrik come out of the cabin, Josef wanted to make for the door at once, but Yitzhak held him back. "Wait! Let him get out of earshot!"

The gun in Tovah's hand was heavy and slippery with sweat. She couldn't stop swallowing. It had been crazy for Yitzhak to decide that she was the one to hold it. Why had he—

"Yes!" Yitzhak whispered.

All of a sudden, the situation became unreal, like a high-school play. As Yitzhak and Josef stepped forward and she joined them as rehearsed, it felt as if she stepped onto a stage, leaving her real self behind. She knew the role by heart, only it wasn't she. The stage wasn't real. The gun wasn't real. But neither was the fear she had felt; it suddenly left her.

She gripped the gun firmly and tiptoed behind Josef and Yitzhak to the door of the captain's cabin. There, they waited until the others joined them. She was ready and eager to go now, now!

"Ssh!" Yitzhak warned. "Handcuffs ready?"

There was a soft clinking of metal.

"Ssh!"

Everyone froze.

"Josef—you cover her left . . . "

Yitzhak threw open the door.

It was like the rising of a curtain. Cool, collected, coiled like a spring, she stepped inside; the others slipped in beside her, Josef on the left, Yitzhak on the right. The captain was sitting behind the table; she raised her hand with the gun and spoke her line calmly, in control: "Be quiet, Captain. Don't make a sound."

The captain looked at the gun. He did not move.

She stepped forward and heard the others slip into the cabin. She heard the door close. "Captain," the next line ran, "nothing will happen to you if you do exactly as we tell you. Stay where you are." Without losing sight of him, the gun steady as a rock, she said, "Now."

"Josef!" Yitzhak whispered beside her.

The captain's eyes shifted from the gun to the boy coming toward him with a pair of handcuffs.

Suddenly, the high-school play seemed to slip back into reality. "Captain," she said, her voice trembling with a mad elation, "you are relieved of your command. We are taking over the ship!"

Yitzhak continued, "We're going to lock you up in this cabin, after we've handcuffed you to your chair. Then we'll haul down the flag and raise the Star of David. Anyone who comes near the ship will be shot at, until the Americans agree to let us in."

The captain's eyes changed. His heavy, muscular body seemed to stiffen. He did not move, but suddenly he frightened her. They had made a mistake somewhere.

"Stand up, Captain," Josef said, handcuffs at the ready.

The captain singled her out and stared at her with something in his eyes that made her want to shout a warning; then Josef touched his arm and he exploded.

With a roar, he leaped to his feet, grabbed the chair that was bolted to the floor, tore it loose and hurled it at her. She ducked, numb with shock, and heard a yelp behind her as the chair hit someone. The captain roared, roared; there was a splintering sound as he tore loose another chair and hurled it at Josef, who fled; it hit the lamp, the light went out, the cabin went dark. "Bastards!" he roared. "Jew bastards! Get out! I'll smash you to a fucking pulp, you goddam kikes! Get out, or I'll kill you! I'll kill you! Get out, you bastards! *Get out!!*"

Terrified out of her senses, Tovah dropped the gun as another chair crashed against the wall. She crawled to the door, fighting the others to get out, stricken with blind panic. The crashing, the banging, the terrible curses grew in fury behind her; finally, she managed to fight her way out. They ran for their lives, streaked down the steps to the deck and piled up by the winch on the forecastle. Anna was weeping, Yitzhak cursing; she herself shivered uncontrollably. Only in the most brutal days of her German past had she been subjected to such violence.

As they huddled close together, stunned, listening to the distant sounds of the madman demolishing his cabin, she was overcome by a sense of loss. In that one moment of mad elation, she had at last realized what Yakov in Palestine was all about; it had been shattered by the captain going berserk. That had been their mistake: they had taken him for a quiescent Christian, expecting him to protest but not resist; nothing had prepared them for the exploding madman. She had seen him change in front of her eyes; she had seen his eyes go mad, his face contort into that of a raging brute, the face of the pogrom.

"Let's go find the others," Yitzhak said, keeping his voice low. "We need to talk."

"No," Anna whispered shakily, "I'm going to lie down. I feel sick."

They went down the steps to the deck, back to the holds, the Jews of Masada surrendering.

7

Head in hands, Kuiper sat in the dark amidst the ruins of his world. The beast within had reclaimed him. All his beautiful slogans, his Christian pretensions had turned to ashes. When the chips were down, he had turned out to be no better than the worst of his crew. No better than the hateful creatures he had watched with such horror in Hamburg, who had spat at the ship and cried foul curses, the same soul-sick words he had shouted at those youngsters. If he had managed to get hold of one of those kids, God only knew what he would have done to him, or her. God only knew to what unspeakable depths he would have fallen.

Well—here it was again, the old, weary litany of yore: broken chairs, smashed glass, screaming women. All that was lacking was the police, trying to handcuff him, stumbling back with nosebleeds, until someone hit him from behind, felling him like an ox.

He felt like weeping, but there were no tears. He felt like praying, but hid his head in shame. Now what? What was to become of him? Return to the old life? That would be worse than death. Plead with God, go through another conversion? He'd never find that childlike faith and certainty again. Not after what had happened.

Well, he should be glad of it. He would not have to sacrifice his ship, his Master's Certificate, his life, after all. He would go up to the bridge now and check the course and make sure of their time of arrival off Ambrose. There, the Coast Guard would escort them to an anchorage, restock and refuel them, fill the tanks with drinking water, and then he would take the Jews back to Germany. A financial loss, but he would survive. He'd find money somewhere. So, was he not pleased, after all?

No. He was destroyed, steeped in damnation.

"Oh Christ, dear Jesus," he whispered, "come back to me! I didn't know what I was doing! Don't leave me! Forgive me! I repent, I repent! Come back to me!"

But there was no response, no sense of the presence. There never would be, never again. Never another angel standing behind him. Never anything but the old life of a dumb drunk. He had kept his ship, but lost his soul. All that remained was a heap of ashes. Even if the Pentecostal flame were to descend upon him now, the ashes would not take fire.

Wearily, he rose. On his way to the door, he tripped over an upturned chair. He put it back on its feet, but even in the dark he could feel that it tilted. In the dark, he found his cap.

8

Peering over the edge of the lifeboat in which he was hiding, Henky had seen the kids go into the cabin, heard the terrifying sounds of the captain's rage, and understood that the kids had copped it when he saw them come tumbling out the door and run for their lives.

Now all was quiet. The door to the cabin stood ajar. It was dark inside. Had the captain gone to the bridge while he ducked out of sight as the kids raced past? Here he was with his urgent message, which he had memorized and repeated continuously so as not to forget it; now was the time to get it to the captain, but he didn't dare go in there. Yells and curses did not faze him; people yelled and cursed at him all the time. But he had never heard the captain in a rage, and did not know what he was likely to find.

The door of the cabin opened wide and the captain stepped outside. Now or never!

He clambered out of the lifeboat, slid down the davit and managed to get to the captain before he climbed the steps to the bridge.

"Captain! Captain, write it down! *Luke fourteen twenty-six hugs Annie kiss Arnold kiss kiss Jantje meow Philip.* That's it! That's what it says!"

The captain frowned. "What are you jabbering about?"

"The telegram, sir! That's what it says: *Luke fourteen twenty-six hugs Annie kiss Arnold—*"

"My wife! Where is it?!"

"*—kiss kiss Jantje meow Philip—*"

The captain grabbed him by the arm and cried, "Where is it, boy?!"

"I—I haven't got it, Captain! Mr. Davelaar has it, in his pocket! Mr. Wybrands read it to Mr. Palstra, Mr. Davelaar to Mr. Meyer, and then he read it again, and I was listening, and I—"

"What does it say?! Tell me!"

The captain shook him fiercely, it hurt, but Henky managed to start all over again: "*Luke fourteen twenty-six hugs* . . . Or was it *twenty-six fourteen hugs* . . . ? *Luke* . . . *Philip* . . . Oh, Captain!" he cried. "I've forgotten!"

"Luke fourteen, verse twenty-six—that's what you said the first time. Is that it?"

"Yes, Captain, yessir! *Luke fourteen twenty-six hugs Annie kiss—*"

The captain ran back to the cabin; Henky heard him stumble as he tripped on something. Then his voice bellowed, "Boy!"

Henky hurried over to the cabin door. It was pitch dark inside. He could hear the captain rummage somewhere.

"Get me some light!" the voice shouted.

"Yessir . . . " Henky found the switch and flicked it, but nothing happened. "It won't work, sir! The bulb must be . . . Wait! Wait, sir!" He stepped over the threshold, fumbling in his pockets. "I've got a box of match—" He tripped on something. "Godda—sorry Captain! Sorry, sir! I've got matches! Wait—" He struck a match on the seat of his pants; the flame took hold and lit up the cabin; what he saw made him say, "Geez . . . "

The cabin was a shambles. Overturned chairs, drawers pulled out, their contents spilled on the floor, glass everywhere . . .

"Come here!" The captain was standing by his bunk, a book in his hands. Then the match went out.

"Sorry, sir! Right here, sir . . . Here I come . . . " He struck another match, let the flame take hold in his cupped hands, then, cautiously, made his way through the wreckage to where the captain was standing. The flame went out again.

The third match flamed bright; by its light, he joined the captain. "Here you are, sir . . . Is this all right, sir . . . ?"

The captain flicked the pages of the book; Henky saw it was a Bible. "Is Philip—is Luke in the Bible, sir? I thought—ouch!" The match burned his fingers, he dropped it. "Sorry, Sir . . . sorry . . . here . . . " He struck another.

The captain had found what he was looking for. He read: "*If any man come to me, and hate not his father, and mother, and wife, and children, and brethren, and sisters, yea, and his own life also, he cannot be my disciple. And whosoever doth not bear his cross and come after me, cannot be my disciple—*" The match went out once more.

"Sorry, Sir! . . . Just a minute . . . "

"It's not necessary, boy. I've read enough." The captain's voice sounded weary.

"Yessir. Who said that, sir?"

"What?"

"What you just read, sir. Philip?"

"Jesus."

"Who to, sir? To Luke?"

"To me."

He heard the captain's boots crunch on glass.

"Ask the Rabbi to come and see me. Quick!"

"Yessir!" Henky picked his way toward the door in the dark, tripping over a chair.

"And Mr. Meyer, Chief Davelaar, the doc—"

"Yessir!"

"Mr. Jablonski, Mrs. Goldstein and those two kids: the girl with the red hair and the boy that goes with her."

"Yessir! Yes!"

Henky dashed out the door.

9

It was all there: all of Anna. It was as if she had been standing over him as he lay defeated.

If any man come to me and hate not his wife and children . . .

It was as clear a signal as she could send. It was as if she said outright: 'Choose between Him and us.' She had added the hugs and kisses and Flip's meow as a reminder of what he would lose if he did what Christ demanded of him.

But there were no longer any choices. The dead ashes had, miraculously, flamed to life, but a life that was no longer his own.

He groped his way to the corner cupboard, found a lightbulb and exchanged it for the broken one. When the light flooded the cabin, he saw, all around him, the traces of the beast. Broken chairs, scattered papers, bedclothes half out of his bunk, and, to his shocked surprise, the glass in front of his father's portrait shattered. He went to have a look at it.

The stern old man stared at him through the shards. *I'll be standing behind you on the bridge.* Maybe so, but no longer as an elder brother in Christ; rather, as a powerless, ranting ghost protesting the murder of his ship.

He proceeded to clear up the wreckage; the ship's council should not see the cabin like this. He ended up in front of the picture of Anna and the children. There she was, with her secretive smile, her silver whistle, her left hand twisted to hold Jantje's. His sense of loss became so acute that he turned his back on them, went to the desk and took from the drawer the declaration he had drawn up.

I, Kuiper, Joris, skipper next to God of the vessel Star of Peace . . .

But he was no longer her skipper. God had taken over command of *Star of Peace.*

10

The cabin boy came darting out of the darkness crying, "Hey! Hey, you!" He singled Tovah out for his breathless message, "The captain wants you, at once! Go on up! He's waiting for you in his cabin!"

Tovah recoiled. No, not that! Not meekly, like a lamb to slaughter!

Yitzhak took her by the arm. "Let's go."

"No!" she said fiercely, shaking herself free. "I won't go! I've heard enough!"

"But, Tovah—"

"No! I'm not going in there to be raked over the coals!"

"But who says—"

"I *won't* go back in there! I—" She stopped as people on their way to the lower bridge passed the corner where they were standing. The Rabbi, Mr. Jablonski, old Goldstein. They climbed the steps, the Rabbi knocked on the captain's door, they went inside.

"You see," Yitzhak said, "it's not just us, it's everybody! Three guesses what he has to tell us. Well, we'd better go and face the music." Again he took her by the arm; again she pulled away.

Then two men came hurrying by, Hendrik and Mr. Meyer. Hendrik knocked on the cabin door, they too went in.

"You see?" Yitzhak said.

This time, she let herself be led up the steps, but with intense reluctance. This could only mean one thing: after what they had done, the captain had decided to take them back to Germany.

Yitzhak knocked on the door; the captain's voice called, "Come in!" They entered the cabin and joined a small crowd waiting around the table; the captain stood behind it with a sheet of paper in his hand. Steps came hurrying; there was a bang on the door; in came Mr. Davelaar and Mr. Palstra. "What the hell is going on?" Mr. Davelaar asked. "The whole ship—"

"I have a statement to make," the captain said.

Her heart sank. Tears were running freely now. She heard Mr. Davelaar say, "Oh—I see!" in a way that indicated he had come to the same conclusion she had: the captain was about to announce that they were to be taken back to Germany. She could not suppress a sob; she didn't want to stay around for this and make a spectacle of herself. She turned away; somebody took her hand and held her back. She thought it was Yitzhak, then she realized to her amazement that it was old Goldstein.

"Ladies and gentlemen," the captain said, "I have called you in for an official announcement. Three times I have tried to put my passengers ashore in the United States, three times I have failed. Convinced that any further attempts would be futile, I have come to the following decision. Tomorrow morning, at daybreak, a fleet of sailboats will pass through this area, racing for Ambrose Lightship off New York. There will be powerboats meeting them with reporters on board. There will be planes overhead to film the finish of the race. There will be radio reporters to broadcast what they see. What they'll see will be the following sequence of events. As soon as the yachts are sighted, I will order everyone into the boats, send out an S.O.S., take my vessel into their midst and scuttle it. The passengers will be picked up by the yachts and the powerboats and thereby find themselves on American territory in the full light of public opinion. This is the only way left to me to give you your freedom, with dignity."

Mrs. Goldstein squeezed her hand, hard; Mr. Davelaar cried, "You can't do that! You don't have the right!"

The captain continued, "As owner of this ship, I do not need the approval of the ship's council. But to avoid adverse consequences for my staff, I have drawn up this official declaration which should relieve you of all responsibility: *I, Kuiper, Joris, skipper next to God of the vessel Star of Peace, hereby declare that I have decided with all deliberation to scuttle my ship, overriding the energetic protest of the ship's council. I declare myself to be solely and uniquely responsible for this operation. Drawn up on board Star of Peace and signed by the following witnesses. . . .* " He held out a pen. "Meyer."

"Aye, aye, Cap—"

"Sign here."

"But, Cap, look here—"

"Sign."

Mr. Meyer shrugged his shoulders, obeyed and turned to go; the captain stopped him. "Wait!" He went to his desk, pulled open a drawer and took out a rolled-up flag. "Here, hoist this flag in the foretop."

"You're crazy!" Mr. Davelaar shrieked. "I told you, that flag is blasphemy! You're crazy! Hey, listen, everybody! This lunatic —you can't let him do this! He's going to kill the ship!"

"Sign, Davelaar," the captain said calmly.

"Never! Do you hear? Never, never in a thousand years!"

"This is an order."

"I refuse!"

"You refuse to protest? That makes you an accessory to the crime."

"I don't give a damn!"

"As you wish. Palstra?"

"Yes, Captain?"

"Sign the document, then go below and put three ice bombs in the propeller-shaft tunnel, with five-minute fuses. That's to say, unless the chief wants to do so himself."

The chief gazed at the captain in horror and disbelief. "You want *me* to do it? I am to kill the ship with my own goddam hands? The ship I've sailed for forty years? I've got nothing else in the world! I've no wife, no children! I have no God!"

"If you don't want to do it, I will," Palstra said.

The old man cried hoarsely, "No!" and ran out the door.

"Doctor, would you sign, please?"

"Skipper, I must say—"

The captain cut him short. "Sign, please."

Hendrik signed.

"Thank you. When the time comes, arrange for the transfer of the sick to the boats as usual. Make sure that when the foghorn goes, nobody's left in the holds. Appoint someone in each hold to make certain everyone's out. Understood?"

"Yes."

"Rabbi?"

The Rabbi looked at the captain in a state of shock. "But—but *why?*" he asked.

"Hush, Rebbe," Mrs. Goldstein whispered, "don't argue."

"Huh? Oh, no—yes—no, no . . . " The Rabbi, confused, took the pen and bent over the paper to sign it. But suddenly he dropped the pen, covered his face with his hands and started to cry.

Mrs. Goldstein let go of Tovah's hand and put her arm around the Rabbi's shoulders. "Hush, Rebbe," she said. "It's all right. We're not going back." Then she asked the captain, "Do you need his signature, or will mine do?"

"Yours will do."

"I—I—thank you." She obviously wanted to say more, but couldn't find the words; she took up the pen and signed. "Come, Tovah," she said.

But the captain's voice stopped them. "I want your signature too."

Tovah looked at him, baffled. "Me?"

"Yes." He held out the pen to her; after a moment's hesitation, she took it with a rush of pride and added her name at the bottom of the list; then she gave the pen to Yitzhak and ran out of the cabin.

Outside, it was dark, and full of stars. There was an excited hubbub of voices all around her as the others gathered on the boat deck.

II

Hendrik hurried down the boat deck, down the steps to the midships, down the passage to the infirmary, shaking off excited passengers who tried to stop him asking if it was true, was it really true?

"Yes, it's true! Yes, he's going to do it! Yes, he's going through with it!"

In the infirmary, he found Susan looking young and beautiful in her white uniform; when he told her the news, her eyes went wide with astonishment. "You can't be serious! He's actually going to *scuttle* this ship?"

"Yes!" Mr. Brandeis cheered from his bed, where he was being catheterized. "The captain is going to sink his ship and we're going to be picked up by sailboats and we're going to New York! All of us!"

"Now, now, Mr. Brandeis," Susan said with the authority of the head nurse, "don't thrash about, or you'll hurt yourself. Now stay calm—we have plenty of time." She turned to Hendrik. "We do, I hope?"

"Oh, yes, yes, it won't be until dawn tomorrow. You and I should get together and discuss what has to be done. I've gone through this drill before, but you should know exactly what the procedure is. Also, there are changes . . . "

She smiled. "See, Mr. Brandeis? Plenty of time. Now relax and let me do my job. I don't want to hurt you, and if it's going to be tomorrow, we want you in good shape."

"It *is* true, is it?" Mr. Brandeis asked, his beseeching eyes suddenly full of tears. "Is it?"

"Yes," Hendrik said.

"But—but *why?* Why is he doing this? For us?"

"Yes, for you."

"But *why?*"

It was a question that Hendrik was not ready to answer. "We'll talk about that some other time, Mr. Brandeis," he said. "Now, please let the nurse do her work so she and I can sit down and make the necessary plans. You understand that, don't you? That we do need time to get everything ready?"

"Oh, yes, yes!" Mr. Brandeis replied hastily. "Of course. I only wanted to know exactly—"

"Hush!" Susan said. "Now you be quiet and keep still, or it's going to hurt."

"*Zu Befehl, Schwester . . .* " Mr. Brandeis closed his eyes, stretched out and suddenly looked dead. His emaciated cheeks, his sunken eyes, the look of bewilderment on his face even though his eyes were closed brought home to Hendrik the terrible strain the old man was under, having to go through all this stress and torment, pawn in a world-large political game the meaning of which totally escaped him and now, catheter, bag and all, to be lowered into a lifeboat from a ship that was about to be sunk— and all that at an age when he should be secure and sheltered in a home for the aged, playing checkers with his peers. Kuiper's decision, crazy as it was, could not have been postponed any longer, or Mr. Brandeis and others like him would simply not have survived.

Yet, the whole thing seemed unreal, a dreamlike illusion, until Susan and he finally sat down together in the consulting room, facing each other across the gyn table, and she said, "So your superstitious old doctor was right after all."

"Who?"

"The old G.P. you told us about that night in Le Havre. The one whose place you took, and who was afraid you'd sue him if the ship actually went down. Or was that just a story you made up?"

"Good God, no! You're right! Old Halbertsma's vision! I'd forgotten all about it . . . "

So he had; now, suddenly, with hallucinatory clarity, there he was: small, swarthy pugilist, observing him from behind his desk with the blank stare of glasses mirroring the window. *I have reason*

to believe that the ship concerned will sink after an explosion. What
did you say your name was?

"My God . . . What an extraordinary thing!"

She reached across the gyn table, patted his hand and said,
"Enough of that. We've got work to do."

CHAPTER TWO

I

Hendrik worked with her through the night, going through patients' charts, Susan making notes on women who needed watching. There were a Mrs. Spiegel and her baby; a Mrs. Schlachter, senile dementia; a Mrs. Kohnstamm, blind and confused. Hendrik suggested that Susan take up position at the bottom of the ladder in the women's hold to make sure the kids, who had that responsibility, were there to help the feeble; ultimately, she would make sure that everyone was safely up on deck before leaving.

During their deliberations, Susan's excitement grew. Casual lovers, lack of professional challenge, rich old women making degrading demands, all the boredom and sense of unreality of shipboard life on an ocean liner were wiped out by the drama of the present. It was all so *real:* the small, work-worn ship, the holds full of ecstatic people who treated her as if she had been with them from the start, embracing her, kissing her in the elation of the incredible grace that had been bestowed upon them at the very last moment. The infectious joy of the passengers fueled her as she worked in the holds, checked on patients, memorized the layout of the aisles between the bunks, made an exploratory tour of washrooms, playroom, latrines so as to know exactly where to

343

look when the time came to make sure everyone was out and on deck before she herself climbed the ladder. She practiced climbing that scary ladder a few times until, short of breath, she felt confident she could do it in the dark.

When finally she emerged on deck and saw that the dark night was faintly clearing, she was suddenly struck by the realization that this was the daydream she had indulged in on the radio deck of *Tubantia* after the scruffy freighter had been escorted out to sea by the Uruguayan Navy. She remembered leaning over the rail, looking across the turquoise rectangle of the swimming pool and the dashes of orange of the deck chairs at the distant horizon and the small black dot of the ship sailing into nowhere. She remembered thinking 'What a waste,' and then realizing that the waste was she: idle on the radio deck, safe, comfortable and uninvolved, while out there on the darkening ocean a ship full of frightened people was sailing into the night. She remembered feeling that she belonged with them: nursing the sick, helping mothers giving birth, caring for their babies, watching over the lonely at dead of night in those holds stacked full of humanity. Well, here she was.

She realized how self-centered her excitement was when she confronted the captain in the chartroom. She had been called in, together with Hendrik, for a briefing. As she entered the small cabin, no more than a closet compared to the chartroom on board *Tubantia,* she found it filled with people, yet there were only five all told: the two representatives of the Jews, Hendrik, herself and the captain. The captain, who seemed very young and somehow uninvolved as if it concerned someone else's ship, briefed them as to where *Star of Peace* would be scuttled, how it would be done and the exact procedure of evacuation. The boats and the rafts should be well clear of the ship, he said, before he activated the foghorn: the signal that the fuses to the bombs were lit, five minutes before the explosion. He explained about the fuses: a tunnel ran from the engine room to the stern of the ship in which the propeller shaft turned. At the far end of it, the chief engineer had put three bombs, called 'ice bombs' because they were intended to dynamite pack ice in fjord or bay. He went to great lengths to make clear to the passengers exactly what would happen and when: the spark of the fuses would take five minutes to reach the bombs, but by then everyone would be in the boats except the chief engineer and himself. The chief would light the fuses, hurry out of the tunnel, up the stairs to the deck; here he would join the captain. Together, they would go down the scramble net and be picked up by the bo'sun's lifeboat, after it had towed its rafts to safety. The five minutes were ample to allow for the chief to get up on deck, for the two of them to be picked up and for the boat to scurry out of the way before the explosion. If all went according to plan, the three bombs would go off simultaneously and blow the stern out of the ship. It was hard to say exactly what effect the explosion would have and what the extent of damage would be, but in any case the ship would go down stern first—either in a matter of minutes, or settling slowly for as long as half an hour. But by then this should no longer concern anyone, for all the passengers would have been taken on board by the yachts and the Coast Guard cutter, obliged by law to come to their aid.

Susan listened to it all, taking in each detail. She watched the captain's profile, wondering at his detachment, as if to him it wasn't an emotional issue at all, just a matter of following someone else's orders. Only as he addressed her directly: "And you, Nurse? You know now what to do?" she realized he was not detached at all. It was as if in those blue eyes *Star of Peace* was already going down, stern first, with all he had, all he was. "Do you?"

"Yes, sir. Yes, I do."

"You're stationed at the bottom of the ladder in the women's hold?"

"Yes, sir."

"So you'll be the last to leave."

"Yes."

"I presume you'll make a quick final check, then come up and go to the starboard gangway. You'll have to disembark with one of the rafts."

"Yes, sir."

"Doctor, you leave with which boat?"

"Port number one, with the serious patients."

"That'll be the first to be lowered away. Correct?"

"Yes."

"Okay." The captain straightened up and put his pencil down on the chart. "Well, that seems to be all. Passengers should now begin to line up and prepare for the evacuation. It's going to be—" he glanced at the clock over the chart table—"another, say, twenty-five minutes. We are being overtaken by the fleet of sailboats; it will depend on the actions of the Coast Guard cutter when exactly I give the signal to light the fuses. I'll begin by sending out an S.O.S. the moment we swing out the boats. Thank you. Good luck."

"Captain," the old Jewish woman said in an emotional voice, "I want you to know how we—"

"Excuse me." He made his way through the small crowd to the door and went out; the Jewish man put his arm around the woman's shoulder and gave her a reassuring hug.

"Well," Hendrik said, "twenty-five minutes. I think you'd better go down, Sue. If I were you, I wouldn't make a production of that final round of inspection. Just a quick look around and get the hell up that ladder. Did I give you a flashlight?"

"No, you didn't."

"Okay, let's go get one."

She got one from a closet marked FLARE CUPBOARD. It was hard to get at because of the passengers jamming the corridor. They all wore life jackets and were obviously already in the process of lining up for disembarkation.

They made Susan's goodbye to Hendrik somewhat sketchy; she suddenly wanted to kiss him when they reached the women's hold, but there were too many people about. "Goodbye," she said lamely.

"Goodbye, sweetheart. See you in the boats. Godspeed." He looked down at her for a long moment as she descended into the hold; then he turned and walked away.

When she reached the bottom of the ladder, she looked up and saw that dawn was breaking in the sky.

2

Kuiper watched the day break over the horizon; the small dots of the sailboat fleet were silhouetted against the orange sky. As the night rose like a curtain, revealing the coast of Long Island on the starboard side, the flashing light of Ambrose Lightship far ahead where darkness lingered, he saw the white ghost of the Coast Guard cutter shadowing them. He had become accustomed to the sight of *Trygona* at first light every morning; this morning, there was a difference. Something about the ship's behavior seemed to betray a heightened vigilance, almost nervousness. There were more people on her bridge than usual; crew members were lined up on deck as if standing by for a maneuver. Was it to watch the regatta? They could not intervene, not officially, outside the three-mile limit, and he was well outside. Even so, the situation suddenly seemed so tense that Kuiper decided to accelerate the operation.

He put the engine-room telegraph from DEAD SLOW AHEAD onto FULL SPEED, told Johansen at the wheel to swing the ship around and head for the black dots on the horizon, then he blew into the speaking tube to the engine room. It took a while before Davelaar's distorted voice quacked, "Engine room."

"Davelaar, listen carefully. We may have problems with the Coast Guard. They're looking very edgy. Have you laid out your fuses?"

It took so long before the tube answered that he blew into it again, but there was no resistance of a whistle at the other end. The old man must be standing by the speaking tube, thinking. Then the voice from below quacked, "Are you sure, now? Have you thought it through?"

"I have. We must maneuver quickly, these guys are on our heels. Be ready to go ahead within the next ten minutes. Hurry." He stuffed the whistle back into the tube, half expecting it to squeal, but it did not.

As the ship gathered speed on her new course, the cutter

increased speed also and edged closer; on her bridge, binoculars were being trained on him. Kuiper checked the situation on deck, saw the passengers lined up for the rafts and those allotted to the boats climbing into them in an orderly manner. He called through the megaphone, "Meyer! Wybrands! To the bridge, please!"

The two came hurrying. "What's going on?" Meyer asked, panting. "Are they going to stop us?"

"They may try. Let me know when the boats are ready to be swung out. How about the gangways, Wybrands?"

"Ready to go."

"The scramble nets. Ready too?"

"Yes, Captain," Wybrands answered. "The moment the boats are gone, I'll have the nets heaved over the side."

"Only one is needed. Make it the starboard side. The only ones likely to need it will be the chief and myself. By that time, the gangways may be gone."

"You want me to hang on too?" Meyer asked anxiously.

Kuiper looked at the bloated face, the eyes full of fear. "No," he said. "You take command of the starboard boats. Wybrands, you take the port ones, but send out the S.O.S. first. When the boats are free of the ship, I'll signal Davelaar to light the fuses. Get with it, Meyer. I think that cutter is up to no good. You wait here, Wybrands."

Meyer hurried to the boat deck; Wybrands stayed. The cutter was now clearly edging closer. At least five pairs of binoculars were trained on *Star*.

3

Susan, in the women's hold, had finished her swift final inspection and was satisfied that there was no one left in the dormitory, the washrooms or the latrines. She was about to climb the ladder to the deck when she heard running footsteps somewhere in the empty hold. Startled, she looked around; there was no one to be seen in the dark cavity with its tiers of bunks, naked lightbulbs and crazy, surrealist shadows. It gave her an eerie feeling, for she had gone through all the rooms, shone her flashlight into all corners. "Who's there?" she called. "Is there someone left here?"

The footsteps stopped. She paused, decided she had imagined it, started to climb the ladder; then a voice called, "Nurse! Help!"

A distraught woman came running toward her out of the gloom, her hair undone, her eyes wild, her clothes in disarray.

"The child! Nurse! I can't find the child anywhere! She's running around somewhere here, but I can't find her! For God's sake, help!"

The woman's anguish was such that Susan's training asserted itself. "How old is she?" she asked calmly.

"Six! She got away as we were going up the ladder; now she's running around back there! She *knows* we're leaving, but she's hiding somewhere! Please go upstairs and stop everything, please, for God's sake! Don't let them do anything before you find her!"

Although it was getting close, she had no choice but to go and look for the child herself. This was what she had feared all along: that one of the little ones, unaware of the seriousness of the situation, would wander off and start playing games. But the last thing she wanted was to have this distraught woman hugging her footsteps while she made the rounds again. "You go on up," she said firmly. "Please, at once. Take your place in the boats. I'll find her."

"She *always* does this! She always—"

"Up the ladder, come on! Up you go! Hurry now!" Susan pushed her up the ladder; muttering and weeping, the woman obeyed. When Susan was sure the poor soul would not turn around and come down again, she took her flashlight and turned to go back. "What did you say her name was?" she shouted after the woman, now almost up to the deck.

"Lieschen!" the woman shouted back.

"All right! Go upstairs and join the others."

"Promise you won't leave without her! Promise!"

"Of course not! I'll find her! Don't worry! *Go!*"

She switched on her flashlight and ran down the first of the long, narrow corridors, calling, "Lieschen! Come out of there, love! Come on now, we want you to go for a boat ride!"

No reply. Her voice echoed eerily in the empty hold.

"Come on, love! Stop playing games! Come out, wherever you are!"

No reply. Oh God . . . where *was* the child?

4

The fleet of sailboats was drawing rapidly closer in the light of the rising sun. They were running downwind; their billowing spinnakers looked like a flight of balloons sweeping low over the water. From the west, a small fleet of powerboats was approaching; overhead, Kuiper heard the sound of an airplane. Then the Coast Guard cutter made her move.

Suddenly gathering speed, she came foaming toward them. When she was close, she stopped, and the bullhorn bellowed, "*Star of Peace!* Change course to a southerly direction! You are in the restricted zone! Get out of the way! Get out of the way!"

It was the moment he had to show his hand. It had come too early and he felt the beginning of panic. With a conscious effort of will, he forced himself to analyze the situation coolly. The cutter, realizing he was not changing course, gathered speed, raced ahead and swung broadside, putting herself squarely across his bow. The moment was now. 'Calm,' he said to himself, 'calm down, don't panic. Think clearly.'

He took the megaphone. "Everyone stand by! Make sure everyone is out of the holds! I'm broadcasting the S.O.S.!" Then he turned to Wybrands. "All right, send it. Put the transmitter on automatic and get yourself to the boats."

"Aye, aye, Captain."

Kuiper trained his binoculars on the cutter. There she lay, stopped dead, long, low and white between him and the rapidly approaching cloud of sails.

"Sir?" a voice asked beside him. It was Henky with coffee.

"Not now, boy, put it down."

"Yessir."

The sudden interruption of his concentration brought the panic to his throat. But again he managed to suppress it.

The Coast Guard cutter expected that putting herself in that position would force him to veer away; if he refused to change course, she would have to give way, be it at the very last moment. He had to see it through.

The tension on board was such that everybody seemed to have frozen where they were standing. All were looking at the Coast Guard cutter, right ahead of them. *Star* was bearing down on her, full speed.

The bullhorn bellowed, *"Star!* Are you crazy!? Change course! Change course over starboard! *Now!"*

"Steady as you go, Johansen," Kuiper said without looking at the helmsman.

"Aye, aye, Captain."

The cutter was now so close that from where Kuiper stood he was losing sight of her hull.

"Change course!" the bullhorn bellowed with a sound of frenzy. "You're ramming us!"

But the panic had subsided; he was cool now, collected. He knew exactly what he was doing and, more important, what the other would do.

They must have been sure of themselves, for it was a close shave indeed. Only at the very last moment, just as he was expecting, incredulously, the crunch of a collision, did the masts of the Coast Guard cutter move out of the way.

They made it in the nick of time. He saw the cutter reappear over starboard, her stern deep in the water, a high tail of foam spouting upward as she thundered off at top speed. She made a wide curve, heeling over on her side, doubled back and headed for him, her bow-wave as high as her deck, sparkling in the sun.

"Everyone ready to go?" Kuiper shouted at the boat deck.

"Yessir!" Not just Meyer and Wybrands answered, but the passengers themselves. Kuiper realized that they were in a state of extreme tension.

The cutter swerved alongside about six boat-lengths away; then the bow-wave collapsed, the bow sank and she stopped. There was a lot of activity on her deck; then a flash, the thunder of an explosion, a whistling sound, the splash of the shell hitting the sea between *Star* and the approaching cloud of white sails.

"Steady as you go," Kuiper said calmly.

The bullhorn shrieked, "The next round will hit you! Stop! *Star of Peace,* stop!"

Some women passengers in the boats swung out in the davits began to scream.

Kuiper took his megaphone. "Pay no attention! That vessel is not going to hit us! I *guarantee* they will not! Steady as you go! *Now* show me that you are Jews!"

He did not know what made him shout that; the effect, however, was magical. Instant quiet descended over the ship. Not another sound was heard. Everybody gazed up at him, waiting for instructions.

The Coast Guard cutter suddenly gathered speed again and came foaming toward them. "Stop!" the bullhorn bellowed. "*Star of Peace,* stop! You're being boarded!"

It gave him a shock: it was the one eventuality he had not taken into account. Even at *Star*'s top speed, the way she was running now, the cutter's skipper could ease his vessel alongside, throw grappling hooks and send an armed boarding party swarming up her flank. This unforeseen development forced his hand.

He ran to the engine-room telegraph and yanked it onto STOP. He grabbed the megaphone. "Lower away boats! Ditch rafts! Drop starboard and port gangways! Away! Away all! We're going!"

The Coast Guard cutter was beginning to edge closer now, adjusting her speed to his; in a minute or so, they would be close enough to board. He pulled the telegraph three times: FINISHED WITH ENGINES. There was no confirming answer.

He felt that the ship was losing speed. Now . . . now . . . He took a deep breath, ran to the engine-room speaking tube, blew, and put his ear to the mouthpiece.

"Yes! Yes!" He could hear the tension in Davelaar's voice, despite the distortion on the tube.

He put his mouth to the mouthpiece and asked calmly, "Are the fuses ready?"

"Yes! Yes!"

"All right, light them."

As he turned away to go to the port wing, he saw the mess-room boy, clutching his tray, staring at him with eyes full of tears. He patted the child's shoulder and said, "Go. Get to your boat. Hurry!"

"Yessir." Clutching his tray, the boy obeyed.

Kuiper took the megaphone and shouted, "Lower away! All boats stay clear of the ship! She's going!"

Wybrands waved from his lifeboat.

Over on the starboard side, the cutter moved in; but the boats were going down, pulleys squealing. The rafts flew overboard and hit the water. The gangways went down.

"Scramble net!" Kuiper shouted, and there it went, sending up a cloud of dust as it unrolled overboard. The cutter backed off with a roar of engines. Kuiper looked out forward: the cloud of sails was almost upon them. Aft, two Chris Craft came foaming toward him. One of them had a man in the bow, frantically waving a red flag. A small airplane circled overhead.

All boats were down, the rafts were off and away. He ran to the wheelhouse and pulled the line of the foghorn. A gurgle, a splash of water on the roof, and there came the deafening bray. It was the end of verbal commands; over the ear-splitting roar, nobody would be able to hear any more what he was shouting. It was the end, he could no longer function as a captain. He had better get off the bridge, go to the starboard scramble net and wait for Davelaar. It was strange, but he felt nothing. No sense of triumph, no regret; he was as objective and uninvolved as if it weren't his ship any more. At the rail, he scanned the sea. All boats were well away, towing the rafts. Even the Coast Guard cutter had had the sense to pull away. All had gone as planned.

5

Chief Davelaar, on his knees in the crawl space of the propeller-shaft tunnel, put down his flashlight and, hands shaking, struck another match. The three innocuous-looking lengths of twine lay on the floor in front of him. All he need do was to put the flame to each of the frayed ends and *Star*'s fate would be sealed, but the damn matches wouldn't light.

He felt like crawling back, running upstairs, shouting, 'No, goddammit, no! No, no! I can't do it!' But it would simply mean that Joris himself would take over. Setting his jaw, he struck a third match, grimly picked up one of the fuses, held it in the sputtering flame, which promptly died.

He struck a fourth, grabbed another fuse; his eyesight blurred by tears, he did not register the exact moment the flame took, but suddenly, with a spitting hiss, a vicious spark sprang to life and began to consume the fuse, spitting, hissing, sending up a trail of smoke as it raced into the long, dark culvert of the tunnel. He had not expected the fuses to burn that fast. He lit the other two; each of them sprang to life with a spark that raced off, spitting, hissing. The first one was no more than a faint glow in the smoky distance.

For a moment, he sat motionless, mesmerized by the sight of death racing toward *Star*'s gut; then, in sudden panic, he scrambled backward out of the hatch and into the engine room, yelling, "They're lit! They're lit! Out! Everybody out! Out! Out! Out!" He opened the iron door to the stokehold, yelling, "Get out! Get out! Get out, all of you!" But his voice echoed back in the empty darkness; everybody was already gone. The fire doors hung open, glowing coal was spilling onto the plate; the bastards had dropped everything and just made off. He was fit to be tied; then he realized that it didn't matter any more, nothing mattered any more; in a few minutes, the ship would be dead. Sobbing, he clambered up the ringing steps to the deck. As he came out, the foghorn stopped.

Down below, in the engine room, steam hissed past motion-less pistons. The clock over the workbench ticked away in the stillness.

6

Susan had reached the end of the last aisle and shone her flashlight at the upper bunks. "Lieschen! Are you up there? Come out at once! I'll get *very* angry! This is no time to play ga—"

A tremendous explosion, more an upheaval than a sound, threw her on her back, knocking the flashlight from her hand. All lights went out; there was a sound of gushing water. Suddenly, utter terror overwhelmed her. My God! The ship was going down!

She scrambled to her feet in the darkness, clutched an upright of the scaffolding of the bunks and shouted, "Lieschen! Here! Lieschen, here I am! Here! Quick! Here! Here!" There was another explosion, more violent than the first. Part of the scaffold-ing came crashing down. She heard the splintering of wood; the floor tilted under her feet; she clutched the upright with all her might and realized: 'I don't know where I am! My God! God! I'm lost! I'll drown!'

The mere thought sent her into total panic. In her terror, she tried to climb the scaffolding. She managed to heave herself onto what must be the second bunk. She heard water gushing right below her. The structure to which she was clinging began to collapse. She screamed, screamed, "Help! Help! For God's sake! Help! *Help!*" There was no answer, only the roar of gushing water, the stench of latrines spilling over, the foul, stinking dark-ness of death. "Help! Help!" She managed to swing herself one layer higher as cold water gripped her ankles. Then the ship heeled over steeply, the structure collapsed and, screaming, screaming, she tumbled down with it. The wreckage pinned her down. Powerless, terrified, water rising around her, she thrashed her arms, splashed, screamed, "I'm drowning! I'm drowning!

God! *The child . . . !*" Then paralysis overwhelmed her, and total darkness, and swirling, ice-cold terror.

7

From the boat with the sick and the senile, Hendrik saw *Star* go down. It was an awesome sight. She settled, stern first, with unexpected rapidity. All sorts of incongruous things broke loose from her decks as she sank, bow upward, masts tilting back, the white flag with the black cross fluttering from the foretop. The objects that came floating by were all familiar to him: the life-jacket chest, a dining table, benches, a blue-and-white parasol. It was as if the contents of a house were being thrown out in a frantic effort to save them from a fire. Deck chairs, hatch covers, another table . . .

Then the stern went under. With it disappeared, below the turbulent waves created by the sinking, the Dutch flag. He had never considered himself a patriot, the flag had never meant much to him; now the sight of it going under brought tears to his eyes and blurred the spectacle of the mammoth death he was witness-ing. But they could not blot it out, for there was the sound: a sustained roar of escaping air, cascading water, a tremendous hissing, like geysers, from portholes in the midships; suddenly, there was another explosion. Huge objects were hurled at the sky and came tumbling down again: the scooped ventilators of the engine room on the boat deck. Jets of water and foam, higher than the funnel, shot up like gigantic fountains from their bases. Then he spotted two manikins clinging to the scramble net on the foreflank, already half submerged: the captain and Chief Dave-laar. They clumsily worked their way down the huge mazes; a lifeboat steered by the bo'sun was heading for them. It was a terrifying sight: any moment now, the ship could go down. But they made it. Sailors pulled the two men on board, then rowed the boat frantically away from the wreck.

"What's happening, *Herr Doktor?*" a quavering voice asked, like a child.

"Nothing, *Frau* Schlachter," Hendrik said soothingly. "Nothing at all. Everybody's safe, everybody's happy. You'll be in America soon."

"Lieschen . . . " the old lady sobbed. "Lieschen . . . I hope she found her . . . "

"Of course, *Frau* Schlachter," he said, putting his arm around her protectively. "Don't you worry now, Lieschen's just fine."

8

Ever since Lieschen Schlachter's burial, Tovah had wondered who had painted the Star of David on the sheet that covered the child's body; now, suddenly, the mystery was solved. Singing *Eretz Israel* with a ringing voice, Mrs. Goldstein lifted an oar with, flapping from it like a flag, the bedsheet with the Star of David.

The sight of it was so unexpected, heartbreaking and glorious that Tovah jumped to her feet and joined in the Zionist anthem, tears streaming down her face. Everyone joined in until it sounded like a mighty chorus; and so, while all the Jews sang their hearts out, shakily standing in their wallowing boats and even, clumsily, in the rafts, *Star of Peace*, hissing steam from holes in her bow like a whale spouting, slid backward under the sea. The last of her to be seen was the white flag with the black cross in the foretop, then that was gone too.

The moment the ship had gone down, the boats and rafts were surrounded by billowing white sails, motorboats with people filming, flashing lightbulbs, shouts, commands, sirens. So eager were the yachts to take them on board that they bumped into each other; there were squeals and cries and whistles. Tovah herself was hoisted on board by two men with funny hats and blue-and-white-striped tee shirts who looked as if they were taking part in a masked ball.

"My God! What happened? What happened to that ship?" one of them asked.

All she could answer was, "We made it! God, dear God: we made it!"

After she and several others had been pulled on board and been given coffee, her confusion started to clear and she suddenly remembered Mrs. Schlachter. She felt a twinge of guilt, for she had lost sight of her in the hold and had gone to find David instead of looking for her. It spoiled the joy of the moment. She looked around to scan the boats, but they were surrounded by yachts and motorboats; she could not recognize anyone, there seemed to be thousands of people. Then she became aware of someone tugging at her sleeve. It was David.

"Tovah! Tovah!"

"Yes, what is it?"

"I have to go to the bathroom!"

"Okay," she said, "let's go and find one."

9

From the lifeboat, Joris Kuiper had watched his ship die.

He felt numb and drained of emotion; then a jeering voice said at his elbow, "*Now* look at him, the skipper next to God! His ship gone, his money gone, his father gone—what does he say *now?*"

As if in a dream, he heard himself say, "The Lord gave, the Lord has taken away, praised be the name of the Lord."

Then grief overwhelmed him. He put his head in his hands. He felt totally alone, shattered, bereft. Suddenly, an arm was put around his shoulders; he looked up and saw it was Davelaar.

"It's okay, Joris," the old man said. "It's okay. You did what you believed was right."

When the bobbing boat slammed against the flank of the Coast Guard cutter, Kuiper let everyone else go first, then he grabbed the Jacob's ladder and climbed aloft, surprised at how heavy he was; he was soaking wet. He took a long time to reach the deck; when finally he heaved himself over the coaming, exhausted, he heard the squeal of a bo'sun's whistle. Unsteady on his feet, dripping with water, hatless, he found himself face to face with the American lieutenant, behind whom the crew of the cutter were lined up, standing to attention.

The lieutenant saluted. "Hats off, Captain," he said in a low voice; then, loudly, "You're under arrest! Sir!"

The bo'sun's whistle squealed. A voice shouted, "At *ease!*"

Back in that dream, Kuiper followed the officer to wherever he was being taken.

CHAPTER THREE

I

The sinking of *Star of Peace* and the dramatic rescue of her passengers would have been the top story of September 2, 1939, but for the fact that the night before, at twenty minutes to midnight Eastern Standard Time, Germany had invaded Poland. As a result, the papers and the radio failed to give the incident the prominence it would have received under normal circumstances. As Bruinsma soothingly pointed out to his guests gathered for cocktails in his sitting room on board *Tubantia*, nobody out there gave a damn.

But the ambassador, his naval attaché, his press officer and the Line's New York agent were all in high dudgeon. Requests had come in from the news media for an interview with the master of the shipwrecked vessel, and that of course must be prevented at all costs.

"Why?" Bruinsma asked. "The young man might have something pertinent to say, especially right now."

The ambassador, a shrill-voiced old man fired by three vodka martinis, reacted as if the commodore had suggested national treason. "For God's sake!" he cried. "Can you imagine what *that* would do to the Americans?"

"Which Americans? The State Department?"

"I said 'the Americans,' " the ambassador retorted testily, "I was not naming names."

It was foolish to goad the man, but Bruinsma was getting tired of him. "As far as I can see, the Americans have been bending over backward to accommodate you. Kuiper should have been kept in custody for their own Maritime Board of Inquiries."

"Not so!" the naval attaché said. "The incident took place in international waters. The Dutch government—"

"The Dutch government had no role in their decision!" The ambassador now seemed to suspect microphones behind the porthole curtains; that's what three of Bruinsma's martinis did to a man. "It was entirely the Americans' own idea—"

"To sweep the whole affair under the rug, Jewish immigrants and all?" Bruinsma asked. "The papers haven't even cottoned on to the fact that the guy scuttled his ship! 'Explosion in the engine room.' Of what? The chief's intestinal gas? The whole thing is a disgrace." He finished his whiskey, his fourth. The agent registered it and started to make preparatory motions for the evacuation of the visitors. "Well," the agent said cheerfully, "as we all seem to agree to disagree, why don't we—"

"You understand, Commodore?" the ambassador persisted. "The orders from your government are clear: under *no* circumstance is any reporter or photographer to be allowed access to your prisoner, under any pretext. He is to remain incommunicado, in total isolation, until delivered into the hands of the proper authorities in Amsterdam. Is that clear, Commodore?"

Bruinsma looked from one to the other and was overcome by a feeling of disgust. They had only one goal in mind: how to cover their own behinds. No one seemed to be aware of the sacrifice of young Hamlet, now confined in the prison cell on B deck, or of the momentousness of this act of divine folly.

"The trouble the man has caused!" the ambassador cried. "The *provocation* his act presents to the Germans! They are invading Poland, war may break out any moment, Holland *must* remain neutral, as we did during the World War! To have this fanatic, this quasi-Christian lunatic thumb his nose at the Germans by provoking anti-Nazi reactions in the American press is

—is a danger to the Fatherland! Do you understand, Commodore? Incommunicado!"

Bruinsma put his glass down and rose. "Your Excellency," he said, "I sympathize with your discomfort, but my vessel has already been held up twelve hours because of the international situation. If war breaks out between England and Germany, I'll be stopped and inspected by the British Navy in the Downs, which will take another twelve hours. So if you'll excuse me—"

"I want your solemn promise!" The ambassador rose also, handing his glass to the naval attaché without looking at him. "I will not leave until you give me your word that you will not allow any contact whatsoever between the prisoner and the outside world!"

"Come, come, now," Bruinsma said deliberately, opening the door. "The man's locked up in a cell. My crew follows orders. The orders are: no visitors. Now, please allow me to look after my own urgent business. Goodbye, Your Excellency."

The agent, well acquainted with the commodore's flashpoint, ushered the ambassador out.

Alone at last, Bruinsma broke out a new bottle of Scotch, splashed a generous helping into his glass, dropped in some fresh ice, picked up the telephone and dialed a number. "Commodore here. Are all the crew members of *Star* on board? . . . *Star of Peace*, you idiot! The shipwrecked sailors we're taking back to Holland . . . Who? . . . Well, tell Dr. Willemse to report to me the moment he receives the list of the crew members . . . What was that? *Who* wants to see me? . . . All right, send him in."

The door was opened after a knock and an old man in a dirty coverall was ushered in by the purser.

"Yes? What do you want?"

The old man shuffled uncomfortably. "I'm Davelaar, sir. Chief Davelaar. You remember me?"

"Er, yes, of course. Sit down—no! Wait. Is your coverall dirty? Then sit over there on the leather sofa. What was it you wanted to see me about?"

"Just Joris, sir. I mean, he's locked up, is he?"

"Who? Oh, you mean your captain. Ah, now I know who

you are. Yes, indeed he's locked up. Orders from the government."

"I tried to go and see him, but they wouldn't let me. Would
it be possible for me to just—well—say hello, or take him a bar
of chocolate, or something?"

"Chief, if it was up to me, your captain could have the run
of the ship. I think the whole thing is nonsense, but I am under
orders. You know about the international situation. Everybody
connected with the Dutch government or my company has their
backs up. Let's get out of here; as soon as we're past Ambrose
Lightship, I'll release him. Drink?"

"Ah, yes. Yes, please, sir . . . So you don't think . . . ?"

"Indeed I don't think," Bruinsma said, filling a glass. "I never
think until I've passed Ambrose. Straight up, or on the rocks?"

"Excuse me?"

"Do you want ice in your whiskey?"

"Oh, yes, yes—please, sir . . . " It was obvious the old man
was not a Scotch addict. He looked gray and weary, he smelled
of steam engines and old age. "Thank you, sir. Well—er—
cheers."

"Cheers." They drank. "Is that all you've got in the way of
clothes—what you're wearing?"

"Yessir."

"Go and see my chief engineer. Tell him to lend you his
number-two uniform. Tell him I said so. The rest went down
with the ship, I take it?"

"Everything, sir. Everything . . . " The man's voice was
suddenly thick with tears. "All my mementoes: my glass ball with
the Eiffel Tower, my Indian cuspidor—well, everything. My
mother."

"Your mother?"

"I had a picture of her in my bunk. I couldn't take it, there
was no time. It was screwed on, you see. Four screws, and they
had rusted. It would have taken a drill to get it off." He took a
big swallow, startling his Adam's apple. "Joris tried to take his
Annie, but same thing: screws." He took another swallow. His
teeth chattered on the glass.

"You mean the girl with the whistle?"

"Ah . . . " As if he had spoken a magic word, the old man gazed at him with a conspiratorial look. "You saw that, eh? Yeah, you saw that." Another swallow, then he looked to the left, to the right, at the door, leaned over close and whispered, breathing a mixture of Johnnie Walker and chewing tobacco, "The Old Man gave it to her!"

"You don't say."

"He was a rascal, the Old Man. A great captain, a great sailor. But, God forbid, a great one for the women. Almost eighty years old he was, and there was this girl, his own son's wife—"

"Look, Mr. Davelaar, why don't you—"

But the old chief was not to be stopped. "If you ask me, sir, women *want* to be treated like slaves. But you have to be a real master, like the Old Man. Would you believe it: even after he had his stroke—"

"He's dead? Well, then, why don't we—"

"Even when he was totally paralyzed, he still treated her like a slave. He could move his head just a little and grope for that whistle with his lips, and he blew it whenever he felt like—well —whatever it was, and she'd come running. And here's the boy, scuttling his ship, losing all his money, his license, going to prison, because he thought that's what the Old Man would want him to do. For years, he's tried to do what he thought the Old Man wanted him to do. Innocent as a lamb, he was. He couldn't see what was going on under his very nose."

Bruinsma had had enough. It was as if the maggots had already started on the one truly noble, selfless act he had witnessed in his life. He took the glass from the old chief's hand and said, "Let me show you how to get to the first engineer."

The old man did not seem to hear him. His face was flushed; he looked sick and very tired. It occurred to Bruinsma that he might be shellshocked; the trauma of the sinking of the ship he had sailed on for maybe half a century must have been devastating. "Come, Chief," he said kindly. "How about going to see my chief engineer and getting yourself that uniform?"

"Oh—oh, yes, sir. Yes . . . " He rose, unsteady on his feet.

Bruinsma put a hand on his shoulder and guided him to the door. "After that, get yourself a nice, warm bath, go to the gym and get a massage. Then off to the barber shop for a shave. You're the company's guest now. If there's anything else you want, let me know."

"I didn't mean to," the old man said in the doorway. "I didn't mean to say anything. Don't tell him. Don't ever tell him."

"I don't have the foggiest idea what you're talking about. So, have a bath, have a shave, get yourself a uniform and live it up. You're a passenger, Cabin Class. The chief's one flight down, right turn, end of the passage."

It was doubtful whether the old man registered any of it. Bruinsma stood watching him stagger off down the corridor when, behind his back, the telephone rang.

"Commodore here."

"Sir, this is Willemse. I have the list of passengers that were picked up by the powerboat *Me Fluffy Too*—"

"What's that?"

"Roman figure two, sir. The one that delivered some of the passengers and crew members of *Star of Peace* in Manasquan, New Jersey. I'm afraid Miss Foster is not on it. She wasn't on any of the other lists either."

"Is everyone else accounted for?"

"Yessir."

"Have you contacted the Coast Guard?"

"No, sir."

"Go to the radio room, call the Coast Guard, tell them who you are and say we're looking for a missing crew member of *Star of Peace*. She's sure to have been picked up by somebody, it's just a matter of tracing her. Get with it; we sail at two hundred hours."

"Yessir. I hope nothing's wrong, sir . . . "

"Goddammit, man! Call the Coast Guard!"

He slammed down the phone and walked over to the window. The Hudson River was busy with boats and gulls. A neon sign winking on the roof of a warehouse in Hoboken told him that Lucky Strike was MFT. If he hadn't overheard Myrtle saying

"Now he asks permission to lay alongside" that time she failed to put down the telephone properly, the girl with the dark brown eyes would still be on board.

But she had to be somewhere! She was probably hob-nobbing with her rescuers—women always turned up at the very last moment. In his years at sea, he had lost a good many crew members, but never a woman. They were the key to man's survival.

Grabbing the phone again, he called the radio room, left the message for Dr. Willemse that he would telephone the district commander of the Coast Guard himself and asked to be put through. He was connected to the right man in record time, even though to Coast Guard telephone operators the word "commodore" evoked the president of a yacht club. But even at headquarters there was no record of a female crew member Foster, Susan, twenty-six, dark brown hair, brown eyes, five-four, a hundred and ten pounds, no birthmarks, no scars, being picked up after the sinking of the Netherlands vessel *Star of Peace* off Long Island. Everyone else had been accounted for. "Sorry, sir. Have you tried Manasquan?"

"We have," Bruinsma said. "Thanks." He put the phone down. Brown eyes. He remembered them. Where could she be? The Coast Guard should have known.

Across the river, the first lights went on in office windows—small yellow squares that would soon be reflected in the darkening water.

"Bouke?" Myrtle stood in the doorway in her white uniform: young, frightened, obscenely desirable. "Any news?"

"No. But don't worry, she'll turn up. Some of the passengers were taken to different hospitals."

"I've called all the hospitals. She's not listed in any of them."

"Well, try again. She may have come in later. Some yacht may have taken a shortcut to dry her out or something."

"Yes . . . Yes, all right . . . You don't think . . . "

"I don't. She'll turn up. Go ahead, start telephoning."

She turned around. For some reason, as he looked at her slender young legs walking out the door, he knew that the girl with the brown eyes was dead.

2

The restaurant was hot and noisy. Hendrik could barely hear the others' voices over the din; the tables were jammed together, there was an atmosphere of anxious excitement in the smoke-hazy room, everywhere around him people were talking at the top of their voices about the Germans and the English and Poland and war.

"Come on, ducks, drink up!" Myrtle shouted to him between two candle flames. She added, seeing his eyes, "Don't worry! She'll turn up!"

Willemse, on the other side of the candles, shouted, "What are you having? This one's on me!"

Hendrik protested half-heartedly. Willemse grinned and shouted back that it wasn't every night he entertained ship-wrecked colleagues. And so he drank his martini and ordered another and after that another and then the meal came, which he consumed without thinking. Maybe it was the drink, maybe a reaction to the stress and the tension of the day, but he began to talk. 'Talk' hardly described it—it was as if the spigot had been pulled out of a barrel. It was Myrtle who set him off with her reminder of old Dr. Halbertsma who had foretold the sinking of the ship. Speaking at the top of his voice like everyone else in the restaurant, he told the story of his visit to the eccentric old doctor all over again; then, without a pause, eating, slurping wine, he told of Molly and Mrs. Karelsen, who had foreseen the cloud of white sails, thinking they were balloons, and then some crazy stuff about a barn in a flood and a girl trying to climb to a hayloft in the dark and the barn collapsing . . .

His heart skipped a beat. All thought stopped, not wanting to cross the threshold into consciousness.

Just then, the couple at the next table were leaving and the woman suddenly bent down and stood up again. "Is this yours?" she said to Myrtle, holding out a handbag.

Myrtle looked at it and shook her head.

"Then it must have been the lady sitting behind you," the

woman said, "I'd better give it to the *maître d'*, don't you think?"

"Try the hatcheck girl," Myrtle suggested.

"That's a good idea. I hope she finds her."

And there was Mrs. Schlachter, in the lifeboat, his arm around her shoulders. *"Lieschen, Lieschen—I hope she found her."* Who had found who?

He jumped to his feet. "Please excuse me, I must go! I'm sorry, I must! She's in a hospital in Staten Island!"

"What's the matter, Hendrik? Who is?"

"Mrs. Schlachter! I must talk to her at once!"

"But why, Hendrik, why?" Myrtle shouted, holding on to him as he started past her chair.

"Because she knows! She knows what happened to Susan! Don't you understand?"

Of course they didn't understand. They insisted on going with him and he tried to explain in the taxi as the three were being driven to the ferry to Staten Island. It was obvious that they thought he had cracked up, he caught a look between them which seemed to say so.

But during that wild, panic-stricken flight through the night, the truth slowly dawned. By the time they reached the hospital, he thought he knew, almost knew, what had happened in the dark barn heeling in the flood Mrs. Karelsen had seen.

3

Tovah was sitting beside Mrs. Schlachter's bed in the hospital room. She had almost managed to lull the old lady to sleep by reading aloud from the only German book the head nurse had managed to rustle up from the hospital library: *Menschen im Hotel* by Vicki Baum. Mrs. Schlachter's eyes were closed, the wrinkled hand on the bedcover twitched as Tovah read, *"and then, after going through a white and green hell of pain—"* Suddenly, the door burst open and there stood Hendrik, disheveled, distraught. "I must talk to her! Is she sedated?"

"No, just asleep . . . "

"Let me talk to her!"

Startled, Tovah stood up; he took her place at the bedside, put his hand on Mrs. Schlachter's; then, instead of addressing her, he turned to Tovah and asked, "Did she mention her granddaughter?"

"No . . . " Come to think of it, that was strange. Mrs. Schlachter hadn't mentioned Lieschen at all since her arrival. "Why?"

He was no longer listening to her. "Mrs. Schlachter," he said, gently but urgently. "Mrs. Schlachter, this is Dr. Richters." His voice was calm, yet there was about him a terrible anguish.

Mrs. Schlachter opened her eyes, slowly focused on his face, then she gave him a wan smile and whispered, *"Herr Doktor* . . . how kind. You are a good person . . . " She closed her eyes again and dozed off.

"Mrs. Schlachter," Hendrik urged, "Mrs. Schlachter, may I ask you a question? Please?"

"Question?" The old lady opened her eyes again—warily, it seemed.

"Mrs. Schlachter? Are you listening?"

"Oh, yes . . . " the old lady said. "I'm listening. I know what you want to ask me. But don't worry, *lieber Freund.* She's safe now. All is well, all is well . . . "

Hendrik stared at her as if she had given him some terrible news. "Tell me, Mrs. Schlachter," he said, his voice hoarse. "Tell me what happened. Please."

"There's nothing to tell . . . " Mrs. Schlachter's eyelids were drooping. "She was upset . . . frightened . . . so alone. She had no idea where to go, running back and forth all the time. They wanted me to leave her, but I couldn't, you know. I hid in Mrs. Gobel's bunk. Up top."

"Then what? Please, Mrs. Schlachter! What happened?"

"That nurse found me."

"Tell me what happened next! Please, Mrs. Schlachter! It's very important."

The old lady opened her eyes again, gazed at Hendrik with

a sleepy smile and said, "Lieschen is home. Not frightened, not lost any more. She's gone home. She no longer needs me."

The eyes closed again, but the smile hovered.

"Why, Mrs. Schlachter?" Hendrik urged. "Tell me, why does she no longer need you? Have you any idea?"

"The nurse," the old lady said, her eyes still closed. "The nurse must have found her and showed her the way."

"What happened to the nurse? Mrs. Schlachter, please: we cannot find Nurse Foster anywhere. She was not in any of the boats or the rafts; you must be the last to have seen her. Now, please tell me what happened. Nobody will blame you, everybody understands, but please, Mrs. Schlachter: did you tell Nurse Foster that Lieschen was still down there?"

Mrs. Schlachter opened her eyes. She gazed at Hendrik with a look of horror, then covered her face with her hands. "*O mein Gott. Mein Gott! Mein lieber Gott im Himmel . . .* "

"You asked her to go and look for Lieschen, didn't you?"

The old woman nodded, her hands on her face; her frail body heaved with sobs. "*O mein Gott,*" she sobbed. "*Ach, du lieber Gott . . .* "

"And Nurse Foster went to look for her."

"I—I was mad! I have gone mad . . . "

Hendrik rose wearily, his hand on her shoulder. "No, Mrs. Schlachter, you're not mad. Believe me, I do understand. I just needed to know. Now, go to sleep. Would you like something to help you sleep?"

The old lady nodded. Hendrik turned to Tovah. "I'll tell the head nurse to give her a sedative. Will you stay with her until she goes over?"

"Oh my God . . . " Tovah said in a whisper. "It's my fault! I should have stayed with her!"

"It's all right." He put his arm around her shoulders. "Don't blame yourself. We mustn't blame ourselves. *Que será, será.* " He kissed her hair. "See you sometime." He went to the door. "In Palestine."

Then he opened the door and was gone.

CHAPTER FOUR

I

In his cell on board *Tubantia*, Kuiper was aware of the ship's departure and progress down the Hudson. Then the tugs left her; then the pilot.

The sounds were familiar to him: the long-drawn-out roar of the foghorn signaling the visitors to leave; the staccato exchanges between the tugboats' and the ship's hooters. He felt the tremor of the engine reversing, stopping, going into slow ahead, then half-speed ahead, then stopping again to allow the pilot to go down the Jacob's ladder to his launch, off Ambrose Lightship. Finally, the nervous surge to full ahead, and soon thereafter the cradling swell of the open ocean.

He could see none of it, for the cell had no porthole. It was a pleasant little cabin, painted white and yellow, with a comfortable bed and its own private bathroom. The only sign that the cabin was a cell was a peephole in the door; but as far as he knew, no one had made use of it. The food was brought in by a uniformed steward who called him "Sir." Then Commodore Bruinsma came to pay him a visit.

He arrived soon after the Atlantic swell had started to rock the ship. "Well, lad," he said, "I've come to release you from your golden cage. How about joining me on the bridge?"

"Aren't I supposed to remain locked up?"

Bruinsma patted his shoulder. "We're at sea now. Come along."

Kuiper followed the commodore down the passage, into the elevator and up to the bridge deck.

On the bridge, he saw that dawn was breaking. Suddenly, there were the vast orb of the morning, the fading stars, the restless red hue of the portside running light in the wisps of haze whisking by with the speed of the ship. "Let's have a look at the chart," Bruinsma said.

The chartroom was larger than his living room at home. In the dim light, the reverent figures of junior officers fell silent at their entrance.

"Come and have a look."

Kuiper joined Bruinsma at the chart. As he bent over it in the light of the chart lamp, he realized why he had been asked in. On the pencil line of the course was drawn a small circle, with the letters *S.O.P.*, followed by a cross.

"We'll be passing over her in about ten minutes."

Kuiper looked up. Bruinsma's face showed no emotion. "Thank you," he said.

"Go and have a breath of air."

"Yes, I'll do that." He went to the door to the bridge, turned around and said, "Thanks."

Out on the bridge, in the whirling turbulence of the speed wind deflected by the coaming, Kuiper took a deep breath of fresh morning air; then he sensed that someone had joined him. The laconic voice of Bruinsma said, "By the way: I hate to tell you this, but there was one casualty when she went down."

Kuiper looked, numb with shock, at the white figure beside him in the light of the dawn. "Who?"

"One of my nurses, called Foster. The one who volunteered to join you after your medic was taken off; you signed for her transfer. Seems she was held up in the women's hold; when the explosions came, she must have lost her way. In any case, she didn't make it." There was a short silence; then he added, "It was not your fault, but it may influence the attitude of the Maritime Court. Sorry about that. Sorry about the girl. Well, I have to get back. If you want me, I'm in the wheelhouse."

Kuiper wandered over to the starboard wing and gazed at the sun rising over the ocean. At first, all he felt was shock. Then he realized that the ultimate sacrifice had been hers, not his. Then the presence made itself felt beside him.

It was the very first time; so far, he had always sensed it standing behind his back. The feeling was so strong that he looked; but there was only the empty sea, sunlit and serene.

2

Bruinsma observed the lonely figure leaning over the rail at the far end of the bridge. Even from this distance, the man's anguish was evident. Poor sod! It would not be long before it penetrated to him that it had been a needless sacrifice, not just of the girl's life but of his ship and his future. The ambassador had put it with unappealing bluntness the previous evening over his second martini: 'If only the damn fool had held his horses twenty-four hours longer, the Jews would have been admitted as a matter of course. After Poland, no U.S. government could have afforded to send those Jews back to Germany. The whole thing has been for nothing. Nothing at all.'

There he stood, young Hamlet, tinged with gold by the rising sun. Bruinsma wondered if Hamlet's father had been a scoundrel too, deserving to be done in by his scoundrel brother. Maybe *Papa's spook* had had a silver whistle too, to blow with pale, dying lips when he wanted his son's adulterous wife. My God, the dark secrets of humdrum lives.

That was the true enigma: the smallness of the people who did magnificent deeds. Maybe it was ever thus. Maybe Jeanne d'Arc had been just a dairymaid with delusions. Maybe Alexander the Great had been Alexander the small. Maybe all saints had been neurotics sublimating their complexes.

But this morning, he knew that this simply was not so.

3

Vinkemans looked ghastly. His head, with feverish eyes in sunken sockets, looked like a death's-head. His hair was matted on his forehead; his bony hands clutched the bedcovers in nervous spasms. "Doctor!" he croaked, in a voice hoarse with disuse.

"Hello there, old friend. How are you?" Hendrik shook the thin, hot hand. "I can't tell you how great it is to see you! Are you having a good rest? How are you feeling?"

Vinkemans looked confused by the questions. "I—I'm so glad to see you, Doctor," he said. "I've been lying here—well, just lying here." It was obvious from his anguished eyes that the poor guy had heard about Susan and now was in a torment of regret and sorrow.

"Well, you've heard, I suppose: His Nibs did it. So our Jews are safely in the United States, and old *Star* has gone to her eternal rest somewhere a few hundred feet down on the continental shelf, playground for young fish." It had been the wrong thing to say; suddenly, he was struck by the sheer horror of a vision: Susan, now at the stage where her body would have risen to the surface, bobbing in the dark against the underside of the deck. He looked up, startled, when Vinkemans touched his knee; a thin, skeletal arm reached out to him in a gesture of understanding. "I heard, Doc," he said. "I'm so terribly sorry."

"It's tough. It's not that there was anything serious between us, but, well, I liked her a lot. I think it was mutual; we might well have . . . Oh, the hell with it. The bloody hell with it."

"I know what it means, Doc. Believe me, I know." Vinkemans paused, then went on, "I blame myself, you know. If I hadn't deserted—"

"Oh, for God's sake, Vinkemans! Of course you're not to blame. I'm not to blame. Nobody is to blame. It's just—well—the waste of it. The bloody waste."

They sat in silence for a while. Then Hendrik said, "I went to a palmist, you know. Before we sailed."

"Who? Ah, yes . . . And what did the palmist say?"

"She saw those yachts coming out of the sunrise, white spin-nakers—'a swarm of balloons swept low by the wind,' that's what she said. Pretty accurate. She also . . . Well, never mind. It was all pretty hairy. I hope to God she was right."

"What do you mean, Doc?"

"Well, in her trance she described a young woman in panic and terror of death, in a dark barn collapsing in a flood. I wasn't really listening any more by that time, as I thought it was all nonsense, but suddenly the girl was in a sunny field or meadow, with children playing, I believe, and there was a smell of flowers. The woman went on and on about those flowers; when we were going down the stairs, she yelled after us, 'Honeysuckle! The flowers are honeysuckle!' Well, it gives a feeling of comfort, I suppose. If she was accurate on the first part, maybe there is a sunny meadow on the other side, with flowers and children play-ing, and—well—peace."

They sat for a while in silence, then the door opened and a British voice said, "Come on, ducks! Stop spoiling my patients. Come with us to the aft deck. Hurry up now."

Myrtle and Willemse stood in the doorway, Willemse carry-ing a champagne bottle and two glasses, she a small bouquet of flowers.

"Come on," Myrtle said, "bring the glass from the washstand, over there."

"But what . . . ?"

"We're planning a little ceremony," Willemse said.

"Ceremony?"

"Come!" Myrtle said. "We owe it to her; it's the only memo-rial service she'll ever have."

"Oh," he said. "I see . . . " He didn't, not really, but fetched the glass from the washstand in the corner. Then he turned to Vinkemans and said, "Sorry. I'll be back. We have a lot more to talk about."

Vinkemans lifted a weary hand. "Good luck, Doc," he said.

Outside in the corridor, Myrtle took Hendrik's arm; together, the three of them walked down the passage and took the elevator to the main deck. They walked past groups of people in deck chairs gravely talking, down to the stern, as far as they could go.

On the poopdeck, underneath the thin, high flagpole with the Dutch ensign crackling overhead, there was no one except the seagulls planing over the wake.

"Well," Willemse said, checking his wristwatch, "I suppose here's more or less where it was. Anyhow, there she goes." He undid the gold paper collar of the champagne bottle and the little wire basket, then he wrenched the cork out. A squirt of white foam gushed out, from which he backed off, holding the bottle at arm's length. "All right," he said, "glasses."

He filled the three glasses, raised his and said, "Here's to a great girl. May she, wherever she is, rest in peace . . . To Susan."

"To Susan," they said, and drank, but Hendrik couldn't make it. He threw his glass over the rail and covered his face with his hands.

Myrtle threw her glass away too and put her arm around him. Willemse stood for a moment in doubt, then threw both his glass and the bottle overboard and self-consciously put his hand on Hendrik's shoulder.

"Goodbye, Susan," Myrtle said, her voice breaking, and she threw the small bouquet over the rail.

So they stood, close together, the mighty pulse of the propellers throbbing underfoot, and watched the gold neck of the bottle and the small, colorful patch in the turbulent wake, until there was nothing left to see.

About the Author

Jan de Hartog, born in Haarlem, Holland, the second son of a Calvinist minister and a Quaker mother, ran off to sea at the age of ten. At sixteen he entered Amsterdam Naval College, ending up as a junior mate in the Dutch ocean-going tugboat service. When war broke out, in 1940, and Holland was occupied by the Nazis, de Hartog was trapped in his native country. During this time he wrote and published his first major novel, *Holland's Glory*, which became an instant and historic bestseller and a symbol of the Dutch Resistance. (The German occupying forces banned the book in 1942, but it went on selling in large quantities on the underground market.) When he escaped to London in 1943, he was appointed war correspondent for the Dutch merchant marine. There he gathered the material for his postwar novels *The Distant Shore* and *The Captain*, of which over a million copies were sold in the United States alone.

In 1956 he and his wife, Marjorie, crossed the Atlantic on assignment for a number of European magazines, and after a year decided to become permanent residents of the United States. In 1962 de Hartog accepted a post as professor of English at the University of Houston, teaching creative playwriting there and at all-black Texas Southern University. His wife became a volunteer nurses' aide in the local charity hospital; de Hartog followed her and served three years as an orderly in the emergency room. Later, after publication of his book *The Hospital*, conditions in the charity hospital vastly improved and, for the first time, blacks were admitted as members to the board.

In the late sixties de Hartog, himself a Quaker, undertook the ambitious project of a multivolume novel on the history of the Religious Society of Friends. *The Peaceable Kingdom* was the first book, followed by *The Lamb's War*.

De Hartog has written many plays, among which the most famous is *The Fourposter* (later turned into the musical *I Do! I Do!*), and several volumes of essays, the best-known being *A Sailor's Life* (memories of life at sea before World War II) and *The Children* (a personal record for the benefit of the adoptive parents of Asian children).

Mr. and Mrs. de Hartog live in New Jersey.